THE HORUS HERESY®
SIEGE OF TERRA

Book 1 – THE SOLAR WAR
John French

Book 2 – THE LOST AND THE DAMNED
Guy Haley

Book 3 – THE FIRST WALL
Gav Thorpe

Book 4 – SATURNINE
Dan Abnett

Book 5 – MORTIS
John French

Book 6 – WARHAWK
Chris Wraight

SONS OF THE SELENAR (Novella)
Graham McNeill

FURY OF MAGNUS (Novella)
Graham McNeill

THE HORUS HERESY®

Book 1 – HORUS RISING
Dan Abnett

Book 2 – FALSE GODS
Graham McNeill

Book 3 – GALAXY IN FLAMES
Ben Counter

Book 4 – THE FLIGHT OF THE EISENSTEIN
James Swallow

Book 5 – FULGRIM
Graham McNeill

Book 6 – DESCENT OF ANGELS
Mitchel Scanlon

Book 7 – LEGION
Dan Abnett

Book 8 – BATTLE FOR THE ABYSS
Ben Counter

Book 9 – MECHANICUM
Graham McNeill

Book 10 – TALES OF HERESY
edited by Nick Kyme and Lindsey Priestley

Book 11 – FALLEN ANGELS
Mike Lee

Book 12 – A THOUSAND SONS
Graham McNeill

Book 13 – NEMESIS
James Swallow

Book 14 – THE FIRST HERETIC
Aaron Dembski-Bowden

Book 15 – PROSPERO BURNS
Dan Abnett

Book 16 – AGE OF DARKNESS
edited by Christian Dunn

Book 17 – THE OUTCAST DEAD
Graham McNeill

Book 18 – DELIVERANCE LOST
Gav Thorpe

Book 19 – KNOW NO FEAR
Dan Abnett

Book 20 – THE PRIMARCHS
edited by Christian Dunn

Book 21 – FEAR TO TREAD
James Swallow

Book 22 – SHADOWS OF TREACHERY
edited by Christian Dunn and Nick Kyme

Book 23 – ANGEL EXTERMINATUS
Graham McNeill

Book 24 – BETRAYER
Aaron Dembski-Bowden

Book 25 – MARK OF CALTH
edited by Laurie Goulding

Book 26 – VULKAN LIVES
Nick Kyme

Book 27 – THE UNREMEMBERED EMPIRE
Dan Abnett

Book 28 – SCARS
Chris Wraight

Book 29 – VENGEFUL SPIRIT
Graham McNeill

Book 30 – THE DAMNATION OF PYTHOS
David Annandale

Book 31 – LEGACIES OF BETRAYAL
edited by Laurie Goulding

Book 32 – DEATHFIRE
Nick Kyme

Book 33 – WAR WITHOUT END
edited by Laurie Goulding

Book 34 – PHAROS
Guy Haley

Book 35 – EYE OF TERRA
edited by Laurie Goulding

Book 36 – THE PATH OF HEAVEN
Chris Wright

Book 37 – THE SILENT WAR
edited by Laurie Goulding

Book 38 – ANGELS OF CALIBAN
Gav Thorpe

Book 39 – PRAETORIAN OF DORN
John French

Book 40 – CORAX
Gav Thorpe

Book 41 – THE MASTER OF MANKIND
Aaron Dembski-Bowden

Book 42 – GARRO
James Swallow

Book 43 – SHATTERED LEGIONS
edited by Laurie Goulding

Book 44 – THE CRIMSON KING
Graham McNeill

Book 45 – TALLARN
John French

Book 46 – RUINSTORM
David Annandale

Book 47 – OLD EARTH
Nick Kyme

Book 48 – THE BURDEN OF LOYALTY
edited by Laurie Goulding

Book 49 – WOLFSBANE
Guy Haley

Book 50 – BORN OF FLAME
Nick Kyme

Book 51 – SLAVES TO DARKNESS
John French

Book 52 – HERALDS OF THE SIEGE
edited by Laurie Goulding and Nick Kyme

Book 53 – TITANDEATH
Guy Haley

Book 54 – THE BURIED DAGGER
James Swallow

Other Novels and Novellas

PROMETHEAN SUN
Nick Kyme

AURELIAN
Aaron Dembski-Bowden

BROTHERHOOD OF THE STORM
Chris Wright

THE CRIMSON FIST
John French

CORAX: SOULFORGE
Gav Thorpe

PRINCE OF CROWS
Aaron Dembski-Bowden

DEATH AND DEFIANCE
Various authors

TALLARN: EXECUTIONER
John French

SCORCHED EARTH
Nick Kyme

THE PURGE
Anthony Reynolds

THE HONOURED
Rob Sanders

THE UNBURDENED
David Annandale

BLADES OF THE TRAITOR
Various authors

TALLARN: IRONCLAD
John French

RAVENLORD
Gav Thorpe

THE SEVENTH SERPENT
Graham McNeill

WOLF KING
Chris Wright

CYBERNETICA
Rob Sanders

SONS OF THE FORGE
Nick Kyme

*Many of these titles are also available as abridged and unabridged audiobooks.
Order the full range of Horus Heresy novels and audiobooks from*
blacklibrary.com

Also available

THE SCRIPTS: VOLUME I
edited by Christian Dunn

THE SCRIPTS: VOLUME II
edited by Laurie Goulding

VISIONS OF HERESY
Alan Merrett and Guy Haley

MACRAGGE'S HONOUR
Dan Abnett and Neil Roberts

Audio Dramas

THE DARK KING
Graham McNeill

THE LIGHTNING TOWER
Dan Abnett

RAVEN'S FLIGHT
Gav Thorpe

GARRO: OATH OF MOMENT
James Swallow

GARRO: LEGION OF ONE
James Swallow

BUTCHER'S NAILS
Aaron Dembski-Bowden

GREY ANGEL
John French

GARRO: BURDEN OF DUTY
James Swallow

GARRO: SWORD OF TRUTH
James Swallow

THE SIGILLITE
Chris Wraight

HONOUR TO THE DEAD
Gav Thorpe

CENSURE
Nick Kyme

WOLF HUNT
Graham McNeill

HUNTER'S MOON
Guy Haley

THIEF OF REVELATIONS
Graham McNeill

TEMPLAR
John French

ECHOES OF RUIN
Various authors

MASTER OF THE FIRST
Gav Thorpe

THE LONG NIGHT
Aaron Dembski-Bowden

THE EAGLE'S TALON
John French

IRON CORPSES
David Annandale

RAPTOR
Gav Thorpe

GREY TALON
Chris Wraight

THE EITHER
Graham McNeill

THE HEART OF THE PHAROS/
CHILDREN OF SICARUS
L J Goulding and
Anthony Reynolds

RED-MARKED
Nick Kyme

THE THIRTEENTH WOLF
Gav Thorpe

VIRTUES OF THE SONS/
SINS OF THE FATHER
Andy Smillie

The BINARY SUCCESSION
David Annandale

ECHOES OF IMPERIUM
Various Authors

ECHOES OF REVELATION
Various authors

DARK COMPLIANCE
John French

BLACKSHIELDS: THE FALSE WAR
Josh Reynolds

BLACKSHIELDS: THE RED FIEF
Josh Reynolds

HUBRIS OF MONARCHIA
Andy Smillie

NIGHTFANE
Nick Kyme

BLACKSHIELDS: THE BROKEN CHAIN
Josh Reynolds

Download the full range of Horus Heresy audio dramas from
blacklibrary.com

THE HORUS HERESY®

Graham McNeill

FALSE GODS

The heresy takes root

BLACK LIBRARY

A BLACK LIBRARY PUBLICATION

First published in 2006.
This edition published in Great Britain in 2022 by
Black Library, Games Workshop Ltd., Willow Road,
Nottingham, NG7 2WS, UK.

Represented by: Games Workshop Limited – Irish branch,
Unit 3, Lower Liffey Street, Dublin 1,
D01 K199, Ireland.

17

Produced by Games Workshop in Nottingham.
Cover illustration by Philip Sibbering.

See Black Library on the internet at

blacklibrary.com

Find out more about Games Workshop
and the worlds of Warhammer at

games-workshop.com

Printed and bound by CPI Group (UK) Ltd, Croydon, CR0 4YY

To Dan. Thanks for the illumination.

THE HORUS HERESY®

It is a time of legend.

Mighty heroes battle for the right to rule the galaxy.

The vast armies of the Emperor of Earth have conquered the galaxy in a Great Crusade – the myriad alien races have been smashed by the Emperor's elite warriors and wiped from the face of history.

The dawn of a new age of supremacy for humanity beckons.

Gleaming citadels of marble and gold celebrate the many victories of the Emperor. Triumphs are raised on a million worlds to record the epic deeds of his most powerful and deadly warriors.

First and foremost amongst these are the primarchs, superheroic beings who have led the Emperor's armies of Space Marines in victory after victory. They are unstoppable and magnificent, the pinnacle of the Emperor's genetic experimentation. The Space Marines are the mightiest human warriors the galaxy has ever known, each capable of besting a hundred normal men or more in combat.

Organised into vast armies of tens of thousands called Legions, the Space Marines and their primarch leaders conquer the galaxy in the name of the Emperor.

Chief amongst the primarchs is Horus, called the Glorious, the Brightest Star, favourite of the Emperor, and like a son unto him. He is the Warmaster, the commander-in-chief of the Emperor's military might, subjugator of a thousand thousand worlds and conqueror of the galaxy. He is a warrior without peer, a diplomat supreme.

Horus is a star ascendant, but how much further can a star rise before it falls?

~ DRAMATIS PERSONAE ~

The Sons of Horus

THE WARMASTER HORUS

	Commander of the Sons of Horus Legion
EZEKYLE ABADDON	First Captain of the Sons of Horus
TARIK TORGADDON	Captain, 2nd Company, Sons of Horus

IACTON QRUZE, 'THE HALF-HEARD'

	Captain, 3rd Company, Sons of Horus
HASTUR SEJANUS	Captain, 4th Company, Sons of Horus (Deceased)

HORUS AXIMAND, 'LITTLE HORUS'

	Captain, 5th Company, Sons of Horus
SERGHAR TARGOST	Captain, 7th Company, Sons of Horus, lodge master
GARVIEL LOKEN	Captain, 10th Company, Sons of Horus
LUC SEDIRAE	Captain, 13th Company, Sons of Horus

TYBALT MARR, 'THE EITHER'

	Captain, 18th Company, Sons of Horus

VERULAM MOY, 'THE OR'

	Captain, 19th Company, Sons of Horus

KALUS EKADDON, CAPTAIN

        Catulan Reaver Squad, Sons of Horus

FALKUS KIBRE, 'WIDOWMAKER'

        Captain, Justaerin Terminator Squad, Sons of Horus

NERO VIPUS   Sergeant, Locasta Tactical Squad, Sons of Horus

MALOGHURST 'THE TWISTED'

        Equerry to the Warmaster

The Primarchs

ANGRON   Primarch of the World Eaters

FULGRIM   Primarch of the Emperor's Children

Other Space Marines

EREBUS   First Chaplain of the Word Bearers

KHÂRN   Captain, 8th Assault Company of the World Eaters

The Legio Mortis

PRINCEPS ESAU TURNET

        Commander of the *Dies Irae*, an Imperator-class Titan

MODERATI PRIMUS CASSAR

        One of the senior crew of the *Dies Irae*

MODERATI PRIMUS ARUKEN

> Another of the *Dies Irae*'s crew

The Davinites

LODGE PRIESTESS AKSHUB

> Leader of the Lodge of the Serpent

TSI REKH — Davinite liaison

TSEPHA — A cultist of Davin and facilitator for Akshub

Non-Astartes Imperials

PETRONELLA VIVAR — Palatina Majoria of House Carpinus – one of the scions of a wealthy noble family of Terra

MAGGARD — Bodyguard to Petronella

LORD COMMANDER VARVARAS

> Commander of Imperial Army forces attached to Horus's Legion

MECHANICUM ADEPT REGULUS

> Mechanicum representative to Horus, he commands the Legion's robots and maintains its fighting machines

PART ONE

THE BETRAYER

I was there the day that Horus fell…

'It is the folly of men to believe that they are great players on the stage of history, that their actions might affect the grand procession that is the passage of time. It is an insulating conceit a powerful man might clasp tight to his bosom that he might sleep away the night, safe in the knowledge that, but for his presence, the world would not turn, the mountains would crumble and the seas dry up. But if the remembrance of history has taught us anything, it is that, in time, all things will pass. Unnumbered civilisations before ours are naught but dust and bones, and the greatest heroes of their age are forgotten legends. No man lives forever and even as memory fades, so too will any remembrance of him.

'It is a universal truth and an unavoidable law that cannot be denied, despite the protestations of the vain, the arrogant and the tyrannical.

'Horus was the exception.'

– Kyril Sindermann, *Preface to the Remembrancers*

'It would take a thousand clichés to describe the Warmaster, each one truer than the last.'

– Petronella Vivar,
Palatina Majoria of House Carpinus

'Everything degenerates in the hands of men.'

– Ignace Karkasy, *Meditations on the Elegiac Hero*

ONE

Scion of Terra/Colossi/Rebel moon

CYCLOPEAN MAGNUS, ROGAL Dorn, Leman Russ: names that rang with history, names that *shaped* history. Her eyes roamed further up the list: Corax, Night Haunter, Angron... and so on through a legacy of heroism and conquest, of worlds reclaimed in the name of the Emperor as part of the ever-expanding Imperium of Man.

It thrilled her just to hear the names in her head.

But greater than any of them was the name at the top of the list.

Horus: the Warmaster.

Lupercal, she heard his soldiers now called him – an affectionate nickname for their beloved commander. It was a name earned in the fires of battle: on Ullanor, on Murder, on Sixty-Three Nineteen, – a world the deluded inhabitants had, in their ignorance, known as Terra – and a thousand other battles she had not yet committed to her mnemonic implants.

The thought that she was so very far from the sprawling family estates of Kairos and would soon set foot on the *Vengeful Spirit* to record living history took her breath away. But she was here to do more than simply record history unfolding; she knew, deep in her soul, that Horus *was* history.

She ran a hand through her long, midnight black hair, swept up in a style considered chic in the Terran court – not that anyone this far out in space would know, allowing her fingernails to trace a path down her smooth, unblemished skin. Her olive skinned features had been carefully moulded by a life of wealth and facial sculpting to be regal and distinguished, with just the fashionable amount of aloofness crafted into the proud sweep of her jawline.

Tall and striking, she sat at her maplewood escritoire, a family heirloom her father proudly boasted had been a gift from the Emperor to his great, great grandmother after the great oath-taking in the Urals. She tapped on her dataslate with a gold tipped mnemo-quill, its reactive nib twitching in response to her excitement. Random words crawled across the softly glowing surface, the quill's organic stem-crystals picking up the surface thoughts from her frontal lobes.

Crusade… Hero… Saviour… Destroyer.

She smiled and erased the words with a swipe of an elegantly manicured nail, the edge smooth down to the fractal level, and began to write with pronounced, cursive sweeps of the quill.

It is with great heart and a solemn sense of honour that I, Petronella Vivar, Palatina Majoria of House Carpinus do pen these words. For many a long year I have journeyed from Terra, enduring many travails and inconveniences…

Petronella frowned and quickly erased the words she had written, angry at having copied the unnatural affectedness that so infuriated her in the remembrancers' scripts that had been sent back from the leading edge of the Great Crusade.

Sindermann's texts in particular irritated her, though of late they had become few and far between. Dion Phraster produced some passable symphonics – nothing that would enjoy more than a day or so of favour in the Terran ballrooms – but pleasing enough; and the landscapes of Keland Roget were certainly vibrant, but possessed a hyperbole of brush stroke that she felt was unwarranted.

Ignace Karkasy had written some passable poems, but they painted a picture of the Crusade she often thought unflattering to such a wondrous undertaking (especially *Blood Through Misunderstanding*) and she often asked herself why the Warmaster allowed him to pen such words. She wondered if perhaps the subtexts of the poetry went over his head, and then laughed at the thought that anything could get past one such as Horus.

She sat back on her chair and placed the quill in the Lethe-well as a sudden, treacherous doubt gnawed at her. She was so critical of the other remembrancers, but had yet to test her own mettle amongst them.

Could she do any better? Could she meet with the greatest hero of the age – a god some called him, although that was a ridiculous, outmoded concept these days – and achieve what they had, in her opinion, singularly failed to do? Who was she to believe that her paltry skill could do justice to the mighty tales the War-master was forging, hot on the anvil of battle?

Then she remembered her lineage and her posture straightened. Was she not of House Carpinus, finest and most influential of the noble houses in Terran aristocracy? Had not House Carpinus chronicled the rise of the Emperor and his domain throughout the Wars of Unification, watching it grow from a planet-spanning empire to one that was even now reaching from one side of the galaxy to the other to reclaim mankind's lost realm?

As though seeking further reassurance, Petronella opened a flat blotting folder with a monogrammed leather cover and slid a sheaf of papers from inside it. At the top of the pile was a pict image of a fair-haired Astartes in burnished plate, kneeling before a group of his peers as one of them presented a long, trailing parchment to him. Petronella knew that these were called oaths of moment, vows sworn by warriors before battle to pledge their skill and devotion to the coming fight. An intertwined 'EK' device in the corner of the pict identified it as one of Euphrati Keeler's images, and though she was loath to give any of the remembrancers credit, this piece was simply wondrous.

Smiling, she slid the pict to one side, to reveal a piece of heavy grain cartridge paper beneath. The paper bore the familiar double-headed eagle watermark, representing the union of the Mechanicum of Mars and the Emperor, and the script was written in the short, angular strokes of the Sigillite's hand, the quick pen strokes and half-finished letters speaking of a man writing in a hurry. The upward slant to the tails of the high letters indicated that he had a great deal on his mind, though why that should be so, now that the Emperor had returned to Terra, she did not know.

She smiled as she studied the letter for what must have been the hundredth time since she had left the port at Gyptus, knowing that it represented the highest honour accorded to her family.

A shiver of anticipation travelled along her spine as she heard far distant klaxons, and a distorted automated voice, coming from the gold-rimmed speakers in the corridor outside her suite, declared that her vessel had entered high anchor around the planet.

She had arrived.

Petronella pulled a silver sash beside the escritoire and, barely a moment later, the door chime rang and she smiled, knowing without turning that only Maggard would have answered her summons so quickly. Though he never uttered a word in her presence – nor ever would, thanks to the surgery she'd had the family chaperones administer – she always knew when he was near by the agitated jitter of her mnemo-quill as it reacted to the cold steel bite of his mind.

She spun around in her deeply cushioned chair and said, 'Open.'

The door swung smoothly open and she let the moment hang as Maggard waited for permission to stand in her presence.

'I give you leave to enter,' she said and watched as her dour bodyguard of twenty years smoothly crossed the threshold into her frescoed suite of gold and scarlet. His every move was controlled and tight, as though his entire body – from the hard, sculpted muscles of his legs, to his wide, powerful shoulders – was in tension.

He moved to the side as the door shut behind him, his dancing, golden eyes sweeping the vaulted, filigreed ceiling and the adjacent anterooms in a variety of spectra for anything suspect. He kept one hand on the smooth grip of his pistol, the other on the grip of his gold-bladed Kirlian rapier. His bare arms bore the faint scars of augmetic surgery, pale lines across his dark skin, as did the tissue around his eyes where house chirurgeons had replaced them with expensive biometric spectral enhancers to enable him better to protect the scion of House Carpinus.

Clad in gold armour of flexing, ridged bands and silver mail, Maggard nodded in unsmiling acknowledgement that all was clear, though Petronella could have told him that without all his fussing. But since his life was forfeit should anything untoward befall her, she supposed she could understand his caution.

'Where is Babeth?' asked Petronella, slipping the Sigillite's letter back into the blotter and lifting the mnemo-quill from the Lethe-well. She placed the nib on the dataslate and cleared her mind, allowing Maggard's thoughts to shape the words his throat could not, frowning as she read what appeared.

'She has no business being asleep,' said Petronella. 'Wake her. I am to be presented to the mightiest hero of the Great Crusade and I'm not going before him looking as though I've just come from some stupid pilgrim riot on Terra. Fetch her and have her bring the velveteen gown, the crimson one with the high collars. I'll expect her within five minutes.'

Maggard nodded and withdrew from her presence, but not before she felt the delicious thrill of excitement as the mnemo-quill twitched in her grip and scratched a last few words on the dataslate.

...*ing bitch*...

IN ONE OF the ancient tongues of Terra its name meant 'Day of Wrath' and Jonah Aruken knew that the name was well deserved. Rearing up before him like some ancient god of a forgotten time, the *Dies Irae* stood as a vast monument to war and destruction, its armoured head staring proudly over the assembled ground crew that milled around it like worshippers.

The Imperator-class Titan represented the pinnacle of the Mechanicum's skill and knowledge, the culmination of millennia of war and military technology. The Titan had no purpose other than to destroy, and had been designed with all the natural affinity for the business of killing that mankind possessed. Like some colossal armoured giant of steel, the Titan stood forty-three metres tall on crenellated bastion legs, each one capable of mounting a full company of soldiers and their associated supporting troops.

Jonah watched as a long banner of gold and black was unfurled between the Titan's legs, like the loincloth of some feral savage, emblazoned with the death's head symbol of the Legio Mortis. Scores of curling scrolls, each bearing the name of a glorious victory won by the Warmaster, were stitched to the honour banner and Jonah knew that there would be many more added before the Great Crusade was over.

Thick, ribbed cables snaked from the shielded power cores in the hangar's ceiling towards the Titan's armoured torso, where the mighty war engine's plasma reactor was fed with the power of a caged star.

Its adamantine hull was scarred and pitted with the residue of battle, the tech-adepts still patching it up after the fight against the megarachnid. Nevertheless, it was a magnificent and humbling sight, though not one that could dull the ache in his head and the churning in his belly from too much amasec the night before.

Giant, rumbling cranes suspended from the ceiling lifted massive hoppers of shells and long, snub-nosed missiles into the launch bays of the Titan's weapon mounts. Each gun was the size of a hab-block, massive rotary cannons, long-range howitzers and a monstrous plasma cannon with the power to level cities. He watched the ordnance crews prep the weapons, feeling the familiar flush of pride and excitement as he made his way towards the Titan, and smiled at the obvious masculine symbolism of a Titan being made ready for war.

He jumped as a gurney laden with Vulkan bolter shells sped past him, just barely avoiding him as it negotiated its way at speed through the organised chaos of ground personnel, Titan crews and deck hands. It squealed to a halt and the driver's head snapped around.

'Watch where the hell you're going, you damn fool!' shouted the driver, rising from his seat and striding angrily towards him. 'You Titan crewmen think you can swan about like pirates, well this is my–'

The words died in the man's throat and he snapped to attention as he saw the garnet studs and the winged skull emblem on the shoulder boards of Jonah's uniform jacket that marked him as a moderati primus of the *Dies Irae*.

'Sorry,' smiled Jonah, spreading his arms in a gesture of amused apology as he watched the man fight the urge to say more. 'Didn't see you there, chief, got a hell of a hangover. Anyway, what the devil are you doing driving so fast? You could have killed me.'

'You just walked out in front of me, sir,' said the man, staring fixedly at a point just over Jonah's shoulder.

'Did I? Well… just… be more careful next time,' said Jonah, already walking away.

'Then watch where you're going…' hissed the man under his breath, before climbing back onto his gurney and driving off.

'You be careful now!' Jonah called after the driver, imagining the colourful insults the man would already be cooking up about 'those damned Titan crewmen' to tell his fellow ground staff.

The hangar, though over two kilometres in length, felt cramped to Jonah as he made his way towards the *Dies Irae*, the scent of engine oil, grease and sweat not helping one whit with his hangover.

A host of Battle Titans of the Legio Mortis stood ready for war: fast, mid-range Reavers, snarling Warhounds and the mighty Warlords – as well as some newer Night Gaunt-class Titans – but none could match the awesome splendour of an Imperator-class Titan. The *Dies Irae* dwarfed them all in size, power and magnificence, and Jonah knew there was nothing in the galaxy that could stand against such a terrifying war machine.

Jonah adjusted his collar and fastened the brass buttons of his jacket, straightening it over his stocky frame before he reached the Titan's wide feet. He ran his hands through his shoulder-length black hair, trying to give the impression, at least, that he hadn't slept in his clothes. He could see the thin, angular form of Titus Cassar, his fellow moderati primus, working behind a monitoring terminal, and had no wish to endure another lecture on the ninety-nine virtues of the Emperor.

Apparently, smartness of appearance was one of the most important.

'Good morning, Titus,' he said, keeping his tone light.

Cassar's head bobbed up in surprise and he quickly slid a folded pamphlet beneath a sheaf of readiness reports.

'You're late,' he said, recovering quickly. 'Reveille was an hour ago and punctuality is the hallmark of the pious man.'

'Don't start with me, Titus,' said Jonah, reaching over and snatching the pamphlet that Cassar had been so quick to conceal. Cassar made to stop him, but Jonah was too quick, brandishing the pamphlet before him.

'If Princeps Turnet catches you reading this, you'll be a gunnery servitor before you know what's hit you.'

'Give it back, Jonah, please.'

'I'm not in the mood for another sermon from this damned *Lectitio Divinitatus* chapbook.'

'Fine, I'll put it away, just give it back, alright?'

Jonah nodded and held the well-thumbed paper out to Cassar, who snatched it back and quickly slid it inside his uniform jacket.

Rubbing his temples with the heel of his palms, Jonah said, 'Anyway, what's the rush? It's not as though the old girl's even ready for the pre-deployment checks, is she?'

'I pray you'll stop referring to it as a she, Jonah, it smacks of pagan anthropomorphising,' said Cassar. 'A

Titan is a war machine, nothing more: steel, adamantine and plasma with flesh and blood controlling it.'

'How can you say that?' asked Aruken, sauntering over to a steel plated leg section and climbing the steps to the arched gates that led within. He slapped his palm on the thick metal and said, 'She's obviously a she, Titus. Look at the shapely legs, the curve of the hips, and doesn't she carry us within her like a mother protecting her unborn children?'

'In mockery are the seeds of impiety sown,' said Cassar without a trace of irony, 'and I will not have it.'

'Oh, come on, Titus,' said Aruken, warming to his theme. 'Don't you feel it when you're inside her? Don't you hear the beat of her heart in the rumble of her reactor, or feel the fury of her wrath in the roar of her guns?'

Cassar turned back to the monitoring panel and said, 'No, I do not, and I do not wish to hear any more of your foolishness, we are already behind on our pre-deployment checks. Princeps Turnet will have our hides nailed to the hull if we are not ready.'

'Where is the princeps?' asked Jonah, suddenly serious.

'With the War Council,' said Cassar.

Aruken nodded and descended the steps of the Titan's foot, joining Cassar at the monitoring station and letting fly with one last jibe. 'Just because you've never had the chance to enjoy a woman doesn't mean I'm not right.'

Cassar gave him a withering glare, and said, 'Enough. The War Council will be done soon, and I'll not have it said that the Legio Mortis wasn't ready to do the Emperor's bidding.'

'You mean Horus's bidding,' corrected Jonah.

'We have been over this before, my friend,' said Cassar. 'Horus's authority comes from the Emperor. We forget that at our peril.'

'That's as maybe, but it's been many a dark and bloody day since we've fought with the Emperor beside us, hasn't it? But hasn't Horus always been there for us on every battlefield?'

'Indeed he has, and for that I'd follow him into battle beyond the Halo stars,' nodded Cassar. 'But even the Warmaster has to answer to the God-Emperor.'

'God-Emperor?' hissed Jonah, leaning in close as he saw a number of the ground crew turn their heads towards them. 'Listen, Titus, you have to stop this God-Emperor rubbish. One day you're going to say that to the wrong person and you'll get your skull cracked open. Besides, even the Emperor himself says he's not a god.'

'Only the truly divine deny their divinity,' said Cassar, quoting from his book.

Jonah raised his hands in surrender and said, 'Alright, have it your way, Titus, but don't say I didn't warn you.'

'The righteous have nothing to fear from the wicked, and–'

'Spare me another lesson on ethics, Titus,' sighed Jonah, turning away and watching as a detachment of Imperial Army soldiers marched into the hangar, lasrifles on canvas slings hanging from their shoulders.

'Any word yet on what we're going to be fighting on this rock?' asked Jonah, changing the subject, 'I hope it's the green skin. We still owe them for the destruction of *Vulkas Tor* on Ullanor. Do you think it will be the green skin?'

Cassar shrugged. 'I don't know, Jonah. Does it matter? We fight who we are ordered to fight.'

'I just like to know.'

'You will know when Princeps Turnet returns,' said Cassar. 'Speaking of which, hadn't you better prepare the command deck for his return?'

Jonah nodded, knowing that his fellow moderati was right and that he'd wasted enough time in baiting him.

Senior Princeps Esau Turnet's reputation as a feared, ruthless warrior was well deserved and he ran a tight ship on the *Dies Irae*. Titan crews might be permitted more leeway in their behaviour than the common soldiery, but Turnet brooked no such laxity in the crew of his Titan.

'You're right, Titus, I'm sorry.'

'Don't be sorry,' said Cassar, pointing to the gateway in the Titan's leg. 'Be ready.'

Jonah sketched a quick salute and jogged up the steps, leaving Cassar to finish prepping the Titan for refuelling. He made his way past embarking soldiers who grumbled as he pushed them aside. Some raised their voices, but upon seeing his uniform, and knowing that their lives might soon depend on him, they quickly silenced their objections.

Jonah halted at the entrance to the Titan, taking a second to savour the moment as he stood at the threshold. He tilted his head back and looked up the height of the soaring machine, taking a deep breath as he passed through the tall, eagle and lightning bolt wreathed gateway and entered the Titan.

HE WAS BATHED in red light as he entered the cold, hard interior of the Titan and began threading his way through the low-ceilinged corridors with a familiarity borne of countless hours learning the position of every rivet and bolt that held the *Dies Irae* together. There wasn't a corner of the Titan that Jonah didn't know: every passageway, every hatch and every secret the old girl had in her belonged to him. Even Titus and Princeps Turnet didn't know the *Dies Irae* as well as he did.

Reaching the end of a narrow corridor, Jonah approached a thick, iron door guarded by two soldiers in burnished black breastplates over silver mail shirts. Each wore a mask fashioned in the shape of the Legio's death's head and was armed with a short jolt-stick and a holstered shock-pistol. They tensed as he came into view, but relaxed a fraction as they recognised him.

Jonah nodded to the soldiers and said, 'Moderati primus moving from lower levels to mid levels.'

The nearest soldier nodded and indicated a glassy, black panel beside the door as the other drew his pistol. Its muzzle was slightly flared, and two silver steel prongs protruded threateningly, sparks of blue light flickering between them. Arcs of light could leap out and sear the flesh from a man's bones in a burst of lightning, but wouldn't dangerously ricochet in the cramped confines of a Titan's interior.

Jonah pressed his palm against the panel and waited as the yellow beam scanned his hand. A light above the door flashed green and the nearest soldier reached over and turned a hatch wheel that opened the door.

'Thanks,' said Jonah and passed through, finding himself in one of the screw-stairs that climbed the inside of the Titan's leg. The narrow iron mesh stairs curled around thick, fibre-bundle muscles and throbbing power cables wreathed in a shimmering energy field, but Jonah paid them no mind, too intent on his roiling stomach as he climbed the hot, stuffy stairs. He had to pause to catch his breath halfway up, and wiped a hand across his sweaty brow before reaching the next level.

This high up, the air was cooler as powerful recyc-units dispersed the heat generated by the venting of plasma gasses from the reactor. Hooded adepts of the Mechanicum tended to flickering control panels as they carefully built up the plasma levels in the reactor. Crewmen passed him along the cramped confines of the Titan's interior, saluting as they passed him. Good men crewed the *Dies Irae*, they had to be good – Princeps Turnet would never have picked them otherwise. All the men and women onboard the Titan had been chosen personally for their expertise and dedication.

Eventually, Jonah reached the Moderati Chambers in the heart of the Titan and slid his authenticator into the slot beside the door.

'Moderati Primus Jonah Aruken,' he said.

The lock mechanism clicked and, with a chime, the door slid open. Inside was a brilliant domed chamber with curving walls of shining metal and half a dozen openings spaced evenly throughout the ceiling.

Jonah stood in the centre of the room and said, 'Command Bridge, Moderati Primus Jonah Aruken.'

The floor beneath him shimmered and rippled like mercury, a perfectly circular disc of mirror-like metal forming beneath his feet and lifting him from the ground. The thin disc climbed into the air and Jonah rose through a hole in the ceiling, passing along the transport tube towards the summit of the Titan. The walls of the tube glowed with their own inner light, and Jonah stifled a yawn as the silver disc came to a halt and he emerged onto the command deck.

The interior of the *Dies Irae*'s head section was wide and flat, with recessed bays in the floor to either side of the main gangway, where hooded adepts and servitors interfaced directly with the deep core functions of the colossal machine.

'And how is everyone this fine morning?' he asked no one in particular. 'Ready to take the fight to the heathens once more?'

As usual, no one answered him and Jonah shook his head with a smile as he made his way to the front of the bridge, already feeling his hangover receding at the thought of meshing with the command interface. Three padded chairs occupied a raised dais before the glowing green tactical viewer, each with thick bundles of insulated cables trailing from the arms and headrests.

He slid past the central chair, that of Princeps Turnet, and sat in the chair to the right, sliding into the comfortable groove he'd worn in the creaking leather over the years.

'Adepts,' he said. 'Link me.'

Red-robed adepts of the Mechanicum appeared, one on either side of him, their movements slow and in perfect concert with one another, and slotted fine micro-cellular gauntlets over his hands, the inner, mnemonic surfaces meshing with his skin and registering his vital signs. Another adept lowered a silver lattice of encephalographic sensors onto his head, and the touch of the cool metal against his skin was a welcome sensation.

'Hold still, moderati,' said the adept behind him, his voice dull and lifeless. 'The cortical-dendrites are ready to deploy.'

Jonah heard the hiss of the neck clamps as they slid from the side of the headrest, and, from the corners of his eyes, he could see slithering slivers of metal emerging from the clamps. He braced himself for the momentary pain of connection as they slid across his cheek like silver worms reaching towards his eyes.

Then he could see them fully: incredibly fine silver wires, each no thicker than a human hair, yet capable of carrying vast amounts of information.

The clamps gripped his head firmly as the silver wires descended and penetrated the corners of his eyes, worming down past his optic nerve and into his brain, where they finally interfaced directly with his cerebral cortex.

He grunted as the momentary, icy pain of connection passed through his brain, but relaxed as he felt the body of the Titan become one with his own. Information flooded through him, the cortical-dendrites filtering it through portions of his brain that normally went unused, allowing him to feel every part of the gigantic machine as though it were an extension of his own flesh.

Within microseconds, the post-hypnotic implants in the subconscious portions of his brain were already running the pre-deployment checks, and the insides of his eyeballs lit up with telemetry data, weapon readiness status, fuel levels and a million other nuggets of information that would allow him to command this beautiful, wonderful Titan.

'How do you feel?' asked the adept, and Jonah laughed.

'It's good to be the king,' he said.

As THE FIRST pinpricks of light flared in the sky, Akshub knew that history had come to her world. She gripped her fetish-hung staff tightly in her clawed hand, knowing that a moment in time had dawned that mankind would never forget, heralding a day when the gods themselves would step from myth and legend to hammer out the future in blood and fire.

She had waited for this day since the great warriors from the sky had brought word of the sacred task appointed to her when she was little more than a babe in arms. As the great red orb of the sun rose in the north, hot, dry winds brought the sour fragrance of bitter blossoms from the tomb-littered valleys of long-dead emperors.

Standing high in the mountains, she watched this day of days unfold below her, tears of rapture spilling down her wrinkled cheeks from her black, oval eyes, as the pinpricks of light became fiery trails streaking across the clouds towards the ground.

Below her, great herds of horned beasts trekked across the verdant savannah, sweeping towards their watering holes in the south before the day grew too hot for them to move and the swift, razor-fanged predators emerged from their rocky burrows. Flocks of wide-pinioned birds wheeled over the highest peaks of the mountains above her, their cries raucous, yet musical, as this momentous day grew older.

All the multitudinous varieties of life carried on in their usual ways, oblivious to the fact that events that would change the fate of the galaxy were soon to unfold on this unremarkable world.

On this day of days, only she truly appreciated it.

THE FIRST WAVE of drop-pods landed around the central massif at exactly 16:04 zulu time, the screaming jets of their retros bringing them in on fiery pillars as they breached the lower atmosphere. Stormbirds followed, like dangerously graceful birds of prey swooping in on some hapless victim.

Black and scorched by the heat of re-entry, the thirty drop-pods sent up great clouds of dust and earth from their impacts, their wide doors opening with percussive booms and clanging down on the steppe.

Three hundred warriors in thick, plate armour swiftly disembarked from the drop-pods and fanned out with mechanical precision, quickly linking up with other squads, and forming a defensive perimeter around an unremarkable patch of ground in the centre of their landing pattern. Stormbirds circled above in overlapping racetrack patterns, as though daring anything to approach.

At some unseen signal, the Stormbirds broke formation and rose into the sky as the boxy form of a Thunderhawk descended from the clouds, its belly blackened and trailing blue-white contrails. The larger craft surrounded the smaller one, like mother hens protecting a chick, escorting it to the surface, where it landed in a billowing cloud of red dust.

The Stormbirds screamed away on prescribed patrol circuits as the forward ramp of the Thunderhawk groaned open, the hiss of pressurised air gusting from within. Ten warriors clad in the comb-crested helms and shimmering plate armour of the Sons of Horus marched from the gunship, cloaks of many colours billowing at their shoulders.

Each carried a golden bolter across his chest, and their heads turned from left to right as they searched for threats.

Behind them came a living god, his armour gleaming gold and ocean green, with a cloak of regal purple framing him perfectly. A single, carved red eye stared out from his breastplate and a wreath of laurels sat upon his perfect brow.

'Davin,' sighed Horus. 'I never thought I'd see this place again.'

TWO

**You bleed/A good war/Until the galaxy burns/
A time to listen**

MERSADIE OLITON FORCED herself to watch the blade stab towards Loken, knowing that this strike must surely end his life. But, as always, he swayed aside from the lethal sweep with a speed that belied his massive Astartes frame, and raised his sword in time to block yet another stabbing cut. A heavy cudgel looped down at his head, but he had obviously anticipated the blow and ducked as it slashed over him.

The armatures of the practice cage clattered as the weapons swung, stabbed and slashed through the air, mindlessly seeking to dismember the massive Astartes warrior who fought within. Loken grunted, his hard-muscled body shining with a gleaming layer of sweat as a blade scored his upper arm, and Mersadie winced as a thin line of blood ran from his bicep.

As far as she could remember, it was the first time she had ever seen him wounded in the practice cages.

The smirking blond giant, Sedirae, and Loken's friend Vipus had long ago left the training halls, leaving her alone with the Captain of 10th Company. Flattered as she was that he'd asked her to watch him train, she soon found herself wishing that he would finish this punishing ritual so that they could talk about what had happened on Davin and the events that now led them to war on its moon. Sitting on the cold, iron benches outside the practice cages, she had already blink-clicked more images to store in her memory coils than she would ever need.

Moreover, if she was honest, the sheer… obsessiveness of Loken's desperate sparring was somehow unsettling. She had watched him spar before, but it had always been an adjunct to their normal discussions, never the focus. This… this was something else. It was as though the Captain of the Luna Wolves–

No, not the Luna Wolves, she reminded herself: the Sons of Horus.

As Loken deflected yet another slashing blade, she checked her internal chronometer again and knew that she would have to leave soon. Karkasy wouldn't wait, his prodigious appetite outweighing any notion of courtesy towards her, and he would head for the Iterators' Luncheon in the ship's staterooms without her. There would be copious amounts of free wine there and, despite Ignace's newfound dedication to the cause of remembrance, she did not relish the thought of such a smorgasbord of alcohol landing in his path again.

She pushed thoughts of Karkasy aside as the hissing mechanical hemispheres of the sparring cage withdrew and a bell began chiming. Loken stepped from the cage, his fair hair, longer than she had seen it before, plastered to his scalp, and his lightly freckled face flushed with exertion.

'You're hurt,' she said, passing him a towel from the bench.

He looked down, as though unaware of the wound.

'It's nothing,' he said, wiping away the already clotted blood. His breathing came in short bursts and she tried to mask her surprise. To see an Astartes out of breath was utterly alien to her. How long had he been training before she had arrived in the halls?

Loken wiped the sweat from his face and upper body as he made his way to his personal arming chamber. Mersadie followed him and, as usual, could not help but admire the sheer physical perfection of his enhanced physique. The ancient tribes of the Olympian Hegemony were said to have called such specimens of physical perfection Adonian, and the word fit Loken like a masterfully crafted suit of Mark IV plate. Almost without thinking, Mersadie blink-clicked the image of his body.

'You're staring,' said Loken, without turning.

Momentarily flustered, she said, 'Sorry, I didn't mean–'

He laughed. 'I'm teasing. I don't mind. If I am to be remembered, I'd like it to be when I was at my peak rather than as a toothless old man drooling into my gruel.'

'I didn't realise Astartes aged,' she replied, regaining her composure.

Loken shrugged, picking up a carved vambrace and a polishing cloth. 'I don't know if we do either. None of us has ever lived long enough to find out.'

Her sense for things unsaid told her that she could use this angle in a chapter of her remembrances, if he would talk more on the subject. The melancholy of the immortal, or the paradox of an ageless being caught in the flux of constantly changing times – struggling flies in the clotting amber of history.

She realised she was getting ahead of herself and asked, 'Does that bother you, not getting old? Is there some part of you that wants to?'

'Why would I want to get old?' asked Loken, opening his tin of lapping powder and applying it to the vambrace, its new colour, a pale, greenish hued metallic still unfamiliar to her. 'Do you?'

'No,' she admitted, unconsciously reaching up to touch the smooth black skin of her hairless augmetic scalp. 'No, I don't. To be honest, it scares me. Does it scare you?'

'No. I've told you, I'm not built to feel like that. I am powerful now, strong. Why would I want to change that?'

'I don't know. I thought that if you aged maybe you'd be able to, you know, retire one day. Once the Crusade is over I mean.'

'Over?'

'Yes, once the fighting is done and the Emperor's realm is restored.'

Loken didn't answer immediately, instead continuing to polish his armour. She was about to ask the question again when he said, 'I don't know that it ever will be over, Mersadie. Since I joined the Mournival, I've spoken to a number of people who seem to think we'll never finish the Great Unification. Or if we do, that it won't last.'

She laughed. 'Sounds like you've been spending too much time with Ignace. Has his poetry taken a turn for the maudlin again?'

He shook his head. 'No.'

'Then what is it? What makes you think like this? Those books you've been borrowing from Sindermann?'

'No,' repeated Loken, his pale grey eyes darkening at the mention of the venerable primary iterator, and she sensed that he would not be drawn any further on the subject. Instead, she stored this conversation away for another time, one when he might be more forthcoming on these uncharacteristically gloomy thoughts.

She decided to ask another question and steer the conversation in a more upbeat direction, when a looming

shadow fell over the pair of them and she turned to see
the massive, slab-like form of First Captain Abaddon
towering over her.

As usual, his long hair was pulled up in its silver-
sheathed topknot, the rest of his scalp shaved bare. The
captain of the First Company of the Sons of Horus was
dressed in simple sparring fatigues and carried a monstrous sword with a toothed edge.

He glared disapprovingly at Mersadie.

'First Captain Abaddon–' she began, bowing her head,
but he cut her off.

'You bleed?' said Abaddon and took Loken's arm in
his powerful grip, the sonorous tone of his voice only
accentuating his massive bulk. 'The sparring machine
drew Astartes blood?'

Loken glanced at the bulging muscle where the blade
had cut across the black, double-headed eagle tattoo
there. 'Yes, Ezekyle, it was a long session and I was getting tired. It's nothing.'

Abaddon grunted and said, 'You're getting soft, Loken.
Perhaps if you spent more time in the company of warriors than troublesome poets and inquisitive scriveners
you'd be less inclined to such tiredness.'

'Perhaps,' agreed Loken, and Mersadie could sense the
crackling tension between the two Astartes. Abaddon
nodded curtly to Loken and gave her a last, barbed
glance before turning away to the sparring cages, his
sword buzzing into throaty life.

Mersadie watched Loken's eyes as they followed Abaddon, and saw something she never expected to see there:
wariness.

'What was all that about?' she asked. 'Did it have anything to do with what happened on Davin?'

Loken shrugged. 'I can't say.'

✠ ✠ ✠

DAVIN. THE MELANCHOLY ruins scattered throughout its deserts told of its once civilised culture, but the anarchy of Old Night had destroyed whatever society had once prospered many centuries before. Now Davin was a feral world swept by hot, arid winds and baking under the baleful red eye of a sun. It had been six decades since Loken had last set foot on Davin, though back then it had been known as Sixty-Three Eight, being the eighth world brought into compliance by the 63rd Expeditionary force.

Compliance had not improved it much in his opinion.

Its surface was hard, baked clay clumped with scrubby vegetation and forests of tall, powerfully scented trees. Habitation was limited to primitive townships along the fertile river valleys, though there were many nomadic tribes that made their lonely way across the mighty, serpent-infested deserts.

Loken well remembered the battles they'd fought to bring this world into compliance, short sharp conflicts with the autochthonic warrior castes who made war upon one another, and whose internecine conflicts had almost wiped them out. Though outnumbered and hopelessly outclassed, they had fought with great courage, before offering their surrender after doing all that honour demanded.

The Luna Wolves had been impressed by their courage and willingness to accept the new order of their society and the commander – not yet the Warmaster – had decreed that his warriors could learn much from these brave opponents.

Though the tribesmen were separated from the human genome by millennia of isolation, and shared few physical traits with the settlers that came after the Astartes, Horus had allowed the feral tribesmen to remain, in light of their enthusiastic embracing of the Imperial way of life.

Iterators and remembrancers had not yet become an official part of the Crusade fleets, but the civilians and scholars who hung on the coattails of the expeditionary forces moved amongst the populace and promulgated the glory and truth of the Imperium. They had been welcomed with open arms, thanks largely to the dutiful work undertaken by the chaplains of the XVII Legion, the Word Bearers, in the wake of the conquest.

It had been a good war; won rapidly and, for the Luna Wolves, bloodlessly. The defeated foe was brought into compliance quickly and efficiently, allowing the commander to leave Kor-Phaeron of the Word Bearers to complete the task of bringing the light of truth and enlightenment to Davin.

Yes, it had been a good war, or so he had thought.

Sweat trickled down the back of his head and ran down the inside of his armour, its greenish, metallic sheen still new and startling to him, even though it had been months since he had repainted it. He could have left the job to one of the Legion's many artificers, but had known on some bone-deep level that he must look to his battle gear himself, and thus had painstakingly repainted each armoured segment single-handedly. He missed the pristine gleam of his white plate, but the Warmaster had decreed that the new colour be adopted to accompany the Legion's new name: the Sons of Horus.

Loken remembered the cheers and the cries of adoration laid at the feet of the Warmaster as his announcement had spread through the Expedition. Fists punched the air and throats were shouted hoarse with jubilation. Loken had joined in with the rest of his friends, but a ripple of unease had passed through him upon hearing his beloved Legion's new name.

Torgaddon, ever the joker, had noticed the momentary shadow pass over his face and said, 'What's the matter, you wanted it to be the Sons of Loken?'

Loken had smiled and said, 'No, it's just–'

'Just what? Don't we deserve this? Hasn't the commander earned this honour?'

'Of course, Tarik,' nodded Loken, shouting to be heard over the deafening roar of the Legion's cheers. 'More than anyone, he has earned it, but don't you think the name carries a whiff of self aggrandisement to it?'

'Self aggrandisement?' laughed Torgaddon. 'Those remembrancers that follow you around like whipped dogs must be teaching you new words. Come on, enjoy this and don't be such a starch arse!'

Tarik's enthusiasm had been contagious and Loken had found himself once again cheering until his throat was raw.

He could almost feel that rawness again as he took a deep breath of the sour, acrid winds of Davin that blew from the far north, wishing he could be anywhere else right now. It was not a world without beauty, but Loken did not like Davin, though he could not say what exactly bothered him about it. A sour unease had settled in his belly on the journey from Xenobia to Davin, but he had pushed it from his thoughts as he marched ahead of the commander onto the planet's surface.

To someone from the nightmarish, industrial caverns of Cthonia, Loken could not deny that Davin's wide-open spaces were intoxicatingly beautiful. To the west of them, soaring mountain peaks seemed to scrape the stars and further north, Loken knew that there were valleys that plumbed the very depths of the earth, and fantastical tombs of ancient kings.

Yes, they had waged a good war on Davin.

Why then had the Word Bearers brought them here again?

SOME HOURS BEFORE, ON the bridge of the *Vengeful Spirit*, Maloghurst had activated the data-slate he held in his twisted claw of a hand; the skin fused and wet pink, despite the best efforts of the Legion apothecaries to restore it. He had scanned the contents of the communiqué within the slate once more, angry at the turn of phrase used by the petitioner.

He did not relish the prospect of showing the message to the Warmaster and briefly wondered if he could ignore it or pretend the missive had never come before him, but Maloghurst had not risen to become the Warmaster's equerry by insulating him from bad news. He sighed; these days the words of bland administrators carried the weight of the Emperor and, as much as Maloghurst wanted to, he could not ignore this message in particular.

The Warmaster would never agree to it, but Maloghurst had to tell him. In a moment of weakness, Maloghurst turned and limped across the Strategium deck towards the Warmaster's sanctum chamber. He would leave the slate on the Warmaster's table, for him to find in his own time.

The sanctum doors slid smoothly aside, revealing the dark and peaceful interior.

Maloghurst enjoyed the solitude of the sanctum, the coolness of the air easing the pain of his raw skin and twisted spine. The only sound that broke the stillness of the sanctum was the breath rasping in his throat, the abnormal rearward curvature of his spine placing undue pressure on his lungs.

Maloghurst shuffled painfully along the length of the smooth surfaced oval table, reaching out to place the slate at its head, where the Warmaster sat.

It has been too long since the Mournival gathered here, thought Maloghurst.

'Evening, Mal,' said a voice from the shadows, sombre and tired.

Maloghurst turned in surprise towards the source of the voice, dropping the slate to the table, ready to rebuke whoever had seen fit to violate the Warmaster's sanctum.

A shape resolved out of the darkness and he relaxed as he saw the familiar features of the commander, eerily red-lit from below by the light of his gorget.

Fully armoured in his battle plate, the Warmaster sat at the back of the darkened sanctum, his elbows resting on his knees and his head held in his hands.

'My lord,' said Maloghurst. 'Is everything alright?'

Horus stared at the terrazzo-tiled floor of the sanctum and rubbed the heels of his palms across his shaved skull. His noble, tanned face and wide spaced eyes were deep in shadow and Maloghurst waited patiently for the Warmaster's answer.

'I don't know anymore, Mal,' said Horus.

Maloghurst felt a shiver travel down his ruined spine at the Warmaster's words. Surely, he had misheard. To imagine that the Warmaster did not know something was inconceivable.

'Do you trust me?' asked Horus suddenly.

'Of course, sir,' answered Maloghurst without pause.

'Then what do you leave here for me that you don't dare bring me directly?' asked Horus, moving to the table and lifting the fallen data-slate.

Maloghurst hesitated. 'Another burden you do not need, my lord. A remembrancer from Terra, one with friends in high places it would seem: the Sigillite for one.'

'Petronella Vivar of House Carpinus,' said Horus, reading the contents of the slate. 'I know of her family. Her ancestors chronicled my father's rise, back in the days before Unification.'

'What she demands,' spat Maloghurst, 'is ridiculous.'

'Is it, Maloghurst? Am I so insignificant that I don't require remembrance?'

Maloghurst was shocked. 'Sir, what are you talking about? You are the Warmaster, chosen by the Emperor, beloved by all, to be his regent in this great endeavour.

The remembrancers of this fleet may record every fact they witness, but without you, they are nothing. Without you, all of it is meaningless. You are above all men.'

'Above all men,' chuckled Horus. 'I like the sound of that. All I've ever wanted to do was to lead this Crusade to victory and complete the work my father left me.'

'You are an example to us all, sir,' said Maloghurst, proudly.

'I suppose that's all a man can hope for during his lifetime,' nodded Horus, 'to set an example, and when he is dead, to be an inspiration for history. Perhaps she will help me with that noble ideal.'

'Dead? You are a god amongst men, sir: immortal and beloved by all.'

'I know!' shouted Horus, and Maloghurst recoiled before his sudden, volcanic rage. 'Surely the Emperor would not have created such a being as me, with the ability to grasp the infinite, to exist only for this short span! You're right, Mal, you and Erebus both. My father made me for immortality and the galaxy should know of me. Ten thousand years from now I want my name to be known all across the heavens.'

Maloghurst nodded, the Warmaster's furious conviction intoxicating, and dropped painfully to one knee in supplication.

'What would you have me do, my lord?'

'Tell this Petronella Vivar that she may have her audience, but it must be now,' said Horus, his fearsome outburst quite forgotten, 'and tell her that if she impresses me, I will allow her to be my personal documentarist for as long as she desires it.'

'Are you sure about this, sir?'

'I am, my friend,' smiled Horus. 'Now get up off your knees, I know it pains you.'

Horus helped Maloghurst rise to his feet and gently placed his armoured gauntlet on his equerry's shoulder.

'Will you follow me, Mal?' asked the Warmaster. 'No matter what occurs?'

'You are my lord and master, sir,' swore Maloghurst. 'I will follow you until the galaxy burns and the stars themselves go out.'

'That's all I ask, my friend,' smiled Horus. 'Now let's get ready to see what Erebus has to say for himself. Davin, eh? Who'd have thought we'd ever be back here?'

Two HOURS AFTER making planetfall on Davin.

The communication from Erebus of the Word Bearers that had brought the 63rd Expedition to Davin had spoken of an old tally, the settling of a dispute, but had said nothing of its cause or participants.

After the carnage on Murder and the desperate extraction from the Extranus, Loken had expected a warzone of unremitting ferocity, but this warzone, if indeed it could be called that, was deathly quiet, hot and... peaceful.

He didn't know whether to be disappointed or relieved.

Horus had come to the same conclusion not long after they had landed, sniffing the air of Davin with a look of recognition.

'There is no war here,' he had said.

'No war?' Abaddon had asked. 'How can you tell?'

'You learn, Ezekyle,' said Horus. 'The smell of burnt meat and metal, the fear and the blood. There is none of that on this world.'

'Then why are we here?' asked Aximand, reaching up to lift his plumed helmet clear of his head.

'It would seem we are here because we have been summoned,' replied Horus, his tone darkening, and Loken had not liked the sound of the word 'summoned' coming from the Warmaster's lips.

Who would dare to summon the Warmaster?

The answer had come when a column of dust grew on the eastern horizon and eight boxy, tracked vehicles rumbled across the steppe towards them. Shadowed by the Stormbirds that had flown in with the Warmaster, the dark, brushed steel vehicles trailed guidons from their vox-antenna, emblazoned with the heraldry of an Astartes Legion.

From the lead Rhino, a great, devotional trophy rack stood proud of the armoured glacis, hung with golden eagles and books, and sporting jagged lightning bolts picked out in lapis lazuli.

'Erebus,' spat Loken.

'Hold your tongue,' warned Horus as the Rhinos had drawn closer, 'and let me do the talking.'

BIZARRELY, THE YURT smelled of apples, although Ignace Karkasy could see no fruit in any of the carved wooden trays, just heaped cuts of meat that looked a little on the raw side for his epicurean palate. He could swear he smelled apples. He glanced around the interior of the yurt, wondering if perhaps there was some local brew of cider on offer. A hairy-faced local with impenetrable black eyes had already offered him a shallow bowl of the local liquor, a foul-looking brew that smelled like curdled milk, but after catching a pointed glance from Euphrati Keeler he'd politely declined.

Like the drink, the yurt was crude, but had a primitive majesty to it that appealed to the romantic in him, though he was savvy enough to know that primitive was all very well and good unless you had to live there. Perhaps a hundred people filled the yurt – army officers, strategium adepts, a few remembrancers, scribes and military aides.

All come for the commander's War Council.

Casting his gaze around the smoky interior, Karkasy had seen that he was in illustrious company indeed: Hektor

Varvarus, Lord Commander of the Army, stood next to a hunched Astartes giant swathed in cream coloured robes who Karkasy knew must be the Warmaster's equerry, Maloghurst.

An unsmiling figure in the black uniform of a Titan commander stood to attention at the forefront of the gathering, and Karkasy recognised the jowly features of Princeps Esau Turnet, commander of the Imperator Titan, *Dies Irae*. Turnet's Titan had led the armada of enormous battle machines into the heart of the megarachnid territory on Murder and had earned the Legio Mortis the lion's share of the glory.

Karkasy remembered the huge Titan that towered over the architectural presentation that Peeter Egon Momus had given back on Sixty-Three Nineteen, and shivered. Even motionless, it had provoked an intense reaction in him, and the thought of such incredible destructive power being unleashed didn't bear thinking about.

The hissing collection of silver struts and whirling cogs that encased scraps of flesh in a vaguely humanoid form must be the Mechanicum adept, Regulus, and Karkasy saw enough brass and medals hanging from puffed out, uniformed chests to equip a battalion.

Despite the presence of such luminaries, Karkasy found himself stifling a yawn as he and the rest of the audience listened to the Davinite lodge master, Tsi Rekh, performing an elaborate chant in the local tongue. As interesting as it had been to see the bizarre, almost-human locals, Karkasy knew that simply bearing witness to this interminable ceremony of welcome couldn't be the reason why Captain Loken had authorised his presence at the War Council.

A bland faced iterator named Yelten translated the lodge priest's speech into Imperial Gothic, the precisely modulated timbre of his voice carrying the words to the very edges of the yurt.

Say what you like about the iterators, thought Karkasy, they can certainly enunciate to the back row.

'How much longer is this going to go on for?' whispered Euphrati Keeler, leaning towards him. Dressed in her ubiquitous combat fatigues, chunky army boots and tight white vest top, Keeler looked every inch the spunky frontierswoman. 'When is the Warmaster going to get here?'

'No idea,' said Ignace, sneaking a look down her cleavage. A thin silver chain hung around her neck, whatever was hanging on it, hidden beneath the fabric of her top.

'My face is up here, Ignace,' said Euphrati.

'I know, my dear Euphrati,' he said, 'but I'm terribly bored now and this view is much more to my liking.'

'Give it up, Ignace, it's never going to happen.'

He shrugged. 'I know, but it is a pleasant fiction, my dear, and the sheer impossibility of a quest is no reason to abandon it.'

She smiled, and Ignace knew that he was probably a little in love with Euphrati Keeler, though the time since the xeno beast had attacked her in the Whisperheads had been hard for her, and to be honest, he was surprised to see her here. She'd lost weight and wore her blonde hair scraped back in a tight ponytail, still beautifully feminine, despite her best attempts to disguise the fact. He'd once written an epic poem for the marchioness Xorianne Delaquis, one of the supposed great beauties of the Terran court – a despicable commission that he'd loathed, but one that had paid handsomely – but her beauty was artificial and hollow compared to the vitality he now saw in Keeler's face, like someone born anew.

Well out of his league, he knew, what with his generously proportioned physique, hangdog eyes and plain, round face; but his looks had never deterred Ignace Karkasy from attempting to seduce beautiful women – they just made it more of a challenge.

He had made some conquests by riding the adulation for his earlier work, *Reflections and Odes* garnering him several notable carnal tales, while other, more easily impressed members of the opposite sex had been seduced by his witty badinage.

He already knew that Euphrati Keeler was too smart to fall for such obvious flattery, and contented himself with counting her simply as a friend. He smiled as he realised that he didn't think he'd ever had a woman as a friend before.

'To answer your question seriously, my dear,' he said. 'I hope the Warmaster will be here soon. My mouth's as dry as a Tallarn's sandal and I could use a bloody drink.'

'Ignace...' said Euphrati.

'Spare us from those of moral fibre,' he sighed. 'I didn't mean anything alcoholic, though I could fair sink a bottle of that swill they drank on Sixty-Three Nineteen right about now.'

'I thought you hated that wine,' said Keeler. 'You said it was tragic.'

'Ah, yes, but when you've been reduced to drinking the same vintage for months, it's surprising what you'll be willing to drink for a change.'

She smiled, placing her hand over whatever lay at the end of the chain around her neck and said, 'I'll pray for you, Ignace.'

He felt a flicker of surprise at her choice of words, and then saw an expression of rapt adoration settle over her as she raised her picter at something behind him. He turned to see the door flap of the yurt pushed aside and the massive bulk of an Astartes duck down as he entered. Karkasy did a slow double take as he saw that the warrior's shining plate armour was not that of the Sons of Horus, but was the carved granite grey of the Word Bearers. The warrior carried a staff crowned with a book draped in oath paper, over which wound a long sash of purple cloth. He had his helmet tucked into the crook of his arm, and seemed surprised to see all the remembrancers there.

Karkasy could see that the Astartes's wide-featured face was earnest and serious, his skull shaved and covered with intricate scriptwork. One shoulder guard of his armour was draped in heavy parchment, rich with illuminated letters, while the other bore the distinctive icon of a book with a flame burning in its centre. Though he knew it symbolised enlightenment springing forth from the word, Karkasy instinctively disliked it.

It spoke to his poet's soul of the Death of Knowledge, a terrible time in the history of ancient Terra when madmen and demagogues burned books, libraries and wordsmiths for fear of the ideas they might spread with their artistry. By Karkasy's way of thinking, such symbols belonged to heathens and philistines, not Astartes charged with expanding the frontiers of knowledge, progress and enlightenment.

He smiled to himself at this delicious heresy, wondering if he could work it into a poem without Captain Loken realising, but even as the rebellious thought surfaced, he quashed it. Karkasy knew that his patron was showing his work to the increasingly reclusive Kyril Sindermann. For all his dreariness, Sindermann was no fool when it came to the medium, and he would surely spot any risqué references.

In that case, Karkasy would quickly find himself on the next bulk hauler on its way back to Terra, regardless of his Astartes sponsorship.

'So who's that?' he asked Keeler, returning his attention to the new arrival as Tsi Rekh stopped his chanting and bowed towards the newcomer. The warrior in turn raised his long staff in greeting.

Keeler gave him a sidelong glance, looking at him as though he had suddenly sprouted another head.

'Are you serious?' she hissed.

'Never more so, my dear, who is he?'

'That,' she said proudly, snapping off another pict of the Astartes warrior, 'is Erebus, First Chaplain of the Word Bearers.'

And suddenly, with complete clarity, Ignace Karkasy knew why Captain Loken had wanted him here.

STEPPING ONTO THE dusty hardpan of Davin, Karkasy had been reminded of the oppressive heat of Sixty-Three Nineteen. Moving clear of the propwash of the shuttle's atmospheric rotors, he'd half run, half stumbled from beneath its deafening roar with his exquisitely tailored robes flapping around him.

Captain Loken had been waiting for him, resplendent in his armour of pale green and apparently untroubled by the heat or the swirling vortices of dust.

'Thank you for coming at such short notice, Ignace.'

'Not at all, sir,' said Karkasy, shouting over the noise of the shuttle's engines as it lifted off the ground. 'I'm honoured, and not a little surprised, if I'm honest.'

'Don't be. I told you I wanted someone familiar with the truth, didn't I?'

'Yes, sir, indeed you did, sir,' beamed Karkasy. 'Is that why I'm here now?'

'In a manner of speaking,' agreed Loken. 'You're an inveterate talker, Ignace, but today I need you to listen. Do you understand me?'

'I think so. What do you want to me to listen to?'

'Not what, but who.'

'Very well. Who do you want me to listen to?'

'Someone I don't trust,' said Loken.

THREE

**A sheet of glass/A man of fine character/
Hidden words**

ON THE DAY before making planetfall to the surface of Davin, Loken sought out Kyril Sindermann in Archive Chamber Three to return the book he had borrowed from him. He made his way through the dusty stacks and piles of yellowed papers, lethargic globes of weak light bobbing just above head height, his heavy footsteps echoing loudly in the solemn hush. Here and there, a lone scholar clicked through the gloom in a tall stilt chair, but none was his old mentor.

Loken travelled through yet another dizzyingly tall lane of manuscripts and leather bound tomes with names like *Canticles of the Omniastran Dogma*, *Meditations on the Elegiac Hero* and *Thoughts and Memories of Old Night*. None of them was familiar, and he began to despair of ever finding Sindermann amidst this labyrinth of the arcane, when he saw the iterator's familiar, stooped form hunched over a long table and surrounded by collections of loose parchment bound with leather cords, and piles of books.

Sindermann had his back to him and was so absorbed in his reading that, unbelievably, he didn't appear to have heard Loken's approach.

'More bad poetry?' asked Loken from a respectful distance.

Sindermann jumped and looked over his shoulder with an expression of surprise and the same furtiveness he had displayed when Loken had first met him here.

'Garviel,' said Sindermann, and Loken detected a note of relief in his tone.

'Were you expecting someone else?'

'No. No, not at all. I seldom encounter others in this part of the archive. The subject matter is a little lurid for most of the serious scholars.'

Loken moved around the table and scanned the papers spread before Sindermann – tightly curled, unintelligible script, sepia woodcuts depicting snarling monsters and men swathed in flames. His eyes flicked to Sindermann, who chewed his bottom lip nervously at Loken's scrutiny.

'I must confess to have taken a liking to the old texts,' explained Sindermann. 'Like *The Chronicles of Ursh* I loaned you, it's bold, bloody stuff. Naïve and overly hyperbolic, but stirring nonetheless.'

'I have finished reading it, Kyril,' said Loken, placing the book before Sindermann.

'And?'

'As you say, it's bloody, garish and sometimes given to flights of fantasy…'

'But?'

'But I can't help thinking that you had an ulterior motive in giving me this book.'

'Ulterior motive? No, Garviel, I assure you there was no such subterfuge,' said Sindermann, though Loken could not be sure that he believed him.

'Are you sure? There are passages in there that I think have more than a hint of truth to them.'

'Come now, Garviel, surely you can't believe that,' scoffed Sindermann.

'The murengon,' stated Loken. 'Anult Keyser's final battle against the Nordafrik conclaves.'

Sindermann hesitated. 'What about it?'

'I can see from your eyes that you already know what I'm going to say.'

'No, Garviel, I don't. I know the passage you speak of and, while it's certainly an exciting read, I hardly think you can take its prose too literally.'

'I agree,' nodded Loken. 'All the talk of the sky splitting like silk and the mountains toppling is clearly nonsense, but it talks of men becoming daemons and turning on their fellows.'

'Ah... now I see. You think that this is another clue as to what happened to Xavyer Jubal?'

'Don't you?' asked Loken, turning one of the yellowed parchments around to point at a fanged daemon figure clothed in fur with curling ram's horns and a bloody, skull-stamped axe.

'Jubal turned into a daemon and tried to kill me! Just as happened to Anult Keyser himself. One of his generals, a man called Wilhym Mardol, became a daemon and killed him. Doesn't that sound familiar?'

Sindermann leaned back in his chair and closed his eyes. Loken saw how tired he looked, his skin the colour of the parchments he perused and his clothes hanging from his body as though draped across his bare bones.

Loken realised that the venerable iterator was exhausted.

'I'm sorry, Kyril,' he said, also sitting back. 'I didn't come here to pick a fight with you.'

Sindermann smiled, reminding Loken of how much he had come to rely on his wise counsel. Though not a tutor as such, Sindermann had filled the role of Loken's mentor and instructor for some time, and it had come as a great shock to discover that Sindermann did not have all the answers.

'It's alright, Garviel, it's good that you have questions, it shows you are learning that there is often more to the truth than what we see at first. I'm sure the Warmaster values that aspect of you. How is the commander?'

'Tired,' admitted Loken. 'The demands of those crying for his attention grow more strident every day. Communiqués from every expedition in the Crusade seek to pull him in all directions, and insulting directives from the Council of Terra seek to turn him into a damned administrator instead of the Warmaster. He carries a huge burden, Kyril; but don't think you can change the subject that easily.'

Sindermann laughed. 'You are becoming too quick for me, Garviel. Very well, what is it you want to know?'

'The men in the book who were said to use sorcerous powers, were they warlocks?'

'I don't know,' admitted Sindermann. 'It's certainly possible. The powers they used certainly do not sound natural.'

'But how could their leaders have sanctioned the use of such powers? Surely they must have seen how dangerous it was?'

'Perhaps, but think on this: we know so little on the subject and we have the light of the Emperor's wisdom and science to guide us. How much less must they have known?'

'Even a barbarian must know that such things are dangerous,' said Loken.

'Barbarian?' said Sindermann. 'A pejorative term indeed, my friend. Do not be so quick to judge, we are not so different from the tribes of Old Earth as you might think.'

'Surely you're not serious,' asked Loken. 'We are as different from them as a star from a planet.'

'Are you so sure, Garviel? You believe that the wall, separating civilisation from barbarism is as solid as steel, but it is not. I tell you the division is a thread, a sheet of glass. A touch here, a push there, and you bring back the reign of pagan superstition, fear of the dark and the worship of fell beings in echoing fanes.'

'You exaggerate.'

'Do I?' asked Sindermann, leaning forward. 'Imagine a newly compliant world that experiences a shortage of some vital resource, such as fuel, water or food, how long would it take before civilised behaviour broke down and barbaric behaviour took over? Would human selfishness cause some to fight to get that resource at all costs, even if it meant harm to others and trafficking with evil? Would they deprive others of this resource, or even destroy them in an effort to keep it for themselves? Common decency and civil behaviour are just a thin veneer over the animal at the core of mankind that gets out whenever it has the chance.'

'You make it sound like there's no hope for us.'

'Far from it Garviel,' said Sindermann, shaking his head. 'Mankind continually stands bewildered in the presence of its own creation, but, thanks to the great works of the Emperor, I firmly believe that the time will come when we will rise to mastery of all before us. The time that has passed since civilisation began is but a fragment of the duration of our existence, and but a fragment of the ages yet to come. The rule of the Emperor, brotherhood in society, equality in rights and privileges, and universal education foreshadow the higher plane of society to which our experience, intelligence and knowledge are steadily tending. It will be a revival, in a higher form, of the liberty, equality and fraternity of the ancient tribes of Man before the rise of warlords like Kalagann or Narthan Dume.'

Loken smiled, 'And to think I thought you were in despair.'

Sindermann returned Loken's smile and said, 'No, Garviel, far from it. I admit I was shaken after the Whisperheads, but the more I read, the more I see how far we have come and how close we are to achieving everything we ever dreamed of. Each day, I am thankful that we have the light of the Emperor to guide us into this golden future. I dread to think what might become of us were he to be taken from us.'

'Don't worry,' said Loken. 'That will never happen.'

AXIMAND LOOKED THROUGH a gap in the netting and said, 'Erebus is here.'

Horus nodded and turned to face the four members of the Mournival. 'You all know what to do?'

'No,' said Torgaddon. 'We've completely forgotten. Why don't you remind us.'

Horus's eyes darkened at Tarik's levity and he said, 'Enough, Tarik. There is a time for jokes, and this isn't it, so keep your mouth shut.'

Torgaddon looked shocked at the Warmaster's outburst, and shot a hurt glance at his fellows. Loken was less shocked, having witnessed the commander raging at subordinates many times in the weeks since they had departed the marches of the interex. Horus had known no peace since the terrible bloodshed amid the House of Devices on Xenobia, and the deaths and the missed opportunity of unification with the interex haunted him still.

Since the debacle with the interex, the Warmaster had withdrawn into a sullen melancholy, remaining more and more within his inner sanctum, with only Erebus to counsel him. The Mournival had barely seen their commander since returning to Imperial space and they all keenly felt their exclusion from his presence.

Where once they had offered the Warmaster their guidance, now, only Erebus whispered in his ear.

Thus, it was with some relief that the Mournival heard that Erebus would take his leave of the Expedition and journey ahead with his own Legion to Davin.

Even while en route to the Davin system, the Warmaster had not had a moment's peace. Repeated requests for aid or tactical assistance came to him from all across the galaxy, from brother primarchs, Army commanders and, most loathed of all, the army of civil administrators who followed in the wake of their conquests.

The eaxectors from Terra, led by a high administratrix called Aenid Rathbone, plagued the Warmaster daily for assistance in their dispersal throughout the compliant territories to begin the collection of the Emperor's Tithe. Everyone with an ounce of common sense knew that such a measure was premature, and Horus had done all he could to stall Rathbone and her eaxectors, but there was only so long they could be kept at bay.

'If I had my choice,' Horus had told Loken one evening as they had discussed fresh ways of delaying the taxation of compliant worlds, 'I would kill every eaxector in the Imperium, but I'm sure we would be getting tax bills from hell before breakfast.'

Loken had laughed, but the laughter had died in his throat when he realised that Horus was serious.

They had reached Davin, and there were more important matters to deal with.

'Remember,' said Horus. 'This plays out exactly as I have told you.'

A REVERED HUSH fell on the assemblage and every person present dropped to one knee as the Emperor's chosen proxy made his entrance. Karkasy felt faint at the sight of the living god, arrayed as he was in a magnificent suit of plate armour the colour of a distant ocean and a cloak of deepest purple. The Eye of Terra shone on his breast, and Karkasy was overcome by the magisterial beauty of the Warmaster.

To have spent so long in the 63rd Expedition and only now to lay eyes upon the Warmaster seemed the grossest waste of his time, and Karkasy resolved to tear out the pages he'd written in the Bondsman number 7 this week and compose an epic soliloquy on the nobility of the commander.

The Mournival followed him, together with a tall, statuesque woman in a crimson velveteen gown with high collars and puffed sleeves, her long hair worn in an impractical looking coiffure. He felt his indignation rise as he realised this must be Vivar, the remembrancer from Terra that they had heard about.

Horus raised his arms and said, 'Friends, I keep telling you that no one need kneel in my presence. Only the Emperor is deserving of such an honour.'

Slowly, as though reluctant to cease their veneration of this living god, the crowd rose to its feet as Horus passed amongst those closest to him, shaking hands and dazzling them with his easy charm and spontaneous wit. Karkasy watched the faces of those the Warmaster spoke to, feeling intense jealousy swell within his breast at the thought of not being so favoured.

Without thinking, he began pushing his way through the crowd towards the front, receiving hostile glares and the odd elbow to the gut for his troubles. He felt a tug on the collar of his robe and craned his neck to rebuke whoever had thought to handle his expensive garments so roughly. He saw Euphrati Keeler behind him and, at first, thought she was attempting to pull him back, but then he saw her face and smiled as he realised that she was coming with him, using his bulk like a plough.

He managed to get within six or seven people of the front, when he remembered why he had been allowed within this august body in the first place. He tore his eyes from the Warmaster to watch Erebus of the Word Bearers.

Karkasy knew little of the XVII Legion, save that its primarch, Lorgar, was a close and trusted brother of Horus. Both Legions had fought and shed their blood together many times for the glory of the Imperium. The members of the Mournival came forward and, one by one, embraced Erebus as a long lost brother. They laughed and slapped each other's armour in welcome, though Karkasy saw a measure of reticence in the embrace between Loken and Erebus.

'Focus, Ignace, focus...' he whispered to himself as he found his gaze straying once again to the glory of the Warmaster. He tore his eyes from Horus in time to see Abaddon and Erebus shake hands one last time and saw a gleam of silver pass between their palms. He couldn't be sure, it had happened so fast, but it had looked like a coin or medal of some sort.

The Mournival and Vivar then took up positions a respectful distance behind the Warmaster, as Maloghurst assumed his place at his master's side. Horus lifted his arms and said, 'You must bear with me once again, my friends, as we gather to discuss our plans to bring truth and light to the dark places.'

Polite laughter and clapping spread towards the edges of the yurt as Horus continued. 'Once again we return to Davin, site of a great triumph and the eighth world brought into compliance. Truly it is–'

'Warmaster,' came a voice from the centre of the yurt.

The word was spoken softly, and the audience let out a collective gasp at such a flagrant breach of etiquette.

Karkasy saw the Warmaster's expression turn thunderous, understanding that he was obviously unused to being interrupted, before switching his scrutiny back to the speaker.

The crowd drew back from Erebus, as though afraid that mere proximity to him might somehow taint them with his temerity.

'Erebus,' said Maloghurst. 'You have something to say.'

'Merely a correction, equerry,' explained the Word Bearer.

Karkasy saw Maloghurst give the Warmaster a wary sidelong glance. 'A correction you say. What would you have corrected?'

'The Warmaster said that this world is compliant,' said Erebus.

'Davin is compliant,' growled Horus.

Erebus shook his head sadly and, for the briefest instant, Karkasy detected a trace of dark amusement in his next pronouncement.

'No,' said Erebus. 'It is not.'

LOKEN FELT HIS choler rise at this affront to their honour and sensed the anger of the Mournival in the stiffening of their backs. Surprisingly, Aximand went so far as to reach for his sword, but Torgaddon shook his head and Little Horus reluctantly removed his hand from his weapon.

He had known Erebus for only a short time, but Loken had seen the respect and esteem the softly spoken chaplain of the Word Bearers commanded. His counsel had been sage, his manner easy and his faith in the Warmaster unshakeable; but Erebus's subtle infiltration to the Warmaster's side had unsettled Loken in ways beyond simple jealousy. Since taking counsel from the first chaplain, the commander had become sullen, needlessly argumentative and withdrawn. Maloghurst himself had expressed his concern to the Mournival over the Word Bearer's growing influence upon the Warmaster.

After a conversation with Erebus in the *Vengeful Spirit's* forward observation deck, Loken had known that there

was more to the first chaplain than met the eye. Seeds of
suspicion had been planted in his heart that day, and
Erebus's words were now like fresh spring rain upon
them.

After the influence he had accumulated since Xenobia,
Loken could hardly believe that Erebus would now
choose to behave in such a boorish manner.

'Would you care to elaborate on that?' asked Maloghurst, visibly struggling to keep his temper. Loken had
never admired the equerry more.

'I would,' said Erebus, 'but perhaps these might be
matters best discussed in private.'

'Say what you have to say, Erebus, this is the War
Council and there are no secrets here,' said Horus, and
Loken knew that whatever role the Warmaster had
planned for them was an irrelevance now. He saw that
the other members of the Mournival realised this too.

'My lord,' began Erebus, 'I apologise if–'

'Save your apology, Erebus,' said Horus. 'You have a
nerve to come before me like this. I took you in and gave
you a place at my War Council and this is how you repay
me, with dishonour? With insolence? I'll not stand for it,
I'll tell you that right now. Do you understand me?'

'I do, my lord, and no dishonour was intended. If you
would allow me to continue, you will see that I mean no
insult.'

A crackling tension filled the yurt, and Loken silently
willed the Warmaster to put an end to this farce and
retire to somewhere more secluded, but he could see the
Warmaster's blood was up and there would be no backing down from this confrontation.

'Go on,' said Horus through gritted teeth.

'As you know, we left here six decades ago, my lord.
Davin was compliant and seemed as though it would
become an enlightened part of the Imperium. Sadly that
has not proven to be the case.'

'Get to the point, Erebus,' said Horus, his fists clenching in murderous balls.

'Of course. En route to Sardis and our rendezvous with the Two Hundred and Third fleet, the revered Lord Kor Phaeron bade me detour to Davin that I might ensure the Word of the Emperor, beloved by all, was being maintained by Commander Temba and the forces left with him.'

'Where is Temba anyway?' demanded Horus. 'I gave him enough men to pacify any last remnants of resistance. Surely if this world was no longer compliant I would have heard about it?'

'Eugan Temba is a traitor, my lord,' said Erebus. 'He is on the moon of Davin and no longer recognises the Emperor as his lord and master.'

'Traitor?' shouted Horus. 'Impossible. Eugan Temba was a man of fine character and admirable martial spirit, I chose him personally for this honour. He would never turn traitor!'

'Would that that were true, my lord,' said Erebus, sounding genuinely regretful.

'Well, what in the name of the Emperor is he doing on the moon?' asked Horus.

'The tribes on Davin itself were honourable and readily accepted compliance, but those on the moon did not,' explained Erebus. 'Temba led his men in a glorious, but ultimately foolhardy, expedition to the moon to bring the tribes there into line.'

'Why foolhardy? Such is the duty of an Imperial commander.'

'It was foolhardy, my lord, for the tribes of the moon do not understand respect as we do and it appears that when Temba attempted an honourable parley with them, they employed… means to twist the perceptions of our men and turn them against you.'

'Means? Speak plainly, man!' said Horus.

'I hesitate to name them, my lord, but they are what might be described in the ancient texts as, well, sorcery.'

Loken felt the humours in his blood swing wildly out of balance at this mention of sorcery, and a gasp of disbelief swept around the yurt at such a notion.

'Temba now serves the master of Davin's moon and has spat on his oaths of loyalty to the Emperor. He names you as the lackey of a fallen god.'

Loken had never met Eugan Temba, but he felt his hatred of the man rise like a sickness in his gorge at this terrible insult to the Warmaster's honour. An astonished wailing swept round the yurt as the assembled warriors felt this insult as keenly as he did.

'He will pay for this!' roared Horus. 'I will tear his head off and feed his body to the crows. By my honour I swear this!'

'My lord,' said Erebus. 'I am sorry to be the bearer of such ill news, but surely this is a matter best left to those appointed beneath you.'

'You would have me despatch others to avenge this stain upon my honour, Erebus?' demanded Horus. 'What sort of a warrior do you take me for? I signed the Decree of Compliance here and I'll be damned if the only world to backslide from the Imperium is one that I conquered!'

Horus turned to the Mournival. 'Ready a Speartip – now!'

'Very well, my lord,' said Abaddon. 'Who shall lead it?'

'I will,' said Horus.

THE WAR COUNCIL was dismissed; all other concerns and matters due before it shelved by this terrible development. A frantic vigour seized the 63rd Expedition as commanders returned to their units and word spread of Eugan Temba's treachery.

Amid the urgent preparations for departure, Loken found Ignace Karkasy in the yurt so recently vacated by the incensed War Council. He sat with an open book before him, writing with great passion and pausing only to sharpen his nib with a small pocket knife.

'Ignace,' said Loken.

Karkasy looked up from his work, and Loken was surprised at the amusement he saw in the remembrancer's face. 'Quite a meeting, eh? Are they all that dramatic?'

Loken shook his head. 'No, not usually. What are you writing?'

'This, oh, just a quick poem about the vile Temba,' said Karkasy. 'Nothing special, just a stream of consciousness kind of thing. I thought it appropriate given the mood of the expedition.'

'I know. I just can't believe anyone could say such a thing.'

'Nor I, and I think that's the problem.'

'What do you mean?'

'I'll explain,' said Karkasy, rising from his seat and making his way towards the untouched bowls of cold meat and helping himself to a plateful. 'I remember a piece of advice I heard about the Warmaster. It was said that a good trick upon meeting him was to look at his feet, because if you caught his eye you'd quite forget what it was you were going to say.'

'I have heard that too. Aximand told me the same thing.'

'Well it's obviously a good piece of advice, because I was quite taken aback when I saw him up close for the first time: quite magnificent. Almost forgot why I was there.'

'I'm not sure I understand,' said Loken, shaking his head as Karkasy offered him some meat from the plate.

'Put it this way, can you imagine anyone who had actually met Horus – may I call him Horus? I hear you're not too fond of us mere mortals calling him that – saying such a thing as this Temba person is supposed to have said?'

Loken struggled to keep up with Karkasy's rapid delivery, realising that his anger had blinded him to the simple fact of the Warmaster's glory.

'You're right, Ignace. No one who'd met the Warmaster could say such things.'

'So the question then becomes, why would Erebus say that Temba had said it?'

'I don't know. Why would he?'

Karkasy swallowed some of the meat on his plate and washed it down with a drink of the white liquor.

'Why indeed?' asked Karkasy, warming to the weaving of his tale. 'Tell me, have you had the "pleasure" of meeting Aeliuta Hergig? She's a remembrancer – one of the dramatists – and pens some dreadfully overwrought plays. Tedious things if you ask me, but I can't deny that she has some skill in treading the boards herself. I remember watching her play Lady Ophelia in *The Tragedy of Amleti* and she was really rather good, though–'

'Ignace,' warned Loken. 'Get to the point.'

'Oh, yes, of course. My point is that as talented an actress as Ms Hergig is, she couldn't hold a candle to the performance given by Erebus today.'

'Performance?'

'Indeed. Everything he did from the moment he entered this yurt was a performance. Didn't you see it?'

'No, I was too angry,' admitted Loken. 'That's why I wanted you there. Explain it to me simply and without digressions, Ignace.'

Karkasy beamed in pride before continuing.

'Very well. When he first spoke of Davin's non-compliance, Erebus suggested taking the matter somewhere more private, yet he had just broached this highly provocative subject in a room full of people. And did you notice? Erebus said that Temba had turned against him, Horus, not the Emperor: Horus. He made it personal. '

'But why would he seek to provoke the Warmaster so?'

'Perhaps to unbalance his humour in order to bring his choler to the fore, it's not like he wouldn't have known what his reaction would be. I think Erebus wanted the Warmaster in a position where he wasn't thinking clearly.'

'Be careful, Ignace. Are you suggesting that the Warmaster does not think clearly?'

'No, no, no,' said Karkasy. 'Only that with his humours out of balance, Erebus was able to manipulate him.'

'Manipulate him to what end?'

Karkasy shrugged. 'I don't know, but what I do know is that Erebus *wants* Horus to go to Davin's moon.'

'But he counselled against going there. He even had the nerve to suggest that others go in the Warmaster's place.'

Karkasy shook his hand dismissively. 'Only so as to look like he had tried to stop him from his course of action, while knowing full well that the Warmaster couldn't back down from this insult to his honour.'

'And nor should he, remembrancer,' said a deep voice at the entrance to the yurt.

Karkasy jumped, and Loken turned at the sound of the voice to see the First Captain of the Sons of Horus resplendent and huge in his plate armour.

'Ezekyle,' said Loken. 'What are you doing here?'

'Looking for you,' said Abaddon. 'You should be with your company. The Warmaster himself is to lead the speartip, and you waste time with scriveners who call into question the word of an honourable Astartes.'

'First Captain Abaddon,' breathed Karkasy, lowering his head. 'I meant no disrespect. I was just apprising Captain Loken of my impressions of what I heard.'

'Be silent, worm,' snapped Abaddon. 'I should kill you where you stand for the dishonour you do to Erebus.'

'Ignace was just doing what I asked him to do,' Loken pointed out.

'You put him up to this, Garviel?' asked Abaddon. 'I'm disappointed in you.'

'There's something not right about this, Ezekyle,' said Loken. 'Erebus isn't telling us everything.'

Abaddon shook his head. 'You would take this fool's word over that of a brother Astartes? Your dalliance with petty wordsmiths has turned your head around, Loken. The commander shall hear of this.'

'I sincerely hope so,' said Loken, his anger growing at Abaddon's easy dismissal of his concerns. 'I will be standing next to you when you tell him.'

The first captain turned on his heel and made to leave the yurt.

'First Captain Abaddon,' said Karkasy. 'Might I ask you a question?'

'No, you may not,' snarled Abaddon, but Karkasy asked anyway.

'What was the silver coin you gave Erebus when you met him?'

FOUR

Secrets and hidden things/Chaos/Spreading the word/Audience

ABBADON FROZE AT Karkasy's words.

Loken recognised the signs and quickly moved to stand between the first captain and the remembrancer.

'Ignace, get out of here,' he shouted, as Abaddon turned and lunged for Karkasy.

Abaddon roared in anger and Loken grabbed his arms, holding him at bay as Karkasy squealed in terror and bolted from the yurt. Abaddon pushed Loken back, the first captain's massive strength easily greater than his; Loken tumbled away, but he had achieved his objective in redirecting Abaddon's wrath.

'You would raise arms against a brother, Loken?' bellowed Abaddon.

'I just saved you from making a big mistake, Ezekyle,' replied Loken as he climbed to his feet. He could see that Abaddon's blood was up and knew that he must tread warily. Aximand had told him of Abaddon's berserk rages during the desperate extraction of the commander from the Extranus, and his temper was becoming more and more unpredictable.

'A mistake? What are you talking about?'

'Killing Ignace,' said Loken. 'Think what would have happened if you'd killed him. The Warmaster would have had your head for that. Imagine the repercussions if an Astartes murdered a remembrancer in cold blood.'

Abaddon furiously paced the interior of the yurt like a caged animal, but Loken could see that his words had penetrated the red mist of his friend's anger.

'Damn it, Loken… Damn it,' hissed Abaddon.

'What was Ignace talking about, Ezekyle? Was it a lodge medal that passed between you and Erebus?'

Abaddon looked directly at Loken and said, 'I can't say.'

'Then it was.'

'I. Can't. Say.'

'Damn you, Ezekyle. Secrets and hidden things, my brother, I can't abide them. This is exactly why I can't return to the warrior lodge. Aximand and Torgaddon have both asked me to, but I won't, not now. Tell me: is Erebus part of the lodge now? Was he always part of it or did you bring him in on the journey here?'

'You heard Serghar's words at the meeting. You know I can't speak of what happens within the circles of the lodge.'

Loken stepped in close to Abaddon, chest plate to chest plate, and said, 'You'll tell me now, Ezekyle. I smell something rank here and I swear if you lie to me I'll know.'

'You think to bully me, little one?' laughed Abaddon, but Loken saw the lie in his bluster.

'Yes, Ezekyle, I do. Now tell me.'

Abaddon's eyes flickered to the entrance of the yurt.

'Very well,' he said. 'I'll tell you, but what I say goes no further.'

Loken nodded and Abaddon said, 'We did not bring Erebus into the lodge.'

'No?' asked Loken, his disbelief plain.

'No,' repeated Abaddon. 'It was Erebus who brought us in.'

EREBUS, BROTHER ASTARTES, First Chaplain of the Word Bearers...

Trusted counsellor of the Warmaster...

Liar.

No matter how much he tried to blot the word out with his battle meditation it kept coming back to haunt him. In response, Euphrati Keeler's words, from the last time they had spoken, swirled around his head, over and over.

She had stared him down and asked, 'If you saw the rot, a hint of corruption, would you step out of your regimented life and stand against it?'

Keeler had been suggesting the impossible, and he had denied that anything like what she was suggesting could ever take place. Yet here he was entertaining the possibility that a brother Astartes – someone the Warmaster valued and trusted – was lying to them for reasons unknown.

Loken had tried to find Kyril Sindermann to broach the subject with him, but the iterator was nowhere to be found and so Loken had returned to the training halls despondent. The smiling killer, Luc Sedirae, was cleaning the dismantled parts of his bolter; the 'twins', Moy and Marr, were conducting a sword drill; and Loken's oldest friend, Nero Vipus, sat on the benches polishing his breastplate, working out the scars earned on Murder.

Sedirae and Vipus nodded in acknowledgement as he entered.

'Garvi,' said Vipus. 'Something on your mind?'

'No, why?'

'You look a little strung out, that's all.'

'I'm fine,' snapped Loken.

'Fine, fine,' muttered Vipus. 'What did I do?'

'I'm sorry, Nero,' Loken said. 'I'm just…'

'I know, Garvi. The whole company's the same. They can't wait to get in theatre and be the first to get to grips with that bastard, Temba. Luc's already bet me he'll be the one to take his head.'

Loken nodded noncommittally and said, 'Have either of you seen First Captain Abaddon?'

'No, not since we got back,' replied Sedirae without looking up from his work. 'That remembrancer, the black girl, she was looking for you though.'

'Oliton?'

'Aye, that's her. Said she'd come back in an hour or so.'

'Thank you, Luc,' said Loken, turning back to Vipus, 'and again, I'm sorry I snapped at you, Nero.'

'Don't worry,' laughed Vipus. 'I'm a big boy now and my skin's thick enough to withstand your bad moods.'

Loken smiled at his friend and opened his arming cage, stripping off his armour and carefully peeling away the thick, mimetic polymers of his sub-suit body glove until he was naked but for a pair of fatigues. He lifted his sword and stepped towards the training cage, activating the weapon as the iron-grey hemispheres lifted aside and the tubular combat servitor descended from the centre of the dome's top.

'Combat drill Epsilon nine,' he said. 'Maximum lethality.'

The combat machine hummed to life, long blade limbs unfolding from its sides in a manner that reminded him of the winged clades of Murder. Spikes and whirring edges sprouted from the contraption's body and Loken swivelled his neck and arms in readiness for the coming fight.

He needed a clear head if he was to think through all that had happened, and there was no better way to achieve purity of thought than through combat. The battle machine began a soft countdown and Loken dropped into a fighting crouch as his thoughts once again turned to the First Chaplain of the Word Bearers.

Liar...

IT HAD BEEN on the fifteenth day since leaving interex space, and a week before reaching Davin, that Loken finally had the chance to speak with Erebus alone. He awaited the First Chaplain of the Word Bearers in the forward observation deck of the *Vengeful Spirit*, watching smudges of black light and brilliant darkness slide past the great, armoured viewing bay.

'Captain Loken?'

Loken turned, seeing Erebus's open, serious face. His shaved, tattooed skull gleamed in the swirling vortices of coloured light shining through the glass of the observation bay; rendering his armour with the patina of an artist's palette.

'First chaplain,' replied Loken, bowing low.

'Please, my given name is Erebus; I would be honoured if you would call me by it. We have no need of such formality here.'

Loken nodded as Erebus joined him in front of the great, multicoloured vista laid out before them.

'Beautiful, isn't it?' said Erebus.

'I used to think so,' nodded Loken. 'But in truth I can't look on it now without dread.'

'Dread? Why so?' asked Erebus, placing his hand on Loken's shoulder. 'The warp is simply the medium through which our ships travel. Did not the Emperor, beloved by all, reveal the ways and means by which we might make use of it?'

'Yes, he did,' agreed Loken, glancing at the tattooed script on Erebus's skull, though the words were in a language he did not understand.

'They are the pronouncements of the Emperor as interpreted in the *Book of Lorgar* and rendered in the language of Colchis,' said Erebus, answering Loken's unasked question. 'They are as much a weapon as my bolter and blade.'

Seeing Loken's incomprehension, Erebus said, 'On the battlefield I must be a figure of awe and majesty, and by bearing the Word of the Emperor upon my very flesh, I cow the xeno and unbeliever before me.'

'Unbeliever?'

'A poor choice of word,' shrugged Erebus dismissively, 'perhaps misanthrope would be a better term, but I suspect that you did not ask me here to admire the view or my scripture.'

Loken smiled and said, 'No, you're right, I didn't. I asked to speak to you because I know the Word Bearers to be a Legion with many scholars among their ranks. You have sought out many worlds that were said to be seats of learning and knowledge and brought them to compliance.'

'True,' agreed Erebus slowly. 'Though we destroyed much of that knowledge as profane in the fires of war.'

'But you are wise in matters esoteric and I desired your counsel on a… a matter I thought best spoken of privately.'

'Now I am intrigued,' said Erebus. 'What is on your mind?'

Loken pointed towards the pulsing, spectral light of the warp on the other side of the observation bay's glass. Clouds of many colours and spirals of darkness spun and twisted like blooms of ink in water, constantly churning in a maelstrom of light and shadow. No coherent forms existed in the mysterious otherworld beyond the ship, which, but for the power of the Geller field, would destroy the Warmaster's vessel in the blink of an eye.

'The warp allows us to travel from one side of the galaxy to the other, but we don't really understand it at all, do we?' asked Loken. 'What do we really know about the things that lurk in its depths? What do we know of Chaos?'

'Chaos?' repeated Erebus, and Loken detected a moment of hesitation before the Word Bearer answered. 'What do you mean by that term?'

'I'm not sure,' admitted Loken. 'It was something Mithras Tull said to me back on Xenobia.'

'Mithras Tull? I don't know the name.'

'He was one of Jephta Naud's subordinate commanders,' explained Loken. 'I was speaking to him when everything went to hell.'

'What did he say, Captain Loken? Exactly.'

Loken's eyes narrowed at the first chaplain's tone and he said, 'Tull spoke of Chaos as though it were a distinct force, a primal presence in the warp. He said that it was the source of the most malevolent corruption imaginable and that it would outlive us all and dance on our ashes.'

'He used a colourful turn of phrase.'

'That he did, but I believe he was serious,' said Loken, gazing out into the depths of the warp.

'Trust me: Loken; the warp is nothing more than mindless energy churning in constant turmoil. That is all there is to it. Or is there something else that makes you believe his words?'

Loken thought of the slavering creature that had taken the flesh of Xavyer Jubal in the water fane under the mountains of Sixty-Three Nineteen. That had not been mindless warp energy given form. Loken had seen a monstrous, thirsting intelligence lurking within the horrid deformity that Jubal had become.

Erebus was staring at him expectantly and as much as the Word Bearer had been welcomed within the ranks of the Sons of Horus, Loken wasn't yet ready to share the horror beneath the Whisperheads with an outsider.

Hurriedly he said, 'I read of battles between the tribes of men on old Terra, before the coming of the Emperor, and they were said to use powers that were–'

'Was this in *The Chronicles of Ursh*?' asked Erebus.

'Yes. How did you know?'

'I too have read it and I know of the passages to which you refer.'

'Then you also know that there was talk of dark, primordial gods and invocations to them.'

Erebus smiled indulgently. 'Yes, and it is the work of outrageous taletellers and incorrigible demagogues to make their farragoes as exciting as possible, is it not? *The Chronicles of Ursh* is not the only text of that nature. Many such books were written before Unification and each writer filled page after page with the most outrageous, blood-soaked terrors in order to outdo his contemporaries, resulting in some works of... dubious value.'

'You don't think there's anything to it then?'

'Not at all,' said Erebus.

'Tull said that the Immaterium, as he called it, was the root of sorcery and magic.'

'Sorcery and magic?' laughed Erebus before locking his gaze with Loken. 'He lied to you, my friend. He was a fraterniser with xenos breeds and an abomination in the sight of the Emperor. You know the word of an enemy cannot be trusted. After all, did the interex not falsely accuse us of stealing one of the kinebrach's swords from the Hall of Devices? Even after the Warmaster himself vouchsafed that we did not?'

Loken said nothing as ingrained bonds of brotherhood warred with the evidence of his own senses.

Everything Erebus was saying reinforced his long held beliefs in the utter falsehood of sorcery, spirits and daemons.

Yet he could not ignore what his instincts screamed at him: *that Erebus was lying to him and the threat of Chaos was horribly real.*

Mithras Tull had become an enemy and Erebus was a brother Astartes, and Loken was astonished to find that he more readily believed the warrior of the interex.

'As you have described it to me, there is no such thing as Chaos,' promised Erebus.

Loken nodded in agreement, but despaired as he realised that no one, not even the interex, had said exactly what kind of weapon had been stolen from the Hall of Devices.

'DID YOU HEAR?' asked Ignace Karkasy, pouring yet another glass of wine. 'She's got full access... to the Warmaster! It's disgraceful. Here's us, breaking our backs to create art worthy of the name, in the hope of catching the eye of someone important enough to matter, and she bloody swans in without so much as a by your leave and gets an audience with the Warmaster!'

'I heard she has connections,' nodded Wenduin, a petite woman with red hair and an hourglass figure that ship scuttlebutt had down as a firecracker between the sheets. Karkasy had gravitated towards her as soon as he had realised she was hanging on his every bitter word. He'd forgotten exactly what it was she did, though he vaguely remembered something about 'compositions of harmonic light and shade' – whatever that meant.

Honestly, he thought, they'll let anyone be a remembrancer these days.

The Retreat was, as usual, thick with remembrancers: poets, dramatists, artists and composers, which had made for a bohemian atmosphere, while off-duty Army officers, naval ratings and crew were there for the civilians to impress with tales of books published, opening night ovations and scurrilous backstage hedonistic excess.

Without its audience, the Retreat revealed itself as an uncomfortably vandalised, smoky bar filled with people who had nothing better to do. The gamblers had scraped the arched columns bare of gilt to make gambling chips (of which Karkasy now had quite a substantial pile back in his cabin) and the artists had whitewashed whole areas of the walls for their own daubings – most of which were either lewd or farcical.

Men and women filled all the available tables, playing hands of merci merci while some of the more enthusiastic remembrancers planned their next compositions. Karkasy and Wenduin sat in one of the padded booths along the wall and the low buzz of conversation filled the Retreat.

'Connections,' repeated Wenduin sagely.

'That's it exactly,' said Karkasy, draining his glass. 'I heard the Council of Terra – the Sigillite too.'

'Throne! How'd she get them?' asked Wenduin. 'The connections I mean?'

Karkasy shook his head. 'Don't know.'

'It's not like you don't have connections either. You could find out,' Wenduin pointed out, filling his glass once more. 'I don't know what you have to be worried about anyway. You have one of the Astartes looking after you. You're a fine one to be casting aspersions!'

'Hardly,' snorted Karkasy, slapping a palm on the table. 'I have to show him everything I damn well write. It's censorship, that's what it is.'

Wenduin shrugged. 'Maybe it is, maybe it isn't, but you got to go to the War Council didn't you? A little censorship's worth that, I'll bet.'

'Maybe,' said Karkasy, unwilling to be drawn on the subject of the events on Davin and his terror at the sight of an enraged First Captain Abaddon coming to tear his head off.

In any event, Captain Loken had later found him, trembling and afraid, in the commissariat tent, making inroads into a bottle of distilac. It had been a little ridiculous really. Loken had ripped a page from the Bondsman number 7 and written on it in large, blocky letters before handing it to him.

'This is an oath of moment, Ignace,' Loken had said. 'Do you know what that means?'

'I think so,' he had replied, reading the words Loken had written.

'It is an oath that applies to an individual action. It is very specific and very precise,' Loken had explained. 'It is common for an Astartes to swear such an oath before battle when he vows to achieve a certain objective or uphold a certain ideal. In your case, Ignace, it will be to keep what passed here tonight between us.'

'I will, sir.'

'You must swear, Ignace. Place your hand on the book and the oath and swear the words.'

He had done so, placing a shaking hand atop the page, feeling the heavy texture of the page beneath his sweating palm.

'I swear not to tell another living soul what passed between us,' he said.

Loken had nodded solemnly and said, 'Do not take this lightly, Ignace. You have just made an oath with the Astartes and you must never break it. To do so would be a mistake.'

He'd nodded and made his way to the first transport off Davin.

Karkasy shook his head clear of the memory, any warmth or comfort the wine had given him suddenly, achingly, absent.

'Hey,' said Wenduin. 'Are you listening to me? You looked a million miles away there.'

'Yes, sorry. What were you saying?'

'I was asking if there was any chance you could put in a good word for me to Captain Loken? Maybe you could tell him about my compositions? You know, how good they are.'

Compositions?

What did that mean? He looked into her eyes and saw a dreadful avarice lurking behind her façade of interest, now seeing her for the self-interested social climber she was. Suddenly all he wanted to do was get away.

'Well? Could you?'

He was saved from thinking of an answer by the arrival of a robed figure at the booth.

Karkasy looked up and said, 'Yes? Can I help–' but his words trailed off as he eventually recognised Euphrati Keeler. The change in her since the last time he had seen her was remarkable. Instead of her usual ensemble of boots and fatigues, she wore the beige robe of a female remembrancer, and her long hair had been cut into a modest fringe.

Though more obviously feminine, Karkasy was disappointed to find that the change was not to his liking, preferring her aggressive stylings to the strange sexless quality this attire granted her.

'Euphrati? Is that you?

She simply nodded and said, 'I'm looking for Captain Loken. Have you seen him today?'

'Loken? No, well, yes, but not since Davin. Won't you join us?' he said, ignoring the viperous glare Wenduin cast in his direction.

His hopes of rescue were dashed when Euphrati shook her head and said, 'No, thank you. This place isn't really for me.'

'Nor me, but here I am,' smiled Karkasy. 'You sure I can't tempt you to some wine or a round of cards?'

'I'm sure, but thanks anyway. See you around, Ignace, and have a good night,' said Keeler with a knowing smile. Karkasy gave her a lopsided grin and watched her as she made her way from booth to booth before leaving the Retreat.

'Who was that?' asked Wenduin, and Karkasy was amused at the professional jealousy he heard in her voice.

'That was a very good friend of mine,' said Karkasy, enjoying the sound of the words.

Wenduin nodded curtly.

'Listen, do you want to go to bed with me or not?' she asked, all pretence of actual interest in him discarded in favour of blatant ambition.

Karkasy laughed. 'I'm a man. Of course I do.'

'And you'll tell Captain Loken of me?'

If you're as good as they say you are, you can bet on it, he thought.

'Yes, my dear, of course I will,' said Karkasy, noticing a folded piece of paper on the edge of the booth. Had it been there before? He couldn't remember. As Wenduin eased herself from the booth, he picked up the paper and unfolded it. At the top was some kind of symbol, a long capital 'I' with a haloed star at its centre. He had no idea what it meant and began to skim the words, thinking it might be some remembrancer's discarded scribblings.

Such thoughts faded, however, as he read the words written on the paper.

'The Emperor of Mankind is the Light and the Way, and all his actions are for the benefit of mankind, which is his people. The Emperor is God and God is the Emperor, so it is taught in this, the...'

'What's that?' asked Wenduin.

Karkasy ignored her, pushing the paper into his pocket and leaving the booth. He looked around the retreat and saw several identical pamphlets on various tables around the room. Now he was convinced that the paper hadn't been on his table before Euphrati's visit and he began making his way around the bar, gathering up as many of the dog-eared papers as he could find.

'What are you doing?' demanded Wenduin, watching him with her arms folded impatiently across her chest.

'Piss off!' snarled Karkasy, heading for the exit. 'Find some other gullible fool to seduce. I don't have time.'

If he hadn't been so preoccupied, he might have enjoyed her look of surprise.

SOME MINUTES LATER, Karkasy stood before Euphrati Keeler's billet, deep in the labyrinth of arched companionways and dripping passages that made up the residential deck. He noticed the symbol from the pamphlet etched on the bulkhead beside her billet and hammered his fist on her shutter until at last it opened. The smell of scented candles wafted into the corridor.

She smiled, and he knew she had been expecting him.

'Lectitio Divinitatus?' he said, holding up the pile of pamphlets he'd gathered from the Retreat. 'We need to talk.'

'Yes, Ignace, we do,' she said, turning and leaving him standing at the threshold.

He went inside after her.

HORUS'S PERSONAL CHAMBERS were surprisingly modest, thought Petronella, simple and functional with only a few items that might be considered personal. She hadn't expected lavish ostentation, but had thought to see more than could be found in any Army soldier's billet. A stack of yellowed oath papers filled a footlocker against one wall and some well thumbed books sat on the shelves beside the cot bed, its length and breadth massive to her, but probably barely sufficient for a being with the inhuman scale of a primarch.

She smiled at the idea of Horus sleeping, wondering what mighty visions of glory and majesty one of the Emperor's sons might dream. The idea of a primarch sleeping was distinctly humanising, though it had never crossed her mind that one such as Horus would even need to rest. Petronella had assumed that, as well as never aging, the primarchs did not tire either. She decided the bed was an affectation, a reminder of his humanity.

In deference to her first meeting with Horus, Petronella wore a simple dress of emerald green, its skirts hung with silver and topaz netting, and a scarlet bodice with a scandalous décolletage. She carried her dataslate and gold tipped mnemo-quill in a demure reticule of gold cord draped over her shoulder, and her fingers itched to begin their work. She had left Maggard outside the chambers, though she knew the thought of being denied the chance to stand in the presence of such a sublime warrior as Horus was galling to him. Being in such close proximity to the Astartes had been a powerful intoxicant to her bodyguard, who she could tell looked up to them as gods. She regarded his pleasure at being amongst such powerful warriors as quietly endearing, but wanted the Warmaster all to herself today.

She ran her fingertips across the wooden surface of Horus's desk, anxious to begin this first session of documenting him. The desk's proportions were as enlarged as those of his bed, and she smiled as she imagined the many great campaigns he had planned here, and the commands for war signed upon its stained and faded surface.

Had he written the order granting her previous audience here, she wondered?

She remembered well receiving that instruction to attend upon the Warmaster immediately; she remembered her terror and elation as Babeth was run ragged with half a dozen rapid changes of costume for her. In the end she had settled for something elegant yet demure – a cream dress with an ivory panelled bodice that pushed her bosom up, and a webbed necklace of red gold that reached up her neck before curling over her forehead in a dripping cascade of pearls and sapphires. Eschewing the Terran custom of powdering her face, she opted instead for a subtle blend of powdered antimony sulphide to darken the rims of her eyes and a polychromatic lip-gloss.

Horus had obviously appreciated her sartorial restraint, smiling broadly as she was ushered into his presence. Her breath, had it not already been largely stolen by the constriction of her bodice, would have been snatched away by the glory of the Warmaster's physical perfection and palpable charisma. His hair was short, and his face open and handsome, with dazzling eyes that fixed her with a stare that told her she was the most important thing to him right now. She felt giddy, like a debutante at her first ball.

He wore gleaming battle armour the colour of a winter sky, its rims formed of beaten gold, and bas-relief text filling each shoulder guard. Bright against his chest plate was a staring red eye, like a drop of blood on virgin snow, and she felt transfixed by its unflinching gaze.

Maggard stood behind her, resplendent in brightly polished gold plate and silver mail. Of course, he carried no weapons, his swords and pistols already surrendered to Horus's bodyguards.

'My lord,' she began, bowing her head and making an elaborate curtsey, her hand held palm down before him in expectation of a kiss.

'So you are of House Carpinus?' asked Horus.

She recovered quickly, disregarding the Warmaster's breach of etiquette in ignoring her hand and asking her a question before formal introductions had been made. 'I am indeed, my lord.'

'Don't call me that,' said the Warmaster.

'Oh… of course… how should I address you?'

'Horus would be a good start,' he said, and she looked up to see him smiling broadly. The warriors behind him tried unsuccessfully to hide their amusement, and Petronella realised that Horus was toying with her. She forced herself to return his smile, masking her annoyance at his informality, and said, 'Thank you. I shall.'

'So you want to be my documentarist do you?' asked Horus.

'If you will permit me to fulfil such a role, yes.'

'Why?'

Of all the questions she'd anticipated, this simple query was one she hadn't been expecting to be thrown so baldly at her.

'I feel this is my vocation, my lord,' she began. 'It is my destiny as a scion of House Carpinus to record great things and mighty deeds, and to encapsulate the glory of this war – the heroism, the danger, the violence and the full fury of battle. I desire to–'

'Have you ever seen a battle, girl?' asked Horus suddenly.

'Well, no. Not as such,' she said, her cheeks flushing angrily at the term "girl".

'I thought not,' said Horus. 'It is only those who have neither fired a shot nor heard the shrieks and groans of the dying who cry aloud for blood, vengeance and desolation. Is that what you want? Is that your "vocation"?'

'If that is what war is, then yes,' she said, unwilling to be cowed before his boorish behaviour. 'I want to see it all. See it all and record the glory of Horus for future generations.'

'The glory of Horus,' repeated the Warmaster, obviously relishing the phrase.

He held her pinned by his gaze and said, 'There are many remembrancers in my fleet, Miss Vivar. Tell me why I should give you this honour.'

Flustered by his directness once more, she searched for words, and the Warmaster chuckled at her awkwardness. Her irritation rose to the surface again and, before she could stop herself she said, 'Because no one else in the ragtag band of remembrancers you've managed to accumulate will do as good a job as I will. I will immortalise you, but if you think you can bully me with your bad manners and high and mighty attitude then you can go to hell… sir.'

A thunderous silence descended.

Then Horus laughed, the sound hard, and she knew that, in one flash of anger, she had destroyed her chances of being able to accomplish the task she had appointed herself.

'I like you, Petronella Vivar of House Carpinus,' he said. 'You'll do.'

Her mouth fell open and her heart fluttered in her breast.

'Truly?' she asked, afraid that the Warmaster was playing with her again.

'Truly,' agreed Horus.

'But I thought…'

'Listen, lass, I usually make up my mind about a person within ten seconds and I very rarely change it. The minute you walked in, I saw the fighter in you. There is something of the wolf in you, girl, and I like that. Just one thing…'

'Yes?'

'Not so formal next time,' he smirked. 'We are a ship of war, not the parlours of Merica. Now I fear I must excuse myself, as I have to head planetside to Davin for a council of war.'

And with that, she had been appointed.

It still amazed her that it had been so easy, though it meant most of the formal gowns she had brought now seemed wholly inappropriate, forcing her to dress in unbearably prosaic dresses more at home in the alms houses of the Gyptus spires. The dames of society wouldn't recognise her now.

She smiled at the memory as her trailing fingers reached the end of the desk and rested on an ancient tome with a cracked leather binding and faded gilt lettering. She opened the book and idly flipped a couple of pages, stopping at one showing a complex astrological diagram of the orbits of planets and conjunctions, below which was the image of some mythical beast, part man, part horse.

'My father gave me that,' said a powerful voice behind her.

She turned, guiltily snatching her hand back from the book.

Horus stood behind her, his massive form clad in battle plate. As ever, he was almost overwhelmingly intimidating, physical and masculine, and the thought of sharing a room with such a powerful specimen of manhood in the absence of a chaperone gave her guilt a delicious edge.

'Sorry,' she said. 'That was impolite of me.'

Horus waved his hand. 'Don't worry,' he said. 'If there was anything I didn't want you to see I wouldn't have left it out.'

Despite his easy reassurance, he gathered up the book and slipped it onto the shelves above his bed. She immediately sensed great tension in him, and though he appeared outwardly calm, her heart raced as she felt his furious anger. It bubbled beneath his skin like the fires of a once dormant volcano on the verge of unleashing its terrible fury.

Before she could say anything in reply, he said, 'I'm afraid I can't sit and speak to you today, Miss Vivar. Matters have arisen on Davin's moon that require my immediate attention.'

She tried to cover her disappointment, saying, 'No matter, we can reschedule a meeting for when you have more time.'

He laughed, the sound harsh and, she thought, a little too sad to be convincing.

'That may not be for a while,' he warned.

'I'm not someone who gives up easily,' she promised. 'I can wait.'

Horus considered her words for a moment, and then shook his head.

'No, that won't be necessary,' he said with a smile. 'You said you wanted to see war?'

She nodded enthusiastically and he said, 'Then accompany me to the embarkation deck and I'll show you how the Astartes prepare for war.'

FIVE

Our people/A leader/Speartip

THE BRIDGE OF the *Vengeful Spirit* bustled with activity, the business of ferrying troops and war machines back from the surface of Davin complete, and plans now drawn for the extermination of Eugan Temba's rebellious forces.

Extermination. That was the word they used, not subjugation, not pacification: extermination.

And the Legion was more than ready to carry out that sentence.

Sleek and deadly warships broke anchor with Davin under the watchful gaze of the Master of the Fleet, Boas Comnenus. Moving such a fleet even a short distance in formation was no small undertaking, but the ship's masters appointed beneath him knew their trade and the withdrawal from Davin was accomplished with the precision of a surgeon wielding a scalpel.

Not all the Expedition fleet vacated Davin's orbit, but enough followed the course of the *Vengeful Spirit* to ensure that nothing would be able to stand before the Astartes speartip.

The journey was a mercifully short one, Davin's moon a dirty, yellow brown smudge of reflected light haloed against the distant red sun.

To Boas Comnenus their destination looked like a terrible, bloated pustule against the heavens.

FEVERISH ACTIVITY FILLED the embarkation deck as fitters, deck hands and Mechanicum adepts made last minute pre-flight checks to the growling Stormbirds. Engines flared and strobing arc lights bathed the enormous, echoing deck in a pale, washed out industrial glow. Hatches were slammed shut, arming pins were removed from warheads, and fuel lines were disconnected from rumbling engines. Six of the monstrous flyers sat hunched at the end of their launch rails, cranes delivering the last of their ordnance payloads, while gunnery servitors calibrated the cannons slung beneath the cockpit.

The captains and warriors selected to accompany the Warmaster's speartip followed ground crews around the Stormbirds, checking and rechecking their machines. Their lives would soon depend on these aircraft and no one wanted to wind up dead thanks to something as trivial as mechanical failure. Along with the Mournival, Luc Sedirae, Nero Vipus and Verulam Moy – together with specialised squads from their companies – would travel to Davin's moon to fight once more in the name of the Imperium.

Loken was ready. His mind was full of new and disturbing thoughts, but he pushed them to one side in preparation for the coming fight. Doubt and uncertainty clouded the mind and an Astartes could afford neither.

'Throne, I'm ready for this,' said Torgaddon, clearly relishing the prospect of battle.

Loken nodded. Something still felt terribly wrong to him, but he too longed for the purity of real combat, the chance to test his warrior skills against a living opponent. Though if their intelligence was correct, all they would be facing was perhaps ten thousand rebellious Army soldiers, no match for even a quarter this many Astartes.

The Warmaster, however, had demanded the utter destruction of Temba's forces, and five companies of Astartes, a detachment of Varvarus's Byzant Janizars and a battle group of Titans from the Legio Mortis were to unleash his fiery wrath. Princeps Esau Turnet had pledged the *Dies Irae* itself.

'I've not seen a gathering of might like this since before Ullanor,' said Torgaddon. 'Those rebels on the moon are already as good as dead.'

Rebels...

Whoever thought to hear such a word?

Enemies yes, but rebels... never.

The thought soured his anticipation of battle as they made their way to where Aximand and Abaddon checked the arms inventory of their Stormbird, arguing over which munitions would be best suited to the mission.

'I'm telling you, the subsonic shells will be better,' said Aximand.

'And what if they have armour like those interex bastards?' demanded Abaddon.

'Then we use mass reactive. Tell him, Loken!'

Abaddon turned at Loken and Torgaddon's approach and nodded curtly.

'Aximand's right,' Loken said. 'Supersonic shells will pass through a man before they have time to flatten and create a killing exit wound. You might fire three of these through a target and still not put him down.'

'Just because the last few fights have been against armoured warriors, Ezekyle wants them,' said Aximand, 'but I keep telling him that this battle will be fought against men no more armoured than our own Army soldiers.'

'And let's face it,' sniggered Torgaddon. 'Ezekyle needs all the help he can get putting an enemy down.'

'I'll bloody well put you down, Tarik,' said Abaddon, his grim exterior finally cracking into a smile. The first captain's hair was pulled back in a long scalp lock in preparation for donning his helmet, and Loken could see that he too was fiercely anticipating the coming bloodshed.

'Doesn't this bother any of you?' asked Loken, unable to contain himself any longer.

'What?' asked Aximand.

'This,' said Loken, waving an arm around the deck at the preparations for war that were being made all around them. 'Don't you realise what we're about to do?'

'Of course we do, Garvi,' bellowed Abaddon. 'We're going to kill some damned fool that insulted the Warmaster!'

'No,' said Loken. 'It's more than that, don't you see? These people we're going to kill, they're not some xeno empire or a lost strand of humanity that doesn't want to be brought to compliance. They're ours; it's our people we'll be killing.'

'They're traitors,' said Abaddon, needlessly emphasising the last word. 'That's all there is to it. Don't you see? They have turned their back on the Warmaster and the Emperor, and for that reason, their lives are forfeit.'

'Come on, Garvi,' said Torgaddon. 'You're worrying about nothing.'

'Am I? What do we do if it happens again?'

The other members of the Mournival looked at one another in puzzlement.

'If what happens again?' asked Aximand finally.

'What if another world rebels in our wake, then another and another after that? This is Army, but what happens if Astartes rebel? Would we still take the fight to them?'

The three of them laughed at that, but Torgaddon answered. 'You have a fine sense of humour, my brother. You know that could never happen. It's unthinkable.'

'And unseemly,' said Aximand, his face solemn. 'What you suggest might be considered treason.'

'What?'

'I could report you to the Warmaster for this sedition.'

'Aximand, you know I would never…'

Torgaddon was the first to crack. 'Oh, Garvi, you're too easy!' he said, and they all laughed. 'Even Aximand can get you now. Throne, you're so straight up and down.'

Loken forced a smile and said, 'You're right. I'm sorry.'

'Don't be sorry,' said Abaddon. 'Be ready to kill.'

The first captain held his hand out into the middle of the group and said, 'Kill for the living.'

'Kill for the dead,' said Aximand, placing his hand on top of Abaddon's.

'To hell with the living and the dead,' said Torgaddon, following suit. 'Kill for the Warmaster.'

Loken felt a great love for his brothers and nodded, placing his hand into the circle, the confraternity of the Mournival filling him with pride and reassurance.

'I will kill for the Warmaster,' he promised.

THE SCALE OF it took her breath away. Her own vessel boasted three embarkation decks, but they were poor things compared to this, capable of handling only skiffs, cutters and shuttles.

To see so much martial power on display was humbling.

Hundreds of Astartes surrounded them, standing before their allocated Stormbirds – monstrous, fat-bodied flyers with racks of missiles slung under each wing and wide, rotary cannons seated in forward pintle mounts. Engines screamed as last minute adjustments were carried out, and each group of Astartes warriors, massive and powerful, began final weapons checks.

'I never dreamed it could be like this,' said Petronella, watching as the gargantuan blast door at the far end of the launch rails deafeningly rumbled open in preparation for the launch. Through the shimmering integrity field, she could see the leprous glow of Davin's moon against a froth of stars, as blackened jet blast deflectors rose up from the floor on hissing pneumatic pistons.

'This?' said Horus. 'This is nothing. At Ullanor, six hundred vessels anchored above the planet of the green skin. My entire Legion went to war that day, girl. We covered the land with our soldiers: over two million Army soldiers, a hundred Titans of the Mechanicum and all the slaves we freed from the green skin labour camps.'

'And all led by the Emperor,' said Petronella.

'Yes,' said Horus. 'All led by the Emperor...'

'Did any other Legions fight on Ullanor?'

'Guilliman and the Khan, their Legions helped clear the outer systems with diversionary attacks, but my warriors won the day, the best of the best slogging through blood and dirt. It was I who led the Justaerin speartip to final victory.'

'It must have been incredible.'

'It was,' agreed Horus. 'Only Abaddon and I walked away from the fight against the green skin warlord. He was a tough bastard, but I illuminated him and then threw his body from the highest tower.'

'This was before the Emperor granted you the title of Warmaster?' asked Petronella, her mnemo-quill frantically trying to keep up with Horus's rapid delivery.

'Yes.'

'And you led this... what did you call it? Speartip?'

'Yes, a speartip. A precision strike to tear out the enemy's throat and leave him leaderless and blind.'

'And you'll lead it again here?'

'I will.'

'Is that not a little unusual?'

'What?'

'Someone of such high rank taking to the field of battle?'

'I have had this same argum… discussion with the Mournival,' said Horus, ignoring her look of confusion at the term. 'I am the Warmaster and I did not attain such a title by keeping myself away from battle. For men to follow me and obey my orders without question as the Astartes do, they must see that I am right there with them, sharing the danger. How can any warrior trust me to send him into battle if he feels that all I do is sign orders, without appreciating the dangers he must face?'

'Surely there comes a time when considerations of rank must necessarily remove you from the battlefield? If you were to fall –'

'I will not.'

'But if you did.'

'I will not,' repeated Horus, and she could feel the force of his conviction in every syllable. His eyes, always so bright and full of power met hers and she felt the light of her belief in him swell until it illuminated her entire body.

'I believe you,' she said.

'Tell me, would you like to meet the Mournival?'

'The what?'

Horus smiled. 'I'll show you.'

'ANOTHER DAMNED REMEMBRANCER,' sneered Abaddon, shaking his head as he saw Horus and a woman in a green and red dress enter the embarkation deck. 'It's bad enough you've got a gaggle of them hanging round you, Loken, but the Warmaster? It's disgraceful.'

'Why don't you tell him that yourself?' asked Loken.

'I will, don't worry,' said Abaddon.

Aximand and Torgaddon said nothing, knowing when to leave the first captain to his choler and when to back off. Loken, however, was still relatively new to regular contact with Abaddon, and his anger with him over his defence of Erebus was still raw.

'You don't feel the remembrancer program has any merit at all?'

'Pah, it's a waste of our time to babysit them. Didn't Leman Russ say something about giving them all a gun? That sounds a damn sight more sensible to me than having them write stupid poems or paint pictures.'

'It's not about poems and pictures, Ezekyle, it's about capturing the spirit of the age. It's about history that we are writing.'

'We're not here to write history,' answered Abaddon, 'We're here to make it.'

'Exactly. And they will tell it.'

'Well what use is that to us?'

'Perhaps it's not for us,' said Loken. 'Did you ever think of that?'

'Then who's it for?' demanded Abaddon.

'It's for the generations who come after us,' said Loken. 'For the Imperium yet to be. You can't imagine the wealth of information the remembrancers are gathering: libraries worth of achievements chronicled, galleries worth of artistry and countless cities raised for the glory of the Imperium. Thousands of years from now, people will look back at these times and they will know us and understand the nobility of what we set out to do. Ours will be an age of enlightenment that men will weep to know they were not a part of it. All that we have achieved will be celebrated and people will remember the Sons of Horus as the founders of a new age of illumination and progress. Think of that,

Ezekyle, the next time you dismiss the remembrancers so quickly.'

He locked eyes with Abaddon, daring him to contradict him.

The first captain met his gaze then laughed. 'Maybe I should get one too. Wouldn't want anyone to forget my name in the future, eh?'

Torgaddon clapped both of them on the shoulders and said, 'No, who'd want to know about you, Ezekyle? It's me they'll remember, the hero of Spiderland who saved the Emperor's Children from certain death at the hands of the megarachnids. That's a tale worth telling twice, eh, Garvi?'

Loken smiled, glad of Tarik's intervention. 'It's a grand tale right enough, Tarik.'

'I wish it was only twice we had to hear it,' put in Aximand. 'I've lost count of how many times I've heard you tell that tale. It's getting to be as bad as that joke you tell about the bear.'

'Don't,' warned Loken, seeing Torgaddon about to launch into a rendition of the joke.

'There was this bear, the biggest bear you can imagine,' started Torgaddon. 'And a hunter...'

The others didn't give him a chance to continue, bundling him with shouts and whoops of laughter.

'This is the Mournival,' said a powerful voice and their play fighting ceased immediately.

Loken released Torgaddon from a headlock and straightened before the sound of the Warmaster's voice. The remainder of the Mournival did likewise, guiltily standing to attention before the commander. The dark complexioned woman with the black hair and fanciful dress stood at his side, and though she was tall for a mortal, she still only just reached the lower edges of his chest plate. She stared at them in confusion, no doubt wondering what she had just seen.

'Are your companies ready for battle?' demanded Horus.

'Yes, sir,' they chorused.

Horus turned to the woman and said, 'This is Petronella Vivar of House Carpinus. She is to be my documentarist and I, unwisely it seems now, decided it was time for her to meet the Mournival.'

The woman took a step towards them and gave an elaborate and uncomfortable looking curtsey, Horus waiting a little behind her. Loken caught the amused glint concealed behind his brusqueness and said, 'Well are you going to introduce us, sir? She can't very well chronicle you without us can she?'

'No, Garviel,' smiled Horus. 'I wouldn't want the chronicles of Horus to exclude you, would I? Very well, this insolent young pup is Garviel Loken, recently elevated to the lofty position of the Mournival. Next to him is Tarik Torgaddon, a man who tries to turn everything into a joke, but mostly fails. Aximand is next. "Little Horus" we call him, since he is lucky enough to share some of my most handsome features. And finally, we come to Ezekyle Abaddon, Captain of my First Company.'

'The same Abaddon from the tower at Ullanor?' asked Petronella, and Abaddon beamed at her recognition.

'Yes, the very same,' answered Horus, 'though you wouldn't think it to look at him now.'

'And this is the Mournival?'

'They are, and for all their damned horseplay, they are invaluable to me. They are a voice of reason in my ear when all around me is confusion. They are as dear to me as my brother primarchs and I value their counsel above all others. In them are the humours of choler, phlegm, melancholia and sanguinity mixed in exactly the right amount I need to keep me on the side of the angels.'

'So they are advisors?'

'Such a term is too bland for the place they have in my heart. Learn this, Petronella Vivar, and your time with me will not have been in vain: without the Mournival, the office of Warmaster would be a poor thing indeed.'

Horus stepped forward and pulled something from his belt, something with a long strip of parchment drooping from it.

'My sons,' said Horus, dropping to one knee and holding the waxen token towards the Mournival. 'Would you hear my oath of moment?'

Stunned by the magnanimity of such an act, none of the Mournival dared move. The other Astartes on the embarkation deck saw what was happening and a hush spread throughout the chamber. Even the background noise of the deck seemed to diminish at the incredible sight of the Warmaster kneeling before his chosen sons.

Eventually, Loken reached out a trembling gauntlet and took the seal from the Warmaster's hand. He glanced over at Torgaddon and Aximand either side of him, quite dumbfounded by the Warmaster's humility.

Aximand nodded and said, 'We will hear your oath, Warmaster.'

'And we will witness it,' added Abaddon, unsheathing his sword and holding it out before the Warmaster.

Loken raised the oath paper and read the words the commander had written.

'Do you, Horus, accept your role in this? Will you take your vengeance to those who defy you and turn from the glory of all you have helped create? Do you swear that you shall leave none alive who stand against the future of humanity and do you pledge to do honour to the XVI Legion?'

Horus looked up into Loken's eyes and removed his gauntlet, clenching his bare fist around the blade Abaddon held out.

'On this matter and by this weapon, I swear,' said Horus, dragging his hand along the sword blade and opening the flesh of his palm. Loken nodded and handed the wax seal to the Warmaster as he rose to his feet.

Blood welled briefly from the cut and Horus dipped the oath paper in the clotting red fluid before affixing the oath paper to his breastplate and grinning broadly at them all.

'Thank you, my sons,' he said, coming forward to embrace them all one by one.

Loken felt his admiration for the Warmaster fill his heart, all the hurt at their exclusion from his deliberations on the way here forgotten as he held each of them close.

How could they ever have doubted him?

'Now, we have a war to wage, my sons,' shouted Horus. 'What say you?'

'Lupercal!' yelled Loken, punching the air.

The others joined in and the chant spread until the embarkation deck reverberated with the deafening roars of the Sons of Horus.

'Lupercal! Lupercal! Lupercal! Lupercal!'

THE STORMBIRDS LAUNCHED in sequence, the Warmaster's bird streaking from its launch rails like a predator unleashed. At intervals of seven seconds, each Stormbird fired until all six were launched. The pilots kept them close to the *Vengeful Spirit*, waiting for the remaining assault craft to launch from the other embarkation decks. So far, there had been no sign of the *Glory of Terra*, Eugan Temba's flagship, or any of the other vessels left behind, but no one was taking any chances that their might be wolf pack squadrons of cruisers or fighters lurking nearby.

Presently, another twelve Stormbirds of the Sons of Horus took up position with the Warmaster's squadron as well as two belonging to the Word Bearers. The formation complete, the Astartes craft banked sharply, altering course to take them to the surface of Davin's moon. The mighty, cliff-like flanks of the Warmaster's flagship receded and, like swarms of bright insects, hundreds of Army drop ships detached from their bulk transporters – each one carrying a hundred armed men.

But greatest of all were the lander vessels of the Mechanicum.

Vast, monolithic structures as big as city blocks, they resembled snub-nosed tubes fitted with a wealth of heat resistant technologies and recessed deceleration burners. Inertial dampening fields held their cargoes secure and explosive bolts on internal anti-motion scaffolding were primed to release on impact.

In the wake of the militant arm of the launch came the logistics of an invasion, ammunition carriers, food and water tankers, fuel haulers and a myriad other support vessels essential for the maintenance of offensive operations.

Such was the proliferation of craft heading for the surface that no one could keep track of them all, not even the bridge crew under Boas Comnenus, and thus the gold-skinned landing skiff that launched from the civilian bay of the *Vengeful Spirit* went unnoticed.

The invasion fleet mustered in low orbit, orbital winds clutching at streamers of atmospheric gases and spinning them in lazy coils beneath the vessels.

As always, it was the Astartes who led the invasion.

THE WAY IN was rough. Atmospheric disturbances and storms wracked the skies and the Astartes Stormbirds were tossed like leaves in a hurricane. Loken felt the craft vibrate wildly around him, grateful for the restraint harness that held him fast to his cage seat. His bolter was stowed above him and there was nothing to do but wait until the Stormbird touched down and the attack began.

He slowed his breathing and cleared his mind of all distractions, feeling a hot energy suffuse his limbs as his armour prepared his metabolism for imminent battle.

The warriors of Nero Vipus's Locasta squad and Brakespur squad surrounded him, immobile, yet representing the peak of humanity's martial prowess. He loved them all dearly and knew that they wouldn't let him down. Their conduct on Murder and Xenobia had been exemplary and many of the newly elevated novitiates had been blooded on those desperate battlefields.

His company was battle tested and sure.

'Garviel,' said Vipus over the inter-armour link. 'There's something you should hear.'

'What is it?' asked Loken, detecting a tone of warning in his friend's voice.

'Switch to channel 7,' said Vipus. 'I've isolated it from the men, but I think you ought to hear this.'

Loken switched internal channels, hearing nothing but a wash of grainy static, warbling and constant. Pops and crackles punctuated the hiss, but he could hear nothing else.

'I don't hear anything,'

'Wait. You will,' promised Vipus.

Loken concentrated, listening for whatever Nero was hearing.

And then he heard it.

Faint, as though coming from somewhere impossibly far away was a voice, a gargling, wet voice.

'...the ways of man. Folly... seek... doom of all things. In death and rebirth shall mankind live forever...'

Though he was not built to feel fear, Loken was suddenly and horribly reminded of the approach to the Whisperheads when the air had been thick with the taunting hiss of the thing called Samus.

'Oh no...' whispered Loken as the watery, rasping voice came again. 'Thus do I renounce the ways of the

Emperor and his lackey the Warmaster of my own free will. If he dares come here, he will die. And in death shall he live forever. Blessed be the hand of Nurgh-leth. Blessed be. Blessed be…'

Loken hammered his fist against the release bolt on his cage seat and rose to his feet, swaying slightly as he felt a strange nausea cramp his belly. His genhanced body allowed him to compensate for the wild motion of the Stormbird, and he made his way swiftly along the ribbed decking towards the pilots' compartment, determined that they wouldn't walk blind into the same horror as had been waiting for them on Sixty-Three Nineteen.

He pulled open the hatch where the flight officers and hardwired pilots fought to bring them in through the swirling yellow storm clouds. He could hear the same, repeating phrase coming over the internal speakers here.

'Where's it coming from?' he demanded.

The nearest flight officer turned and said, 'It's a vox, plain and simple, but…'

'But?'

'It's coming from a ship vox,' said the man, pointing at a wavering green waveform on the waterfall display before him. 'From the patterning it's one of ours. And it's a powerful one, a transmitter designed for inter-ship communication between fleets.'

'It's an actual vox transmission?' said Loken, relieved it wasn't ghost chatter like the hateful voice of Samus.

'Seems to be, but a ship's vox unit that size shouldn't be anywhere near the surface of a planet. Ships that big don't come this far down into the atmosphere. Leastways if they want to keep flying they don't.'

'Can you jam it?'

'We can try, but like I said, it's a powerful signal, it could burn through our jamming pretty quickly.'

'Can you trace where it's coming from?'

The flight officer nodded. 'Yes, that won't be a problem. A signal that powerful we could have traced from orbit.'

'Then why didn't you?'

'It wasn't there before,' protested the officer. 'It only started once we hit the ionosphere.'

Loken nodded. 'Jam it as best you can. And find the source.'

He turned back to the crew compartment, unsettled by the uncanny similarities between this development and the approach to the Whisperheads.

Too similar to be accidental, he thought.

He opened a channel to the other members of the Mournival, receiving confirmation that the signal was being heard throughout the speartip.

'It's nothing, Loken,' came the voice of the Warmaster from the Stormbird at the leading edge of the speartip. 'Propaganda.'

'With respect, sir, that's what we thought in the Whisperheads.'

'So what are you suggesting, Captain Loken? That we turn around and head back to Davin? Ignore this stain on my honour?'

'No, sir,' replied Loken. 'Just that we ought to be careful.'

'Careful?' laughed Abaddon, his hard Cthonic laughter grating even over the vox. 'We are Astartes. Others should be careful around us.'

'The first captain is right,' said Horus. 'We will lock onto this signal and destroy it.'

'Sir, that might be exactly what our enemies want us to try.'

'Then they'll soon realise their error,' snapped Horus, shutting off the connection.

Moments later, Loken heard the Warmaster's orders come through the vox and felt the deck shift under him as the Stormbirds smoothly changed course like a pack of hunting birds.

He made his way back to his cage seat and strapped himself in, suddenly sure that they were walking into a trap.

'What's going on, Garvi?' asked Vipus.

'We're going to destroy that voice,' said Loken, repeating the Warmaster's orders. 'It's nothing, just a vox transmitter. Propaganda.'

'I hope that's all it is.'

So do I, thought Loken.

THE STORMBIRD TOUCHED down with a hard slam, lurching as its skids hit soft ground and fought for purchase. The harness restraints disengaged and the warriors of Locasta smoothly rose from their cage seats and turned to retrieve their stowed weaponry as the debarking ramp dropped from the rear of the Stormbird.

Loken led his men from their transport, hot steam and noxious fumes fogging the air as the blue glow of the Stormbird's shrieking engines filled the air with noise. He stepped from the hard metal of the ramp and splashed down onto the boggy surface of Davin's moon. His armoured weight sank up to mid calf, an abominable stench rising from the wet ground underfoot.

The Astartes of Locasta and Brakespur dispersed from the Stormbird with expected efficiency, spreading out to form a perimeter and link up with the other squads from the Sons of Horus.

The noise of the Stormbirds diminished as their engines spooled down and the blue glow faded from beneath their wings. The billowing clouds of vapour they threw up began to disperse and Loken had his first view of Davin's moon.

Desolate moors stretched out as far as the eye could see, which wasn't far thanks to the rolling banks of yellow mist clinging to the ground and moist fog that restricted visibility to less than a few hundred metres. The Sons of Horus were forming up around the magnificent figure of the Warmaster, ready to move out, and spots of light in the yellow sky announced the imminent arrival of the Army drop ships.

'Nero, get some men forward to scout the edges of the mist,' Loken ordered. 'I don't want anything coming at us without prior warning.'

Vipus nodded and set about establishing scouting parties as Loken opened a channel to Verulam Moy. The Captain of the 19th Company had volunteered some of his heavy weapon squads and Loken knew he could rely on their steady aim and cool heads. 'Verulam? Make sure your Devastators are ready and have good fields of fire, they won't get much of a warning through this fog.'

'Indeed, Captain Loken,' replied Moy. 'They are deploying as we speak.'

'Good work, Verulam,' he said, shutting off the vox and studying the landscape in more detail. Wretched bogs and dank fens rendered the landscape a uniform brown and sludgy green, with the occasional blackened and withered tree silhouetted against the sky. Clouds of buzzing insects hovered in thick swarms over the black waters.

Loken tasted the atmosphere via his armour's external senses, gagging on the rank smell of excrement and rotten meat. The senses in his armour's helmet quickly filtered them out, but the breath he'd taken told him that the atmosphere was polluted with the residue of decaying matter, as though the ground beneath him was slowly rotting away. He took a few ungainly steps through the swampy ground, each step sending up a bubbling ripple of burps and puffs of noxious gasses.

As the noise of the Stormbirds faded, the silence of the moon became apparent. The only sounds were the splashing of the Astartes through the swampy bogs and the insistent buzz of the insects.

Torgaddon splashed towards him, his armour stained with mud and slime from the swamps and even though his helmet obscured his features, Loken could feel his friend's annoyance at this dismal location.

'This place reeks worse than the latrines of Ullanor,' he said.

Loken had to agree with him; the few breaths he'd taken before his armour had isolated him from the atmosphere still lingered in the back of his throat.

'What happened here?' wondered Loken. 'The briefing texts didn't say anything about the moon being like this.'

'What did they say?'

'Didn't you read them?'

Torgaddon shrugged. 'I figured I'd see what kind of place it was once we landed.'

Loken shook his head, saying, 'You'll never make an Ultramarine, Tarik.'

'No danger of that,' replied Torgaddon. 'I prefer to form plans as I go and Guilliman's lot are even more starch-arsed than you. But leaving my cavalier attitude to mission briefings aside, what's this place supposed to look like then?'

'It's supposed to be climatologically similar to Davin – hot and dry. Where we are now should be covered in forests.'

'So what happened?'

'Something bad,' said Loken, staring out into the foggy depths of the moon's marshy landscape. 'Something very bad.'

PART TWO

PLAGUE MOON

SIX

Land of decay/Dead things/*Glory of Terra*

THE ASTARTES SPREAD out through the fog, moving as swiftly as the boggy conditions allowed and following the source of the vox signal. Horus led from the front, a living god marching tall through the stinking quagmires and rank swamps of Davin's moon, untroubled by the noxious atmosphere. He disdained the wearing of a helmet, his superhuman physique easily able to withstand the airborne poisons.

Four blocks of Astartes marched, phalanx-like, into the mists, with each member of the Mournival leading nearly two hundred warriors. Behind them came the soldiers of the Imperial army, company after company of red-jacketed warriors with gleaming lasguns and silver tipped lances. Each man was equipped with rebreather apparatus after it was discovered that their mortal constitutions were unable to withstand the moon's toxic atmosphere. Initial landings of armour proved to be disastrous, as tanks sank into the marshland and dropships found themselves caught in the sucking mud.

Though the greatest of all the engines of war were those that emerged from the Mechanicum landers. Even the Astartes had paused in their advance to watch the descent of the three monstrously huge craft. Slowly dropping through the yellow skies in defiance of gravity like great primeval monoliths, the blackened hulks travelled on smoking pillars of fire as their colossal retros fought to slow them down. Even with such fiery deceleration, the ground shook with the hammerblow of their impacts, geysers of murky water thrown hundreds of metres into the air along with blinding clouds as the swamps flashed to steam. Massive hatches blew open and the motion resistant scaffolding fell away as the Titans of the Legio Mortis stepped from their landing craft and onto the moon's surface.

The *Dies Irae* led the *Death's Head* and *Xestor's Sword*, Warlord Titans with long, fluttering honour rolls hung from their armoured thorax. Each thunderous footstep of the mighty Titans sent shockwaves through the swamps for kilometres in all directions, their bastion legs sinking several metres through the marshy ground to the bedrock beneath. Their steps churned huge gouts of mud and water, their appearance that of awesome gods of war come to smite the Warmaster's enemies beneath their mighty tread.

Loken watched the arrival of the Titans with a mixture of awe and unease: awe for the majesty of their colossal appearance, unease for the fact that the Warmaster felt it necessary to deploy such powerful engines of destruction.

THE ADVANCE WAS slow going, trudging through clinging mud and stinking, brackish water, all the while unable to see much more than a few dozen metres. The thick fog banks deadened sound such that something close by might be inaudible while Loken could clearly hear the splash of warriors from Luc Sedirae's men, far to his right. Of course he couldn't see them through the yellow mist, so each company kept in regular vox contact to try and ensure they weren't separating.

Loken wasn't sure it was helping though. Strange groans and hisses, like the expelled breath of a corpse, bubbled from the ground and blurred shadow forms moved in the mist. Each time he raised his bolter to take aim in readiness, the mist would part and an armoured figure in the green of the Sons of Horus or the steel grey of the Word Bearers would be revealed. Erebus had led his warriors to Davin's moon in support of the Warmaster and Horus had welcomed their presence.

The mist gathered in thickness with unsettling speed, slowly swallowing them up until all Loken could see were warriors from his own company. They passed through a dark forest of leafless, dead trees, the bark glistening and wet looking. Loken paused to examine one, pressing his gauntlet against the tree's surface and grimacing as its bark sloughed off in wet chunks. Writhing maggots and burrowing creatures curled and wriggled within the rotten sapwood.

'These trees…' he said.

'What about them?' asked Vipus.

'I thought they were dead, but they're not.'

'No?'

'They're diseased. Rotten with it.'

Vipus shrugged and carried onwards, and once again Loken was struck by the certainty that something terrible had happened here. And looking at the diseased heartwood of the tree, he wasn't sure that it was over. He wiped his stained gauntlet on his leg armour and set off after Vipus.

The eerily silent march continued through the fog and, assisted by the servo muscles of their armour, the Astartes quickly began to outpace the soldiers of the

Imperial Army, who were finding the going much more difficult.

'Mournival,' said Loken over the inter-suit link. 'We need to slow our advance, we're leaving too big a gap between ourselves and the Army detachments.'

'Then they need to pick up the pace,' returned Abaddon. 'We don't have time to wait for lesser men. We're almost at the source of the vox.'

'Lesser men,' said Aximand. 'Be careful, Ezekyle, you're starting to sound a little like Eidolon now.'

'Eidolon? That fool would have come down here on his own to gain glory,' snarled Abaddon. 'I'll not be compared to him!'

'My apologies, Ezekyle. You're obviously nothing like him,' deadpanned Aximand.

Loken listened with amusement to his fellow Mournival's bantering, which, together with the quiet of Davin's moon began to reassure him that his concerns over their deployment here might be unfounded. He lifted his armoured boot from the swamp and took another step forward, this time feeling something crack under his step. Glancing down, he saw something round and greenish white bob upwards in the water.

Even without turning it over he could see it was a skull, the paleness of bone wreathed in necrotic strands of rotted flesh and muscle. A pair of shoulders rose from the depths behind it, the spinal column exposed beneath a layer of bloated green flesh.

Loken's lip curled in disgust as the decomposed corpse rolled onto its back, its sightless eye sockets filled with mud and weeds. Even as he saw the rotted cadaver, more bobbed to the surface, no doubt disturbed from their resting places on the bottom of the swamps by the footfalls of the Titans.

He called a halt and opened the link to his fellow commanders once again as yet more bodies, hundreds now, floated to the surface of the swamp. Grey and lifeless meat still clung to their bones and the impacts of the Titans' footfalls gave their dead limbs a horrid animation.

'This is Loken,' he said. 'I've found some bodies.'

'Are they Temba's men?' asked Horus.

'I can't tell, sir,' answered Loken. 'They're too badly decomposed. It's hard to tell. I'm checking now.'

He slung his bolter and leaned forwards, gripping the nearest corpse and lifting it from the water. Its bloated, rancid flesh was alive with wriggling motion, burrowing carrion insects and larvae nesting within it. Sure enough, mouldering scraps of a uniform hung from it and Loken wiped a smear of mud from its shoulder.

Barely legible beneath the scum and filth of the swamps he found a sewn patch bearing the number sixty-three emblazoned over the outline of a snarling wolf's head.

'Yes, 63rd Expedition,' confirmed Loken. 'They're Temba's, but I–'

Loken never finished the sentence as the bloated body suddenly reached up and fastened its bony fingers around his neck, its eyes filled with lambent green fire.

'LOKEN?' SAID HORUS as the link was suddenly cut off. 'Loken?'

'Something amiss?' asked Torgaddon.

'I don't know yet, Tarik,' answered the Warmaster.

Suddenly the hard bangs of bolter fire and the whoosh of flame units could be heard from all around them.

'Second Company!' shouted Torgaddon. 'Stand to, weapons free!'

'Where's it coming from?' bellowed Horus.

'Can't say,' replied Torgaddon. 'The mist's playing merry hell with the acoustics.'

'Find out,' ordered the Warmaster.

Torgaddon nodded, demanding contact reports from all companies. Garbled shouts of impossible things came over the link, along with the louder bark of heavy bolter fire.

Gunfire sounded to his left and he spun to face it, his bolter raised before him. He could see nothing but the staccato flashes of weapon fire and the occasional blue streak of a plasma shot. Even the external senses of his armour were unable to penetrate the creeping mist.

'Sir, I think we–'

Without warning the swamp exploded as something vast and bloated erupted from the water before him. Its gangrenous, rotten flesh barrelled into him, its bulk sufficient to knock him onto his back and into the swamp.

Before he went under the dark water, Torgaddon had the fleeting impression of a yawning mouth filled with hundreds of fangs and a glaucous, cyclopean eye beneath a horn of yellowed bone.

'I DON'T KNOW. The command net just went crazy,' said Moderati Primus Aruken in response to Princeps Turnet's question. The external surveyors had suddenly and shockingly filled with returns that hadn't been there a second ago and his princeps had demanded to know what was going on.

'Well find out, damn you!' ordered Turnet. 'The Warmaster's out there.'

'Main guns spooled up and ready to fire,' reported Moderati Primus Titus Cassar.

'We need a damn target first, I'm not about to fire into that mess without knowing what I'm shooting at,' said Turnet. 'If it was Army I'd risk it, but not Astartes.'

The bridge of the *Dies Irae* was bathed in a red light, its three command officers seated upon their control seats on a raised dais before the green glow of the tactical plot. Wired into the very essence of the Titan, they could feel its every motion as though it were their own.

Despite the mighty war machine beneath him, Jonah Aruken suddenly felt powerless as this unknown enemy arose to engulf the Sons of Horus. Expecting armoured opposition and an enemy they could see, they had been little more than a focus for the Imperial forces to rally around so far. For all the Titan's overwhelming superiority in firepower, there was little they could do to aid their fellows.

'Getting something,' reported Cassar. 'Incoming signal.'

'What is it? I need better information than that, damn you,' shouted Turnet.

'Aerial contact. Signal's firming up. Fast moving and heading towards us.'

'Is it a Stormbird?'

'No, sir. All Stormbirds are accounted for in the deployment zone and I'm not picking up any military transponder signals.'

Turnet nodded. 'Then it's hostile. Do you have a solution, Aruken?'

'Running it now, princeps.'

'Range six hundred metres and closing,' said Cassar. 'God-Emperor protect us, it's coming right for us.'

'Aruken! That's too damn close, shoot it down.'

'Working on it, sir.'

'Work faster!'

THE DENSE MISTS made looking through the frontal windshield pointless; nevertheless, there was an irresistible fascination in looking out at an alien world – not that there was much, or indeed anything, to see. Thus, Petronella's first impressions upon breaching the upper atmosphere were of disappointment, having expected exotic vistas of unimaginable alien strangeness.

Instead, they had been buffeted by violent storm winds and could see nothing but the yellow skies and banks of fog that seemed to be gathered around another unremarkable patch of brown swampland ahead.

Though the Warmaster had politely, but firmly, declined her request to travel to the surface with the warriors of the speartip, she had been sure there was a glint of mischief in his eye. Taking that for a sign of tacit approval, she had immediately gathered Maggard and her flight crew in the shuttle bay in preparation for descent to the moon below.

Her gold-skinned landing skiff launched in the wake of the Army dropships, losing itself in the mass of assault craft heading to the moon's surface. Unable to keep pace with the invasion force, they had been forced to follow the emission trails and now found themselves circling deep in a soup of impenetrable fog that rendered the ground below virtually invisible.

'Getting some returns from up ahead, my lady,' said the first officer. 'I think it's the speartip.'

'At last,' she said. 'Get as close as you can then set us down. I want to get out of this mist so I can see something worth writing about.'

'Yes, ma'am.'

Petronella settled back into her seat as the skiff angled its course towards the source of the surveyor return, irritably altering the position of her restraint harness to try to avoid creasing the folds of her dress. She gave up, deciding that the dress was beyond saving, and returned her gaze to the windshield as the pilot gave a sudden yell of terror.

Hot fear seethed in her veins as the mist before them cleared and she saw a huge mechanical giant before them, its proportions massive and armoured. Saw-toothed bastions and towers filled her vision, massive cannons and a terrible, snarling face of dark iron.

'Throne!' cried the pilot, hauling on the controls in a desperate evasive manoeuvre as roaring fire and light horrifyingly filled the windshield.

Petronella's world exploded in pain and broken glass as the guns of the *Dies Irae* opened fire and blasted her skiff from the yellow skies.

LOKEN SURGED BACKWARDS in horror and disgust as the cadaver attempted to strangle the life from him with its slimy fingers. For something as apparently fragile as a rotted corpse, the thing was possessed of a fearsome strength and he was dragged to his knees by the weight and power of the creature.

With a thought, he flooded his metabolism with battle stimms and fresh strength surged into his limbs. He gripped the arms of his attacker and pulled them from its reeking torso in a flood of dead fluids and a wash of brackish blood. The fire died in the thing's eyes and it flopped lifeless to the swamp.

He pushed himself to his feet and took stock of the situation, his Astartes training suppressing any notion of panic or disorientation. From all around them, the bodies he had previously thought to be lifeless were rising from the dark waters and launching themselves at his warriors.

Bolters blasted chunks of mouldered flesh from their bodies or tore limbs from putrefied torsos, but still they kept coming, tearing at the Astartes with diseased, yellowed claws. More of the things were rising all around them and Loken shot three down with as many shots, shattering skulls and exploding chests with mass-reactive shells.

'Sons of Horus, on me!' he yelled. 'Form on me.'

The warriors of 10th Company calmly began falling back to their captain, firing as they went at the necrotic horrors rising from the swamp like creatures from their worst nightmares. Hundreds of dead things surrounded them, mouldering corpses and bloated, muttering abominations, each with a single milky, distended eye and a scabrous horn sprouting from its forehead.

What were they? Monstrous xeno creatures with the power to reanimate dead flesh or something far worse? Thick, buzzing clouds of flies flew round them, and Loken saw an Astartes go down, the feeds on his helmet thick with fat bodied insects. The warrior frenziedly tore his helmet off and Loken was horrified to see his flesh rotting away with an unnatural rapidity, his skin greying and peeling away to reveal the liquefying tissue beneath.

The bark of bolter fire focussed him and he returned his attention to the battle before him, emptying magazine after magazine into the shambling mass of repulsive creatures before him.

'Head shots only!' he cried as he put another of the dead things down, its skull a ruin of blackened bone and sloshing ooze. The tide of the battle began to turn as more and more of the shambling horrors went down and stayed down. The green-fleshed things with grotesquely distended bellies took more killing, though it seemed to Loken that they dissolved into stinking matter as they fell into the water of the swamp.

More shapes moved through the mist as a thunderous roar of heavy cannon fire came from behind them, followed by the bright flare of an explosion high above. Loken looked up to see a golden landing skiff trailing smoke and fire wobble in the sky, though he had not the time to wonder what a civilian craft was doing in a warzone as yet more of the dead things climbed from the water.

Too close for bolters, he drew his sword and brought the monstrously toothed blade to life with a press of the activation stud. A ghastly thing of decomposed flesh and rotten meat hurled itself at him and he swung his blade two handed for its skull.

The blade roared as it slew, gobbets of wet, grey meat spattering his armour as he ripped the sword through from brainpan to groin. He swung at another creature, the green fire of its eyes flickering out as he hacked it in two. All about him, Sons of Horus went toe to toe with the terrible creatures that had once been members of the 63rd Expedition.

Rotted hands clamped onto his armour from beneath the water and Loken felt himself being dragged down. He roared and reversed his grip on his sword, stabbing it straight down into leering skulls and rotted faces, but incredibly their strength was the greater and he could not resist their pull.

'Garvi!' shouted Vipus, hacking enemies from his path as he forged through the swamp towards him.

'Luc! Help me!' cried Vipus, grabbing onto Loken's outstretched arm. Loken gripped onto his friend's hand as he felt another set of hands grip him around his chest and haul backwards.

'Let go, you bastards!' roared Luc Sedirae, hauling with all his might.

Loken felt himself rising and kicked out as the swamp creatures finally released him. He scrambled back and clambered to his feet. Together, he, Luc and Nero fought with bludgeoning ferocity, although there was no shape to the battle now, if there ever had been. It was nothing more than butcher work, requiring no swordsmanship or finesse, just brute strength and a determination not to fall. Bizarrely, Loken thought of Lucius, the swordsman of the Emperor's Children Legion, and of how he would have hated this inelegant form of war.

Loken returned his attention to the battle and, with Luc Sedirae and Nero Vipus in the fight, he was able to gain some space and time to reorganise.

'Thanks, Luc, Nero. I owe you,' he said in a lull in the fighting. The Sons of Horus reloaded bolters and cleaned chunks of dead flesh from their swords. Sporadic bursts of gunfire still sounded from the swamp and strobing flashes lit the fog with firefly bursts. Off to their left Loken saw a burning pyre where the skiff had come down, its flames acting as a beacon in the midst of the obscuring fog.

'No problem, Garvi,' said Sedirae, and Loken knew that he was grinning beneath his helmet. 'You'll do the same for me before we're out of this shit-storm, I'll wager.'

'You're probably right, but let's hope not.'

'What's the plan, Garvi?' asked Vipus.

Loken held up his hand for silence as he attempted to make contact with his Mournival brothers and the War-master once more. Static and desperate cries filled the vox, terrified voices of army soldiers and the damned, gurgling voices that kept saying, 'Blessed be Nurgh-leth...' over and over.

Then a voice cut across every channel and Loken almost cried aloud in relief to hear it.

'All Sons of Horus, this is the Warmaster. Converge on this signal. Head for the flames!'

At the sound of the Warmaster's voice, fresh energy filled the tired limbs and hearts of the Astartes, and they moved off in good order towards the burning pillar of fire coming from the wrecked skiff they had seen earlier. Loken killed with a methodical precision, each shot felling an opponent. He began to feel that they finally had the measure of this grotesque enemy.

Whatever fell energy bestowed animation upon these diseased nightmares was clearly incapable of giving them much more than basic motor functions and an unremit-ting hostility.

Loken's armour was covered in deep gouges and he wished he knew how many men he had lost to the loath-some hunger of the dead things.

He vowed that this Nurgh-leth would pay dearly for each of their deaths.

SHE COULD BARELY breathe, her chest hiking as she drew in convulsive gulps of air from the respirator Maggard was pushing against her face. Petronella's eyes stung, tears of pain coursing down her cheeks as she tried to push herself into a sitting position.

All she remembered was a fury of noise and light, a metallic shriek and a bone jarring impact as the skiff crashed and broke into pieces. Blood filled her senses and she felt excruciating pain all down her left side. Flames leapt around her, and her vision blurred with the sting of the atmosphere and smoke.

'What happened?' she managed, her voice muffled through the respirator's mouthpiece.

Maggard didn't answer, but then she remembered that he couldn't and twisted her head around to gain a better appreciation of their current situation. Torn up bodies clothed in her livery littered the ground – the pilots and flight crew of her skiff – and there was a lot of blood covering the wreckage. Even through the respirator, she could smell the gore.

Cloying banks of leprous fog surrounded them, though the heat of the flames appeared to be clearing it in their immediate vicinity. Shambling shapes surrounded them and relief flooded her as she realised that they would soon be rescued.

Maggard spun, drawing his sword and pistol, and Petronella tried to shout at him that he must stand down, that these were their rescuers.

Then the first shape emerged from the smoke and she screamed as she saw its diseased flesh and the rotted innards hanging from its opened belly. Nor was it the worst of the approaching things. A cavalcade of cadavers with bloated, ruptured flesh and putrid, diseased bodies sloshed through the mud and wreckage towards them, clawed hands outstretched.

The green fire in their eyes spoke of monstrous appetites and Petronella felt a gut-wrenching terror greater than anything she had ever known.

Only Maggard stood between her and the walking, diseased corpses, and he was but one man. She had watched him train in the gymnasia of Kairos many times, but she had never seen him draw his weapons in anger.

Maggard's pistol barked and each shot blasted one of the shambling horrors from its feet, neat holes drilled in its forehead. He fired and fired until his pistol was empty, and then holstered it and drew a long, triangular bladed dagger.

As the horde approached, her bodyguard attacked.

He leapt, feet first, at the nearest corpse and a neck snapped beneath his boot heel. Maggard spun as he landed, his sword decapitating a pair of the monsters, and his dagger ripping the throat from another. His Kirlian rapier darted like a silver snake, its glowing edge stabbing and cutting with incredible speed. Whatever it touched dropped instantly to the muddy ground like a servitor with its dotrina wafer pulled.

His body was always in motion, leaping, twisting and dodging away from the clutching hands of his diseased attackers. There was no pattern to their assault, simply a mindless host of dead things seeking to envelop them. Maggard fought like nothing she had ever seen, his augmetic muscles bulging and flexing as he cut down his foes with quick, lethal strokes.

No matter how many he killed, there were always more pressing in and they steadily forced him back a step at a time. The horde of creatures began to surround them, and Petronella saw that Maggard couldn't possibly hold them all back. He staggered towards her, bleeding from a score of minor wounds. His flesh was blistered and weeping around the cuts and there was an unhealthy pallor to his skin, despite his respirator gear.

She wept bitter tears of horror as the monsters closed in, jaws opening wide to devour her flesh, and grasping hands ready to tear her perfect skin and feast on her innards. This wasn't how it was supposed to be. The Great Crusade wasn't supposed to end in failure and death!

A corpse with mouldering, sagging skin lurched past Maggard, his blade lodged in the belly of a giant, necrotic thing with green flesh that was thick with flies.

She screamed as it reached for her.

Deafening bangs thundered behind her and the creature disintegrated in an explosion of wet meat and bone. Petronella covered her ears as the thunderous roar of gunfire came again and her attackers were torn apart in a series of rancid explosions, falling back into the fires of the skiff and burning with stinking green flames.

She rolled onto her side, crying in pain and fear as the terrifyingly close volleys continued, clearing a path for the massive, armoured warriors of the Sons of Horus.

A giant towered above her, reaching for her with his armoured gauntlet.

He wore no helmet and was silhouetted by a terrible red glow, his awesome bulk haloed by blazing plumes of fire and pillars of black smoke. Even through her tears, the Warmaster's beauty and physical perfection rendered her speechless. Though blood and dark slime covered his armour and his cloak was torn and tattered, Horus towered like a war god unleashed, his face a mask of terrifying power.

He lifted her to her feet as easily as one might lift a babe in arms, while his warriors continued the slaughter of the monstrous dead things. More and more Sons of Horus were converging on the crash site, guns firing to drive the enemy back and forming a protective cordon around the Warmaster.

'Miss Vivar,' demanded Horus. 'What in the name of Terra are you doing here? I ordered you to stay aboard the *Vengeful Spirit*.'

She struggled for words, still in awe of his magnificent presence. He had saved her. The Warmaster had personally saved her and she wept to know his touch.

'I had to come. I had to see – '

'Your curiosity almost got you killed,' raged Horus. 'If your bodyguard had been less capable, you'd already be dead.'

She nodded dumbly, holding onto a twisted spar of metal to keep from collapsing as the Warmaster stepped through the debris towards Maggard. The gold armoured warrior held himself erect, despite the pain of his wounds.

Horus lifted Maggard's sword arm, examining the warrior's blade.

'What's your name, warrior?' asked the Warmaster.

Maggard, of course, did not answer, looking over at Petronella for help in answering.

'He cannot answer you, my lord,' said Petronella.

'Why not? Doesn't he speak Imperial Gothic?'

'He does not speak at all, sir. House Carpinus chaperones removed his vocal chords.'

'Why would they do that?'

'He is an indentured servant of House Carpinus and it is not a bodyguard's place to speak in the presence of his mistress.'

Horus frowned, as though he did not approve of such things, and said, 'Then you tell me what his name is.'

'He is called Maggard, sir.'

'And this blade he wields? How is it that the slightest touch of its edge slays one of these creatures?'

'It is a Kirlian blade, forged on ancient Terra and said to be able to sever the connection between the soul and the body, though I have never seen it used before today.'

'Whatever it is, I think it saved your life, Miss Vivar.'

She nodded as the Warmaster turned to face Maggard once more and made the sign of the aquila before saying, 'You fought with great courage, Maggard. Be proud of what you did here today.'

Maggard nodded and dropped to his knees with his head bowed, tears streaming from his eyes at being so honoured by the Warmaster.

Horus bent down and placed the palm of his hand on the bodyguard's shoulder, saying, 'Rise, Maggard. You have proven yourself to be a warrior, and no warrior of such courage should kneel before me.'

Maggard stood, smoothly reversing the grip of his sword and offering it, hilt first, to the Warmaster.

The yellow sky reflected coldly in his golden eyes, and Petronella shivered as she saw a newfound devotion in her bodyguard's posture, an expression of faith and pride that frightened her with its intensity.

The meaning of the gesture was clear. It said what Maggard himself could not.

I am yours to command.

THUS ASSEMBLED, THE Astartes took stock of their situation. All four phalanxes had rendezvoused around the crash site as the attacks from the diseased and dead things ceased for the time being. The speartip was blunted, but it was still an awesome fighting force and easily capable of destroying what remained of Temba's paltry detachment.

Sedirae volunteered his men to secure the perimeters, and Loken simply waved his assent, knowing that Luc was hungry for more battle and for a chance to shine in front of the Warmaster. Vipus re-formed the scouting parties and Verulam Moy set up fire positions for his Devastators.

Loken was relieved beyond words to see that all four members of the Mournival had survived the fighting, though Torgaddon and Abaddon had both lost their helmets in the furious mêlées. Aximand's armour had been torn open across his side and a splash of red, shockingly bright against the green of his armour, stained his thigh.

'Are you all right?' Torgaddon asked him, his armour stained and blistered, as though someone had poured acid over its plates.

'Just about,' nodded Loken. 'You?'

'Yes, though it was a close run thing,' conceded Torgaddon. 'Bastard got me underwater and was choking the life out of me. Tore my helmet right off and I think I must have drunk about a bucket of that swamp water. Had to gut him with my combat knife. Messy.'

Torgaddon's genhanced body would be unharmed by swallowing the water, no matter what toxins it carried, but it was a stark reminder of the power of these creatures that a warrior as fearsome as him could almost be overcome. Abaddon and Aximand had similar tales of close run things, and Loken desperately wanted the fight to be over. The longer the mission went on, the more it reminded him of Eidolon's abortive first strike on Murder.

Restored communications revealed that the Byzant Janizars had suffered terribly under the assault from the swamp and had hunkered down in defensive positions. Not even the electro-scythes of their discipline masters were able to coerce them forward. The horrific enemy had melted back into the fog, but no one could say with any certainty where the creatures had gone.

The Titans of the Legio Mortis towered over the Astartes; the *Dies Irae* reassuring the assembled warriors by the simple virtue of is immensity.

It was left to Erebus to point the way onwards, he and his depleted warriors staggering into the circle of light surrounding Petronella Vivar's crashed skiff. The first chaplain's armour was stained and battered, its many seals and scripture papers torn from it.

'Warmaster, I believe we have found the source of the transmissions,' reported Erebus. 'There is a... structure up ahead.'

'Where is it and how close?' demanded the Warmaster.

'Perhaps another kilometre to the west.'

Horus raised his sword and shouted, 'Sons of Horus, we have been grossly wronged here and some of our brothers are dead. It is time we avenge them.'

His voice easily carried over the dead waters of the swamps, his warriors roaring their assent and following the Warmaster, as Erebus and the Word Bearers set of into the mists.

Fired with furious energy, the Astartes ploughed through the sodden ground, ready to enact the Warmaster's wrath upon the vile foe that had unleashed such horrors upon them. Maggard and Petronella went with them, none of the Astartes willing to retreat and escort them back to the Army positions. Legion apothecaries tended their wounds and helped them through the worst of the terrain.

Eventually, the mists began to thin and Loken could make out the more distant figures of Astartes warriors through the smudges of fog. The further they marched, the more solid the ground underfoot became, and as Erebus led them onwards, the mist became thinner still.

Then, as quickly as a man might step from one room to another, they were out of it.

Behind them, the banks of fog gathered and coiled, like a theatre curtain in a playhouse waiting to unveil some wondrous marvel.

Before them was the source of the vox transmission, rearing up from the muddy plain like a colossal iron mountain.

Eugan Temba's flagship, the *Glory of Terra*.

SEVEN

Watch our backs/Collapse/The betrayer

RUSTED AND DEAD nearly six decades, the vessel lay smashed and ruined on the cratered mudflats, its once mighty hull torn open and buckled almost beyond recognition. Its towering gothic spires, like the precincts of a mighty city, lay fallen and twisted, its buttresses and archways hung with decaying fronds of huge web-like vines. Its keel was broken, as though it had struck the moon's surface, belly first, and many of the upper surfaces had caved in, the decks below open to the elements.

Swathes of mossy greenery covered the hull and her command spire speared into the sky; warp vanes and tall vox masts bending in the moaning wind.

Loken thought the scene unbearably sad. That this should be the final resting place of such a magnificent vessel seemed utterly wrong to him.

Pieces of debris spotted the landscape, twisted hunks of rusted metal and incongruous personal items that must have belonged to the ship's crew and had been ejected during the massive impact with the ground.

'Throne...' breathed Abaddon.

'How?' was all Aximand could manage.

'It's the *Glory of Terra* alright,' said Erebus. 'I recognise the warp array configuration of the command deck. It's Temba's flagship.'

'Then Temba's already dead,' said Abaddon in frustration. 'Nothing could have survived that crash.'

'Then who's broadcasting that signal?' asked Horus.

'It could have been automated,' suggested Torgaddon. 'Maybe it's been going for years.'

Loken shook his head. 'No, the signal only started once we breached the atmosphere. Someone here activated it when they knew we were coming.'

The Warmaster stared at the massive shape of the wrecked spaceship, as if by staring hard enough he could penetrate its hull and discern what lay within.

'Then we should go in,' urged Erebus. 'Find whoever is inside and kill them.'

Loken rounded on the first chaplain. 'Go inside? Are you mad? We don't have any idea what might be waiting for us. There could be thousands more of those... things inside, or something even worse.'

'What is the matter, Loken?' snarled Erebus. 'Are the Sons of Horus now afraid of the dark?'

Loken took a step towards Erebus and said, 'You dare insult us, Word Bearer?'

Erebus stepped to meet Loken's challenge, but the Mournival took up position behind their newest member and their presence gave the first chaplain pause. Instead of pursuing the matter, Erebus bowed his head and said, 'I apologise if I spoke out of turn, Captain Loken. I sought only to erase the gross stain on the Legion's honour.'

'The Legion's honour is our own to uphold, Erebus,' said Loken. 'It is not for you to tell us how we must act.'

Horus decided the matter before further harsh words could be exchanged.

'We're going in,' he said.

THE RIPPLING FOG bank followed the Astartes as they advanced towards the crashed ship and the Titans of the Legio Mortis followed behind, their legs still wreathed in the mists. Loken kept his bolter at the ready, conscious of the sounds of splashing water behind them, though he told himself that they were just the normal sounds of this world – whatever that meant.

As they closed the gap, he drew level with the Warmaster and said, 'Sir, I know what you will say, but I would be remiss if I didn't speak up.'

'Speak up about what, Garviel?' asked Horus.

'About this. About you leading us into the unknown.'

'Haven't I been doing that for the last two centuries?' asked Horus. 'All the time we've been pushing out into space, hasn't it been to push back the unknown? That's what we're here for, Garviel, to render that which is unknown, known.'

Loken sensed the commander's superlative skills of misdirection at work and kept himself focused on the point. The Warmaster had an easy way of steering conversations away from issues he didn't want to talk about.

'Sir, do you value the Mournival as counsel?' asked Loken, taking a different tack.

Horus paused in his advance and turned to face Loken, his face serious. 'You heard what I told that remembrancer in the embarkation deck didn't you? I value your counsel above all things, Garviel. Why would you even ask such a question?'

'Because so often you simply use us as your war dogs, always baying for blood. Having us play a role, instead of allowing us to keep you true to your course.'

'Then say what you have to say, Garviel, and I swear I will listen,' promised Horus.

'With respect, sir, you should not be here leading this speartip and we should not be going into that vessel without proper reconnaissance. We have three of the Mechanicum's greatest war machines behind us. Can we not at least let them soften up the target first with their cannons?'

Horus chuckled. 'You have a thinker's head on you, my son, but wars are not won by thinkers, they are won by men of action. It has been too long since I wielded a blade and fought in such a battle – against abominations that seek nothing more than our utter destruction. I told you on Murder that had I felt I could not take to the field of battle again, I would have refused the position of Warmaster.'

'The Mournival would have done this thing for you, sir,' said Loken. 'We carry your honour now.'

'You think my shoulders so narrow that I cannot bear it alone?' asked Horus, and Loken was shocked to see genuine anger in his stare.

'No, sir, all I mean is that you don't need to bear it alone.'

Horus laughed and broke the tension. His anger quite forgotten, he said, 'You're right of course, my son, but my glory days are not over, for I have many laurels yet to earn.'

The Warmaster set off once more. 'Mark my words, Garviel Loken, everything achieved thus far in this Crusade will pale into insignificance compared to what I am yet to do.'

DESPITE THE WARMASTER'S insistence on leading the Astartes into the wreck, he consented to Loken's plan of allowing the Titans of the Legio Mortis to engage the target first. All three mighty war engines braced themselves and, at a command from the Warmaster, unleashed a rippling salvo of missiles and cannon fire into the massive ship. Flaring blooms of light and smoke rippled across the ship's immensity and it shuddered with each concussive impact. Fires caught throughout its hull, and thick plumes of acrid black smoke twisted skyward like signal beacons, as though the ship were trying to send a message to its former masters.

Once again, the Warmaster led from the front, the mist following them in like a smoggy cape of yellow. Loken could still hear noises from behind them, but with the thunderous footfalls of the Titans, the crackling of the burning ship and their own splashing steps, it was impossible to be sure what he was hearing.

'Feels like a damned noose,' said Torgaddon, looking over his shoulder and mirroring Loken's thoughts perfectly.

'I know what you mean.'

'I don't like the thought of going in there, I can tell you that.'

'You're not afraid are you?' asked Loken, only half joking.

'Don't be flippant, Garvi,' said Torgaddon. 'For once I think you're right. There's something not right about this.'

Loken saw genuine concern in his friend's face, unsettled at seeing the joker Torgaddon suddenly serious. For all his bluster and informality, Tarik had good instincts and they had saved Loken's life on more than one occasion.

'What's on your mind?' he asked.

'I think this is a trap,' said Torgaddon. 'We're being funnelled here and it feels like it's to get us inside that ship.'

'I said as much to the Warmaster.'

'And what did he say?'

'What do you think?'

'Ah,' nodded Torgaddon. 'Well, you didn't seriously expect to change the commander's mind did you?'

'I thought I might have given him pause, but it's as if he's not listening to us any more. Erebus has made the commander so angry at Temba, he won't even consider any other option than going in and killing him with his bare hands.'

'So what do we do?' asked Torgaddon, and once again, Loken was surprised.

'We watch our backs, my friend. We watch our backs.'

'Good plan,' said Torgaddon. 'I hadn't thought of that. And here I was all set to walk into a potential trap with my guard down.'

That was the Torgaddon that Loken knew and loved.

The rear quarter of the crashed *Glory of Terra* reared up before them, its command decks pitched upwards at an angle, blotting out the diseased sky. It enveloped them in its dark, cold shadow, and Loken saw that getting into the ship would not be difficult. The gunfire from the Titans had blasted huge tears in its hull, and piles of debris had spilled from inside, forming great ramps of buckled steel like the rocky slopes before the walls of a breached fortress.

The Warmaster called a halt and began issuing his orders.

'Captain Sedirae, you and your assaulters will form the vanguard.'

Loken could practically feel Luc's pride at such an honour.

'Captain Moy, you will accompany me. Your flame and melta units will be invaluable in case we need to quickly cleanse an area or breach bulkheads.'

Verulam Moy nodded, his quiet reserve more dignified than Luc's eagerness to impress the Warmaster with his ardour.

'What are your orders, Warmaster?' asked Erebus, his grey armoured Word Bearers at attention behind their first chaplain. 'We stand ready to serve.'

'Erebus, take your warriors over to the other side of the ship. Find a way in and then rendezvous with me in the middle. If that bastard Temba tries to run, I want him crushed between us.'

The first chaplain nodded his understanding and led his warriors off into the shadow of the mighty vessel. Then the Warmaster turned to the Mournival.

'Ezekyle, use the signal locator on my armour to form overlapping echelons around my left. Little Horus, take my right. Torgaddon and Loken, form the rear. Secure this area and our line of withdrawal. Understood?'

The Warmaster delivered the orders with his trademark efficiency, but Loken was aghast at being left to cover the rear of their advance. He could see that the others of the Mournival, especially Torgaddon, were similarly surprised. Was this the Warmaster's way of punishing him for daring to question his orders or for suggesting that he should not be leading the speartip? To be left behind?

'Understood?' repeated Horus and all four members of the Mournival nodded their assent.

'Then let's move out,' snarled the Warmaster. 'I have a traitor to kill.'

LUC SEDIRAE LED the assaulters, the bulky back burners of their jump packs easily carrying them up towards the black tears in the side of the ship. As Loken expected, Luc was first inside, vanishing into the darkness with barely a pause. His warriors followed him and were soon lost to sight, as Abaddon and Aximand found other ways inside, clambering up the debris to reach the still smoking holes that the Titans had torn. Aximand gave him a quick shrug as he led his own squads upwards, and

Loken watched them go, unable to believe that he would not be fighting alongside his brothers as they went into battle.

The Warmaster himself strode up the piled debris as easily as a man might ascend a gently sloping hill, Verulam Moy and his weapons specialists following in his wake.

Within moments, they were alone on the desolate mudflats, and Loken could sense the confusion in his warriors. They stood awkwardly, awaiting orders to send them into the fight, but he had none to give them.

Torgaddon saved him from his stupefaction, bellowing out commands and lighting a fire under the Astartes left behind. They spread out to form a cordon around their position, Nero Vipus's scouts taking up position at the edge of the mist, and Brakespur climbing up the slopes to guard the entrances to the *Glory of Terra*.

'Just what exactly did you say to the commander?' asked Torgaddon, squelching back through the mud towards him.

Loken cast his mind back to the words that had passed between himself and the Warmaster since they had set foot on Davin's moon, searching for some offence that he might have given. He could find nothing serious enough to warrant his and Torgaddon's exclusion from the battle against Temba.

'Nothing,' he said, 'just what I told you.'

'This doesn't make any sense,' said Torgaddon, attempting to wipe some mud from his face, but only serving to spread it further across his features. 'I mean, why leave us out of all the fun. I mean, come on, Moy?'

'Verulam's a competent officer,' said Loken.

'Competent?' scoffed Torgaddon. 'Don't get me wrong, Garvi, I love Verulam like a brother, but he's a file officer. You know it and I know it; and while there's nothing wrong with that and Emperor knows we need good file officers, he's not the sort the Warmaster should have at his side at a time like this.'

Loken couldn't argue with Tarik's logic, having had the same reaction upon hearing the Warmaster's orders. 'I don't know what to tell you, Tarik. You're right, but the commander has given his orders and we are pledged to obey him.'

'Even when we know those orders make no sense?'

Loken had no answer to that.

THE WARMASTER AND Verulam Moy led the van of the speartip through the dark and oppressive interior of the *Glory of Terra*, its arched passageways canted at unnatural angles and its bulkheads warped and rusted with decay. Brackish water dripped through sections open to the elements, and a reeking wind gusted through the creaking hallways like a cadaver's breath. Diseased streamers of black fungus and dangling fronds of rotted matter brushed against their heads and helmets, leaving slimy trails of sticky residue behind.

The perforated floors were treacherous and uneven, but the Astartes made good time, pushing ever upwards through the halls of putrefaction towards the command decks.

Regular, static-laced communication with Sedirae's vanguard informed them of his progress ahead of them, the ship apparently lifeless and deserted. Even though the vanguard was relatively close, Sedirae's voice was chopped with interference, every third word or so unintelligible.

The deeper into the ship they penetrated, the worse it got.

'Ezekyle?' said the Warmaster, opening the vox-mic on his gorget. 'Progress report.'

Abaddon's voice was barely recognisable, as crackling pops and wet hissing overlaid it with meaningless babble.

'Moving… th… gh the lowe… rat… decks… keep… We have… flank… master.'

Horus tapped his gorget. 'Ezekyle? Damn it.'

The Warmaster turned to Verulam Moy and said, 'Try and raise Erebus,' before returning to his own attempts at communication. 'Little Horus, can you hear me?'

More static followed, uninterrupted save for a faint voice. '…ordnance deck… slow… shells. Making safe… but… make… gress.'

'Nothing from Erebus,' reported Moy, 'but he may be on the other side of the ship by now. If the interference we are getting between our own warriors is anything to go by, it is unlikely our armour links will be able to reach him.'

'Damn it,' repeated the Warmaster. 'Well, let's keep going.'

'Sir,' ventured Moy. 'Might I make a suggestion?'

'If it's that we turn back, forget it, Verulam. My honour and that of the Crusade has been impugned and I'll not have it said that I turned my back on it.'

'I know that, sir, but I believe Captain Loken is correct. We are taking a needless risk here.'

'Life is a risk, my friend. Every day we spend away from Terra is a risk. Every decision I make is a risk. We cannot avoid risk, my friend, for if we do, we achieve nothing. If the highest aim of a captain were to preserve his ship, he would keep it in port forever. You are a fine officer, Verulam, but you do not see heroic opportunities as I do.'

'But, sir,' protested Moy, 'we cannot maintain contact with our warriors and we have no idea what might be waiting for us in this ship. Forgive me if I speak out of turn, but delving into the unknown like this does not feel like heroism. It feels like guesswork.'

Horus leaned in close to Moy and said, 'Captain, you know as well as I do that the whole art of war consists of guessing what is on the other side of the hill.'

'I understand that, sir–' began Moy, but Horus was in no mood for interruptions.

'Ever since the Emperor appointed me in the role of Warmaster, people have been telling me what I can and cannot do, and I tell you I am sick and tired of it,' snapped Horus. 'If people don't like my opinions, then that's their problem. I am the Warmaster and I have made up my mind. We go on.'

A squealing shriek of static abruptly sliced through the darkness and Luc Sedirae's voice came over the armour link as clearly as if he stood next to them.

'Throne! They're here!' shouted Sedirae.

Then everything turned upside down.

LOKEN FELT IT through the soles of his boots as a tremendous rumbling that seemed to come from the very foundations of the moon. He turned in horror, hearing metal grind on metal with a deafening screech, and watching geysers of mud spout skyward as buried portions of the starship tore themselves free of the sucking mud. The upper sections of the vessel plummeted towards the ground and the entire ship began tipping over, the colossal rear section arcing downwards with a terrible inevitability.

'Everyone get clear!' bellowed Loken as the massive weight of metal gathered speed.

Astartes scattered from the falling wreck, and Loken felt its massive shadow like a shroud as his armour's senses shut out the roaring noise of the starship's collapse.

He looked back in time to see the wreckage slam into the ground with the force of an orbital strike, the superstructure crumpling under the impact of its own weight and hurling lakes of muddy water through the air. Loken was tossed like a leaf by the shockwave, landing waist deep in a stagnant pool of greenish scum and disappearing beneath the surface.

Rolling to his knees, he saw tsunamis of mud rippling out from the vessel, and watched as dozens of his warriors were buried beneath the brownish sludge. The power of the wrecked starship's impact spread from the crater it had gouged in the mud. A brackish rain of muddy water drizzled down, smearing his helmet's visor and reducing visibility to no more than a few hundred metres.

Loken climbed to his feet, clearing the action of his bolter as he realised the shockwave had dispersed the sulphurous fog that had been their constant companion since landing on this accursed moon.

'Sons of Horus, stand ready!' he shouted, seeing what lay beyond the fog.

Hundreds of the dead things marched relentlessly towards them.

NOT EVEN THE armour of a primarch could withstand the impact of a falling starship, and Horus grunted as he pulled a twisted spar of jagged iron from his chest. Sticky blood coated his armour, the wound sealing almost as soon as he had withdrawn the metal. His genhanced body could easily withstand such trivial punishment, and despite the spinning fall through the decks of the ship, he remained perfectly orientated and in balance on the sloping deck.

He remembered the sound of tearing metal, the clang of metal on armour and the sharp crack of bones snapping as Astartes warriors were thrown around like children in a funhouse.

'Sons of Horus!' he shouted. 'Verulam!'

Only mocking echoes answered him, and he cursed as he realised he was alone. The vox mic on his gorget was shattered, brass wires hanging limply from the empty socket, and he angrily ripped them away.

Verulam Moy was nowhere to be seen, and his squad members were similarly scattered beyond sight. Quickly taking stock of his surroundings, Horus could see that he lay partially buried in metal debris on the armorium vestibule, its ceiling bulging and cracked. Icy water dripped in a cold rain, and he tipped his head back to let it pour over his face.

He was close to the bridge of the ship, assuming it hadn't sheared off on impact with the ground – for surely there could be no other explanation for what had happened. Horus hauled himself from beneath the wreckage and checked to make sure that he was still armed, finding his sword hilt protruding from the detritus of the vestibule.

Pulling the weapon clear, its golden blade caught what little light there was and shone as though an inner fire burned within its core. Forged by his brother, Ferrus Manus of the Tenth Legion, the Iron Hands, it had been a gift to commemorate Horus's investiture as Warmaster.

He smiled as he saw that the weapon remained as unblemished as the day Ferrus had held it out to him, the light of adoration in his steel grey eyes, and Horus had never been more thankful for his brother's skill at the forge's anvil.

The deck creaked beneath his weight, and he suddenly began to question the wisdom of leading this assault. Despite that, he still seethed with molten rage for Eugan Temba, a man whose character he had believed in, and whose betrayal cut his heart with searing knives.

What manner of a man could betray the oath of loyalty to the Imperium?

What manner of base cur would dare to betray *him*?

The deck shifted again, Horus easily compensating for the lurching motion. He used his free hand to haul himself up towards the gaping doorway that led to the warren of passageways that riddled a ship this size. Horus had set foot on the *Glory of Terra* only once before, nearly seventy years ago, but remembered its layout as though it had been yesterday. Beyond this doorway lay the upper gantries of the armorium and beyond that, the central spine of the ship that led through several defensive choke points to the bridge.

Horus grunted as he felt a sharp pain in his chest and realised that the iron spar must have torn through one of his lungs. Without hesitation, he switched his breathing pattern and carried on without pause, his eyesight easily piercing the darkness of the vessel's interior.

This close to the bridge, Horus could see the terrible changes wrought upon the ship, its walls coated in loathsome bacterial slime that ate at the metal like an acidic fungus. Dripping fronds of waving, leech-like organisms suckled at oozing pustules of greenish brown matter, and an unremitting stench of decay hung in the air.

Horus wondered what had happened to this ship. Had the tribes of the moon unleashed some kind of deadly plague on the crew? Were these the means that Erebus had spoken of?

He could taste that the air was thick with lethal bacterial filth and biological contaminants, though none were even close to virulent enough to trouble his incredible metabolism. With the golden light of his sword to illuminate the way, Horus negotiated a path around the gantry, listening out for any signs of his warriors. The occasional distant crack of gunfire or clang of metal told him that he wasn't completely alone, but the whereabouts of the battles was a mystery. The corrupted inner structure of the ship threw phantom echoes and faraway shouts all around him until he decided to ignore them and press on alone.

Horus passed through the armorium and into the starship's central spine, the deck warped and canted at an unnatural angle. Flickering glow-globes and sputtering power conduits sparked and lit the arched passageway with blue electrical fire. Broken doors clanged against their frames with the rocking motion of the ship, making a sound like funeral bells.

Ahead he could hear a low moaning and the shuffle of callused feet, the first sounds he could clearly identify. They came from beyond a wide hatchway, toothed blast doors juddering open and closed like the jaws of some monstrous beast. Crushed debris prevented the doors from closing completely, and Horus knew that whatever was making the noises stood between him and his ultimate destination.

Some trick of the diffuse, strobing light threw jittering shadows from the mouth of the hatchway, and flickering after-images danced on his retinas as though the light came from a pict projector running in slow motion.

As the hatchway rumbled closed once more, a clawed hand reached out and gripped the smeared metal. Long, dripping yellow talons sprouted from the hand, the flesh of the wasted arm maggot-ridden and leprous. Another hand pushed through and clamped onto the metal, wrenching open the blast doors with a strength that belied the frailness of the arms.

The sensation of fear was utterly alien to Horus, but when the horrifying source of the sounds was revealed, he was suddenly seized with the conviction that perhaps his captains had been right after all.

A shambling mob of rotten–fleshed famine victims appeared, their shuffling gaits carrying them forwards in a droning phalanx of corruption. A creeping sensation of hidden power pulsed from their hunger-wasted bodies and swollen bellies, and buzzing clouds of flies surrounded their cyclopean, horned heads. Sonorous doggerel spilled from bloated and split lips, though Horus could make no sense of the words. Green flesh hung from exposed bones, and although they moved with the leaden monotony of the dead things, Horus could see coiled strength in their limbs and a terrible hunger in each monster's cataracted eyeball.

The creatures were less than a dozen metres from him, but their images were blurred and wavering, as though tears misted his vision. He blinked rapidly to clear it, and saw their swords, rusted and dripped with contagion.

'Well you're a handsome bunch and no mistake,' said Horus, raising his sword and throwing himself forward.

His golden sword clove into the monsters like a fiery comet, each blow hacking down a dozen or more without effort. Spatters of diseased meat caked the walls, and the air was thick with the stench of faecal matter, as each monster exploded with rotten bangs of flesh at his every blow. Filthy claws tore at Horus, but his every limb was a weapon. His elbow smashed skulls from shoulders, his knees and feet shattered spines, and his sword struck his foes down as if they were the mindless automatons in the training cages.

Horus did not know what manner of creatures these were, but they had obviously never faced a being as mighty as a primarch. He pushed further up the central spine of the starship, hacking a path through hundreds of organ-draped beasts. Behind him lay the ruin of his passing, shredded meat that reeked of decay and pestilence. Before him lay scores more of the creatures, and the bridge of the *Glory of Terra*.

He lost track of time, the primal brutality of the fight capturing the entirety of his attention, his sword strikes mechanical and bludgeoning. Nothing could stand before him, and with each blow, the Warmaster drew closer to his goal. The corridor grew wider as he pushed through the heaving mass of cyclopean monsters, the golden sheen of his sword and the flickering, uncertain lights of the corridor making it appear that his enemies were becoming less substantial.

His sword chopped through a distended belly, ripping it wide open in a gush of stinking fluids, but instead of bursting open, the meat of the creature simply vanished like greasy smoke in the wind. Horus took another step forwards, but instead of meeting his foes head on with brutal ferocity, the corridor was suddenly and inexplicably empty. He looked around, and where once there had been a host of diseased creatures bent on his death, now there were only the reeking remains of hacked up corpses.

Even they were dissolving like fat on a griddle, vanishing in hissing streamers of green smoke so dark it was almost black.

'Throne,' hissed Horus, revolted by the sickening sight of the liquefying meat, and finally recognising the taint within the ship for what it was – a charnel house of the warp: a spawning ground of the Immaterium.

Horus felt fresh resolve fill his limbs as he drew closer to the multiple blast doors that protected the bridge, more certain than ever that he must destroy Eugan Temba. He expected yet more legions of the warp-spawned things, but the way was eerily quiet, the silence punctuated only by the sounds of more gunfire (which he was now sure was coming from beyond the hull) and the patter of black water on his armour.

Horus made his way forward cautiously, brushing sparking cables from his path as, one by one, the sealed blast doors slowly rumbled open at his approach. The whole thing reeked of a trap, but nothing could deny him his vengeance now, and he pressed onwards.

Stepping onto the bridge of the *Glory of Terra*, Horus saw that its colonnaded immensity had been changed from a place of command to something else entirely. Mouldering banners hung from the highest reaches, with long dead corpses stitched into the torn fabric of each one. Even from here, Horus could see that they wore the lupine grey uniforms of the 63rd Expedition, and he wondered if these poor souls had stayed true to their oaths of loyalty.

'You will be avenged, my friends,' he whispered as he stepped further into the bridge.

The tiered workstations were smashed and broken, their inner workings ripped out and rewired in some bizarre new way, metres-thick bundles of coiled wire rising into the darkness of the arched ceiling.

Throbbing energy pulsed from the cables and Horus realised that he was looking at the source of the vox signal that had so perturbed Loken on the way in.

Indeed, he fancied he could still hear the words of that damned voice whispering on the air like a secret that would turn your tongue black were you to tell it.

Nurgh-leth, it hissed, over and over…

Then he realised that it wasn't some auditory echo from the ship's vox, but a whisper from a human throat.

Horus's eyes narrowed as he sought the source of the voice, his lip curling in revulsion as he saw the massively swollen figure of a man standing before the captain's throne. Little more than a heaving mass of corpulent flesh, a terrific stench of rank meat rose from his fleshy immensity.

Flying things with glossy black bodies infested every fold of his skin, and scraps of grey cloth were stuck to his green grey flesh, gold epaulettes glinting and silver frogging hanging limply over his massive belly.

One hand rested in the glutinous mess of an infected wound in his chest, while the other held a sword with a glitter-sheen like diamond.

Horus dropped to his knees in anger and sorrow as he saw the slumped corpse of an Astartes warrior sprawled before the decayed splendour of the bloated figure.

Verulam Moy, his neck obviously broken and his sightless eyes fixed upon the decaying corpses hanging from the banners.

Even before Horus lifted his gaze to Moy's killer, he knew who it would be: Eugan Temba...

The Betrayer.

EIGHT

Fallen god

LOKEN COULD SCARCELY remember a fight where he and his warriors had expended all their ammunition. Each Astartes carried enough shells to sustain them for most types of engagement, since no shot was wasted and each target would normally fall to a single bolt.

The ammo hoppers were back at the drop site and there was no way they could get through to them. The Warmaster's resolute advance had seen to that.

Loken's full capacity of bolter rounds had long been expended, and he was thankful for Aximand's insistence on subsonic rounds, as they made satisfyingly lethal explosions within the bodies of the dead things.

'Throne, don't they ever stop?' gasped Torgaddon. 'I must have killed a hundred or more of the damned things.'

'You probably keep killing the same one,' replied Loken, shaking his sword free of grey matter. 'If you don't destroy the head, they get back up again. I've cut down half a dozen or more with bolter wounds in them.'

Torgaddon nodded and said, 'Hold on, the Legio's coming again.'

Loken gripped onto a more solid piece of debris, as the Titans began yet another deadly strafing run through the mass of rotted monsters. Like the monstrous giants said to haunt the mists of Barbarus, the Titans emerged from the fog with fists of thunder and fire. Wet explosions mushroomed from the swamp as high explosives hurled the cadavers into the air and the crashing steps of the mighty war machines crushed them to ooze beneath their hammer-blow footsteps.

The very air thrummed with the vibrations of the Titans' attack, avalanches of debris and mud sliding from the *Glory of Terra* with each explosion and titanic footstep. The dead things had gained the slopes of rubble and detritus that led into the starship three times; and three times had they sent them back, first with gunfire, and, when the ammunition had run out, with blades and brute strength. Each time they killed hundreds of their enemies, but each time a handful of Astartes was dragged down and pulled beneath the waters of the swamp.

Under normal circumstances, the Astartes would have had no trouble in dealing with these abominations, but with the Warmaster's fate unknown they were brittle and on edge, unable to think or fight with their customary ferocity. Loken knew exactly what they were feeling, because he felt it too.

Unable to raise the Warmaster, Aximand or Abaddon, the warriors outside the hulk were left paralysed and in disarray without their beloved leader.

'TEMBA,' SAID THE Warmaster, rising to his feet and marching towards his erstwhile planetary governor. With each step, he saw further evidence of Eugan Temba's treachery, clotted blood on the edge of his sword and a fierce grin of anticipation. Where once had been the loyal and upright follower, Horus now saw only a filthy traitor who deserved the most painful of deaths. A fell light grew around Temba, further revealing the corruption of his flesh, and Horus knew that nothing of his former friend was left in the diseased shell that stood before him.

Horus wondered if this was what Loken had experienced beneath the mountains of Sixty-Three Nineteen: the horror of a former comrade succumbing to the warp. Horus had known of the bad blood between Jubal and Loken, now understanding that such enmity, however trivial, had been the chink in Jubal's armour by which the warp had taken him.

What flaw had been Temba's undoing? Pride, ambition, jealousy?

The bloated monster that had once been Eugan Temba looked up from the corpse of Verulam Moy and smiled, thoroughly pleased with its work.

'Warmaster,' said Temba, each syllable glottal and wet, as though spoken through water.

'Do not dare to address me by such a title, abomination.'

'Abomination?' hissed Temba, shaking his head. 'Don't you recognise me?'

'No,' said Horus. 'You're not Temba, you're warp-spawned filth, and I'm here to kill you.'

'You are wrong, Warmaster,' it laughed. 'I am Temba. The so-called friend you left behind. I am Temba, the loyal follower of Horus you left to rot on this backwater world while you went on to glory.'

Horus approached the dais of the captain's throne and dragged his eyes from Temba to the body of Verulam Moy. Blood streamed from a terrible wound in his side, pumping energetically onto the stained floor of the bridge. The flesh of his throat was purple and black, a lump of broken bone pushing at the bruised skin where his neck had been snapped.

'A pity about Moy,' said Temba. 'He would have been a fine convert.'

'Don't say his name,' warned Horus. 'You are not fit to give it voice.'

'If it consoles you, he was loyal until the end. I offered him a place at my side, with the power of Nurgh-leth filling his veins with its immortal necrosis, but he refused. He felt the need to try to kill me; foolish really. The power of the warp fills me and he had no chance at all, but that didn't stop him. Admirable loyalty, even if it was misplaced.'

Horus placed a foot on the first step of the dais, his golden sword held out before him, his fury at this beast drowning out all other concerns. All he wanted to do was throttle the life from this treacherous bastard with his bare hands, but he retained enough sense to know that if Moy had been killed with such apparent ease, then he would be a fool to discard his weapon.

'We don't have to be enemies, Horus,' said Temba. 'You have no idea of the power of the warp, old friend. It is like nothing we ever saw before. It's beautiful really.'

'It is power,' agreed Horus, climbing another step, 'elemental and uncontrollable and therefore not to be trusted.'

'Elemental? Perhaps, but it is far more than that,' said Temba. 'It seethes with life, with ambition and desire. You think it's a wasteland of raging energy that you bend to your will, but you have no idea of the power that lies there: the power to dominate, to control and to rule.'

'I have no desire for such things,' said Horus.

'You lie,' giggled Temba. 'I can see it in your eyes, old friend. Your ambition is a potent thing, Horus. Do not be afraid of it. Embrace it and we will not be enemies, we will be allies, embarking upon a course that will see us masters of the galaxy.'

'This galaxy already has a master, Temba. He is called the Emperor.'

'Then where is he? He blundered across the cosmos in the manner of the barbarian tribes of ancient Terra, destroying anyone who would not submit to his will, and then left you to pick up the pieces. What manner of leader is that? He is but a tyrant by another name.'

Horus took another step, and was almost at the top of the dais, almost within striking distance of this traitor who dared to profane the name of the Emperor.

'Think about it, Horus,' urged Temba. 'The whole history of the galaxy has been the gradual realisation that events do not happen in an arbitrary manner, but that they reflect an underlying destiny. That destiny is Chaos.'

'Chaos?'

'Yes!' shouted Temba. 'Say it again, my friend. Chaos is the first power in the universe and it will be the last. When the first ape creatures bashed each other's brains out with bones, or cried to the heavens in the death throes of plague, they fed and nurtured Chaos. The blissful release of excess and the glee of intrigue – all is grist for the soul mills of Chaos. So long as Man endures, so too does Chaos.'

Horus reached the top of the dais and stood face to face with Temba, a man he had once counted as his friend and comrade in this great undertaking. Though the thing spoke with Temba's voice and its stretched features were still those of his comrade, there was nothing left of that fine man, only this wretched creature of the warp.

'You have to die,' said Horus.

'No, for that is the glory of Nurgh-leth,' chuckled Temba. 'I will never die.'

'We'll soon see about that,' snarled Horus, and drove his sword into Temba's chest, the golden blade easily sliding through the layers of blubber towards the traitor's heart.

Horus ripped his sword free in a wash of black blood and stinking pus, the stench almost too much for even him to bear. Temba laughed, apparently untroubled by such a mortal wound, and brought up his own sword, its glinting, fractured blade like patterned obsidian.

He brought the blade to his blue lips and said, 'The Warmaster Horus.'

With a speed that was unnatural in its swiftness, the tip of the blade speared for the Warmaster's throat.

Horus threw up his sword, deflecting Temba's weapon barely a centimetre from his neck, and took a step backwards as the traitor lurched towards him. Recovering from the surprise attack, Horus gripped his sword two-handed, blocking every lethal thrust and cut that Temba made.

Horus fought like never before, his every move to parry and defend. Eugan Temba had never been a swordsman, so where this sudden, horrifying skill came from Horus had no idea. The two men traded blows back and forth across the command deck, the bloated form of Eugan Temba moving with a speed and dexterity quite beyond anything that should have been possible for someone of such vast bulk. Indeed, Horus had the distinct impression that it was not Temba's skill with a blade that he was up against, but the blade itself.

He ducked beneath a decapitating strike and spun inside Temba's guard, slashing his sword through his opponent's belly, a thick gruel of infected blood and fat spilling onto the deck. The dark blade darted out and struck his shoulder guard, ripping it from his armour in a flash of purple sparks.

Horus danced back from the blow as the return stroke arced towards his head. He dropped and rolled away as Temba turned his bloody, carven body back towards him. Any normal man would have died a dozen times or more, but Temba seemed untroubled by such killing wounds.

Temba's face shone with glistening sweat, and Horus blinked as the monster's outline wavered, like those of the cyclopean monsters that he had fought in the ship's central spine. Frantic motion shimmered and he could see something deep within the monstrously swollen body, the faint outline of a screaming man, his hands clasped to his ears and his face twisted in a rictus grin of horror.

Trailing his innards like gooey ropes, Eugan Temba descended the steps of the dais like a socialite making her entrance at one of the Merican balls. Horus saw the cursed sword gleaming with a terrible hunger, its edges twitching in Temba's hand, as though aching to bury itself in his flesh.

'It doesn't have to end this way, Horus,' gurgled Temba. 'We need not be enemies.'

'Yes,' said Horus. 'We do. You killed my friend and you betrayed the Emperor. It can be no other way.'

Even before the words were out of his mouth, the smoky grey blade streaked towards him, and Horus threw himself back as the razor-sharp edge grazed his breastplate and cut into the ceramite. Horus backed away from Temba, hearing twin cracks as the monstrously bloated traitor's anklebones finally snapped under his weight.

Horus watched as Temba dragged himself forwards unsteadily, the splintered ends of bone jutting from the bloody flesh of his ankles. No normal man could endure such agony, and Horus felt a flickering ember of compassion for his former friend stir within his breast. No man deserved to be abused so, and Horus vowed to end Temba's suffering, seeing again the jagged after-image sputtering within the alien flesh of the warp.

'I should have listened to you, Eugan,' he whispered.

Temba didn't reply. The glimmering blade wove bright patterns in the air, but Horus ignored it, too seasoned a warrior to be caught by such an elementary trick.

Once again, Temba's blade reached out for him, but Horus was now gaining a measure of its hunger to do him harm. It attacked without thought or reason, only the simple lust to destroy. He looped his own blade around the quillons of Temba's sword and swept his arm out in a disarming move, before closing to deliver the deathblow.

Instead of releasing the blade for fear of a shattered wrist, however, Temba retained his grip on the sword, its tip twisting in the air and plunging towards Horus's shoulder.

Both blades pierced flesh at the same instant, Horus's tearing through his foe's chest and into his heart and lungs, as Temba's stabbed into the muscle of Horus's shoulder where his armour had been torn away.

Horus yelled in sudden pain, his arm burning with the shimmering sword's touch, and reacted with all the speed the Emperor had bred into him. His golden sword slashed out, severing Temba's arm just above the elbow and the sword clanged to the deck where it twitched in the grip of the severed arm with a loathsome life of its own.

Temba wavered and fell to his knees with a cry of agony, and Horus reared above his foe with his sword upraised. His shoulder ached and bled, but victory was now his and he roared with anger, as he stood ready to enact his vengeance.

Through the red mist of anger and hurt, he saw the pathetic, weeping and soiled form of Eugan Temba stripped of the loathsome power of the warp that had claimed him. Still bloated and massive, the dark light in his eyes was gone, replaced by tears and pain as the enormity of his betrayal crashed down upon him.

'What have I done?' asked Temba, his voice little more than a whisper.

The anger went out of Horus in an instant and he lowered his sword, kneeling beside the dying man that had once been his trusted friend.

Juddering sobs of agony and remorse wracked Temba's body and he reached up with his remaining hand to grip the Warmaster's armour.

'Forgive me, my friend,' he said. 'I didn't know. None of us did.'

'Hush now, Eugan,' soothed Horus. 'It was the warp. The tribes of the moon must have used it against you. They would have called it magic.'

'No… I'm so sorry,' wept Temba, his eyes dimming as death reached up to claim him. 'They showed us what it could do and I saw the power of it. I saw beyond and into the warp. I saw the powers that dwell there and, Emperor forgive me, I still said yes to it.'

'There are no powers that dwell there, Eugan,' said Horus. 'You were deceived.'

'No!' said Temba, gripping Horus's arm tightly. 'I was weak and I fell willingly, but it is done with me now. There is great evil in the warp and I need you to know the truth of Chaos before the galaxy is condemned to the fate that awaits it.'

'What are you talking about? What fate?'

'I saw it, Warmaster, the galaxy as a wasteland, the Emperor dead and mankind in bondage to a nightmarish hell of bureaucracy and superstition. All is grim darkness and all is war. Only you have the power to stop this future. You must be strong, Warmaster. Never forget that…'

Horus wanted to ask more, but watched impotently as
the spark of life fled Eugan Temba.

His shoulder still burning with fire, Horus rose to his
feet and marched over to the rewired consoles and the
throbbing bundle of cables that reached up to the chamber's roof.

With an aching cry of loss and anger, he severed the
cables with one mighty blow of his sword. They flopped
and spun like landed fish, sparks and green fluids spurt-
ing from internal tubes and cables, and Horus could tell
that the damnable vox transmission had ceased.

Horus dropped his sword and, clutching his injured
shoulder, sat on the deck next to Eugan Temba's dead
body and wept for his lost friend.

LOKEN HACKED HIS sword through another corpse's neck,
dropping the mouldering revenant to the ground as still
more pressed in behind it. He and Torgaddon fought
back to back, their swords coated in the flesh of the dead
things as they were pushed further and further up the
slopes of metal that led inside the starship. Their warriors
fought desperately, each blow leaden and exhausted. The
Titans of the Legio Mortis crushed what they could and
sporadically raked the base of the rubble with sprays of
gunfire, but there was no stopping the horde.

Dozens of Astartes were dead, and there was still no
word from the forces that had entered the *Glory of Terra*.

Garbled vox transmissions from the Byzant Janizars
seemed to indicate that they were finally moving forward, but no one could be sure as to where exactly they
were moving.

Loken fought with robotic movements, his every blow
struck with mechanical regularity rather than skill. His
armour was dented and torn in a dozen places, but still
he fought for victory, despite the utter desperation of
their cause.

That was what Astartes did: they triumphed over insurmountable odds. Loken had lost track of how long they had been fighting, the brutal sensations of this combat having dulled his senses to all but his next attacker.

'We'll have to pull back into the ship!' he shouted.

Torgaddon and Nero Vipus nodded, too busy with their own immediate situations to respond verbally, and Loken turned and began issuing orders across the inter-suit vox, receiving acknowledgements from all his surviving squad commanders.

He heard a cry of anger and, recognising it as belonging to Torgaddon, turned with his sword raised. A mob of stinking cadavers swamped the top of the slopes, overwhelming the Astartes gathered there in a frenzy of clawing hands and biting jaws. Torgaddon was borne to the ground, and the mouths of the corpses fastened on his neck and arms were dragging him down.

'No!' shouted Loken as he leapt towards the furious combat. He shoulder charged in amongst them, sending bodies flying down the slopes. His fists crushed skulls and his sword hacked dead things in two. A gauntleted fist thrust up through grey flesh and he grabbed it, feeling the weight of an armoured Astartes behind it.

'Hold on, Tarik!' he ordered, hauling on his friend's arm. Despite his strength, he couldn't free Torgaddon and felt grasping limbs envelop his legs and waist. He clubbed with his free hand, but he couldn't kill enough of them. Hands tore at his head, smearing blood across his visor and blinding him as he felt himself falling.

Loken thrashed in vain, breaking dead things apart, but unable to prevent himself and Torgaddon from being pulled apart. Claws tore at his armour, the unnatural strength of their enemies piercing his flesh and drawing his precious blood. A grinning, skull faced monster landed on his chest, face to face with him, and its jaws snapped shut on his visor. Unable to penetrate the armoured glass, rivulets of muddy saliva blurred his vision as its jaws worked up and down.

Loken head-butted the thing from his chest and rolled onto his front to gain some purchase. He lost his grip on his sword and bellowed in anger as he finally began to free himself from their intolerable grip. Loken fought with every ounce of his strength, finally gaining a respite and rising to his feet.

All around him, warriors of the Astartes struggled with the dead things, and he knew that they were undone.

Then, at a stroke, every one of the dead things dropped to the ground with a soft sigh of release.

Where seconds before the area around the starship had been a furious battlefield of warriors locked in life or death struggles, now it was an eerily silent graveyard. Bewildered Astartes picked themselves up and looked around at the inert, lifeless bodies surrounding them.

'What just happened?' asked Nero Vipus, disentangling himself from a pile of bludgeoned corpses. 'Why have they stopped?'

Loken shook his head. He had no answer to give him. 'I don't know, Nero.'

'It doesn't make any sense.'

'You'd rather they got back up?'

'No, don't be dense. I just mean that if someone was animating these things, then why stop now? They had us.'

Loken shuddered. For someone to wield a power that could defeat the Astartes was a sobering thought. All the time they had crusaded through the galaxy there had been nothing that could stand against them for long – eventually the enemy's will would break in the face of the overwhelming superiority of the Space Marines.

Would this happen when they met a foe with a will as implacable as their own?

Shaking himself free of such gloomy thoughts, he began issuing orders to dispose of the dead things, and they began hurling them from the wreckage, hacking or tearing heads from shoulders lest they reanimate.

Eventually Aximand and Abaddon led their warriors from the wreckage, battered and bloody from the ship's fall, but otherwise unharmed. Erebus too returned, his Word Bearers similarly abused, but also largely unharmed.

There was still no sign of Sedirae's men or the Warmaster.

'We're going back in there for the Warmaster,' said Abaddon. 'I'll lead.'

Loken was about to protest, but nodded as he saw the unshakable resolve in Ezekyle's face.

'We'll all go,' he said.

THEY FOUND LUC Sedirae and his men trapped in one of the lower decks, hemmed in by fallen bulkheads and tonnes of debris. It took the better part of an hour to move enough of it to grant Luc's assaulters their freedom. On pulling Sedirae from his prison, all he could say was, 'They were here. Monsters with one eye... came out of nowhere, but we killed them, all of them. Now they're gone.'

Luc had suffered casualties; seven of his men were dead and his perpetual grin was replaced by a vengeful expression that reminded Loken of a defiant young boy's. Black, stinking residue coated the walls, and Sedirae had a haunted look to him that Loken did not like at all. It reminded him of Euphrati Keeler in the moments after the warp thing that had taken Jubal almost killed her.

With Sedirae and his warriors in tow, the Mournival pressed on with Loken leading the way, finding signs of battle scattered throughout the ship, bolter impacts and sword cuts that led inexorably towards the ship's bridge.

'Loken,' whispered Aximand. 'I fear what we may find ahead. You should prepare yourself.'

'No,' said Loken. 'I know what you are suggesting, but I won't think of that. I can't.'

'We have to be prepared for the worst.'

'No,' said Loken, louder than he had intended. 'We would know if–'

'If what?' asked Torgaddon.

'If the Warmaster was dead,' said Loken finally.

Thick silence enveloped them as they struggled to come to terms with such a hideous idea.

'Loken's right,' said Abaddon. 'We would know if the Warmaster was dead. You know we would. You of all of us would feel it, Little Horus.'

'I hope you're right, Ezekyle.'

'Enough of this damned misery,' said Torgaddon. 'All this talk of death and we haven't found hide nor hair of the Warmaster yet. Save your gloomy thoughts for the dead that we already know about. Besides, we all know that if the Warmaster was dead, the sky would have fallen, eh?'

That lightened their mood a little and they pressed on, making their way along the central spine of the ship, passing through juddering bulkheads and along corridors with flickering lights, until they reached the blast doors that led to the bridge.

Loken and Abaddon led the way, with Aximand, Torgaddon and Sedirae bringing up the rear.

Inside it was almost dark, only a soft light from ruptured consoles providing any illumination.

The Warmaster sat with his back to them, his glorious plate armour dented and filthy, cradling something vast and bloated in his lap.

Loken drew level with the Warmaster, grimacing as he saw a grotesquely swollen human head in his commander's lap. A great puncture wound pierced the

Warmaster's breastplate and a bloody stab wound on his shoulder leaked blood down the armour of his arm.

'Sir?' said Loken. 'Are you alright?'

The Warmaster didn't answer, instead cradling the head of what Loken could only assume was Eugan Temba. His bulk was immense, and Loken wondered how such a monstrously fat creature could possibly have moved under his own strength.

The Mournival joined Loken, shocked and horrified at the Warmaster's appearance, and at this terrible place. They looked at one another with a growing unease, none quite knowing what to make of this bizarre scene.

'Sir?' said Aximand, kneeling before the weeping Warmaster.

'I failed him,' said Horus. 'I failed them all. I should have listened, but I didn't and now they're all dead. It's too much.'

'Sir, we're going to get you out of here. The dead things have stopped attacking. We don't know how long that's going to last, so we need to get out of this place and regroup.'

Horus shook his head slowly. 'They won't be attacking again. Temba's dead and I cut the vox signal. I don't know how exactly, but I think it was part of what was animating those poor souls.'

Abaddon pulled Loken aside and hissed, 'We need to get him out of here, and we can't let anyone see the state he's in.'

Loken knew that Abaddon was right. To see the Warmaster like this would break the spirit of every Astartes who saw him. The Warmaster was an invincible god of war, a towering figure of legend that could never be brought low.

To see him humbled so would be a blow to morale that the 63rd Expedition might never recover from.

Gently, they prised Eugan Temba's massive body away from the Warmaster and lifted their commander to his feet. Loken slung the Warmaster's arm over his shoulder, feeling a warm wetness against his face from the blood that still dripped from Horus's arm.

Between them, he and Abaddon walked the Warmaster from the bridge.

'Wait,' said the Warmaster, his voice weak and low. 'I'll walk out of this place on my own.'

Reluctantly, they let him go, and though he swayed a little, the Warmaster kept his feet, despite the ashen pallor of his face and the obvious pain he was in.

The Warmaster spared a last look at Eugan Temba and said, 'Gather up Verulam and let's get out of here, my sons.'

MAGGARD SLUMPED AGAINST the steel bulkhead of the *Glory of Terra*, his sword covered in black fluids from the dead things. Petronella fought to hold back tears at the thought of how close they had all come to death on this bleak, Emperor forsaken moon.

Sheltered behind the bulkhead where Maggard had thrust her, she had heard rather than seen the desperate conflict that raged outside – the war cries, the sound of motorised blades tearing into wet meat, the percussive booms and explosive flashes of light from the Titans' weapons.

Her imagination filled in the blanks and though a gut-loosening terror filled her from head to toe, she pictured glorious combats and heroic duels between the towering Astartes giants and the corrupt foes that sought their destruction.

Her breathing came in short, convulsive gasps as she realised she had just survived her first battle, but with that realisation came a strange calm: her limbs stopped shaking and she wanted to smile and laugh. She wiped her hand across her eyes, smearing the kohl that lined them across her cheeks like tribal war paint.

Petronella looked over at Maggard, seeing him now for the great warrior he truly was, barbaric and bloody, and magnificent. She pushed herself to her feet and leaned out beyond her sheltering bulkhead to look at the battlefield below.

It was like a scene from one of Keland Roget's landscapes, and the sublime vision took her breath away. The fog and mist had lifted and the sun was already breaking through to bathe the landscape in its ruddy red glow. The pools of swamp water glittered like shards of broken glass spread across the landscape. The three magnificent Titans of the Legio Mortis watched over squads of Astartes, armed with flamers, putting the corpses of the dead things to the torch, and pyres of the fallen monsters burned with a blue green light.

She was already forming the metaphors and imagery she would use: the Emperor's warriors taking his light into the dark places of the galaxy, or perhaps that the Astartes were his Angels of Death bringing his retribution to the unrighteous.

The words had the right epic tone, but she sensed that such imagery still lacked some fundamental truth, sounding more like propaganda slogans than anything else.

This was what the Great Crusade was all about and the fear of the last few hours was washed away in a swelling wave of admiration for the Astartes and the men and women of the 63rd Expedition.

She turned as she heard heavy footfalls. The officers of the Mournival were marching towards her, a plate armoured body borne upon their shoulders, and the levity she had witnessed in them earlier now utterly absent. Each one's face, even the joker Torgaddon's, was serious and grim.

The cloaked figure of the Warmaster himself followed behind them, and she was shocked rigid at his beaten appearance. His armour was torn and gashed with foulness, and blood spatters matted his face and arm.

'What happened?' she asked as Captain Loken passed her. 'Whose body is that?'

'Be silent,' he snapped, 'and be gone.'

'No,' said the Warmaster. 'She is my documentarist and if that is to mean anything then she must see us at our worst as well as our best.'

'Sir–' began Abaddon, but Horus cut him off.

'I'll not be argued with on this, Ezekyle. She comes with us.'

Petronella felt her heart leap at this inclusion and fell into step with the Warmaster's party as they began their descent to the ground.

'The body is that of Verulam Moy, captain of my 19th Company,' said Horus, his voice weary and filled with pain. 'He fell in the line of duty and will be honoured as such.'

'You have my deepest sorrows, my lord,' said Petronella, her heart aching to see the Warmaster in such pain.

'Was it Eugan Temba?' she asked, fishing out her data-slate and mnemo-quill. 'Did he kill Captain Moy?'

Horus nodded, too weary even to answer her.

'And Temba is dead? You killed him?'

'Eugan Temba is dead,' answered Horus. 'I think he died a long time ago. I don't know exactly what I killed in there, but it wasn't him.'

'I don't understand.'

'I'm not sure I do either,' said Horus, stumbling as he reached the bottom of the slope of debris. She reached out a hand to steady him, before realising what a ridiculous idea that was. Her hand came away bloody and wet,

and she saw that the Warmaster still bled from a wound
in his shoulder.

'I ended the life of Eugan Temba, but damn me if I
didn't weep for him afterwards.'

'But wasn't he an enemy?'

'I have no trouble with my enemies, Miss Vivar,' said
Horus. 'I can take care of my enemies in a fight. But my
so-called allies, my damned allies, they're the ones who
keep me walking the floors at night.'

Legion apothecaries made their way towards the Warmaster as she tried to make sense of what he was saying.
She allowed the mnemo-quill to inscribe his words anyway. She saw the looks she was getting from the
Mournival, but ignored them.

'Did you speak to him before you slew him? What did
he say?'

'He said… that only I had the power… to stop the
future…' said the Warmaster, his voice suddenly faint
and echoing as though coming from the other end of a
long tunnel.

Puzzled, she looked up in time to see the Warmaster's
eyes roll back in their sockets and his legs buckle
beneath him. She screamed, reaching out with her hand
towards him, knowing that she was powerless to help
him, but needing to try to prevent his fall.

Like a slow moving avalanche or a mountain toppling,
the Warmaster collapsed.

The mnemo-quill scratched at the data-slate and she
wept as she read the words there.

I was there the day that Horus fell.

NINE

Silver towers/A bloody return/The veil grows thin

FROM HERE, HE could see the pyramid roof of the Athenaeum, the low evening sun reflecting on its gold panels as if it were ablaze, and even though Magnus knew he used but a colourful metaphor, the very idea gave him a pang of loss. To imagine that vast repository of knowledge lost in the flames was abhorrent and he turned his cyclopean gaze from the pyramid of crystal glass and gold.

Tizca, the so-called City of Light, stretched out before him, its marble colonnades and wide boulevards tree- lined and peaceful. Soaring towers of silver and gold reared above a city of gilded libraries, arched museums and sprawling seats of learning. The bulk of the city was constructed of white marble and gold-veined ouslite, shining like a bejewelled crown in the sun. Its architecture spoke of a time long passed, its buildings shaped by craftsmen who had honed their trades for centuries under the tutelage of the Thousand Sons.

From his balcony on the Pyramid of Photep, Magnus the Red, Primarch of the Thousand Sons, contemplated the future of Prospero. His head still hurt from the ferocity of the nightmare and his eye throbbed painfully in its enlarged socket. He gripped the marble balustrade of the balcony, trying to wish away the visions that assailed him in the night and now chased him into the daylight. Mysteries of the night were revealed in the light of day, but these visions of darkness could not be dragged out so easily.

For as long as Magnus could remember, he had been cursed and blessed with a measure of foresight, and his allegorical interpretation of the Athanaeum ablaze troubled him more than he liked to admit.

He poured himself some wine from a silver pitcher, rubbing a copper-skinned hand through his mane of fiery red hair. The wine helped dull the ache in his heart as well as his head, but he knew it was only a temporary solution. Events were now in motion that he had the power to shape and though much of what he had seen was madness and turmoil, and made no sense, he could make out enough to know that he had to make a decision soon – before events spiralled out of control.

Magnus turned from the view over Tizca and made his way back inside the pyramid, pausing as he caught sight of his reflection in the gleaming silver panels. Huge and red-skinned, Magnus was a towering giant with a lustrous mane of red hair. His patrician features were noble and just, his single eye golden and flecked with crimson. Where his other eye would have sat was blank and empty, though a thin scar ran from the bridge of his nose to the edge of his cheekbone.

Cyclopean Magnus they called him, or worse. Since their inception, the Thousand Sons had been viewed with suspicion for embracing powers that others were afraid of. Powers that, because they were not understood, were rejected as being somehow unclean: rejected ever since the Council of Nikaea.

Magnus threw down his goblet, angry at the memory of his humbling at the feet of the Emperor, when he had been forced to renounce the study of all things sorcerous for fear of what he might learn. Such a notion was surely ridiculous, for was his father's realm not founded on the pursuit of knowledge and reason? What harm could study and learning do?

Though he had retreated to Prospero and sworn to renounce such pursuits, the Planet of the Sorcerers had one vital attribute that made it the perfect place for such studies – it was far from the prying eyes of those who said he dabbled with powers beyond his control.

Magnus smiled at the thought, wishing he could show his persecutors the things he had seen, the wonders and the beauty of what lived beyond the veil of reality. Notions of good and evil fell by the wayside next to such power as dwelled in the warp, for they were the antiquated concepts of a religious society, long cast aside.

He stooped to retrieve his goblet and filled it once more before returning to his chambers and taking a seat at his desk. Inside it was cool and the scent of various inks and parchments made him smile. The wide chamber was walled with bookshelves and glass cabinets, filled with curios and remnants of lost knowledge gleaned from conquered worlds. Magnus himself had penned many of the texts in this room, though others had contributed to this most personal of libraries – Phosis T'kar, Ahriman and Uthizzar to name but a few.

Knowledge had always been a refuge for Magnus, the intoxicating thrill of rendering the unknown down to its constituent parts and, by doing so, rendering it knowable. Ignorance of the universe's workings had created false gods in man's ancient past, and the understanding of them was calculated to destroy them. Such was Magnus's lofty goal.

His father denied such things, kept his people ignorant of the true powers that existed in the galaxy, and though he promulgated a doctrine of science and reason, it was naught but a lie, a comforting blanket thrown over humanity to shield them from the truth.

Magnus had looked deep into the warp, however, and knew different.

He closed his eye, seeing again the darkness of the corrupt chamber, the glitter sheen of the sword, and the blow that would change the fate of the galaxy. He saw death and betrayal, heroes and monsters. He saw loyalty tested, and found wanting and standing firm in equal measure. Terrible fates awaited his brothers and, worst of all, he knew that his father was utterly ignorant of the doom that threatened the galaxy.

A soft knocking came at his door and the red-armoured figure of Ahriman entered, holding before him a long staff topped with a single eye.

'Have you decided yet, my lord?' asked his chief librarian, without preamble.

'I have, my friend,' said Magnus.

'Then shall I gather the coven?'

'Yes,' sighed Magnus, 'in the catacombs beneath the city. Order the thralls to assemble the conjunction and I shall be with you presently.'

'As you wish, my lord,' said Ahriman.

'Something troubles you?' asked Magnus, detecting an edge of reticence in his old friend's tone.

'No, my lord, it is not my place to say.'

'Nonsense. If you have a concern then I give you leave to voice it.'

'Then may I speak freely?'

'Of course,' nodded Magnus. 'What troubles you?'

Ahriman hesitated before answering. 'This spell you propose is dangerous, very dangerous. None of us truly understand its subtleties and there may be consequences we do not yet foresee.'

Magnus laughed. 'I've not known you shirk from the power of a spell before, Ahriman. When manipulating power of this magnitude there will always be unknowns, but only by wielding it can we bring it to heel. Never forget that we are the masters of the warp, my friend. It is strong, yes, and great power lives within it, but we have the knowledge and means to bend it to our will do we not?'

'We do, my lord,' agreed Ahriman. 'Why then do we use it to warn the Emperor of what is to come when he has forbidden us to pursue such matters?'

Magnus rose from his seat, his copper skin darkening in anger. 'Because when my father sees that it is our sorcery that has saved his realm, he will not be able to deny that what we do here is important, nay, vital to the Imperium's survival!'

Ahriman nodded, fearful of his primarch's rage, and Magnus softened his tone. 'There is no other way, my friend. The Emperor's palace is warded against the power of the warp and only a conjuration of such power will breach those wards.'

'Then I will gather the coven immediately,' said Ahriman.

'Yes, gather them, but await my arrival before beginning. Horus may yet surprise us.'

PANIC, FEAR, INDECISION: three emotions previously unknown to Loken seized him as Horus fell. The Warmaster crashed to the ground in slow motion, splashing into the mud as his body went completely limp. Shouts of alarm went up, but a paralysis of inaction held those closest to the Warmaster tightly in its grip, as though time itself had slowed.

Loken stared at the Warmaster lying on the ground before him, inert and corpse-like, unable to believe what he was seeing. The rest of the Mournival stood similarly immobile, rooted to the spot in disbelief. He felt as though the air had become thick and cloying, the cries of fear that spread outwards echoing and distant as though from a holo-picter running too slow.

Only Petronella Vivar seemed unaffected by the inaction that held Loken and his brothers firm. Down on her knees in the mud next to the Warmaster, she was weeping and wailing at him to get back up again.

The knowledge that his commander was down and a mortal woman had reacted before any of the Sons of Horus shamed Loken into action and he dropped to one knee alongside the fallen Horus.

'Apothecary!' shouted Loken, and time snapped back with a crash of shouts and cries.

The Mournival dropped to the ground beside him.

'What's wrong?' demanded Abaddon.

'Commander!' shouted Torgaddon.

'Lupercal!' cried Aximand.

Loken ignored them and forced himself to focus.

This is a battlefield injury and I will treat it as such, he thought.

He scanned the Warmaster's body as the others put their hands on him, pushing the remembrancer out of the way as each struggled to wake their lord and master. Too many hands were interfering, and Loken yelled, 'Stop. Get back!'

The Warmaster's armour was beaten and torn, but Loken could see no other obvious breaches in the armoured plates save where the shoulder guard had been torn away, and where the gaping puncture wound oozed in his chest.

'Help me get his armour off!' he shouted.

The Mournival, bound together as brothers, nodded and, grateful to have a focus for their efforts, instantly obeyed Loken's command. Within moments, they had removed Horus's breastplate and pauldrons and were unstrapping his remaining shoulder guard.

Loken tore off his helmet and cast it aside, pressing his ear to the Warmaster's chest. He could hear the Warmaster's hearts, pounding in a deathly slow double beat.

'He's still alive!' he cried.

'Get out of the way!' shouted a voice behind him, and he turned to rebuke this newcomer before seeing the double helix caduceus symbol on his armour plates. Another apothecary joined the first and the Mournival was unceremoniously pushed aside as they went to work, hissing Narthecium stabbing into the Warmaster's flesh.

Loken stood watching them, impotent and helpless as they fought to stabilise the Warmaster. His eyes filled with tears and he looked around in vain for something to do, something to make him feel he was helping. There was nothing, and he felt like crying out to the heavens for making him so powerful and yet so useless.

Abaddon wept openly, and to see the first captain so unmanned made Loken's fear for the Warmaster all the more terrible. Aximand watched the apothecaries work with a grim stoicism, while Torgaddon chewed his bottom lip and prevented the remembrancer from getting in the way.

The Warmaster's skin was ashen, his lips blue and his limbs rigid, and Loken knew that they must destroy whatever power had felled Horus. He turned and began marching back towards the *Glory of Terra*, determined that he would take the stricken craft apart, piece by piece if need be.

'Captain!' called one of the apothecaries, a warrior Loken knew as Vaddon. 'Get a Stormbird here now! We need to get him to the *Vengeful Spirit*!'

Loken stood immobile, torn between his desire for vengeance and his duty to the Warmaster.

'Now, captain!' yelled the apothecary, and the spell was broken.

He nodded dumbly and opened a channel to the captains of the Stormbirds, grateful to have a purpose in this maelstrom of confusion. Within moments, one of the medical craft was inbound and Loken watched, mesmerised, as the apothecaries fought to save the Warmaster.

He could see from the frantic nature of their ministrations that they were fighting an uphill battle, their Narthecium whirring miniature centrifuges of blood and dispensing patches of syn-skin to treat his wounds. Their conversations passed over him, but he caught the odd familiar word here and there.

'Larraman cells ineffective…'

'Hypoxic poisoning…'

Aximand appeared at his side and placed his hand on Loken's shoulder.

'Don't say it, Little Horus,' warned Loken.

'I wasn't going to, Garviel,' said Aximand. 'He'll be alright. There's nothing this place could throw at the Warmaster that'll keep him down for long.'

'How do you know?' asked Loken, his voice close to breaking.

'I just do. I have faith.'

'Faith?'

'Yes,' answered Aximand. 'Faith that the Warmaster is too strong and too stubborn to be brought low by something like this. Before you know it we'll be his war dogs once again.'

Loken nodded as the howling downdraught of a Stormbird snatched his breath away.

The screaming craft hovered overhead, throwing up sheets of water as it circled on its descent. Landing skids deployed and the craft came down amid a spray of muddy water.

Before it had touched down, the Mournival and apothecaries had lifted Horus between them. Even as the assault ramp came down, they were rushing inside, placing the Warmaster on one of the gurneys as the Stormbird's jets fired to lift it from Davin's moon.

The assault ramp clanged shut behind them, and Loken felt the aircraft lurch as the pilot aimed it for the skies. The apothecaries hooked the Warmaster up to medicae machines, jamming needles and hissing tubes into his arms, and placing a feed line of oxygen over his mouth and nose.

Suddenly superfluous, Loken slumped into one of the armoured bucket seats against the fuselage of the aircraft and held his head in his hands.

Across from him, the Mournival did the same.

To say that Ignace Karkasy was not a happy man was an understatement. His lunch was cold, Mersadie Oliton was late and the wine he was drinking wasn't fit to lubricate the gears of an engine. To top it all off, his pen tapped on the thick paper of the Bondsman number 7 without any inspiration flowing. He'd taken to avoiding the Retreat, partly for fear of running into Wenduin again, but mostly because it just depressed him too much. The vandalism done to the bar lent it an incredibly sad and gloomy aspect and, while some of the remembrancers needed the squalor to inspire their work, Karkasy wasn't one of them.

Instead, he relaxed in the sub-deck where most of the remembrancers gathered for their meals, but which was empty for the better part of the day. The solitude was helping him to deal with all that had happened since he'd challenged Euphrati Keeler about her distributing the *Lectitio Divinitatus* pamphlets – though it certainly wasn't helping him compose any poetry.

She'd been unrepentant when he'd confronted her, urging him to join her in prayer to the God-Emperor, before some kind of makeshift shrine.

'I can't,' he had said. 'It's ridiculous, Euphrati, can't you see that?'

'What's so ridiculous about it, Ig?' she'd asked. 'Think about it, we've embarked upon the greatest crusade known to man. A crusade: a war motivated by religious beliefs!'

'No, no,' he protested, 'it's not that at all. We've moved beyond the need for the crutch of religion, Euphrati and we didn't set out from Terra to take a step backwards into such outmoded concepts of belief. It's only by dispelling the clouds and superstitions of religion that we discover truth, reason and morality.'

'It's not superstition to believe in a god, Ignace,' said Euphrati, holding out another of the *Lectitio Divinitatus* pamphlets. 'Look, read this and then make up your mind.'

'I don't need to read it,' he snapped, throwing the pamphlet to the deck. 'I know what it will say and I'm not interested.'

'But you have no idea, Ignace. It's all so clear to me now. Ever since that thing attacked me, I've been hiding. In my billet and in my head, but I realise now that all I had to do was allow the light of the Emperor into my heart and I would be healed.'

'Didn't Mersadie and I have anything to do with that?' sneered Karkasy. 'All those hours we spent with you weeping on our shoulders?'

'Of course you did,' smiled Euphrati, coming forward and placing her hands on his cheeks. 'That's why I wanted to give you the message and tell you what I'd realised. It's very simple, Ignace. We create our own gods and the blessed Emperor is the Master of Mankind.'

'Create our own gods?' said Karkasy, pulling away from her. 'No, my dear, ignorance and fear create the gods, enthusiasm and deceit adorn them, and human weakness worships them. It's been the same throughout history. When men destroy their old gods they find new ones to take their place. What makes you think this is any different?'

'Because I feel the Emperor's light within me.'

'Oh, well, I can't argue with that, can I?'

'Spare me your sarcasm, Ignace,' said Euphrati, suddenly hostile. 'I thought you might be open to hearing the good word, but I can see you're just a close-minded fool. Get out, Ignace, I don't want to see you again.'

Thus dismissed, he'd found himself outside in the companionway alone, bereft of a friend he'd only just managed to make. That had been the last time she'd spoken to him. He'd seen her only once since then, and she had ignored his greeting.

'Lost in thought, Ignace?' asked Mersadie Oliton, and he looked up in surprise, shaken from his miserable reverie by her sudden appearance.

'Sorry, my dear,' he said. 'I didn't hear you approach. I was miles away; composing another verse for Captain Loken to misunderstand and Sindermann to discard.'

She smiled, instantly lifting his spirits. It was impossible to be too maudlin around Mersadie, she had a way of making a man realise that it was good to be alive.

'Solitude suits you, Ignace, you're far less susceptible to temptation.'

'Oh I don't know,' he said, holding up the bottle of wine. 'There's always room in my life for temptation. I count it a bad day if I'm not tempted by something or other.'

'You're incorrigible, Ignace,' she laughed, 'but enough of that, what's so important that you drag me away from my transcripts to meet here? I want to be up to date by the time the speartip gets back from the moon.'

Flustered by her directness, Karkasy wasn't sure where to begin and thus opted for the softly-softly approach. 'Have you seen Euphrati around recently?'

'I saw her yesterday evening, just before the Storm-birds launched. Why?'

'Did she seem herself?'

'Yes, I think so. I was a little surprised by the change in her appearance, but she's an imagist. I suppose it's what they do every now and again.'

'Did she try to give you anything?'

'Give me anything? No. Look, what's this all about?'

Karkasy slipped a battered pamphlet across the table towards Mersadie, watching her expression change as she read it and recognised it for what it was.

'Where did you get this?' she asked when she'd finished reading it.

'Euphrati gave it to me,' he replied. 'Apparently she wants to spread the word of the God-Emperor to us first because we helped her when she needed support.'

'God-Emperor? Has she taken leave of her senses?'

'I don't know, maybe,' he said, pouring himself a drink. Mersadie pushed over a glass and he filled that too. 'I don't think she was over her experience in the Whisperheads, even if she made out that she was.'

'This is insane,' said Mersadie. 'She'll have her certification revoked. Did you tell her that?'

'Sort of,' said Karkasy. 'I tried to reason with her, but you know how it is with those religious types, never any room for a dissenting opinion.'

'And?'

'And nothing, she threw me out of her billet after that.'

'So you handled it with your usual tact then?'

'Perhaps I could have been more delicate,' agreed Karkasy, 'but I was shaken to know that a woman of intelligence could be taken in by such nonsense.'

'So what do we do about it?'

'You tell me. I don't have a clue. Do you think we should tell someone about Euphrati?'

Mersadie took a long drink of the wine and said, 'I think we have to.'

'Any ideas who?'

'Sindermann maybe?'

Karkasy sighed. 'I had a feeling you were going to suggest him. I don't like the man, but he's probably the best bet these days. If anyone can talk Euphrati around it's an iterator.'

Mersadie sighed and poured another couple of drinks. 'Want to get drunk?'

'Now you're talking my language,' said Karkasy.

They swapped stories and memories of less complicated times for an hour, finishing the bottle of wine and sending a servitor to fetch more when it ran out. By the time they'd drained half the second one, they were already planning a great symphonic work of her documentarist findings embellished with his verse.

They laughed and studiously avoided any talk of Euphrati Keeler and the betrayal they were soon to visit upon her.

Their thoughts were immediately dispelled as chiming alarm bells rang out, and the corridor beyond began to fill with hurrying people. At first, they ignored the noise, but as the number of people grew, they decided to find out what was going on. Picking up the bottle and glasses, Karkasy and Mersadie unsteadily made their way to the hatchway where they saw a scene of utter bedlam.

Soldiers and civilians, remembrancers and ship's crew, were heading for the embarkation decks in a hurry. They saw faces streaked with tears, and huddled weeping figures consoling one another in their shared misery.

'What's going on?' shouted Karkasy, grabbing a passing soldier.

The man rounded on him angrily. 'Get off me, you old fool.'

'I just want to know what's happening,' said Karkasy, shocked at the man's venom.

'Haven't you heard?' wept the soldier. 'It's all over the ship.'

'What is?' demanded Mersadie.

'The Warmaster…'

'What about him? Is he alright?'

The man shook his head. 'Emperor save us, but the Warmaster is dead!'

THE BOTTLE SLIPPED from Karkasy's hands, shattering on the floor, and he was instantly sober. The Warmaster dead? Surely, there had to be some kind of mistake. Surely, Horus was beyond such concerns as mortality. He faced Mersadie and could see exactly the same thoughts running through her head. The soldier he'd stopped shrugged off his grip and ran down the corridor, leaving the two of them standing there, aghast at such a horrific prospect.

'It can't be true,' whispered Mersadie. 'It just can't be.'

'I know. There must be some mistake.'

'What if there isn't?'

'I don't know,' said Karkasy, 'but we have to find out more.'

Mersadie nodded and waited for him to collect the Bondsman before they joined the hurrying throng as it made its mob-like way towards the embarkation decks. Neither of them spoke during the journey, too busy trying to process the impact of the Warmaster's death. Karkasy felt the muse stir within him at such weighty subject matter, and tried not to despise the fact that it came at such a terrible time.

He spotted the corridor leading to the observation deck adjacent to the launch port from where Stormbirds could be seen deploying, or returning. She resisted his pull until he explained his plan.

'There's no way they're going to let us in,' said Karkasy, out of breath from his exertions. 'We can watch the Stormbirds arrive from here and there's an observation gantry that overlooks the deck itself.'

They darted from the human river making its way to the embarkation deck and followed the arched corridor that led to the observation deck. Inside the long chamber, the wide armoured glass wall showed smudges of starlight and the glinting hulls of distant bulk cruisers belonging to the Army and the Mechanicum. Below them was the chasm-like opening of the embarkation deck, its blinking locator lights flashing an angry red.

Mersadie dimmed the lighting, and the details beyond the glass became clearer.

The yellow brown swell of Davin's moon curved away from them, its surface grimy and smeared with clouds. A hazy corona of sickly light haloed the moon and, from here, it looked peaceful.

'I don't see anything,' said Mersadie.

Karkasy pressed himself against the glass to eliminate reflections and tried to see something other than himself and Mersadie. Then he saw it. Like a glimmering firefly, a distant speck of fire was rising out of the moon's corona and heading towards the *Vengeful Spirit*.

'There!' he said, pointing towards the approaching light.

'Where? Oh, wait, I see it!' said Mersadie, blink-clicking the image of the approaching craft.

Karkasy watched as the light drew nearer, resolving itself into the shape of a speeding Stormbird as it angled its approach to the embarkation deck. Even though Karkasy was no pilot, he could tell that its approach was recklessly rapid, the craft's wings folding in at the last moment as it aimed for the yawning, red-lit hatch.

'Come on!' he said, taking Mersadie's hand and leading the way up the steps to the observation gantry. The steps were steep and narrow, and Karkasy had to stop to get his breath back before he reached the top. By the time they reached the gantry, the Stormbird had already been recovered and its assault ramp was descending.

A host of Astartes gathered around the craft as the Bell of Return began ringing and four warriors emerged, the plates of their armour dented and bloodstained. Between them, they carried a body draped in a Legion banner. Karkasy's breath caught in his throat and he felt his heart turn to stone at the sight.

'The Mournival,' said Mersadie. 'Oh no...'

The four warriors were quickly followed by an enormous gurney upon which lay a partially armoured warrior of magnificent stature.

Even from here, Karkasy could tell that the figure upon the gurney was the Warmaster and though tears leapt unbidden to his eyes at the sight of such a superlative warrior laid low, he rejoiced that the shrouded corpse was not the Warmaster. He heard Mersadie blink clicking the images even though he knew there would be no point; her eyes were similarly misted with tears. Behind the gurney came the remembrancer woman, Vivar, her dress torn and bloody, the fine fabric mud stained and ragged, but Karkasy pushed her from his mind as he saw more warriors rush towards the gurney. Armoured in white plate, they surrounded the Warmaster as he was wheeled through the embarkation deck with great haste, and Karkasy's heart leapt as he recognised them as Legion apothecaries.

'He's still alive...' he said.

'What? How do you know?'

'The apothecaries are still working on him,' laughed Karkasy, the relief tasting like the sweetest wine. They threw themselves into each other's arms, embracing with the sheer relief of the Warmaster's survival.

'He's alive,' sobbed Mersadie. 'I knew he had to be. He couldn't be dead.'

'No,' agreed Karkasy. 'He couldn't.'

They broke apart and sagged against the railings as the Astartes escorted the fallen Warmaster across the deck. As the huge blast doors rumbled open, the masses of people gathered outside surged through in a great wave, their cries of loss and pain audible even through the armoured glass of the observation gantry.

'No,' whispered Karkasy. 'No, no, no.'

The Astartes were in no mood to be slowed by this mass of people, and brutally clubbed them aside as they forced a path through the crowd. The Mournival led the gurney through the crowds, mercilessly clearing a bloody path through the people before them. Karkasy saw men and women cast down, trampled underfoot, and their screams were pitiful to hear.

Mersadie held his arm as they watched the Astartes bludgeon their way from the embarkation deck. They vanished through the blast door and were lost to sight as they rushed towards the medical deck.

'Those poor people...' cried Mersadie, sinking to her knees and looking down on a scene like the aftermath of a battle: wounded soldiers, remembrancers and civilians lay where they had fallen, bleeding and broken, simply because they were unlucky enough to be in the path of the Astartes.

'They didn't care,' said Karkasy, still unable to believe the bloody scenes that he'd just witnessed. 'They've killed those people. It was like they didn't care.'

Still in shock at the casual ease with which the Astartes had punched through the crowd, Karkasy gripped the railings, his knuckles white and his jaw clenched with outrage.

'How dare they?' he hissed. 'How *dare* they?'

His anger at the scenes below still seethed close to the surface; however, he noticed a robed figure making her way through the carnage below, reaching out to the injured and stunned.

His eyes narrowed, but he recognised the shapely form of Euphrati Keeler.

She was handing out *Lectitio Divinitatus* pamphlets, and she wasn't alone.

MALOGHURST WATCHED THE recording from the embarkation deck with a grim expression, watching his fellow Sons of Horus batter their way through the crowds that swarmed around the Warmaster's wracked body. The pict replayed again on the viewer set into the table in the Warmaster's sanctum, and each time he watched it, he willed it to be different, but each time the flickering images remained resolutely the same.

'How many dead?' asked Hektor Varvarus, standing at Maloghurst's shoulder.

'I don't have the final figures yet, but at least twenty-one are dead, and many more are badly injured or won't wake from the comas they're in.'

He cursed Loken and the others for their heavy handedness as the image played again, but supposed he couldn't blame them for their ardour. The Warmaster was in a critical condition and no one knew if he would live, so their desperation to reach the medical decks was forgivable, even if many might say that their actions were not.

'A bad business, Maloghurst,' said Varvarus needlessly. 'The Astartes will not come out of this well.'

Maloghurst sighed, and said, 'They thought the Warmaster was dying and acted accordingly.'

'Acted accordingly?' repeated Varvarus. 'I do not think many people will accept that, my friend, once word of this gets out, it will be a crippling blow to morale.'

'It will not get out,' assured Maloghurst. 'I am rounding up everyone who was on that deck and have shut down all non-command vox traffic from the ship.'

Tall and precise, Hektor Varvarus was rake-thin and angular, and his every movement was calculated – traits he carried over into his role as Lord Commander of the Army forces of the 63rd Expedition.

'Trust me, Maloghurst, this will get out. One way or another, it will get out. Nothing remains secret forever. Such things have a habit of wanting to be told and this will be no different.'

'Then what do you suggest, lord commander?' asked Maloghurst.

'Are you genuinely asking me, Mal, or are you just observing a courtesy because I am here?'

'I was genuinely asking,' said Maloghurst, smiling as he realised that he meant it. Varvarus was a canny soldier who understood the hearts and minds of mortal men.

'Then you have to tell people what happened. Be honest.'

'Heads will need to roll,' cautioned Maloghurst. 'People will demand blood for this.'

'Then give it to them. If that's what it takes, give it to them. Someone has to be seen to pay for this atrocity.'

'Atrocity? Is that what we're calling it now?'

'What else would you call it? Astartes warriors have committed murder.'

The enormity of what Varvarus was suggesting staggered Maloghurst, and he lowered himself slowly into one of the chairs at the Warmaster's table.

'You would have me give up an Astartes warrior for this? I cannot do it.'

Varvarus leaned over the table, the decorations and medals of his dress uniform reflecting like gold suns in its black surface.

'Innocent blood has been spilled, and while I can understand the reasons behind the actions of your men, it changes nothing.'

'I can't do it, Hektor,' said Maloghurst, shaking his head.

Varvarus moved to stand next to him. 'You and I both swore the oath of loyalty to the Imperium did we not?'

'We did, but what has that to do with anything?'

The old general locked eyes with Maloghurst and said, 'We swore that we would uphold the ideals of nobility and justice that the Imperium stands for, yes?'

'Yes, but this is different. There were extenuating circumstances...'

'Irrelevant,' snapped Varvarus. 'The Imperium must stand for something, or it stands for nothing. If you turn away from this, then you betray that oath of loyalty. Are you willing to do that, Maloghurst?'

Before he could answer, there was a soft knocking on the glass of the sanctum and Maloghurst turned to see who disturbed them.

Ing Mae Sing, Mistress of Astropathy, stood before them like a skeletal ghost in a hooded white robe, the upper portions of her face shrouded in shadows.

'Mistress Sing,' said Varvarus, bowing deeply towards the telepath.

'Lord Varvarus,' she replied, her voice soft and feather-light. She returned the lord commander's bow and despite her blindness, inclined her head in precisely the right direction – a talent that never failed to unnerve Maloghurst.

'What is it, Mistress Sing?' he asked, though in truth, he was glad of the interruption.

'I bring tidings that must concern you, Sire Maloghurst,' she said, turning her blind gaze upon him. 'The astropathic choirs are unsettled. They sense a powerful surge in the currents of the warp: powerful and growing.'

'What does that mean?' he asked.

'That the veil between worlds grows thin,' said Ing Mae Sing.

TEN

Apothecarion/Prayers/Confession

STRIPPED OUT OF his armour and wearing bloody surgical robes, Vaddon was as close to desperate as he had ever been in his long experience as an apothecary of the Sons of Horus. The Warmaster lay before him on the gurney, his flesh exposed to his knives and to the probes of the medicae machines. Oxygen was fed to the Warmaster through a mask, and saline drips pumped fluids into his body in an attempt to normalise his blood pressure. Medicae servitors brought fresh blood for immediate transfusions and the entire theatre fizzed with tension and frantic activity.

'We're losing him!' shouted Apothecary Logaan, watching the heart monitors. 'Blood pressure is dropping rapidly, heart rate spiking. He's going to arrest!'

'Damn it,' cursed Vaddon. 'Get me more Larraman serum, his blood won't clot, and fix up another fluid line.'

A whirring surgical narthecium swung down from the ceiling, multiple limbs clattering as they obeyed

Vaddon's shouted commands. Fresh Larraman cells were pumped directly into Horus's shoulder and the bleeding slowed, though Vaddon could see it still wasn't stopping completely. Thick needles jabbed into the Warmaster's arms, filling him with super-oxygenated blood, but their supply was dwindling faster than he would have believed possible.

'Stabilising,' breathed Logaan. 'Heart rate slowing and blood pressure is up.'

'Good,' said Vaddon. 'We've got some breathing room then.'

'He can't take much more of this,' said Logaan. 'We're running out of things we can do for him.'

'I'll not hear that in my theatre, Logaan,' snapped Vaddon. 'We're not going to lose him.'

The Warmaster's chest hiked as he clung to life, his breathing coming in short, hyperventilating gasps, more blood pumping from the wound in his shoulder.

Of the two wounds the Warmaster had suffered, it seemed the least severe, but Vaddon knew it was the one that was killing him. The puncture wound in his chest had practically healed already, ultra sonograms showing that his lung had sealed itself off from the pulmonary system while it repaired itself. The Warmaster's secondary lungs were sustaining him for now.

The Mournival hovered like expectant fathers as the apothecaries worked harder than they had ever worked before. Vaddon had never expected to have the Warmaster for a patient. The primarch's biology was as far beyond that of a normal Astartes warrior as his own was from a mortal man, and Vaddon knew that he was out of his depth. Only the Emperor himself had the knowledge to delve into the body of a primarch with confidence, and the enormity of what was occurring was not lost on him.

A green light winked into life on the narthecium machine and he lifted the data-slate from the port in its silver steel surface. Numbers and text scrolled across its glossy surface and though much of it made no sense to him, he felt his spirits fall as what he could comprehend sank in.

Seeing that the Warmaster was stable, he circled the operating slab and joined the Mournival, wishing he had better news for them.

'What's wrong with him?' demanded Abaddon. 'Why is he still lying there?'

'Honestly, first captain, I don't know.'

'What do you mean, "You don't know"?' shouted Abaddon, grabbing Vaddon and slamming him against the theatre wall. Silver trays laden with scalpels, saws and forceps clattered to the tiled floor. 'Why don't you know?'

Loken and Aximand grappled with the first captain as Vaddon felt Abaddon's enormous strength slowly crushing his neck.

'Let go of him, Ezekyle!' cried Loken. 'This isn't helping!'

'You won't let him die!' snarled Abaddon, and Vaddon was amazed to see a terrible fear in the first captain's eyes. 'He is the Warmaster!'

'You think I don't know that?' gasped Vaddon as the others prised Abaddon's grip from his neck. He slid down the wall, already able to feel the swelling in his bruised throat.

'Emperor damn you if you let him die,' hissed Abaddon, stalking the theatre with predatory strides. 'If he dies, I will kill you.'

Aximand led the first captain away from him, speaking soothing words as Loken and Torgaddon helped him to his feet.

'The man's a maniac,' hissed Vaddon. 'Get him out of my theatre, now!'

'He's not himself, apothecary,' explained Loken. 'None of us are.'

'Just keep him away from my team, captain,' warned Vaddon. 'He's not in control of himself, and that makes him dangerous.'

'We will,' Torgaddon promised him. 'Now what can you tell us? Will he survive?'

Vaddon took a moment to compose himself before answering, picking up his fallen data-slate. 'As I said before, I just don't know. We're like children trying to repair a logic engine that's been dropped from orbit. We don't understand even a fraction of what his body is capable of or how it works. I can't even begin to guess what kind of damage it's suffered to have caused this.'

'What's actually happening to him?' asked Loken.

'It's the wound in his shoulder; it won't clot. It's bleeding out and we can't stop it. We found some degraded genetic residue in the wound that might be some kind of poison, but I can't be sure.'

'Might it be a bacteriological or a viral infection?' asked Torgaddon. 'The water on Davin's moon was thick with contaminants. I ought to know, I swallowed a flagon's worth of it.'

'No,' said Vaddon. 'The Warmaster's body is, for all intents and purposes, immune to such things.'

'Then what is it?'

'This is a guess, but it looks like this particular poison induces a form of anaemic hypoxia. Once it enters the bloodstream, it's absorbed exponentially by the red blood cells, in preference to oxygen. With the Warmaster's accelerated metabolism, the toxin was carried efficiently around his system, damaging his tissue cells as it went, so they were unable to make proper use of the reduced oxygen content.'

'So where did it come from?' asked Loken. 'I thought you said the Warmaster was immune to such things.'

'And so he is, but this is like nothing I've ever seen before… it's as though it's been specifically designed to kill him. It's got precisely the right genetic camouflage to fool his enhanced biological defences and allow it to do the maximum amount of damage. It's a primarch killer – pure and simple.'

'So how do we stop it?'

'This isn't an enemy you can take a bolter or sword to, Captain Loken. It's a poison,' he said. 'If I knew the source of the poisoning, we might be able to do something.'

'Then if we found the weapon that did this, would that be of some help?' asked Loken.

Seeing the desperate need for hope in the captain's eyes, Vaddon nodded. 'Maybe. From the wound shape, it looks like a stab wound from a sword. If you can retrieve the blade, then maybe we can do something for him.'

'I'll find it,' swore Loken. He turned from Vaddon and made his way to the theatre door.

'You're going back there?' asked Torgaddon, running to catch up with him.

'Yes, and don't try to stop me,' warned Loken.

'Stop you?' said Torgaddon. 'Don't be such a drama queen, Garvi. I'm coming with you.'

RECOVERING A TITAN after action in the field was a long and arduous process, full of technical, logistical and manual difficulties. Entire fleets of vessels came down from orbit, bringing huge lifters, enormous diggers and loading machines. The delivery vessels had to be dug from their impact craters, and an army of Mechanicum servitors were required to facilitate the process.

Titus Cassar was exhausted. He'd spent the better part of the day prepping the Titan for its recovery and everything was in readiness for their return to the fleet. Until they were recovered, there wasn't much to do except wait, and that had become the hardest part of all for the men left behind on Davin's moon.

With time to wait, there was time to think; and with time to think, the human mind could conjure all manner of things from the depths of its imagination. Titus still couldn't believe that Horus had fallen. A being of such power, like unto a Titan himself, was not meant to fall in battle – he was invincible, the son of a god.

In the shadow of the *Dies Irae*, Titus fished out his *Lectitio Divinitatus* chapbook and, once he was satisfied he was alone, began to read the words there. The badly printed scripture gave him comfort, turning his mind to the glory of the divine Emperor of Mankind.

'Oh Emperor, who is lord and god above us all, hear me in this hour of need. Your servant lies with death's cold touch upon him and I ask you to turn your beneficent gaze his way.'

He fished out a pendant from beneath his uniform jacket as he read. It was a delicately wrought thing of silver and gold that he'd had one of the blank-faced servitors fashion for him. A silver capital 'I' with a golden starburst at its centre, it represented hope and the promise of a better future.

He held it clasped to his breast as he recited more of the words of the *Lectitio Divinitatus*, feeling a familiar warmth suffuse him as he repeated the words.

Titus sensed the presence of other people behind him a second too late and turned to see Jonah Aruken and a group of the Titan's crew.

Like him, they were dirty and tired after the fight against the monsters of this place, but unlike him they did not have faith.

Guiltily, he closed his chapbook and waited for Jonah's inevitable barb. No one said anything, and as he looked closer, he saw a brittle edge of sorrow and the need for comfort in the faces of the men before him.

'Titus,' said Jonah Aruken. 'We... uh... that is... the Warmaster. We wondered if...'

Titus smiled in welcome as understood what they'd come for.

He opened his chapbook again and said, 'Let us pray, brothers.'

THE MEDICAL DECK was a sterile, gleaming wilderness of tiled walls and brushed steel cabinets, a warren of soul-less glass rooms and laboratories. Petronella had completely lost all sense of direction, bewildered by the hasty summons that had brought her from the moon's surface back to the *Vengeful Spirit*.

Passing through the bloody embarkation deck, she saw that the upper levels of the ship were in pandemonium as word of the Warmaster's death had spread from vessel to vessel with all the fearsome rapidity of an epidemic.

Maloghurst the Twisted had issued a fleet-wide communiqué denying that the Warmaster was dead, but hysteria and paranoia had a firm head start on his words. Riots had taken hold aboard several ships as doomsayers and demagogues had arisen proclaiming that these were now the end times. Army units had been ruthlessly quashing such malcontents, but more sprang up faster then they could stop them.

It had been scant hours since the Warmaster's fall, but the 63rd Expedition was already beginning to tear itself apart without him.

Maggard followed Petronella, his wounds bound and sealed with syn-skin by a Legion apothecary on the journey back to the Warmaster's flagship. His skin still had an unhealthy pallor and his armour was dented and torn, but he was alive and magnificent. Maggard was only an indentured servant, but he had impressed her and she resolved to treat him with the respect his talents deserved.

A helmeted Astartes warrior led her through the confusing maze of the medicae deck, eventually indicating that she should enter a nondescript white door marked with a winged staff wrapped in a pair of twisting serpents.

Maggard opened the door for her and she entered a gleaming operating theatre, its circular walls covered, to waist height, in green enamelled tiles. Silver cabinets and hissing, pumping machines surrounded the Warmaster, who lay on the operating slab with a tangled web of tubes and wires attached to his flesh. A stool of gleaming metal sat next to the slab.

Medicae servitors lurked around the circumference of the room, set into niches around the wall, and a gurgling machine suspended above the Warmaster fed fluid and blood into his body.

Her eyes misted to see the Warmaster brought so low, and tears came at this violation of the natural order of things. A giant Astartes warrior in hooded surgical robes approached her and said, 'My name is Apothecary Vaddon, Miss Vivar.'

She brushed her hands across her eyes, conscious of how she must look – her dress torn and caked with mud, her eyes blackened with smudged make-up. She started to hold her hand out for a kiss, but realised how foolish that would be and simply nodded.

'I am Petronella Vivar,' she managed. 'I am the Warmaster's documentarist.'

'I know,' said Vaddon. 'He asked for you by name.'

Sudden hope flared in her breast. 'He's awake?'

Vaddon nodded. 'He is. If it was up to me, you would not be here now, but I do not disobey the word of the commander, and he desires to speak with you.'

'How is he?' she asked.

The apothecary shook his head. 'He fades in and out of lucidity, so do not expect too much of him. If I decide it is time for you to leave, then you leave. Do you understand me?'

'I do,' she said, 'but please, may I speak with him now?'

Vaddon seemed reluctant to let her near the Warmaster, but moved aside and let her pass. She nodded her thanks and took a faltering step towards the operating slab, eager to see the Warmaster, but afraid of what she might find.

Petronella's hand leapt to her mouth to stifle an involuntary gasp at the sight of him. The Warmaster's cheeks were sunken and hollow, his eyes dull and listless. Grey flesh hung from his skull, wrinkled and ancient looking, and his lips were the blue of a corpse.

'Do I look that bad?' asked Horus, his voice rasping and distant.

'No,' she stammered. 'Not at all, I…'

'Don't lie to me, Miss Vivar. If you're to hear my valediction then there must be no deceit between us.'

'Valediction? No! I won't. You have to live.'

'Believe me, there's nothing I'd like more,' he wheezed, 'but Vaddon tells me there's not much chance of that, and I don't intend to leave this life without a proper legacy: a record that says the things that must be said before the end.'

'Sir, your deeds alone stand as an eternal legacy, please don't ask this of me.'

Horus coughed a froth of blood onto his chest, gathering his strength before speaking once more, and his voice was the strong and powerful one she remembered. 'You told me that it was your vocation to immortalise me, to record the glory of Horus for future generations, did you not?'

'I did,' she sobbed.

'Then do this last thing for me, Miss Vivar,' he said.

She swallowed hard and then fished out the data-slate and mnemo-quill from her reticule, before sitting on the high stool next to the operating slab.

'Very well,' she said at last. 'Let's start at the beginning.'

✠ ✠ ✠

'IT WAS TOO much,' began Horus. 'I promised my father I would make no mistakes, and now we have come to this.'

'Mistakes?' asked Petronella, though she suspected she knew the Warmaster's meaning.

'Temba, giving him lordship over Davin,' said Horus. 'He begged me not to leave him behind, claimed it was too much for him. I should have listened, but I was too eager to be away on some fresh conquest.'

'Temba's weakness is not your fault, sir,' she said.

'It is good of you to say that, Miss Vivar, but I appointed him,' said Horus. 'The responsibility lies with me. Throne! Guilliman will laugh when he hears of this: him and the Lion both. They will say that I was not fit to be Warmaster since I could not read the hearts of men.'

'Never!' cried Petronella. 'They wouldn't dare.'

'Oh, they will, girl, believe me. We are brothers, yes, but like all brothers we squabble and seek to outdo one another.'

Petronella could think of nothing to say; the idea of the superhuman primarchs squabbling quite beyond her.

'They were jealous, all of them,' continued Horus. 'When the Emperor named me Warmaster, it was all some of them could do to congratulate me. Angron especially, he was a wild one, and even now I can barely keep him in check. Guilliman wasn't much better. I could tell he thought it should have been him.'

'They were jealous of you?' asked Petronella, unable to believe what the Warmaster was telling her, the mnemo-quill scratching across the data-slate in response to her thoughts.

'Oh yes,' nodded Horus bitterly. 'Only a few of my brothers were gracious enough to bow their heads and mean it. Lorgar, Mortarion, Sanguinius, Fulgrim and Dorn – they are true brothers. I remember watching the

Emperor's Stormbird leaving Ullanor and weeping to see him go, but most of all I remember the knives I felt in my back as he went. I could hear their thoughts as clearly as though they spoke them aloud: why should I, Horus, be named Warmaster when there were others more worthy of the honour?'

'You were made Warmaster *because* you were the most worthy, sir,' said Petronella.

'No,' said Horus. 'I was not. I was simply the one who most embodied the Emperor's need at that time. You see, for the first three decades of the Great Crusade I fought alongside the Emperor, and I alone felt the full weight of his ambition to rule the galaxy. He passed that vision to me and I carried it with me in my heart as we forged our path across the stars. It was a grand adventure we were on, system after system reunited with the Master of Mankind. You cannot imagine what it was like to live in such times, Miss Vivar.'

'It sounds magnificent.'

'It was,' said Horus. 'It was, but it couldn't last. Soon we were being drawn to other worlds where we discovered my brother primarchs. We had been scattered throughout the galaxy not long after our birth and, one by one, the Emperor recovered us all.'

'It must have been strange to be reunited with brothers you had never known.'

'Not as strange as you might think. As soon as I met each one, I had an immediate kinship with him, a bond that not even time or distance had broken. I won't deny that some were harder to like than others. If you ever meet Night Haunter you'll understand what I mean. Moody bastard, but handy in a tight spot when you need some alien empire shitting in its breeches before you attack.

'Angron's not much better, mind; he's got a temper on him like you've never seen. You think you know anger, I tell you now that you don't know anything until you've seen Angron lose his temper. And don't get me started on the Lion.'

'Of the Dark Angels? His is the First Legion is it not?'

'It is,' replied Horus, 'and doesn't he just love to remind everyone of that. I could see in his eyes that he thought he should have been Warmaster because his Legion was the first. Did you know he'd grown up living like an animal in the wilds, little better than a feral savage? I ask you, is that the sort of man you want as your Warmaster?'

'No it's not,' said Horus, answering his own question.

'Then who would you have picked to be Warmaster if not you?' asked Petronella.

Horus appeared to be momentarily perturbed by her question, but said, 'Sanguinius. It should have been him. He has the vision and strength to carry us to victory, and the wisdom to rule once that victory is won. For all his aloof coolness, he alone has the Emperor's soul in his blood. Each of us carries part of our father within us, whether it is his hunger for battle, his psychic talent or his determination to succeed. Sanguinius holds it all. It should have been his…'

'And what part of the Emperor do you carry, sir?'

'Me? I carry his ambition to rule. While the conquest of the galaxy lay before us that was enough, but now we are nearing the end. There is a Kretan proverb that says that peace is always "over there", but that is no longer true: it is within our grasp. The job is almost done and what is left for a man of ambition when the work is over?'

'You are the Emperor's right hand, sir,' protested Petronella. 'His favoured son.'

'No more,' said Horus sadly. 'Petty functionaries and administrators have supplanted me. The War Council is no more and I receive my orders from the Council of

Terra now. Once everything in the Imperium was geared for war and conquest, but now we are burdened with eaexectors, scribes and scriveners who demand to know the cost of everything. The Imperium is changing and I'm not sure I know how to change with it.'

'In what way is the Imperium changing?'

'Bureaucracy and officialdom are taking over, Miss Vivar. Red tape, administrators and clerks are replacing the heroes of the age and unless we change our ways and our direction, our greatness as an empire will soon be a footnote in the history books. Everything I have achieved will be a distant memory of former glory, lost in the mists of time like the civilisations of ancient Terra, remembered kindly for their noble past.'

'But surely the Crusade was but the first step towards creating a new Imperium for mankind to rule the galaxy. In such a galaxy we will need administrators, laws and scribes.'

'And what of the warriors who conquered it for you?' snarled Horus. 'What becomes of us? Are we to become gaolers and peacekeepers? We were bred for war and we were bred to kill. That is what we were created for, but we have become so much more than that. *I* am more than that.'

'Progress is hard, my lord, and people must always adapt to changing times,' said Petronella, uneasy at this change of temper in the Warmaster.

'It is not strange to mistake change for progress, Miss Vivar,' said Horus. 'I was bred with wondrous powers encoded into my very flesh, but I did not dream myself into the man I am today; I hammered and forged myself upon the anvil of battle and conquest. All that I have achieved in the last two centuries will be given away to weak men and women who were not here to shed their blood with us in the dark places of the galaxy. Where is the justice in that? Lesser men will rule what I have conquered, but what will be my reward once the fighting is done?'

Petronella glanced away at Apothecary Vaddon, but he simply watched impassively as she took down Horus's words. She wondered briefly if he was as upset as she was at the Warmaster's anger.

As shocked as she was, her ambitious core realised that she had the makings of the most sensational remembrance imaginable, one that would dispel forever the myth of the Crusade as a united band of brothers forging their destiny among the stars. Horus's words painted a picture of mistrust and disunion that no one had ever dreamed of.

Seeing her expression, Horus reached up with a shaking hand and touched her arm.

'I am sorry, Miss Vivar. My thoughts are not as clear as they ought to be.'

'No,' she said. 'I think they're clearer than ever now.'

'I can tell I'm shocking you. I'm sorry if I have shattered your illusions.'

'I admit I am… surprised by much of what you're saying, sir.'

'But you like it, yes? It's what you came here for?'

She tried to deny it, but the sight of the dying primarch gave her pause and she nodded.

'Yes,' she said. 'It's what I came here for. Will you tell me everything?'

He looked up and met her stare.

'Yes,' he said. 'I will.'

ELEVEN

Answers/A devil's bargain/Anathame

THE THUNDERHAWK'S ARMOURED flanks were not as sleek as those of a Stormbird, but it was functional and would take them back to Davin's moon more swiftly than the bigger craft. Tech servitors and Mechanicum flight crew prepped it for launch and Loken willed them to hurry. Each passing second brought the Warmaster closer to death and he wasn't going to allow that to happen.

Several hours had passed since they had brought the Warmaster aboard, but he hadn't cleaned his armour or weapons, preferring to go back the way he'd come out, though he had replenished his ammunition supply. The deck was still slick with the blood of those they had battered from their path and only now, with time to reflect on what they had done, did Loken feel ashamed.

He couldn't remember any of the faces, but he remembered the crack of skulls and the cries of pain. All the noble ideals of the Astartes... What did they mean when they could be so easily cast off? Kyril Sindermann was right, common decency and civil behaviour were just a thin veneer over the animal core that lurked in the hearts of all men… even Astartes.

If the mores of civilised behaviour could so easily be forgotten, what else might be betrayed with impunity in difficult circumstances?

Looking around the deck, Loken could sense a barely perceptible difference. Though hammers still beat, hatches still banged and gurneys laden with ordnance curled through the deck spaces, there was a subdued atmosphere to the embarkation deck, as though the memory of what had happened still lingered on the air.

The blast doors of the deck were shut tight, but Loken could still hear the muffled chants and songs of the crowds gathered outside.

Hundreds of people maintained a candlelit vigil in the wide corridors surrounding the embarkation deck, and filled the observation bays. Perhaps three score watched him from the windowed gantry above. They carried offerings and votive papers inscribed with pleas for the Warmaster's survival, random scribbles and outpourings of feelings.

Quite who these entreaties were directed at was a mystery, but it seemed to give people a purpose, and Loken could appreciate the value of purpose in these dark hours.

The men of Locasta were already onboard, though their journey to the embarkation deck had nearly sparked a stampede of terrified people – the memory of the last time the Astartes had marched through them still fresh and bloody.

Torgaddon and Vipus performed the last pre-launch checks on their men, and all that remained for him to do was to give the word.

He heard footsteps behind him and turned to see the armoured figure of Tybalt Marr, Captain of the 18th Company, approaching him. Sometimes known as 'the

Either' due to his uncanny resemblance to Verulam Moy – who had been known as 'the Or' – he was cast so firmly in the image of the Warmaster that Loken's breath caught in his throat. He bowed as his fellow captain approached.

'Captain Loken,' said Marr, returning the bow. 'Might I have a word?'

'Of course, Tybalt,' he said. 'I'm sorry about Verulam. He was brave man.'

Marr nodded curtly and Loken could only imagine the pain he must be going through.

Loken had grieved for fallen brothers before, but Moy and Marr had been inseparable, enjoying a symbiotic relationship not unlike identical twins. As friends and brothers, they had fought best as a pair, but once again, Moy had been lucky enough to gain a place in the speartip, and Marr had not.

This time Moy had paid for that luck with his life.

'Thank you, Captain Loken. I appreciate the sentiment,' replied Marr.

'Was there something you wanted, Tybalt?'

'Are you returning to the moon?' asked Marr, and Loken knew exactly why Marr was here. He nodded. 'We are. There may be something there that will help the Warmaster. If there is, we will find it.'

'Is it in the place where Verulam died?'

'Yes,' said Loken. 'I think so.'

'Could you use another sword arm? I want to see where... where it happened.'

Loken saw the aching grief in Marr's eyes and said. 'Of course we could.'

Marr nodded his thanks and they marched up the assault ramp as the Thunderhawk's engines powered up with the shrieking of a banshee's wail.

✠ ✠ ✠

AXIMAND WATCHED ABADDON punch the sparring servitor's shoulder, tearing off its sword limb before closing to deliver a series of rapid hammer blows to its torso. Flesh caved beneath the assault, bone and steel broke, and the construct collapsed in a splintered mess of meat and metal.

It was the third servitor Abaddon had destroyed in the last thirty minutes. Ezekyle had always worked through his angst with his fists and this time was no different. Violence and killing was what the first captain had been bred for, but it had become such a way of life to him that it was the only way he knew how to express his frustrations.

Aximand himself had dismantled and reassembled his bolter six times, slowly and methodically laying each part on an oiled cloth before cleaning it meticulously. Where Abaddon unleashed his pain through violence, Aximand preferred to detach his mind through familiar routines. Powerless to do anything constructive to help the commander, they had both retreated to the things they knew best.

'The Master of Armouries will have your head for destroying his servitors like that,' said Aximand, looking up as Abaddon pummelled what was left of the servitor to destruction.

Sweating and breathing hard, Abaddon stepped from the training cage, sweat lathering his body in gleaming sheets and his silver-wrapped topknot slick with sweat. Even for an Astartes, he was huge, muscular and solid as stone. Torgaddon often teased Abaddon joking that he left leadership of the Justaerin to Falkus Kibre because he was too big to fit in a suit of Terminator armour.

'It's what they're for,' snapped Abaddon.

'I'm not sure you're meant to be that hard on them.'

Abaddon shrugged, lifted a towel from his arming chamber and hung it around his shoulders. 'How can you be calm at a time like this?'

'Trust me, I'm not calm, Ezekyle.'

'You look calm.'

'Just because I'm not smashing things with my fists doesn't mean I'm not choleric.'

Abaddon picked up a piece of his armour, and began polishing it, before hurling it aside with an angry snarl.

'Centre your humours, Ezekyle,' advised Aximand. 'It's not good to go too far out of balance, you might not come back.'

'I know,' sighed Abaddon. 'But I'm all over the place: choleric, melancholic, saturnine; all of them at the same time. I can't sit still for a second. What if he doesn't make it, Little Horus? What if he dies?'

The first captain stood and paced the arming chambers, wringing his hands, and Aximand could see the blood rising in his cheeks as his anger and frustration grew once more.

'It's not fair,' growled Abaddon. 'It shouldn't be like this. The Emperor wouldn't let this happen. He shouldn't let this happen.'

'The Emperor hasn't been here for a long time, Ezekyle.'

'Does he even know what's happened? Does he even care anymore?'

'I don't know what to tell you, my friend,' said Aximand, picking up his bolter once more and pressing the catch that released the magazine, seeing that Abaddon had a new target for his impotent rage.

'It's not been the same since he left us after Ullanor,' raged Abaddon. 'He left us to clean up what he couldn't be bothered to finish, and for what? Some damn project on Terra that's more important than us?'

'Careful, Ezekyle,' warned Aximand. 'You're in dangerous territory.'

'It's true though isn't it? Don't tell me you don't feel the same, I know you do.'

'It's… different now, yes,' conceded Aximand.

'We're out here fighting and dying to conquer the galaxy for him and he won't even stand with us out on the frontier. Where is his honour? Where is his pride?'

'Ezekyle!' said Aximand, throwing down his bolter and rising to his feet. 'Enough. If you were anyone else, I would strike you down for those words. The Emperor is our lord and master. We are sworn to obey him.'

'We are pledged to the commander. Don't you remember your Mournival oath?'

'I remember it well enough, Ezekyle,' retorted Aximand, 'better than you it seems, for we also pledged to the Emperor above all primarchs.'

Abaddon turned away and gripped the wire mesh of the training cage, his muscles bulging and his head bowed. With a cry of animal rage, he tore the mesh panel from the cage and hurled it across the training halls, where it landed at the armoured feet of Erebus, who stood silhouetted in the doorway.

'Erebus,' said Aximand in surprise. 'How long have you been standing there?'

'Long enough, Little Horus, long enough.'

Aximand felt a dagger of unease settle in his heart and said, 'Ezekyle was just angry and upset. His humours are out of balance. Don't–'

Erebus waved his hand to brush off Aximand's words, the dim light reflecting from the brushed steel plates of his armour. 'Fear not, my friend, you know how it is between us. We are all lodge members here. If anyone were to ask me what I heard here today, you know what I would tell them, don't you?'

'I can't say.'

'Exactly,' smiled Erebus, but far from being reassured, Aximand suddenly felt beholden to the First Chaplain of the Word Bearers, as though his silence were some kind of bargaining chip.

'Did you come for anything, Erebus?' demanded Abaddon, his choler still to the fore.

'I did,' nodded Erebus, holding out his palm to reveal his silver lodge medal. 'The Warmaster's condition is deteriorating and Targost has called a meeting.'

'Now?' asked Aximand. 'Why?'

Erebus shrugged. 'I can't say.'

THEY GATHERED ONCE more in the aft hold of the flagship, travelling the lonely service stairwells to the deep decks of the *Vengeful Spirit*. Tapers again lit the way and Aximand found himself desperate to get this over with. The Warmaster was dying and they were holding a meeting?

'Who approaches?' asked a hooded figure from the darkness.

'Three souls,' Erebus replied.

'What are your names?' the figure asked.

'Do we need to bother with this now?' snapped Aximand. 'You know it's us, Sedirae.'

'What are your names?' repeated the figure.

'I can't say,' said Erebus.

'Pass, friends.'

They entered the aft hold, Aximand shooting a venomous glance at the hooded Luc Sedirae, who simply shrugged and followed them in. Candles lit the vast, scaffold-framed area as usual, but instead of the lively banter of warriors, a subdued, solemn atmosphere shrouded the hold. All the usual suspects were there: Serghar Targost, Luc Sedirae, Kalus Ekaddon, Falkus Kibre and many more officers and file troopers he knew or recognised... and Maloghurst the Twisted.

Erebus led the way into the hold, moving to stand in the centre of the group as Aximand nodded towards the Warmaster's equerry.

'It's been some time since I've seen you at a meeting,' said Aximand.

'It has indeed,' agreed Maloghurst. 'I have neglected my duties as a lodge member, but there are matters before us that demand my attendance.'

'Brothers,' said Targost, beginning the meeting. 'We live in grim times.'

'Get to the point, Serghar,' snarled Abaddon. 'We don't have time for this.'

The lodge master glared at Abaddon, but saw the first captain's lurking temper and nodded rather than confront him. Instead, he gestured towards Erebus and addressed the lodge as a whole. 'Our brother of the XVII Legion would speak to us. Shall we hear him?'

'We shall,' intoned the Sons of Horus.

Erebus bowed and said, 'Brother Ezekyle is right, we do not have time to stand on ceremony so I will be blunt. The Warmaster is dying and the fate of the Crusade stands on a knife-edge. We alone have the power to save it.'

'What does that mean, Erebus?' asked Aximand.

Erebus paced around the circumference of the circle as he spoke. 'The apothecaries can do nothing for the Warmaster. For all their dedication, they cannot cure him of this sickness. All they can do is keep him alive, and they cannot do that for much longer. If we do not act now, it will be too late.'

'What do you propose, Erebus?' asked Targost.

'The tribes on Davin,' said Erebus.

'What of them?' asked the lodge master.

'They are a feral people, controlled by warrior castes, but then we all know this. Our own quiet order bears the hallmarks of their warrior lodges in its structure and practices. Each of their lodges venerates one of the autochthonic predators of their lands, and this is where our order differs. In my time on Davin during its compliance, I studied the lodges and their ways in search of corruption or religious profanity. I found nothing of that, but in one lodge I found what I believe might be our only hope of saving the Warmaster.'

Despite himself, Aximand became caught up in Erebus's words, his oratory worthy of the iterators, with the precise modulation of tone and timbre to entrance his audience.

'Tell us!' shouted Luc Sedirae.

The lodge took up the cry until Serghar Targost was forced to restore order with a bellowed command.

'We must take the Warmaster to the Temple of the Serpent Lodge on Davin,' declared Erebus. 'The priests there are skilled in the mystic arts of healing, and I believe they offer the best chance of saving the Warmaster.'

'Mystic arts?' asked Aximand. 'What does that mean? It sounds like sorcery.'

'I do not believe it is,' said Erebus, rounding on him, 'but what if it was, Brother Horus? Would you refuse their aid? Would you allow the Warmaster to die just so we can feel pure? Is the Warmaster's life not worth a little risk?'

'Risk, yes? But this feels wrong.'

'Wrong would be not doing all that we could to save the commander,' said Targost.

'Even if it means tainting ourselves with impure magick?'

'Don't get all high and mighty, Aximand,' said Targost. 'We do this for the Legion. There is no other choice.'

'Then is it already decided?' demanded Aximand, pushing past Erebus to stand in the centre of the circle. 'If so, then why this charade of debate? Why bother even summoning us here?'

Maloghurst limped from Targost's side and shook his head. 'We must all be in accord here, Brother Horus. You know how the lodge operates. If you do not agree to this, then we will go no further and the Warmaster will remain here, but he will die if we do nothing. You know that to be true.'

'You cannot ask this of me,' pleaded Aximand.

'I have to, my brother,' said Maloghurst. 'There is no other way.'

Aximand felt the responsibility of the decision before him crushing him to the floor as every eye in the chamber turned upon him. His eyes meet Abaddon's and he saw that Ezekyle was clearly in favour of doing whatever it took to save the Warmaster.

'What of Torgaddon and Loken?' asked Aximand, trying to buy some time to think. 'They are not here to speak.'

'Loken is not one of us!' shouted Kalus Ekaddon, Captain of the Reaver squads. 'He had his chance to join us, but turned his back on our order. As for Tarik, he will follow our lead in this. There is no time to seek him out.'

Aximand looked into the faces of the men around him, and he realised had no choice. He never had from the moment he had walked into the room.

Whatever it took, the Warmaster had to live. It was that simple.

He knew there would be consequences. There always were in a devil's bargain like this, but any price was worth paying if it would save the commander.

He was damned if he would be remembered as the warrior who stood by and let the Warmaster die.

'Very well,' he said at last. 'Let the Lodge of the Serpent do what it can.'

THE DIFFERENCE IN Davin's moon in the few hours since they had last set foot on it was incredible, thought Loken. The cloying mists and fogs had vanished and the sky was lightening from a musky yellow to bleached white. The stench was still there, but it too was lessened, now just unpleasant rather than overpowering. Had the death of Temba broken some kind of power that held the moon locked in a perpetual cycle of decay?

As the Thunderhawk had skimmed the marshes, Loken had seen that the diseased forests were gone, their trunks collapsed in on themselves without the life-giving corruption holding them together. Without the obscuring mists, it was easy to find the *Glory of Terra*, though thankfully there was no deathly message coming over the vox this time.

They touched down and Loken led Locasta squad, Torgaddon, Vipus and Marr from the Thunderhawk with the confident strides of a natural leader. Though Torgaddon and Marr had held their captaincies longer than Loken, both instinctively deferred to him on this mission.

'What do you expect to find here, Garvi?' asked Torgaddon, squinting up at the collapsed hulk of the ship. He hadn't bothered to find a new helmet and his nose wrinkled at the stench of the place.

'I'm not sure,' he answered. 'Answers, maybe; something to help the Warmaster.'

Torgaddon nodded. 'Sounds good to me. What about you, Marr? What are you looking for?'

Tybalt Marr didn't answer, racking the slide of his bolter and marching towards the crashed vessel. Loken caught up with him and grabbed his shoulder guard.

'Tybalt, am I going to have a problem with you here?'

'No. I just want to see where Verulam died,' said Marr. 'It won't be real until I've seen the place. I know I saw him in the mortuary, but that wasn't a dead man. It was just like looking in a mirror. You understand?'

Loken didn't, but he nodded anyway. 'Very well, take up position in the file.'

They marched towards the dead ship, clambering up the broken ramps of debris to the gaping holes torn in its side.

'Damn, but it feels like a lifetime since we were fighting here,' said Torgaddon.

'It was only three or four hours ago, Tarik,' Loken pointed out.

'I know, but still…'

Eventually they reached the top of the ramp and penetrated the darkness of the ship, the memory of the last time he had done this and what he had found at the end of the journey still fresh in Loken's mind.

'Stay alert. We don't know what else might still be alive in here.'

'We should have bombed the wreck from orbit,' muttered Torgaddon.

'Quiet!' hissed Loken. 'Didn't you hear what I said?'

Tarik raised his hands in apology and they pressed on through the groaning wreck, along darkened hallways, flickering companionways and stinking, blackened corridors. Vipus and Loken led the way, with Torgaddon and Marr guarding the rear. The shadow-haunted wreck had lost none of its power to disturb, though the disgusting, organic growths that coated every surface with glistening wetness now seemed to be dying – drying up and cracking to powder.

'What's going on in here?' asked Torgaddon. 'This place was like the hydroponics bay a few hours ago, now it's…'

'Dying,' completed Vipus. 'Like those trees we saw earlier.'

'More like dead,' said Marr, peeling the husk of one of the growths from the wall.

'Don't touch anything,' warned Loken. 'Something in this ship had the power to harm the commander and until we know what that was, we touch nothing.'

Marr dropped the remains and wiped his hand on his leg as they journeyed deeper inside the ship. Loken's memory of their previous route was faultless and they soon reached the central spine and the route to the bridge.

Shafts of light speared in through holes in the hull and dust motes floated in the air like a glittering wall. Loken led on, ducking beneath protruding bulkheads and sparking cables as they reached their ultimate destination.

Loken could smell Eugan Temba long before they saw him, the reek of his putrefaction and death thick even beyond the bridge. They made their way cautiously onto the bridge, and Loken sent his warriors around the perimeter with directional chops of his hand.

'What are we going to do about those men up there?' asked Vipus, pointing to the dead soldiers stitched to the banners hanging from the roof. 'We can't just leave them like that.'

'I know, but we can't do anything for them just now,' said Loken. 'When we destroy this hulk, they'll be at rest.'

'Is that him?' asked Marr, pointing at the bloated corpse.

Loken nodded, raising his bolter and advancing on the body. A rippling motion undulated beneath the corpse's skin, and Temba's voluminous belly wobbled with internal motion. His flesh was stretched so tightly over his frame that the outlines of fat maggots and larvae could be seen beneath his parchment skin.

'Throne, he's disgusting,' said Marr. 'And this… thing killed Verulam?'

'I assume so,' replied Loken. 'The Warmaster didn't say exactly, but there's nothing else here is there?'

Loken left Marr to his grief and turned to his warriors, saying, 'Spread out and look for something, anything that might give us some clue as to what happened here.'

'You don't have any idea what we're looking for?' asked Vipus.

'No, not really,' admitted Loken. 'A weapon maybe.'

'You know we're going to have to search that fat bastard don't you?' Torgaddon pointed out. 'Who's the lucky sod who gets to do that?'

'I thought that'd be something you'd enjoy, Tarik.'

'Oh no, I'm not putting so much as a finger near that thing.'

'I'll do it,' said Marr, dropping to his knees and peeling away the sodden remnants of Eugan Temba's clothing and flesh.

'See?' said Torgaddon, backing away. 'Tybalt wants to do it. I say let him.'

'Very well. Be careful, Tybalt,' said Loken before turning away from the disgusting sight of Marr pulling apart Temba's corpse.

His men began searching the bridge and Loken climbed the steps to the captain's throne, staring out over the crew pits, now filled with all manner of vile excrescences and filth. It baffled Loken how such a glorious ship and a man of supposedly fine character could come to such a despicable end.

He circled the throne, pausing as his foot connected with something solid.

He bent down and saw a polished wooden casket. Its surfaces were smooth and clean, and it was clearly out of place in this reeking tomb. Perhaps the length and thickness of a man's arm, the wood was rich brown with strange symbols carved along its length. The lid opened on golden hinges and Loken released the delicate catch that held it shut.

The casket was empty, padded with a red velvet insert, and as he stared at its emptiness, Loken realised how thoughtless he'd been in opening it. He ran his fingers along the length of the casket, tracing the outline of the symbols, seeing something familiar in their elegantly cursive forms.

'Over here!' shouted one of Locasta, and Loken quickly gathered up the casket and made his way towards the source of the call. While Tybalt Marr disassembled the traitor's rotten body, Astartes warriors surrounded something that gleamed on the deck.

Loken saw that it was Eugan Temba's severed arm, the fingers still wrapped around the hilt of a strange, glittering sword with a blade that looked like grey flint.

'It's Temba's arm right enough,' said Vipus, reaching down to lift the sword.

'Don't touch it,' said Loken. 'If it laid the Warmaster low, I don't want to know what it could do to us.'

Vipus recoiled from the sword as though it were a snake.

'What's that?' asked Torgaddon, pointing at the casket.

Loken dropped to his haunches, laying the casket next to the sword, unsurprised when he saw that the sword would fit snugly inside.

'I think it once contained this sword.'

'Looks pretty new,' said Vipus. 'And what's that on the side? Writing?'

Loken didn't answer, reaching out to prise Temba's dead fingers from the sword hilt. Though he knew it was absurd, he grimaced with each finger he pried loose, expecting the hand to leap to life and attack him.

Eventually, the sword was free, and Loken gingerly lifted the weapon.

'Careful,' said Torgaddon.

'Thanks, Tarik, and here was me about to throw it about.'

'Sorry.'

Loken slowly lowered the sword into the casket. The handle tingled and he had felt a curious sensation as he had said Tarik's name, a sense of the monstrous harm the weapon could inflict. He snapped the lid shut, letting out a pent-up breath.

'How in the name of Terra did someone like Temba get hold of a weapon like that?' asked Torgaddon. 'It didn't even look human-made.'

'It's not,' said Loken as the familiarity of the symbols on the side of the casket fell horribly into place. 'It's kinebrach.'

'Kinebrach?' asked Torgaddon. 'But weren't they–'

'Yes,' said Loken, carefully lifting the casket from the deck. 'This is the anathame that was stolen from the Hall of Devices on Xenobia.'

THE WORD WENT out across the *Vengeful Spirit* at the speed of thought, and weeping men and women lined their route. Hundreds filled each passageway as the Astartes bore the Warmaster on a bier of kite-shaped shields. Clad in his ceremonial armour of winter white with burnished gold trims and the glaring red eye, the Warmaster's hands were clasped across his golden sword, and a laurel wreath of silver sat upon his noble brow.

Abaddon, Aximand, Luc Sedirae, Serghar Targost, Falkus Kibre and Kalus Ekaddon carried him, and behind the Warmaster came Hektor Varvarus and Maloghurst. Each one wore shining armour and their company cloaks billowed behind them as they walked.

Heralds and criers announced the route of the cortege, and there was no repeat of the bloody scene on the embarkation deck as the Astartes took this slow march with the beloved leader who had fought beside them since the earliest days of the Crusade. They wept as they marched, each one painfully aware that this might be the Warmaster's last journey.

In lieu of flowers, the people threw torn scraps of tearstained paper, each with words of hope and love written on them. Shown that the Warmaster still lived, his people burned herbs said to have healing

properties, hanging them from smoking censers all
along the route, and from somewhere a band played
the Legion March.

Candles burned with a sweet smell and men and
women, soldiers and civilians, tore at themselves in their
grief. Army banners lined the route, each dipped out of
respect for the Warmaster, and pleading chants followed
the procession until at last they came to the embarkation deck. Its vast gateway was wreathed in parchment,
every square centimetre of bulkhead covered with mes-
sages for the Warmaster and his sons.

Aximand was awed by the outpouring of sorrow and
love for the Warmaster, the scale of people's grief at his
wounding beyond anything in his experience. To him
the Warmaster was a figure of magnificence, but first
and foremost, he was a warrior – a leader of men and
one of the Emperor's chosen.

To these mortals, he was so much more. To them, the
Warmaster was a symbol of something noble and
heroic beyond anything they could ever aspire to, a
symbol of the new galaxy they were forging from the
ashes of the Age of Strife.

Horus's very existence promised an end to the suffering and death that had plagued humanity for
centuries.

Old Night was drawing to a close and, thanks to
heroes like the Warmaster, the first rays of a new dawn
were breaking on the horizon.

All that was under threat now, and Aximand knew
he had made the right choice in allowing the others to
take Horus to Davin. The Lodge of the Serpent would
heal the Warmaster, and if that involved powers he
might once have condemned, then so be it.

The die was cast and all he had left to cling to was his
faith that the Warmaster would be restored to them. He
smiled as he remembered something the Warmaster had

said to him on the subject of faith. The Warmaster had typically delivered his words of wisdom at a wholly inappropriate time – right before they had leapt from the belly of a screaming Stormbird into the green skin city on Ullanor.

'When you have come to the edge of all that you know and are about to drop off into the darkness of the unknown, faith is knowing that one of two things will happen,' the Warmaster had told him.

'And what are they?' he had asked.

'That there will be something solid to stand on or you'll be taught to fly,' laughed Horus as he jumped.

The memory made the tears come all the harder as the huge iron gate of the embarkation deck rumbled closed behind them and the Astartes marched towards the Warmaster's waiting Stormbird.

TWELVE

Agitprop/Brothers in suspicion/Serpent and moon

Slipping across the page like a snake, the nib of Ignace Karkasy's pen moved as though it had a mind of its own. For all the conscious thought he was putting into the words, it might as well have. The muse was well and truly upon him, his stream of consciousness flowing into a river of blood as he retold the diabolical events on the embarkation deck. The meter played in his head like a symphony, every stanza of every canto slipping into place as if there could be no other possible arrangement of verse.

Even in his heyday of *Ocean Poems* or *Reflections and Odes* he had not felt this inspired. In fact, now that he looked back on them, he hated them for their frippery, their unconscionable navel gazing and irrelevance to the galaxy at large. These words, these thoughts that now poured from him, this was what mattered, and he cursed that it had taken him this long to discover it.

The truth was what mattered. Captain Loken had told him as much, but he hadn't heard him, not really. The

verses he'd written since Loken had begun his sponsorship of him were paltry things, unworthy of the man
who had won the Ethiopic Laureate, but that was changing now.

After the bloodbath on the embarkation deck, he'd
returned to his quarters, grabbed a bottle of Terran
wine and made his way to the observation deck. Finding it thronged with wailing lunatics, he'd repaired to
the Retreat, knowing that it would be empty.

The words had poured out of him in a flood of
righteous indignation, his metaphors bold and his
lyric unflinching from the awful brutality he'd witnessed. He'd already used up three pages of the
Bondsman, his fingers blotted with ink and his poet's
soul on fire.

'Everything I've done before this was prologue,' he
whispered as he wrote.

Karkasy paused in his work as he pondered the
dilemma: the truth was useless if no one could hear it.
The facilities set aside for the remembrancers included
a presswork where they could submit their work for
large-scale circulation. It was common knowledge that
much of what that passed through it was vetted and
censored, and so few made use of it. Karkasy certainly
couldn't, considering the content of his new poetry.

A slow smile spread across his jowly features and he
reached into the pocket of his robes and pulled out a
crumpled sheet of paper – one of Euphrati Keeler's
Lectitio Divinitatus pamphlets – and spread it out flat
on the table before him with the heel of his palm.

The ink was smeared and the paper reeked of
ammonia, clearly the work of a cheap mechanical
bulk-printer of some kind. If Euphrati could get the
use of one, then so could he.

✠ ✠ ✠

LOKEN PERMITTED TYBALT Marr to torch the body of Eugan Temba before they left the bridge. His fellow captain, streaked with gore and filth, played the burning breath of a flame unit over the monstrous corpse until nothing but ashen bone remained. It was small satisfaction for the death of a brother, not nearly enough, but it would have to do. Leaving behind the smouldering remains, they retraced their footsteps back through the *Glory of Terra*.

The light was fading on Davin's moon by the time they reached the outside, the planet above a pale yellow orb hanging low in the dusky sky. Loken carried the anathame in its gleaming wooden casket, and his warriors followed him from the wreck without any words spoken.

A great rumbling vibration gripped the moon as a trio of towering columns of light and smoke climbed towards the heavens from the Imperial deployment zone where this whole misadventure had started. Loken watched the incredible spectacle of the war machines of the Legio Mortis returning to their armoured berths in orbit, and silently thanked their crews for their aid in the fight against the dead things.

Soon all that was visible of the Titans' carriers was a diffuse glow on the horizon, and only the lap of water and the low growling of the waiting Thunderhawk's engines disturbed the silence. The desolate mudflats were empty for kilometres around, and as Loken made his way down the slope of rubble, he felt like the loneliest man in the galaxy.

Some kilometres away, he could see specks of blue light following the Titan carriers as Army transports ferried the last remaining soldiers back to their bulk transporters.

'We'll soon be done here, eh?' said Torgaddon.

'I suppose,' agreed Loken. 'The sooner the better.'

'How do you suppose that thing got here?'

Loken didn't have to ask what his brother meant, and shook his head, unwilling to share his suspicions with Torgaddon yet. As much as he loved him, Tarik had a big mouth, and Loken didn't want to put his quarry to flight.

'I don't know, Tarik,' said Loken as they reached the ground and made their way towards the Thunderhawk's lowered assault ramp. 'I don't think we'll ever know.'

'Come on, Garvi, it's me!' laughed Torgaddon. 'You're so straight up and down, and that makes you a really terrible liar. I know you've got some idea of what happened. So come on, spill it.'

'I can't, Tarik, I'm sorry,' said Loken. 'Not yet anyway. Trust me. I know what I'm doing.'

'Do you really?'

'I'm not sure,' admitted Loken. 'I think so. Throne, I wish the Warmaster were here to ask.'

'Well he's not,' stated Torgaddon, 'so you're stuck with me.'

Loken stepped onto the ramp, grateful to be off the marshy surface of the moon, and turned to face Torgaddon. 'You're right, I should tell you, and I will, soon. I just need to figure some things out first.'

'Look, I'm not stupid, Garvi,' said Torgaddon, leaning in close so that none of the others could hear. 'I know the only way this thing could have got here is if someone in the expedition brought it. It had to have been here before we arrived. That means there was only one person who was with us on Xenobia and could have got here before we did. You know who I'm talking about.'

'I know who you're talking about,' agreed Loken, pulling Torgaddon aside as the rest of the warriors embarked upon the Thunderhawk. 'What I can't figure out is why? Why go to all the trouble of stealing this thing and then bringing it here?'

'I'm going to break that son of a bitch in two if he had something to do with what's happened to the Warmaster,' snarled Torgaddon. 'The Legion will have his hide.'

'No,' hissed Loken, 'not yet. Not until we find out what this is all about and if anyone else is involved. I just can't believe that someone would dare try and move against the Warmaster.'

'Is that what you think is happening, a coup? You think that one of the other primarchs is making a play for the role of Warmaster?'

'I don't know, it all sounds too far fetched. It sounds like something from one of Sindermann's books.'

Neither man said anything. The idea that one of the eternal brotherhood of primarchs might be attempting to usurp Horus was incredible, outrageous and unthinkable, wasn't it?

'Hey,' called Vipus from inside the Thunderhawk. 'What are you two conspirators plotting?'

'Nothing,' said Loken guiltily. 'We were just talking.'

'Well finish up. We need to go, now!'

'Why, what is it?' asked Loken as he climbed aboard.

'The Warmaster,' said Vipus. 'They're taking him to Davin.'

The Thunderhawk was in the air moments later, lifting off in a spray of muddy water and a flare of blue-hot jet fire. The gunship circled the massive wreck, gaining altitude and speed as it turned towards the sky.

The pilot firewalled the engines and the gunship roared up into the darkness.

THE GREAT RED orb of the sun was dipping below the horizon and hot, dry winds rising from the plains below made it a bumpy ride as they re-entered Davin's atmosphere. The continental mass swelled through the armoured glass of the cockpit, dusty and brown and dry. Loken sat up front in the cockpit with the pilots and watched the avionics

panel as the red blip that represented the location of the
Warmaster's Stormbird drew ever closer.

Far below them, he could see the glittering lights of
the Imperial deployment zone where they had first
made planetfall on Davin, a wide circle of arc lights,
makeshift landing platforms and defensive positions.
The pilot brought them in at a steep angle, speed more
important to Loken than any notion of safe flight, and
they streaked past scores of other landing craft on their
way to the surface.

'Why so many?' wondered Loken as their flight lev-
elled out and they shot past the wide circle of light,
seeing soldiers and servitors toiling to expedite the
approach of so many landing craft.

'No idea,' said the pilot, 'but there's hundreds of them
coming down from the fleet. Looks like a lot of people
want to see Davin.'

Loken didn't reply, but the sight of so many landing
craft en route to Davin was yet another piece of the puz-
zle that he didn't understand. The vox networks were
jammed with insane chatter, weeping voices and groups
claiming that the end was coming, while yet others gave
thanks to the divine Emperor that his chosen champion
would soon rise from his deathbed.

None of it made any sense. He'd tried to make contact
with the Mournival, but no one was answering, and a
terrible foreboding filled him when he couldn't even
reach Maloghurst on the *Vengeful Spirit*.

Their flight soon carried them beyond the Imperial
position, and Loken saw a ribbon of light stretching
north from the landing zone. A host of pinpricks of light
pierced the darkness, and Loken ordered the pilot to fly
lower and reduce speed.

A long column of vehicles: tanks, supply trucks,
transporter flatbeds and even some civilian traffic, drove
along the dusty hardpan, each one swamped with

people, and all heading to the mountains as fast as their engines could carry them. The Thunderhawk powered on through the fading light of day, soon losing sight of the column of vehicles that was heading in the same direction.

'How long until we reach the Warmaster's position?' he asked.

'At current speed, maybe ten minutes or so,' answered the pilot.

Loken tried to collect his thoughts, but they had long since derailed in the midst of all this madness. Ever since leaving the interex, his mind had been a whirlpool, sucking in every random thought and spitting it out with barbs of suspicion. Could it be that he was still suffering the after-effects of what had happened to Jubal? Might the power, unlocked beneath the Whisperheads, be tainting him so that he jumped at shadows where none existed?

He might have been able to believe that, but for the presence of the anathame and his certainty that First Chaplain Erebus had lied to him on the voyage to Davin.

Karkasy had said that Erebus wanted Horus to come to Davin's moon, and his undoubted complicity in the theft of the anathame could lead to only one conclusion. Erebus had wanted Horus to be killed here.

That didn't make any sense either. Why go to such convoluted lengths just to kill the Warmaster, surely there had to be more to it than that...

Facts were slowly accumulating, but none of them fit, and still he had no idea why any of this was happening, only that it was, and that it was by the artifice of human design. Whatever was going on, he would uncover the conspiracy and make those involved pay with their lives.

'We're coming up on the Warmaster's Stormbird,' called the pilot.

Loken shook himself from his venomous reverie. He hadn't been aware of time passing, but immediately turned his attention to what lay beyond the armoured glass of the cockpit.

Tall mountain peaks surrounded them, jagged cliffs of red stone, veined with gleaming strata of gold and quartz. They followed the course of an ancient causeway along the valley, its flagstones split and cracked with the passing of the centuries. Statues of long-dead kings lined the processional way, and toppled columns littered this forgotten highway like fallen guardians. Shadows plumbed the depths of the valley along which they flew and in a gap ahead, he could see a reflected glow in the brazen sky.

The pilot dropped their speed and the gunship flew through the gap into a colossal crater gouged from the landscape like an enormous, flat-bottomed basin. The sheer sides of the crater soared above them, its diameter thousands of metres across.

A huge stone building stood at its centre, carved from the same rock as the mountains and bathed in the light of a thousand flaming torches. The Thunderhawk circled the structure and Loken saw that it was a giant octagonal building, each corner shaped like the bastion of a fortress. Eight towers surrounded a wide dome at its centre and flames burned from their tops.

Loken could see the Warmaster's Stormbird below them, a multitude of torchbearers surrounding it, hundreds, maybe even thousands of people. A clear path stretched from the Stormbird towards the cyclopean archway that led into the building, and Loken saw the unmistakable form of the Warmaster being borne by the Sons of Horus towards it.

'Take us down. Now!' shouted Loken. He rose, made his way back to the crew compartment and snatched his bolter from the rack.

'What's up?' asked Vipus. 'Trouble?'

'Could be,' said Loken, turning to address all the warriors aboard the gunship. 'Once we disembark, take your lead from me.'

His warriors had efficiently prepped for a combat disembarkation, and Loken felt the motion of the Thunderhawk change as it slowed and came in to land. The internal light changed from red to green and the craft slammed hard into the ground. The assault ramp dropped and Loken led the way out, marching confidently towards the building.

Night had fallen, but the air was hot, and the sour fragrances of bitter blossoms filled the air with a beguiling, aromatic scent. He led his men onwards at a quick march. Many of the torchbearers turned quizzically towards them, and Loken now saw that these were the indigenous inhabitants of Davin.

The Davinites were more wiry than most mortal men, tall and hirsute with thin limbs, and elaborate topknots worn in a style similar to Abaddon's. They wore long capes of shimmering, patterned scales, banded armour – of the same lacquered scales – and most were armed with cross-belts of daggers and primitive looking black powder pistols. They parted before the advance of the Astartes, heads bowed in supplication, and it forcibly struck Loken just how close to deviancy these creatures appeared to be.

He hadn't paid much attention to the Davinites the first time he'd landed. He was just a squad captain more concerned with obeying orders and completing the tasks assigned to him than paying attention to the locals. Even this time, his attention had been elsewhere, and the almost bestial appearance of the Davinites had more or less slipped past his notice.

Surrounded by hundreds of the planet's inhabitants, their divergence from the human genome was unmistakeable, and Loken wondered how they had avoided extermination six decades ago, especially since it had been the Word Bearers who had made first contact with Davin – a Legion not noted for its tolerance of anything beyond the norm.

Loken was reminded of Abaddon's furious argument with the Warmaster over the question of the interex, and of how the first captain had demanded that they make war upon them for their tolerance of xenos breeds. If anything, Davin was far more of a textbook case for war, but somehow that hadn't happened.

The Davinites were clearly of human gene-stock, but this offshoot of humanity had diverged into a species almost all of its own. The wide spacing of their features, the dark eyes without pupils and the excessive, almost simian volume of thick hair on their faces and arms put Loken more in the mind of the stable-bred mutants some regiments of the Imperial Army employed. They were crude creatures with the intelligence to swing a sword or fire a clumsy rifle, but not much else.

Loken did not approve of the practice, and though the inhabitants of Davin were clearly possessed of a greater level of intelligence than such beasts, their appearance did not reassure him as to what was going on.

He put the Davinites from his mind as he approached a massive set of steps carved into the rock and lined with statues of coiling serpents and flaming braziers. Three narrow channels filled with rushing water divided the stairs, one to either side and one down the centre.

The Warmaster and his bearers were out of sight on the next level, and Loken led his warriors up the processional stairs, taking them three at a time as he heard a monstrous grinding of stone up ahead. The image of vast, monolithic doors appeared unbidden in his mind and he said, 'We have to hurry.'

Loken neared the top of the steps, the flickering coal braziers casting a ruddy glow over the statues that glinted from the serpents' scales and quartz-chip eyes. The last rays of the dying sun caught the twisting snakes carved around the pillars, making them seem alive, as if slowly descending to the steps. The effect was unsettling, and Loken opened his suit link again, saying, 'Abaddon, Aximand? Can either of you hear me? Respond.'

His earpiece hissed with static, but his hails received no answers and he picked up the pace.

He reached the top of the steps at last, and emerged onto a moonlit esplanade of yet more serpentine statues atop pillars that lined a narrowing roadway leading towards a giant, arched gateway in the face of the massive edifice. Wide gates of carved and beaten bronze with a glistening, spiralled surface rumbled as they swung closed, and Loken felt his skin crawl at the sight of that dread portal, its yawning darkness rich with the promise of ancient, primal power.

He could see a group of Astartes warriors standing before it, watching as the monstrous gate shut. Loken could see no sign of the Warmaster.

'Pick up the pace, battle march,' he ordered, and began the loping, ground-eating stride that the Astartes adopted when there was no vehicle support. Marching at this speed was sustainable over huge distances and still allowed a warrior to fight at the end of it. Loken prayed that he wouldn't be required to fight at the end of this march.

As he drew closer to the gates he saw that, far from being etched with meaningless spirals, each was carved with all manner of images and scenes. Looping serpents twisted from one leaf to another, others circled and swallowed their tails, and yet more were depicted intertwined as though mating.

Only when the gate slammed shut with a thunderous boom of metal did he see the full image. Unlike the commander, Loken was no student of art; nevertheless, he was awed by the full impact of the images worked onto the sealed gateway. Central to its imagery was a great tree with spreading branches, hanging with fruit of all description. Its three roots stretched out beyond the base of the gates and into a wide circular pool that fed the streams running the length of the esplanade, before cascading down the grand stairs.

Twin snakes coiled around the tree, their heads entwined in the branches above, and Loken was struck by its similarity to the symbol borne upon the shoulder guards of the Legion apothecaries.

Seven warriors stood at the edge of the pool of water, before the massive gate. They were armoured in the green of the Sons of Horus, and Loken knew them all: Abaddon, Aximand, Targost, Sedirae, Ekaddon, Kibre and Maloghurst.

None wore their helmets and as they turned, he could see that each one had the same air of helpless desperation. He had walked into hell with these warriors time and time again, and seeing his brothers with such expressions on their faces, drained him of his anger, leaving him hollow and heartbroken.

He slowed his march as he came face to face with Aximand.

'What have you done?' he asked. 'Oh my brothers, what have you done?'

'What needed to be done,' said Abaddon, when Aximand didn't answer.

Loken ignored the first captain and said, 'Little Horus? Tell me what you've done.'

'It is as Ezekyle said. We did what had to be done,' said Aximand. 'The Warmaster was dying and Vaddon couldn't save him. So we brought him to the Delphos.'

'The Delphos?' asked Loken.

'It is the name of this place,' said Aximand. 'The Temple of the Serpent Lodge.'

'Temple?' asked Torgaddon. 'Horus, you brought the Warmaster to a fane? Are you mad? The commander would never have agreed to this.'

'Maybe not,' replied Serghar Targost, stepping forward to stand beside Abaddon, 'but by the end he couldn't even speak. He spoke to that damn remembrancer woman for hours on end before he lost consciousness. We had to place him in a stasis field to keep him alive long enough to bring him here.'

'Is Tarik right?' asked Loken. 'Is this a fane?'

'Fane, temple, Delphos, house of healing, call it what you will,' shrugged Targost. 'With the Warmaster on the threshold of death, neither religion nor its denial seems very significant any more. It is the only hope we have left and what do we have to lose? If we do nothing, the Warmaster dies. At least this way he has a chance of life.'

'And at what price will we buy his life?' demanded Loken, 'By bringing him to a house of false gods? The Emperor tells us that civilisation will only achieve perfection when the last stone of the last church falls upon the last priest, and this is where you bring the Warmaster. This goes against everything we have fought for these last two centuries. Don't you see that?'

'If the Emperor was here, he would do the same,' said Targost, and Loken felt his choler rise to the surface at such hubris.

He stepped threateningly close to Targost. 'You think you know the Emperor's will, Serghar? Does being lodge master of a secret society give you the power to know such a thing?'

'Of course not,' sneered Targost, 'but I know he would want his son to live.'

'By entrusting his life to these… savages?'

'It is from these savages that our own quiet order comes,' pointed out Targost.

'Yet another reason for me to distrust it then,' snapped Loken, turning from the lodge master and addressing Vipus and Torgaddon. 'Come on. We're getting the Warmaster out of there.'

'You can't,' said Maloghurst, limping forward to join Abaddon, and Loken had the distinct impression that his brothers were forming a barrier between him and the gateway.

'What do you mean?'

'It is said that once the Delphos Gate is shut, there is no way to open it save from the inside. A man in need of healing is carried inside and left to whatever the eternal spirits of deceased things decree for him. If it is his destiny to live, he may open the gate himself, if not, it opens in nine days and his remains are burned before being cast into the pool.'

'So you've just left the Warmaster inside? For all the good that will do him, you might just as well have left him on the *Vengeful Spirit*; and "eternal spirits of deceased things" – what does that even mean? This is insane. Can't you see that?'

'Standing by and watching him die would have been insane,' said Maloghurst. 'You judge us for acting out of love. Can't you see that?'

'No, Mal, I can't,' replied Loken sadly. 'How did you even think to bring him here anyway? Was it some secret knowledge your damned lodge is privy to?'

None of his brothers spoke, and as Loken searched their faces for answers, the truth of the matter was suddenly, horribly, clear to him.

'Erebus told you of this place, didn't he?'

'Yes,' admitted Targost. 'He knows of these lodges of old and has seen the power of their healing houses. If the Warmaster lives you will be thankful he spoke of it.'

'Where is he?' demanded Loken. 'He will answer to me for this.'

'He is not here, Garvi,' said Aximand. 'This was for the Sons of Horus to do.'

'Then where is he now, still on the *Vengeful Spirit*?'

Aximand shrugged. 'I suppose so. Why is it important to you?'

'I believe you have all been deceived, my brothers.' said Loken. 'Only the Emperor has the power to heal the Warmaster now. All else is falsehood and the domain of unclean corpse-whisperers.'

'The Emperor is not here,' said Targost bluntly. 'We take what aid we can.'

'What of you, Tarik?' put in Abaddon. 'Will you turn from your Mournival brothers, as Garviel does? Stand with us.'

'Garvi may be a starch-arse, Ezekyle, but he's right and I can't stand with you on this one. I'm sorry,' said Torgaddon as he and Loken turned away from the gate.

'You forget your Mournival oath!' cried Abaddon as they marched away. 'You swore to be true to the Mournival to the end of your lives. You will be oath-breakers!'

The words of the first captain hit Loken with the force of a bolter round and he stopped in his tracks. Oathbreaker... The very idea was hideous.

Aximand came after him, grabbing his arm and pointing towards the pool of water. The black water rippled with motion and Loken could see the yellow crescent of Davin's moon wavering in its surface.

'See?' said Aximand. 'The moon shines upon the water, Loken. The crescent mark of the new moon... It was branded upon your helmet when we swore our Mournival oath. It is a good omen, my brother.'

'Omen?' spat Loken, shrugging off his touch. 'Since when have we put our faith in omens, Horus? The Mournival oath was pantomime, but this is ritual. This is sorcery. I told you then that I would not bow to any fane or acknowledge any spirit. I told you that I owned only the empirical clarity of Imperial Truth and I stand by those words.'

'Please, Garvi,' begged Aximand. 'We are doing the right thing.'

Loken shook his head. 'I believe we will all rue the day you brought the Warmaster here.'

PART THREE

THE HOUSE OF FALSE GODS

THIRTEEN

Who are you?/Ritual/Old friend

HORUS OPENED HIS eyes, smiling as he saw blue sky above him. Pink and orange tinged clouds drifted slowly across his vision, peaceful and relaxing. He watched them for a few moments and then sat up, feeling wet dew beneath his palms as he pushed himself upright. He saw that he was naked, and as he surveyed his surroundings, he lifted his hand to his face, smelling the sweet scent of the grass and the crystal freshness of the air.

A vista of unsurpassed beauty lay before him, towering snow-capped mountains draped in a shawl of pine and fir, magnificent swathes of emerald green forests as far as the eye could see and a wide river of foaming, icy water. Hundreds of shaggy coated herbivores grazed on the plain and wide pinioned birds circled noisily overhead. Horus sat on the low slopes of the foothills at the base of the mountains, the sun warming his face and the grass wondrously soft beneath him.

'So that's it then,' he said calmly to himself. 'I'm dead.'

No one answered him, but then he hadn't expected them to. Was this what happened when a person died? He dimly remembered someone teaching him of the ancient unbelief of 'heaven' and 'hell', meaningless words that promised rewards for obedience and punishment for wickedness.

He took a deep breath, scenting the aroma of good earth: the fragrances of a world unchecked and untamed and of the living things that covered the landscape. He could taste the air and was amazed at its purity. Its crispness filled his lungs like sweet wine, but how had he come here and... where was here?

He had been... where? He couldn't remember. He knew his name was Horus, but beyond that, he knew only fragments and dim recollections that even now grew faint and insubstantial the more he tried to hold onto them.

Deciding that he should try to find out more about his surroundings, he rose to his feet, wincing as his shoulder pulled tight, and he saw a spot of blood soak through the white woollen robes he found himself wearing. Hadn't he been naked a second ago?

Horus put it from his mind and laughed. 'There might be no hell, but this feels like heaven right enough.'

His throat was dry and he set off towards the river, feeling the softness of the grass through newly sandalled feet. He was further away than he thought, the journey taking him longer than expected, but he didn't mind. The beauty of the landscape was worth savouring, and though something insistent nagged at the back of his mind, he ignored it and carried on.

The mountains seemed to reach the very stars, their peaks lost in the clouds and *belching noxious fumes into the air* as he gazed up at them. Horus blinked; the afterimage of dark, smoke wreathed peaks of iron and cement burned onto his retinas like a spliced frame of harsh interference dropped into a mood window. He dismissed it as the newness of his surroundings, and headed across the swaying plains of tall grass, feeling *the bones and waste of uncounted centuries of industry* crunching beneath his feet.

Horus felt ash in his throat, now needing a drink more than ever, the chemical stink growing worse with each step. He tasted benzene, chlorine, hydrochloric acid and vast amounts of carbon monoxide – lethal toxins to any but him it seemed – and briefly wondered how he knew these things. The river was just ahead and he splashed through the shallows, enjoying the biting cold as he reached down and scooped a handful of water into his cupped palms.

The icy water burned his skin, *molten slag dripping in caustic ropes between his fingers*, and he let it splash back into the river, wiping his hands on his robe, which was now soot stained and torn. He looked up and saw that the glittering quartz mountains had become *vast towers of brass and iron, wounding the sky with gateways like vast maws that could swallow and vomit forth entire armies. Streams of toxic filth poured from the towers and poisoned the river, the landscape around it withering and dying in an instant.*

Confused, Horus stumbled from the river, fighting to hold onto the verdant wilderness that had surrounded him and to hold back the vision of this bleak land of dark ruin and despair. He turned from the dark mountain: *the cliff of deepest red and blackened iron, its top hidden in the high clouds above and its base girded with boulders and skulls.*

He fell to his knees, expecting the softness of the grass, but landing heavily *on a fractured hardpan of ash and iron, swirling vortices of dust rising up in great storms.*

'What's happening here?' shouted Horus, rolling onto his back and screaming into a polluted sky striated with ugly bands of ochre and purple. He picked himself up and ran – ran as though his life depended on it. He ran across a landscape that flickered from one of aching beauty to that of a nightmare in the space of a heartbeat, his senses deceiving him from one second to another.

Horus ran into the forest. The black trunks of the trees snapped before his furious charge, images of lashing branches, *high towers of steel and glass, great ruins of mighty cathedrals and rotted palaces left to crumble under the weight of the ages dancing before his eyes.*

Bestial howls echoed across the landscape, and Horus paused in his mad scramble as the sound penetrated the fog in his head, the insistent nagging sensation in the back of his mind recognising it as significant.

The mournful howls echoed across the land, a chorus of voices reaching out to him, and Horus recognised them as wolf howls. He smiled at the sound, dropping to his knees and clutching his shoulder as fiery pain lanced through his arm and into his chest. With the pain came clarity and he held onto it, forcing the memories to come through force of will.

Howling wolf voices came again, and he cried out to the heavens.

'What's happening to me?'

The trees around him exploded with motion and a hundred-strong pack of wolves sprang from the undergrowth, surrounding him, with their teeth bared and eyes wide. Foam gathered around exposed fangs and each wolf bore a strange brand upon its fur, that of a black, double-headed eagle. Horus clutched his shoulder, his arm numb and dead as though it was no longer part of him.

'Who are you?' asked the closest wolf. Horus blinked rapidly as its image fizzled like static, and he saw curves of armour and a single, staring cyclopean eye.

'I am Horus,' he said.

'Who are you?' repeated the wolf.

'I am Horus!' he yelled. 'What more do you want from me?'

'I do not have much time, my brother,' said the wolf as the pack began circling him. 'You must remember before he comes for you. Who are you?'

'I am Horus and if I am dead then leave me be!' he screamed, surging to his feet and running onwards into the depths of the forest.

The wolves followed him, loping alongside him and matching his steady pace as he lurched randomly through the twilight. Again and again, the wolves howled the same question until Horus lost all sense of direction and time.

Horus ran blindly onwards until he finally emerged from the tree line above a wide, high-cliffed crater gouged in the landscape and filled with dark, still water.

The sky above was black and starless, a moon of purest white shining like a diamond in the firmament. He blinked and raised a hand to ward his eyes against its brightness, looking out over the black waters of the crater, certain that some unspeakable horror lurked in its icy depths.

Horus glanced behind him to see that the wolves had followed him from the trees, and he ran on as their howling followed him to the edge of the crater. Far below, the water lay still and flat like a black mirror, and the image of the moon filled his vision.

The wolves howled again, and Horus felt the yawning depths of the water calling out to him with an inevitable attraction. He saw the moon and heard the company of wolves give voice to one last howled question before he hurled himself into the void.

He fell through the air, his vision tumbling and his memory spinning.

The moon, the wolves, Lupercal.

Luna... Wolves...

Everything snapped into place and he cried out, 'I am Horus of the Luna Wolves, Warmaster and regent of the Emperor and I am alive!'

Horus struck the water and it exploded like shards of black glass.

FLICKERING LIGHT FILLED the chamber with a cold glow, the cracked stone walls limned with crawling webs of frost, and the breath of the cultists feathering in the air. Akshub had painted a circle with eight sharp points around its circumference, on the flagstones in quicklime. The mutilated corpse of one of the Davinite priestess's acolytes lay spread-eagled at its centre.

Erebus watched carefully as the priestess's lodge thralls spread around the circle, ensuring that every stage of the ritual was enacted with meticulous care. To fail now, after he had invested so much effort in bringing the Warmaster to this point, would be disastrous, although Erebus knew that his part in the Warmaster's downfall was but one of a million events set in motion thousands of years ago.

This fulcrum point in time was the culmination of billions of seemingly unrelated chains of circumstance that had led to this backwater world that no one had ever heard of.

Erebus knew that that was all about to change. Davin would soon become a place of legend.

The secret chamber in the heart of the Delphos was hidden from prying eyes by potent magic and sophisticated technology received from disaffected Mechanicum adepts, who welcomed the knowledge the Word Bearers could give them – knowledge that had been forbidden to them by the Emperor.

Akshub knelt and cut the heart from the dead acolyte, the lodge priestess expertly removing the still warm organ from its former owner's chest. She took a bite before handing it to Tsepha, her surviving acolyte.

They passed the heart around the circle, each of the cultists taking a bite of the rich red meat. Erebus took the ghastly remains of the heart as it was passed to him. He wolfed down the last of it, feeling the blood run down his chin and tasting the final memories of the betrayed acolyte as the treacherous blade had ended her life. That betrayal had been offered unto the Architect of Fate, this bloody feast to the Blood God, and the unlovely coupling of the doomed acolyte with a diseased swine had called upon the power of the Dark Prince and the Lord of Decay.

Blood pooled beneath the corpse, trickling into channels cut in the floor before draining into a sinkhole at the centre of the circle. Erebus knew that there was always blood, it was rich with life and surged with the power of the gods. What better way was there of tapping into that power than with the vital substance that carried their blessing?

'Is it done?' asked Erebus.

Akshub nodded, lifting the long knife that had cut the heart from the corpse. 'It is. The power of the Ones Who Dwell Beyond is with us, though we must be swift.'

'Why must we hurry, Akshub?' he asked, placing his hand upon his sword. 'This must be done right or all our lives are forfeit.'

'I know this,' said the priestess. 'There is another presence near, a one-eyed ghost who walks between worlds and seeks to return the son to his father.'

'Magnus, you old snake,' chuckled Erebus, looking up towards the chamber's roof. 'You won't stop us. You're too far away and Horus is too far gone. I have seen to that.'

'Who do you speak with?' asked Akshub.

'The one-eyed ghost. You said there was another presence near.'

'Near, yes,' said Akshub, 'but not here.'

Tired of the old priestess's cryptic answers, Erebus snapped, 'Then where is he?'

Akshub reached up and tapped her head with the flat of her blade. 'He speaks to the son, though he cannot yet reach him fully. I can feel the ghost crawling around the temple, trying to break the magic keeping his full power out.'

'What?' cried Erebus.

'He will not succeed,' said Akshub, walking towards him with the knife outstretched. 'We have spirit-walked in the realm beyond for thousands of years and his knowledge is a paltry thing next to ours.'

'For your sake, it had better be, Akshub.'

She smiled and held the knife out. 'Your threats mean nothing here, warrior. I could boil the blood in your veins with a word, or rip your body inside out with a thought. You need me to send your soul into the world beyond, but how will you return if I am dead? Your soul will remain adrift in the void forever, and you are not so full of anger that you do not fear such a fate.'

Erebus did not like the sudden authority in her voice, but he knew she was right and decided he would kill her once her purpose was served. He swallowed his anger and said, 'Then let us begin.'

'Very well,' nodded the priestess, as Tsepha came forward and anointed Erebus's face with crystalline antimony.

'Is this for the veil?'

'Yes,' said Akshub. 'It will confound his senses and he will not see your likeness. He will see a face familiar and beloved to him.'

Erebus smiled at the delicious irony of the thought, and closed his eyes as Tsepha daubed his eyelids and cheeks with the stinging, silver-white powder.

'The spell that will allow your passage to the void requires one last thing,' said Akshub.

'What last thing?' asked Erebus, suddenly suspicious.

'Your death,' said Akshub, slashing her knife across his throat.

HORUS OPENED HIS eyes, smiling as he saw blue sky above him. Pink and orange tinged clouds drifted slowly across his vision, peaceful and relaxing. He watched them for a few moments and then sat up, feeling wet dew beneath his palms as he pushed himself upright. He saw that he was fully armoured in his frost white plate, and as he surveyed his surroundings, he lifted his hand to his face, smelling the sweet scent on the grass and the crystal freshness of the air.

A vista of unsurpassed beauty lay before him, towering snow-capped mountains draped in a shawl of pine and fir, magnificent swathes of emerald green forests as far as the eye could see and a wide river of foaming, icy water. Hundreds of shaggy coated herbivores grazed on the plain and wide pinioned birds circled noisily overhead. Horus sat on the low slopes of the foothills at the base of the mountains, the sun warming his face and the grass wondrously soft beneath him.

'To hell with this,' he said as he got to his feet. 'I know I'm not dead, so what's going on?'

Once again, no one answered him, though this time he *had* expected an answer. The world still smelled sweet and fragrant, but with the memory of his identity came the knowledge of its falsehood. None of this was real, not the mountains or the river or the forests that covered the landscape, though there was something oddly familiar to it.

He remembered the dark, iron backdrop that lay behind this illusion and found that if he willed it, he could see the suggestion of that nightmarish vision behind the beauty of the world laid out before him.

Horus remembered thinking – a lifetime ago, it seemed – that perhaps this place might have been some netherworld between heaven and hell, but now laughed at the idea. He had long ago accepted the principle that the universe was simply matter, and that which was not matter was nothing. The universe was everything, and therefore nothing could exist beyond it.

Horus had the wit to see why some ancient theologian had claimed that the warp was, in fact, hell. He understood the reasoning, but he knew that the Empyrean was no metaphysical dimension; it was simply an echo of the material world, where random vortices of energy and strange breeds of malign xenos creatures made their homes.

As pleasing an axiom as that was, it still didn't answer the question of where he was.

How had he come to this place? His last memory was of speaking to Petronella Vivar in the apothecarion, telling her of his life, his hopes, his disappointments and his fears for the galaxy – conscious that he had told her those incendiary things as his valediction.

He couldn't change that, but he would damn well get to the bottom of what was happening to him now. Was it a fever dream brought on by whatever had wounded him? Had Temba's sword been poisoned? He dismissed that thought immediately; no poison could lay him low.

Surveying his surroundings, he could see no sign of the wolves that had chased him through the dark forests, but suddenly remembered a familiar form that had ghosted behind the face of the pack leader. For the briefest instant, it had looked like Magnus, but surely he was back on Prospero licking his wounds after the Council of Nikaeal?

Something had happened to Horus on Davin's moon, but he had no idea what. His shoulder ached and he rotated it within his armour to loosen the muscle, but the motion served only to further aggravate it. Horus set off in the direction of the river once more, still thirsty despite knowing that he walked in an illusory realm.

Cresting the rise that then began to slope gently down towards the river, Horus pulled up sharply as he saw something startling: an armoured Astartes warrior floating face down in the water. Wedged in the shallows of the riverbank, the body rose and fell with the swell of the water, and Horus swiftly made his way towards it.

He splashed into the river and gripped the edges of the figure's shoulder guards, turning the body over with a heavy splash.

Horus gasped, seeing that the man was alive, and that it was someone he knew.

A beautiful man was how Loken had described him, a beautiful man who had been adored by all who knew him. The noblest hero of the Great Crusade had been another of his epithets.

Hastur Sejanus.

LOKEN MARCHED AWAY from the temple, angry at what his brothers had done and furious with himself: he should have known that Erebus would have had plans beyond the simple murder of the Warmaster.

His veins surged with the need to do violence, but Erebus was not here, and no one could tell Loken where he was. Torgaddon and Vipus marched alongside him, and even through his anger, Loken could sense his friends' astonishment at what had happened before the great gate of the Delphos.

'Throne, what's happening here?' asked Vipus as they reached the top of the processional steps. 'Garvi, what's happening? Are the first captain and Little Horus our enemies now?'

Loken shook his head. 'No, Nero, they are our brothers, they are simply being used. As I think we all are.'

'By Erebus?' asked Torgaddon.

'Erebus?' said Vipus. 'What has he got to do with this?'

'Garviel thinks that Erebus is behind what's happening to the Warmaster,' said Torgaddon.

Loken shot him an exasperated stare.

'You're joking?'

'Not this time, Nero,' said Torgaddon.

'Tarik,' snapped Loken. 'Keep your voice down or everyone will hear.'

'So what if they do, Garvi?' hissed Torgaddon. 'If Erebus is behind this, then everyone should know about it: we should expose him.'

'And we will,' promised Loken, watching as the pinpricks of vehicle headlights appeared at the mouth of the valley they had only recently flown up.

'So what do we do?' asked Vipus.

That was the question, realised Loken. They needed more information before they could act, and they needed it now. He fought for calm so that he could think more clearly.

Loken wanted answers, but he had to know what questions to ask first, and there was one man who had always been able to cut through his confusion and steer him in the right direction.

Loken set off down the steps, heading back towards the Thunderhawk. Torgaddon, Vipus and the warriors of Locasta followed him. As he reached the bottom of the steps, he turned to them and said, 'I need you two to stay here. Keep an eye on the temple and make sure that nothing bad happens.'

'Define "bad",' said Vipus.

'I'm not sure,' said Loken. 'Just… bad, you know? And contact me if you get so much as a glimpse of Erebus.'

'Where are you going?' asked Torgaddon.

'I'm going back to the *Vengeful Spirit*.'

'What for?'

'To get some answers,' said Loken.

'HASTUR!' CRIED HORUS, reaching down to lift his fallen friend from the water. Sejanus was limp in his arms, though Horus could tell he lived by the pulse in his throat and the colour in his cheeks. Horus dragged Sejanus from the water, wondering if his presence might be another of the strange realm's illusions or if his old friend might in fact be a threat to him.

Sejanus's chest hiked convulsively as he brought up a lungful of water, and Horus rolled him onto his side, knowing that the genhanced physique of an Astartes warrior made it almost impossible for him to drown.

'Hastur, is it really you?' asked Horus, knowing that in this place, such a question was probably meaningless, but overcome with joy to see his beloved Sejanus again. He remembered the pain he had felt when his most favoured son had been hacked down upon the onyx floor of the false Emperor's palace on Sixty-Three Nineteen, and the Cthonic bellicosity that had demanded blood vengeance.

Sejanus heaved a last flood of water and propped himself up on his elbow, sucking great lungfuls of the clean air. His hand clutched at his throat as though searching for something, and he looked relieved to find that it wasn't there.

'My son,' said Horus as Sejanus turned towards him. He was exactly as Horus remembered him, perfect in every detail: the noble face, wide set eyes and firm, straight nose that could be a mirror for the Warmaster himself.

Any thoughts that Sejanus might be a threat to him were swept away as he saw the silver shine of his eyes and knew that this surely was Hastur Sejanus. How such a thing was possible was beyond him, but he did not question this miracle for fear that it might be snatched away from him.

'Commander,' said Sejanus, rising to embrace Horus.

'Damn me, boy, it's good to see you,' said Horus. 'Part of me died when I lost you.'

'I know, sir,' replied Sejanus as they released each other from the crushing embrace. 'I felt your sorrow.'

'You're a sight for sore eyes, my boy,' said Horus, taking a step back to admire his most perfect warrior. 'It gladdens my heart to see you, but how can this be? I watched you die.'

'Yes,' agreed Sejanus. 'You did, but, in truth, my death was a blessing.'

'A blessing? How?'

'It opened my eyes to the truth of the universe and freed me from the shackles of living knowledge. Death is no longer an undiscovered country, my lord, it is one from which this traveller has returned.'

'How is such a thing possible?'

'They sent me back to you,' said Sejanus. 'My spirit was lost in the void, alone and dying, but I have come back to help you.'

Conflicting emotions surged through Horus at the sight of Sejanus. To hear him speak of spirits and voids struck a note of warning, but to see him alive once more, even if it wasn't real, was something to be cherished.

'You say you're here to help me? Then help me to understand this place. Where are we?'

'We don't have much time,' said Sejanus, climbing the slope to the rise that overlooked the plains and forests, and taking a long look around. 'He'll be here soon.'

'That's not the first time I've heard that recently,' said Horus.

'From where else have you heard it?' demanded Sejanus, turning back to face him with a serious expression. Horus was surprised at the vehemence of the question.

'A wolf said it to me,' said Horus. 'I know, I know, it sounds ridiculous, but I swear it really did speak to me.'

'I believe you, sir,' said Sejanus. 'That's why we need to move on.'

Horus sensed evasion, a trait he had never known in Sejanus before now and said, 'You're avoiding my question, Hastur, now tell me where we are.'

'We don't have time, my lord,' urged Sejanus.

'Sejanus,' said Horus, his voice that of the Warmaster. 'Tell me what I want to know.'

'Very well,' said Sejanus, 'but quickly, for your body lies on the brink of death within the walls of the Delphos on Davin.'

'The Delphos? I've never heard of it, and this doesn't look like Davin.'

'The Delphos is a place sacred to the Lodge of the Serpent,' said Sejanus. 'A place of healing. In the ancient tongues of Earth its name means "the womb of the world", where a man may be healed and renewed. Your body lies in the Axis Mundi chamber, but your spirit is no longer tied to your flesh.'

'So we're not really here?' asked Horus. 'This world isn't real?'

'No.'

'Then this is the warp,' said Horus, finally accepting what he had begun to suspect.

'Yes. None of this is real,' said Sejanus, waving his hand around the landscape. 'All this is but fragments of your will and memory that have given shape to the formless energy of the warp.'

Horus suddenly knew where he had seen this land before, remembering the wondrous geophysical relief map of Terra they had found ten kilometres beneath a dead world almost a decade ago. It hadn't been the Terra of their time, but one of an age long past, with green fields, clear seas and clean air.

He looked up into the sky, half expecting to see curious faces looking down on him from above like students studying an ant colony, but the sky was empty, though it was darkening at an unnatural rate. The world around him was changing before his eyes from the Earth that had once existed to the barren wasteland of Terra.

Sejanus followed his gaze and said, 'It's beginning.'

'What is?' asked Horus.

'Your mind and body are dying and this world is beginning to collapse into Chaos. That's why they sent me back, to guide you to the truth that will allow you to return to your body.'

Even as Sejanus spoke, the sky began to waver and he could see hints of the roiling sea of the Immaterium seething behind the clouds.

'You keep saying "they",' said Horus. 'Who are "they" and why are they interested in me?'

'Great intelligences dwell in the warp,' explained Sejanus, casting wary glances at the dissolution of the sky. 'They do not communicate as we do and this is the only way they could reach you.'

'I don't like the sound of this, Hastur,' warned Horus.

'There is no malice in this place. There is power and potential, yes, but no malice, simply the desire to exist. Events in our galaxy are destroying this realm and these powers have chosen you to be their emissary in their dealings with the material world.'

'And what if I don't want to be their emissary?'

'Then you will die,' said Sejanus. 'Only they are powerful enough to save your life now.'

'If they're so powerful, what do they need me for?'

'They are powerful, but they cannot exist in the material universe and must work through emissaries,' replied Sejanus. 'You are a man of strength and ambition and they know there is no other being in the galaxy powerful enough or worthy enough to do what must be done.'

Despite his satisfaction at being so described, Horus did not like what he was hearing. He sensed no deceit in Sejanus, though a warning voice in his head reminded him that the silver-eyed warrior standing before him could not truly be Sejanus.

'They have no interest in the material universe, it is anathema to them, they simply wish to preserve their own realm from destruction,' continued Sejanus as the chemical reek of the world beyond the illusion returned, and a stinking wind arose. 'In return for your aid, they can give you a measure of their power and the means to realise your every ambition.'

Horus saw the lurking world of brazen iron become more substantial as the warp and weft of reality began to buckle beneath his feet. Cracks of dark light shimmered through the splitting earth and Horus could hear the sound of howling wolves drawing near.

'We have to move!' shouted Sejanus as the wolf pack loped from a disintegrating copse of trees. To Horus, it sounded as though their howls desperately called his name.

Sejanus ran back to the river and a shimmering flat oblong of light rose from the boiling water. Horus heard whispers and strange mutterings issuing from beyond it, and a sense of dark premonition seized him as he switched his gaze between this strange light and the wolves.

'I'm not sure about this,' said Horus as the sky shed fat droplets of acid rain.

'Come on, the gateway is our only way out!' cried Sejanus, heading towards the light. 'As a great man once said, "Towering genius disdains the beaten path; it seeks regions hitherto unexplored"'.

'You're quoting me back to myself?' said Horus as the wind blew in howling gusts.

'Why not? Your words will be quoted for centuries to come.'

Horus smiled, liking the idea of being quotable, and set off after Sejanus.

'Where does this gate lead?' shouted Horus over the wind and the howling of wolves.

'To the truth,' replied Sejanus.

THE CRATER BEGAN to fill as the sun finally set, hundreds of vehicles of all descriptions finally completing their journey from the Imperial deployment zone to this place of pilgrimage. The Davinites watched the arrival of these convoys with a mixture of surprise and confusion, incredulous as each vehicle was abandoned, and its passengers made their way towards the Delphos.

Within the hour, thousands of people had gathered, and more were arriving every minute. Most of these new arrivals milled about in an undirected mass until the Davinites began circulating amongst them, helping to find somewhere that belongings could be set down and arranging shelter as a hard rain began to fall.

Headlights stretched all the way along the forgotten causeway and through the valley to the plains below. As night closed in on Davin, songs in praise of the Warmaster filled the air, and the flickering glow of thousands of candles joined the light of the torches ringing the gold-skinned Delphos.

FOURTEEN

The forgotten/Living mythology/Primogenesis

PASSING THROUGH THE gate of light was akin to stepping from one room to another. Where once had been a world on the verge of dissolution, now Horus found himself standing amid a heaving mass of people, in a huge circular plaza surrounded by soaring towers and magnificently appointed buildings of marble. Thousands of people filled the square, and since he was half again as tall as the tallest, Horus could see that thousands more waited to enter from nine arterial boulevards.

Strangely, none of these people remarked on the sudden arrival of two giant warriors in their midst. A cluster of statues stood at the centre of the plaza, and droning chants drifted from corroded speakers set on the buildings, as the mass of humanity marched in mindless procession around them. A pealing clangour of bells tolled from each building.

'Where are we?' asked Horus, looking up at the great eagle-fronted buildings, their golden spires and their

colossal stained glass rosary windows. Each structure
vied with its neighbour for supremacy of height and
ostentation, and Horus's eye for architectural proportion
and elegance saw them as vulgar expressions of devotion.

'I do not know the name of this palace,' said Sejanus.
'I know only what I have seen here, but I believe it to be
some kind of shrine world.'

'A shrine world? A shrine to what?'

'Not what,' said Sejanus, pointing to the statues in the
centre of the plaza. 'Who.'

Horus looked more closely at the enormous statues,
encircled by the thronged masses. The outer ring of statues was carved from white marble, and each gleaming
warrior was clad in full Astartes battle plate. They surrounded the central figure, which was likewise armoured
in a magnificent suit of gold armour that gleamed and
sparkled with precious gems. This figure carried a flaming torch high, the light of it illuminating everything
around him. The symbolism was clear – this central figure was bringing his light to the people, and his warriors
were there to protect him.

The gold warrior was clearly a king or hero of some
kind, his features regal and patrician, though the sculp-
tor had exaggerated them to ludicrous proportions. The
proportions of the statues surrounding the central figure
were similarly grotesque.

'Who is the gold statue meant to be?' asked Horus.

'You don't recognise him?' asked Sejanus.

'No. Should I?'

'Let's take a closer look.'

Horus followed as Sejanus set off into the crowd, making his way towards the centre of the plaza, and the
crowds parted before them without so much as a raised
eyebrow.

'Can't these people see us?' he asked.

'No,' said Sejanus. 'Or if they can, they will forget us in an instant. We move amongst them as ghosts and none here will remember us.'

Horus stopped in front of a man dressed in a thread-bare scapular, who shuffled around the statues on bloodied feet. His hair was tonsured and he clutched a handful of carved bones tied together with twine. A bloody bandage covered one eye and a long strip of parchment pinned to his scapular dangled to the ground.

With barely a pause, the man stepped around him, but Horus put out his arm and prevented his progress. Again, the man attempted to pass Horus, but again he was pre-vented.

'Please, sir,' said the man without looking up. 'I must get by.'

'Why?' asked Horus. 'What are you doing?'

The man looked puzzled, as though struggling to recall what he had been asked.

'I must get by,' he said again.

Exasperated by the man's unhelpful answers, Horus stepped aside to let him pass. The man bowed his head and said, 'The Emperor watch over you, sir.'

Horus felt a clammy sensation crawl along his spine at the words. He pushed through the unresisting crowds towards the centre of the plaza as a terrible suspicion began forming in his gut. He caught up to Sejanus, who stood atop a stepped plinth at the foot of the statues, where a huge pair of bronze eagles formed the backdrop to a tall lectern.

A hugely fat official in a gold chasuble and tall mitre of silk and gold read aloud from a thick, leather-bound book, his words carried over the crowd via silver trumpets held aloft by what looked like winged infants that floated above him.

As Horus approached, he saw that the official was human only from the waist up, a complex series of hissing pistons and brass rods making up his lower half and fusing him with the lectern, which he now saw was mounted on a wheeled base.

Horus ignored him, looking up at the statues, finally seeing them for what they were.

Though their faces were unrecognisable to one who knew them as Horus did, their identities were unmistakable.

The nearest was Sanguinius, his outstretched wings like the pinions of the eagles that adorned every structure surrounding the plaza. To one side of the Lord of the Angels was Rogal Dorn, the unfurled wings haloing his head, unmistakable; on the other, was someone who could only be Leman Russ, his hair carved to resemble a wild mane, and wearing a cloak of wolf pelts draped around his massive shoulders.

Horus circled the statues, seeing other familiar images: Guilliman, Corax, the Lion, Ferrus Mannus, Vulkan and finally Jaghatai Khan.

There could be no doubting the identity of the central figure now, and Horus looked up into the carved face of the Emperor. No doubt the inhabitants of this world thought it magnificent, but Horus knew this was a poor thing, failing spectacularly to capture the sheer dynamism and force of the Emperor's personality.

With the additional height offered by the statues' plinth, Horus looked out over the slowly circling mass of people and wondered what they thought they did in this place.

Pilgrims, thought Horus, the word leaping, unbidden, to his mind.

Coupled with the ostentation and vulgar adornments he saw on the surrounding buildings, Horus knew that this was not simply a place of devotion, but something much more.

'This is a place of worship,' he said as Sejanus joined him at the foot of Corax's statue, the cool marble perfectly capturing the pallid complexion of his taciturn brother.

Sejanus nodded and said, 'It is an entire world given over to the praise of the Emperor.'

'But why? The Emperor is no god. He spent centuries freeing humanity from the shackles of religion. This makes no sense.'

'Not from where you stand in time, but this is the Imperium that will come to pass if events continue on their present course,' said Sejanus. 'The Emperor has the gift of foresight and he has seen this future time.'

'For what purpose?'

'To destroy the old faiths so that one day his cult would more easily supplant them all.'

'No,' said Horus, 'I won't believe that. My father always refuted any notion of divinity. He once said of ancient Earth that there were torches, who were the teachers, but also extinguishers, who were the priests. He would never have condoned this.'

'Yet this entire world is his temple,' Sejanus said, 'and it is not the only one.'

'There are more worlds like this?'

'Hundreds,' nodded Sejanus, 'probably even thousands.'

'But the Emperor shamed Lorgar for behaviour such as this,' protested Horus. 'The Word Bearers Legion raised great monuments to the Emperor and persecuted entire populations for their lack of faith, but the Emperor would not stand for it and said that Lorgar shamed him with such displays.'

'He wasn't ready for worship then: he didn't have control of the galaxy. That's why he needed you.'

Horus turned away from Sejanus and looked up into the golden face of his father, desperate to refute the words he was hearing. At any other time, he would have struck Sejanus down for such a suggestion, but the evidence was here before him.

He turned to face Sejanus. 'These are some of my brothers, but where are the others? Where am I?'

'I do not know,' replied Sejanus. 'I have walked this place many times, but have never yet seen your likeness.'

'I am his chosen regent!' cried Horus. 'I fought on a thousand battlefields for him. The blood of my warriors is on his hands, and he ignores me like I don't exist?'

'The Emperor has forsaken you, Warmaster,' urged Sejanus. 'Soon he will turn his back on his people to win his place amongst the gods. He cares only for himself and his power and glory. We were all deceived. We have no place in his grand scheme, and when the time comes, he will spurn us all and ascend to godhood. While we were fighting war after war in his name, he was secretly building his power in the warp.'

The droning chant of the official – a priest, realised Horus – continued as the pilgrims maintained the slow procession around their god, and Sejanus's words hammered against his skull.

'This can't be true,' whispered Horus.

'What does a being of the Emperor's magnitude do after he has conquered the galaxy? What is left for him but godhood? What use has he for those whom he leaves behind?'

'No!' shouted Horus, stepping from the plinth and smashing the droning priest to the ground. The augmented preacher hybrid was torn from the pulpit and lay screaming in a pool of blood and oil. His cries were carried across the plaza by the trumpets of the floating infants, though none of the crowd seemed inclined to help him.

Horus set off into the crowded plaza in a blind fury, leaving Sejanus behind on the plinth of statues. Once again, the crowd parted before his headlong dash, as unresponsive to his leaving as they had been to his arrival. Within moments he reached the edge of the plaza and made his way down the nearest of the arterial boulevards. People filled the street, but they ignored him as he pushed his way through them, each face turned in rapture to an image of the Emperor.

Without Sejanus beside him, Horus realised that he was completely alone. He heard the howl of a distant wolf, its cry once again sounding as though it called out to him. He stopped in the centre of a crowded street, listening for the wolf howl again, but it was silenced as suddenly as it had come.

The crowds flowed around him as he listened, and Horus saw that once again, no one paid him the slightest bit of attention. Not since Horus had parted from his father and brothers had he felt so isolated. Suddenly he felt the pain of being confronted with the scale of his own vanity and pride as he realised how much he thrived on the adoration of those around him.

On every face, he saw the same blind devotion as he had witnessed in those that circled the statues, a beloved reverence for a man he called father. Didn't these people realise the victories that had won their freedom had been won with Horus's blood?

It should be Horus's statue surrounded by his brother primarchs, not the Emperor's!

Horus seized the nearest devotee and shook him violently by the shoulders, shouting, 'He is not a god! He is not a god!'

The pilgrim's neck snapped with an audible crack and Horus felt the bones of the man's shoulders splinter beneath his iron grip. Horrified, he dropped the dead man and ran deeper into the labyrinth of the shrine world, taking turns at random, as he sought to lose himself in its crowded streets.

Each fevered change of direction took him along thronged avenues of worshippers and marvels dedicated to the glory of the God-Emperor: thoroughfares where every cobblestone was inscribed with prayer, kilometre high ossuaries of gold plated bones, and forests of marble columns, with unnumbered saints depicted upon them.

Random demagogues roamed the streets, one fanatically mortifying his flesh with prayer whips while another held up two squares of orange cloth by the corners and screamed that he would not wear them. Horus could make no sense of any of it.

Vast prayer ships drifted over this part of the shrine city, monstrously bloated zeppelins with sweeping brass sails and enormous prop-driven motors. Long prayer banners hung from their fat silver hulls, and hymns blared from hanging loudspeakers shaped like ebony skulls.

Horus passed a great mausoleum where flocks of ivory-skinned angels with brass-feathered wings flew from dark archways and descended into the crowds gathered in front of the building. The solemn angels swooped over the wailing masses, occasionally gathering to pluck some ecstatic soul from the pilgrims, and cries of adoration and praise followed each supplicant as he was carried through the dread portals of the mausoleum.

Horus saw death venerated in the coloured glass of every window, celebrated in the carvings on every door, and revered in the funereal dirges that echoed from the trumpets of winged children who giggled as they circled like birds of prey. Flapping banners of bone clattered, and the wind whistled through the eye sockets of skulls set into shrine caskets on bronze poles. Morbidity hung like a shroud upon this world, and Horus could not reconcile the dark, gothic solemnity of this new religion with the dynamic force of truth, reason and confidence that had driven the Great Crusade into the stars.

High temples and grim shrines passed him in a blur: cenobites and preachers haranguing the pilgrims from every street corner to the peal of doomsayers' bells. Everywhere Horus looked, he saw walls adorned with frescoes, paintings and bas relief works of familiar faces – his brothers and the Emperor himself.

Why was there no representation of Horus?

It was as if he had never existed. He sank to his knees, raising his fists to the sky.

'Father, why have you forsaken me?'

THE VENGEFUL SPIRIT felt empty to Loken, and he knew it was more than simply the absence of people. The solid, reassuring presence of the Warmaster, so long taken for granted, was achingly absent without him on board. The halls of the ship were emptier, more hollow, as though it were a weapon stripped of its ammunition – once powerful, but now simply inert metal.

Though portions of the ship were still filled with people, huddled in small groups and holding hands around groups of candles, there was an emptiness to the place that left Loken feeling similarly hollowed out.

Each group he passed swarmed around him, the normal respect for an Astartes warrior forgotten in their desperation to know the fate of the Warmaster. Was he dead? Was he alive? Had the Emperor reached out from Terra to save his beloved son?

Loken angrily brushed each group off, pushing through them without answering their questions as he made his way to Archive Chamber Three. He knew Sindermann would be there – he was always there these days – researching and poring over his books like a man possessed. Loken needed answers about the serpent lodge, and he needed them now.

Time was of the essence and he'd already made one stop at the medical deck in order to hand over the anathame to Apothecary Vaddon.

'Be very careful, apothecary,' warned Loken, reverently placing the wooden casket on the steel operating slab between them. 'This is a kinebrach weapon called an anathame. It was forged from a sentient xeno metal and is utterly lethal. I believe it to be the source of the Warmaster's malady. Do what you need to do to find out what happened, but do it quickly.'

Vaddon had nodded, dumbfounded that Loken had returned with something he could actually use. He lifted the anathame by its golden studded pommel and placed it within a spectrographic chamber.

'I can't promise anything, Captain Loken,' said Vaddon, 'but I will do whatever is in my power to find you an answer.'

'That's all I ask, but the sooner the better; and tell no one that you have this weapon.'

Vaddon nodded and turned to his work, leaving Loken to find Kyril Sindermann in the archives of the mighty ship. The helplessness that had seized him earlier vanished now that he had a purpose. He was actively trying to save the Warmaster, and that knowledge gave him fresh hope that there might yet be a way to bring him back unharmed in body and spirit.

As always, the archives were quiet, but now there was a deeper sense of desolation. Loken strained to hear anything at all, finally catching the scratching of a quill-pen from deeper in the stacks of books. Swiftly he made his way towards the sound, knowing before he reached the source that it was his old mentor. Only Kyril Sindermann scratched at the page with such intense pen strokes.

Sure enough, Loken found Sindermann sitting at his usual table and upon seeing him, Loken knew with absolute certainty that he had not left this place since last they had spoken. Bottles of water and discarded food packs lay scattered around the table, and the haggard Sindermann now sported a growth of fine white hair on his cheeks and chin.

'Garviel,' said Sindermann without looking up. 'You came back. Is the Warmaster dead?'

'No,' replied Loken. 'At least I don't think so. Not yet anyway.'

Sindermann looked up from his books, the haphazard piles of which were now threatening to topple onto the floor.

'You don't think so?'

'I haven't seen him since I saw him on the apothecaries' slab,' confessed Loken.

'Then why are you here? It surely can't be for a lesson on the principles and ethics of civilisation. What's happening?'

'I don't know,' admitted Loken. 'Something bad I think. I need your knowledge of... things esoteric, Kyril.'

'Things esoteric?' repeated Sindermann, putting down his quill. 'Now I am intrigued.'

'The Legion's quiet order has taken the Warmaster to the Temple of the Serpent Lodge on Davin. They've placed him in a temple they call the Delphos and say that the "eternal spirits of dead things" will heal him.'

'Serpent Lodge you say?' asked Sindermann, plucking books seemingly at random from the cluttered piles on his desk. 'Serpents... now that is interesting.'

'What is?'

'Serpents,' repeated Sindermann. 'Since the very beginnings of time, on every continent where humanity worshipped divinity, the serpent has been recognised and accepted as a god. From the steaming jungles of the Afrique islands to the icy wastes of Alba, serpents have been worshipped, feared and adored in equal measure. I believe that serpent mythology is probably the most widespread mythology known to mankind.'

'Then how did it get to Davin?' asked Loken.

'It's not difficult to understand,' explained Sindermann. 'You see, myths weren't originally expressed in verbal or written form because language was deemed inadequate to convey the truth expressed in the stories. Myths move not with words, Garviel, but with storytellers and wherever you find people, no matter how primitive or how far they've been separated from the cradle of humanity, you'll always find storytellers. Most of these myths were probably enacted, chanted, danced or sung, more often than not in hypnotic or hallucinatory states. It must have been quite a sight, but anyway, this method of retelling was said to allow the creative energies and relationships behind and beneath the natural world to be brought into the conscious realm. Ancient peoples believed that myths created a bridge from the metaphysical world to the physical one.'

Sindermann flicked through the pages of what looked like a new book encased in fresh red leather and turned the book so Loken could see.

'Here, you see it here quite clearly.'

Loken looked at the pictures, seeing images of naked tribesmen dancing with long snake-topped poles as well as snakes and spirals painted onto primitive pottery. Other pictures showed vases with gigantic snakes winding over suns, moons and stars, while still more showed snakes appearing below growing plants or coiled above the bellies of pregnant women.

'What am I looking at?' he asked.

'Artefacts recovered from a dozen different worlds during the Great Crusade,' said Sindermann, jabbing his finger at the pictures. 'Don't you see? We carry our myths with us, Garviel, we don't reinvent them.'

Sindermann turned the page to show yet more images of snakes and said, 'Here the snake is the symbol of energy, spontaneous, creative energy… and of immortality.'

'Immortality?'

'Yes, in ancient times, men believed that the serpent's ability to shed its skin and thus renew its youth made it privy to the secrets of death and rebirth. They saw the moon, waxing and waning, as the celestial body capable of this same ability, and of course, the lunar cycle has long associations with the life-creating rhythm of the female. The moon became the lord of the twin mysteries of birth and death, and the serpent was its earthly counterpart.'

'The moon…' said Loken.

'Yes,' continued Sindermann, now well into his flow. 'In early rites of initiation where the aspirant was seen to die and be reborn, the moon was the goddess mother and the serpent the divine father. It's not hard to see why the connection between the serpent and healing becomes a permanent facet of serpent worship.'

'Is that what this is,' breathed Loken. 'A rite of initiation?'

Sindermann shrugged. 'I couldn't say, Garviel. I'd need to see more of it.'

'Tell me,' snarled Loken. 'I need to hear all you know.'

Startled by the power of Loken's urging, Sindermann reached for several more books, leafing through them as the 10th Company captain loomed over him.

'Yes, yes…' he muttered, flipping back and forth through the well-thumbed pages. 'Yes, here it is. Ah… yes, a word for serpent in one of the lost languages of old Earth was "nahash", which apparently means, "to guess". It appears that it was then translated to mean a number of different things, depending on which etymological root you believe.'

'Translated to mean what?' asked Loken.

'Its first rendition is as either "enemy" or "adversary", but it seems to be more popularly transliterated as "Seytan".'

'Seytan,' said Loken. 'I've heard that name before.'

'We… ah, spoke of it at the Whisperheads,' said Sindermann in a low voice, looking about him as though someone might be listening. 'It was said to be a nightmarish force of deviltry cast down by a golden hero on Terra. As we now know, the Samus spirit was probably the local equivalent for the inhabitants of Sixty-Three Nineteen.'

'Do you believe that?' asked Loken. 'That Samus was a spirit?'

'Of some form, yes,' said Sindermann honestly. 'I believe that what I saw beneath the mountains was more than simply a xenos of some kind, no matter what the Warmaster says.'

'And what about this serpent as Seytan?'

Sindermann, pleased to have a subject upon which he could illuminate, shook his head and said, 'No. If you look closer, you see the word "serpent" has its origination in the Olympian root languages as "drakon", the cosmic serpent that was seen as a symbol of Chaos.'

'Chaos?' cried Loken. 'No!'

'Yes,' went on Sindermann, hesitantly pointing out a passage of text in yet another of his books. 'It is this "chaos", or "serpent", which must be overcome to create order and maintain life in any meaningful way. This serpentine dragon was a creature of great power and its sacred years were times of great ambition and incredible risk. It's said that events occurring in a year of the dragon are magnified threefold in intensity.'

Loken tried to hide his horror at Sindermann's words, the ritual significance of the serpent and its place in mythology cementing his conviction that what was happening on Davin was horribly wrong. He looked down at the book before him and said, 'What's this?'

'A passage from the *Book of Atum*,' said Sindermann, as though afraid to tell him. 'I only found it quite recently, I swear. I didn't think anything of it, I still don't really... After all, it's just nonsense isn't it?'

Loken forced himself to look at the book, feeling his heart grow heavy with each word he read from its yellowed pages.

I am Horus, forged of the Oldest Gods,
I am he who gave way to Khaos
I am that great destroyer of all.
I am he who did what seemed good to him,
And set doom in the palace of my will.
Mine is the fate of those who move along
This serpentine path.

'I'm no student of poetry,' snapped Loken. 'What does it mean?'

'It's a prophecy,' said Sindermann hesitantly. 'It speaks of a time when the world returns to its original chaos and the hidden aspects of the supreme gods become the new serpent.'

'I don't have time for metaphors, Kyril,' warned Loken.

'At its most basic level,' said Sindermann, 'it speaks about the death of the universe.'

SEJANUS FOUND HIM on the steps of a vaulted basilica, its wide doorway flanked by tall skeletons wrapped in funeral robes and holding flaming censers out before them. Though darkness had fallen, the streets of the city still thronged with worshippers, each carrying a lit taper or lantern to light the way.

Horus looked up as Sejanus approached, thinking that the processions of light through the city would have seemed beautiful at any other time. The pageantry and pomp of the palanquins and altars being carried along the streets would previously have irritated him, were the procession in his honour, but now he craved them.

'Have you seen all you need to see?' asked Sejanus, sitting beside him on the steps.

'Yes,' replied Horus. 'I wish to leave this place.'

'We can leave whenever you want, just say the word,' said Sejanus. 'There is more you need to see anyway, and our time is not infinite. Your body is dying and you must make your choice before you are beyond the help of even the powers that dwell in the warp.'

'This choice.' asked Horus, 'Does it involve what I think it does?'

'Only you can decide that,' said Sejanus as the doors to the basilica opened behind them.

Horus looked over his shoulder, seeing a familiar oblong of light where he would have expected to see a darkened vestibule.

'Very well,' he said, standing and turning towards the light. 'So where are we going now?'

'To the beginning,' answered Sejanus.

STEPPING THROUGH THE light, Horus found himself standing in what appeared to be a colossal laboratory, its cavernous walls formed of white steel and silver panels. The air tasted sterile, and Horus could tell that the temperature of the air was close to freezing. Hundreds of figures encased in fully enclosed white oversuits with reflective gold visors filled the laboratory, working at row upon row of humming gold machines that sat atop long, steel benches.

Hissing puffs of vapour feathered the air above each worker's head, and long tubes coiled around the legs and arms of the white suits before hooking into cumbersome looking backpacks. Though no words were spoken, a sense of the implementation of grand designs was palpable. Horus wandered through the facility, its inhabitants ignoring him as completely as those of the shrine world had. Instinctively, he knew that he and Sejanus were far beneath the surface of whatever world they had travelled to.

'Where are we now?' he asked. 'When are we?'

'Terra,' said Sejanus, 'at the dawn of a new age.'

'What does that mean?'

In answer to his question, Sejanus pointed to the far wall of the laboratory where a shimmering energy field protected a huge silver steel door. The sign of the aquila was etched into the metal, along with strange, mystical looking symbols that were out of place in a laboratory dedicated to the pursuit of science. Just looking at the door made Horus uneasy, as though whatever lay beyond was somehow a threat to him.

'What lies beyond that door?' asked Horus, backing away from the silver portal.

'Truths you will not want to see,' replied Sejanus, 'and answers you will not want to hear.'

Horus felt a strange, previously unknown sensation stir in his belly and fought to quell it as he realised that, despite all the cunning wrought into his creation, the sensation was fear. Nothing good could live behind that door. Its secrets were best forgotten, and whatever knowledge lay beyond should be left hidden.

'I don't want to know,' said Horus, turning from the door. 'It's too much.'

'You fear to seek answers?' asked Sejanus angrily. 'This is not the Horus I followed into battle for two centuries. The Horus I knew would not shirk from uncomfortable truths.'

'Maybe not, but I still don't want to see it,' said Horus.

'I'm afraid you don't have a choice, my friend,' said Sejanus. Horus looked up to see that he now stood in front of the door, wisps of freezing air gusting from its base as it slowly raised and the energy field dissipated. Flashing yellow lights swirled to either side of the door, but no one in the laboratory paid any attention as the door slid up into the panelled wall.

Dark knowledge lay beyond, of that Horus was certain, just as certainly as he knew that he could not ignore the temptation of discovering the secrets it kept hidden. He had to know what it concealed. Sejanus was right; it wasn't in his nature to back away from anything, no matter what it was. He had faced all the terrors the galaxy had to show him and had not flinched. This would be no different.

'Very well,' he said. 'Show me.'

Sejanus smiled and slapped his palm against Horus's shoulder guard, saying, 'I knew we could count on you, my friend. This will not be easy for you, but know that we would not show you this unless it was necessary.'

'Do what you must,' said Horus, shaking off the hand. For the briefest instant, Sejanus's reflection blurred like a shimmering mask in the gleaming metal of the door, and Horus fancied he saw a reptilian grin on his friend's face. 'Let's just get it done.'

They walked through the icy mist together, passing along a wide, steel-walled corridor that led to an identical door, which also slid into the ceiling as they approached.

The chamber beyond was perhaps half the size of the laboratory. Its walls were pristine and sterile, and it was empty of technicians and scientists. The floor was smooth concrete and the temperature cool rather than cold.

A raised central walkway ran the length of the chamber with ten large cylindrical tanks the size of boarding torpedoes lying flat to either side of it, long serial numbers stencilled on their flanks. Steam gusted from the top of each tank like breath. Beneath the serial numbers were the same mystical symbols he had seen on the door leading to this place.

Each tank was connected to a collection of strange machines, whose purpose Horus could not even begin to guess at. Their technologies were unlike anything he had ever seen, their construction beyond even his incredible intellect.

He climbed the metal stairs that led to the walkway, hearing strange sounds like fists on metal as he reached the top. Now atop the walkway, he could see that each tank had a wide hatchway at its end, with a wheel handle in its centre and a thick sheet of armoured glass above it.

Brilliant light flickered behind each block of glass and the very air thrummed with potential. Something about all this seemed dreadfully familiar to Horus and he felt an irresistible urge to know what lay within the tanks while simultaneously dreading what he might see.

'What are these?' he asked as he heard Sejanus climbing up behind him.

'I'm not surprised you don't remember. It's been over two hundred years.'

Horus leaned forward and wiped his gauntlet across the fogged glass of the first tank's hatch. He squinted against the brightness, straining to see what lay within. The light was blinding, a motion blurred shape within twisting like dark smoke in the wind.

Something saw him. Something moved closer.

'What do you mean?' asked Horus, fascinated by the strange, formless being that swam through the light of the tank. Its motion slowed, and it became a silhouette as it moved closer to the glass, its form settling into something more solid.

The tank hummed with power, as though the metal were barely able to contain the energy generated by the creature contained within it.

'These are the Emperor's most secret geno-vaults beneath the Himalayan peaks,' said Sejanus. 'This is where you were created.'

Horus wasn't listening. He was staring through the glass in amazement at a pair of liquid eyes that were the mirror of his own.

FIFTEEN

Revelations/Dissent/Scattering

In the two days since the Warmaster's departure, the *Vengeful Spirit* had become a ghost ship, the mighty vessel having haemorrhaged landers, carriers, skiffs and any other craft capable of making it to the surface to follow Horus to Davin.

This suited Ignace Karkasy fine as he marched with newfound purpose and practiced insouciance through the decks of the ship, a canvas satchel slung over one shoulder. Each time he passed a public area of the ship he would check for anyone watching and liberally spread a number of sheets of paper around on desks, tables and couches.

The ache in his shoulder was lessening the more copies of *The Truth is All We Have* he distributed from the satchel, each sheet bearing three of what he considered to be his most powerful works to date. *Uncaring Gods* was his personal favourite, unfavourably comparing the Astartes warriors to the ancient Titans of myth; a powerful piece that he knew was worthy of a wider audience.

He knew he had to be careful with such works, but the passion burned in him too brightly to be contained.

He'd managed to get his hands on a cheap bulk printer with ridiculous ease, acquiring one from the first junkyard dog he'd approached with no more than a few moments' effort. It was not a good quality machine, or even one he would have looked twice at on Terra, but even so it had cost him the bulk of his winnings at merci merci. It was a poor thing, but it did the job, even though his billet now stank of printers' ink.

Humming quietly to himself, Karkasy continued through the civilian decks, coming at last to the Retreat, careful now that he was entering areas where he was known, and where there might be others around.

His fears were unfounded as the Retreat was empty, making it even more depressing and rundown-looking. One should never see a drinking establishment well lit, he thought, it just makes it look even sadder. He made his way through the Retreat, placing a couple of sheets on each table.

Karkasy froze as he heard the clink of a bottle on a glass, his hand outstretched to another table.

'What are you doing?' asked a cultured, but clearly drunk, female voice.

Karkasy turned and saw a bedraggled woman slumped in one of the booths at the far end of the Retreat, which explained why he hadn't seen her. She was in shadow, but he instantly recognised her as Petronella Vivar, the Warmaster's documentarist, though her appearance was a far cry from when he had last seen her on Davin.

No, that wasn't right, he remembered. He had seen her on the embarkation deck as the Astartes had returned with the Warmaster.

Obviously, the experience hadn't failed to leave its mark on her.

'Those papers,' she said. 'What are they?'

Karkasy guiltily dropped the sheets he had been holding onto the tabletop and shifted the satchel so that it rested at his back.

'Nothing really,' he said, moving down the row of booths towards her. 'Just some poems I'd like people to read.'

'Poetry? Is it any good? I could use something uplifting.'

He knew he should leave her to her maudlin solitude, but the egotist in him couldn't help but respond. 'Yes, I think they're some of my best.'

'Can I read them?'

'I wouldn't right now, my dear' he said. 'Not if you're looking for something light. They're a bit dark.'

'A bit dark,' she laughed, the sound harsh and ugly. 'You have no idea.'

'It's Vivar isn't it?' asked Karkasy, approaching her booth. 'That's your name isn't it?'

She looked up, and Karkasy, an expert in gauging levels of inebriation in others, saw that she was drunk to the point of insensibility. Three bottles sat drained on the table and a fourth lay in pieces on the floor.

'Yes, that's me, Petronella Vivar,' she said. 'Palatina Majoria of House Carpinus, writer and fraud… and, I think, very drunk.'

'I can see that, but what do you mean by fraud?'

'Fraud,' she slurred, taking another drink. 'I came here to tell the glory of Horus and the splendid brotherhood of the primarchs, you know? Told Horus when I met him that if he didn't let me do it he could go to hell. Thought I'd lost my chance right there and then, but he laughed!'

'He laughed?'

She nodded. 'Yes, laughed, but he let me do it anyway. Think he might have thought I'd be amusing to keep around or something. I thought I was ready for anything.'

'And has it proved to be all you hoped it would be, my
dear Petronella?'

'No, not really if I'm honest. Want a drink? I'll tell you
about it.'

Karkasy nodded and fetched himself a glass from the
bar before sitting across from her. She poured him some
wine, getting more on the table than in the glass.

'Thank you,' he said. 'So why is it not what you
thought it would be? There's many a remembrancer
would think such a position would be a documentarist's
dream. Mersadie Oliton would have killed to land such
a role.'

'Who?'

'A friend of mine,' explained Karkasy. 'She's also a documentarist.'

'She wouldn't want it, trust me,' said Petronella, and
Karkasy could see that the puffiness around her eyes was
due as much to tears as to alcohol. 'Some illusions are
best kept. Everything I thought I knew… upside down,
just like that! Trust me, she doesn't want this.'

'Oh, I think she might,' said Karkasy, taking a drink.

She shook her head and took a closer look at him, as
though seeing him for the first time.

'Who are you?' she asked suddenly. 'I don't know you.'

'My name is Ignace Karkasy,' he said, puffing out his
chest. 'Winner of the Ethiopic Laureate and–'

'Karkasy? I know that name…' she said, rubbing the
heel of her palm against her temple as she sought to
recall him. 'Wait, you're a poet aren't you?'

'I am indeed,' he said. 'Do you know my work?'

She nodded. 'You write poetry. Bad poetry I think, I
don't remember.'

Stung by her casual dismissal of his work, he resorted
to petulance and said, 'Well what have you written that's
so bloody great? Can't say I remember reading anything
you've written.'

'Ha! You'll remember what I'm going to write, I'll tell you that for nothing!'

'Really?' quipped Karkasy, gesturing at the empty bottles on the table. 'And what might that be? *Memoirs of an Inebriated Socialite? Vengeful Spirits of the Vengeful Spirit?*'

'You think you're so clever, don't you?'

'I have my moments,' said Karkasy, knowing that there wasn't much challenge in scoring points over a drunken woman, but enjoying it nonetheless. Anyway, it would be pleasant to take this spoiled rich girl – who was complaining about the biggest break of her life – down a peg or two.

'You don't know anything,' she snapped.

'Don't I?' he asked. 'Why don't you illuminate me then?'

'Fine! I will.'

And she told Ignace Karkasy the most incredible tale he'd ever heard in his life.

'WHY DID YOU bring me here?' asked Horus, backing away from the silver tank. The eyes on the other side of the glass watched him curiously, clearly aware of him in a way that everyone else they had encountered on this strange odyssey was not. Though he knew with utter certainty who those eyes belonged to, he couldn't accept that this sterile chamber far beneath the earth was where the glory of his life had begun.

Raised on Cthonia under the black smog of the smelteries – that had been his home, his earliest memories a blur of confusing images and feelings. Nothing in his memory recalled this place or the awareness that must have grown within…

'You have seen the ultimate goal of the Emperor, my friend,' said Sejanus. 'Now it is time for you see how he began his quest for godhood.'

'With the primarchs?' said Horus. 'That makes no sense.'

'It makes perfect sense. You were to be his generals. Like unto gods, you would bestride planets and claim back the galaxy for him. You were a weapon, Horus, a weapon to be cast aside once blunted and past all usefulness.'

Horus turned from Sejanus and marched along the walkway, stopping periodically to peer through the glass of the tanks. He saw something different in each one, light and form indistinguishable, organisms like architecture, eyes and wheels turning in circles of fire. Power like nothing he had known was at work, and he could feel the potent energies surrounding and protecting the tanks, rippling across his skin like waves in the air.

He stopped by the tank with XI stencilled upon it and placed his hand against the smooth steel, feeling the untapped glories that might have lain ahead for what grew within, but knowing that they would never come to pass. He leaned forward to look within.

'You know what happens here, Horus,' said Sejanus. 'You are not long for this place.'

'Yes,' said Horus. 'There was an accident. We were lost, scattered across the stars until the Emperor discovered us.'

'No,' said Sejanus. 'There was no accident.'

Horus turned from the glass, confused. 'What are you talking about? Of course there was. We were hurled from Terra like leaves in a storm. I came to Cthonia, Russ to Fenris, Sanguinius to Baal and the others to the worlds they were raised on.'

'No, you misunderstand me. I meant that it wasn't an accident,' said Sejanus. 'Look around you. You know how far beneath the earth we are and you saw the protective wards carved on the doors that led here. What manner of accident do you think could reach into this facility and scatter you so far across the galaxy? And what were the chances of you all coming to rest on ancient homeworlds of humanity?'

Horus had no answer for him and leaned on the walkway's railing taking deep breaths as Sejanus approached him. 'What are you suggesting?'

'I am suggesting nothing. I am telling you what happened.'

'You are telling me nothing!' roared Horus. 'You fill my head with speculation and conjecture, but you tell me nothing concrete. Maybe I'm being stupid, I don't know, so explain what you mean in plain words.'

'Very well,' nodded Sejanus. 'I will tell you of your creation.'

THUNDERHEADS RUMBLED OVER the summit of the Delphos, and Euphrati Keeler snapped off a couple of quick picts of the structure's immensity, silhouetted against sheets of purple lighting. She knew the picts were nothing special, the composition banal and pedestrian, but she took them anyway, knowing that every moment of this historic time had to be recorded for future generations.

'Are you done?' asked Titus Cassar, who stood a little way behind her. 'The prayer meeting's in a few moments and you don't want to be late.'

'I know, Titus, stop fussing.'

She had met Titus Cassar the day after she had arrived in the valley of the Delphos, following the secret Lectitio Divinitatus symbols to a clandestine prayer meeting he had organised in the shadow of the mighty building. She had been surprised by how many people were part of his congregation, nearly sixty souls, all with their heads bowed and reciting prayers to the Divine Emperor of Mankind.

Cassar had welcomed her into his flock, but people had quickly gravitated to her daily prayers and sermons, preferring them to his. For all his faith, Cassar was no orator and his awkward, spiky delivery left a lot to be desired. He had faith, but he was no iterator, that was for sure. She had worried that he might resent her usurping his group, but he had welcomed it, knowing that he was a follower, not a leader.

In truth, she was no leader either. Like Cassar, she had faith, but felt uncomfortable standing in front of large groups of people. The crowds of the faithful didn't seem to notice, staring at her in rapturous adoration as she delivered the word of the Emperor.

'I'm not fussing, Euphrati.'

'Yes you are.'

'Well, maybe I am, but I have to get back to the *Dies Irae* before I'm missed. Princeps Turnet will have my hide if he finds out what I've been doing here.'

The mighty war engines of the Legio Mortis stood sentinel over the Warmaster at the mouth of the valley, their bulk too enormous to allow them to enter. The crater looked more like the site of a military muster than a gathering of pilgrims and supplicants: tanks, trucks, flatbeds and mobile command vehicles having carried tens of thousands of people to this place over the past seven days.

Together with the bizarre-looking locals, a huge portion of the Expeditionary fleet filled the crater with makeshift camps all around the Delphos. People had, in a wondrous outpouring of spontaneous feeling, made their way to where the Warmaster lay, and the scale of it still had the power to take Euphrati's breath away. The steps of the temple were thick with offerings to the Warmaster, and she knew that many of the people here had given all they had in the hope that it might speed his recovery in some way.

Keeler had a new passion in her life, but she was still an imagist at heart, and some of the picts she had taken here were amongst her finest work.

'Yes, you're right, we should go,' she said, folding up her picter and hanging it around her neck. She ran her hand through her hair, still not used to how short it was now, but liking how it made her feel.

'Have you thought about what you're going to say tonight?' asked Cassar as they made their way through the thronged site to the prayer meeting.

'No, not really,' she answered. 'I never plan that far ahead. I just let the Emperor's light fill me and then I speak from the heart.'

Cassar nodded, hanging on her every word. She smiled.

'You know, six months ago, I'd have laughed if anyone had said things like that around me.'

'What things?' asked Cassar.

'About the Emperor,' she said, fingering the silver eagle on a chain she kept tucked beneath her remembrancer's robes. 'But I guess a lot can happen to a person in that time.'

'I guess so,' agreed Cassar, making way for a group of Army soldiers. 'The Emperor's light is a powerful force, Euphrati.'

As Keeler and Cassar drew level with the soldiers, a thick-necked bull of a man with a shaved head, slammed his shoulder into Cassar and pitched him to the ground.

'Hey, watch where you're going,' snarled the soldier, looming over Cassar.

Keeler stood over the fallen Cassar and shouted, 'Piss off, you cretin, you hit him!'

The soldier turned, backhanding his fist into Euphrati's jaw, and she dropped to the ground, more shocked than hurt. She struggled to rise as blood filled her mouth, but a pair of hands gripped her shoulders and held her firm to the ground. Two soldiers held her down as the others started kicking the fallen Cassar.

'Get off me!' she yelled.

'Shut up, bitch!' said the first soldier. 'You think we don't know what you're doing? Prayers and stuff to the Emperor? Horus is the one you should be giving thanks to.'

Cassar rolled to his knees, blocking the kicks as best he could, but he was facing three trained soldiers and couldn't block them all. He punched one in the groin and swayed away from a thick-soled boot aimed at his head, finally gaining his feet as a chopping hand struck him on the side of the neck.

Keeler struggled in her captors' grip, but they were too strong. One man reached down to tear the picter from around her neck and she bit his wrist as it came into range of her teeth. He yelped and ripped the picter from her as the other wrenched her head back by the roots of her hair.

'Don't you dare!' she screamed, struggling even harder as the soldier swung the picter by its strap and smashed it to pieces on the ground. Cassar was down on one knee, his face bloody and angry. He freed his pistol from its holster, but a knee connected with his face and knocked him insensible, the pistol clattering to the ground beside him.

'Titus!' shouted Keeler, fighting like a wildcat and finally managing to free one arm. She reached back and clawed her nails down the face of the man who held her. He screamed and released his grip on her, and she scrambled on her knees to the fallen pistol.

'Get her!' someone shouted. 'Emperor loving witch!'

She reached the pistol, hearing the thud of heavy impacts, and rolled onto her back. She held the gun out in front of her, ready to kill the next bastard that came near her.

Then she saw that she wouldn't have to kill anyone.

Three of the soldiers were down, one was running for his life through the campsite and the last was held in the iron grip of an Astartes warrior. The soldier's feet flailed a metre off the ground as the Astartes held him round the neck with one hand.

'Five to one doesn't seem very sporting now does it?' asked the warrior, and Keeler saw that it was Captain Torgaddon, one of the Mournival. She remembered snapping some fine images of Torgaddon on the *Vengeful Spirit* and thinking that he was the handsomest of the Sons of Horus.

Torgaddon ripped the name and unit badge from the struggling soldier's uniform, before dropping him and saying, 'You'll be hearing from the Discipline Masters. Now get out of my sight before I kill you.'

Keeler dropped the pistol and scooted over to her picter, cursing as she saw that it and the images contained within it were probably ruined. She pawed through the remains and lifted out the memory coil. If she could get this into the edit engine she kept in her billet quickly enough then perhaps she could save some of the images.

Cassar groaned in pain and she felt a momentary pang of guilt that she'd gone for her smashed picter before him, but it soon passed.

'Are you Keeler?' asked Torgaddon as she slipped the memory coil into her robes.

She looked up, surprised that he knew her name, and said, 'Yes.'

'Good,' he said, offering his hand to help her to her feet.

'You want to tell me what that was all about?' he asked.

She hesitated, not wanting to tell an Astartes warrior the real reason for the assault. 'I don't think they liked the images I was taking,' she said.

'Everyone's a critic, eh?' chuckled Torgaddon, but she could see that he didn't believe her.

'Yeah, but I need to get back to the ship to recover them.'

'Well that's a happy coincidence,' said Torgaddon.

'What do you mean?'

'I've been asked to take you back to the *Vengeful Spirit.*'

'You have? Why?'

'Does it matter?' asked Torgaddon. 'You're coming back with me.'

'You can at least tell me who wants me back, can't you?'

'No, it's top secret.'

'Really?'

'No, not really, it's Kyril Sindermann.'

The idea of Sindermann sending an Astartes warrior to do his bidding seemed ludicrous to Keeler, and there could only be one reason why the venerable iterator wanted to speak to her. Ignace or Mersadie must have blabbed to him about her new faith, and she felt her anger grow at their unwillingness to understand her newfound truth.

'So the Astartes are at the beck and call of the iterators now?' she snapped.

'Hardly,' said Torgaddon. 'It's a favour to a friend and I think it might be in your own best interests to go back.'

'Why?'

'You ask a lot of questions, Miss Keeler,' said Torgaddon, 'and while that's a trait that probably stands you in good stead as a remembrancer, it might be best for you to be quiet and listen for a change.'

'Am I in trouble?'

Torgaddon stirred the smashed remnants of her picter with his boot and said, 'Let's just say that someone wants to give you some lessons in pictography.'

'THE EMPEROR KNEW he would need the greatest warriors to lead his armies,' began Sejanus. 'To lead such warriors as the Astartes needed commanders like gods. Commanders who were virtually indestructible and could command superhuman warriors in the blink of an eye. They would be engineered to be leaders of men, mighty warlords whose martial prowess was only matched by the Emperor's, each with his own particular skills.'

'The primarchs.'

'Indeed. Only beings of such magnitude could even think of conquering the galaxy. Can you imagine the hubris and will required even to contemplate such an endeavour? What manner of man could even consider it? Who but a primarch could be trusted with such a monumental task? No man, not even the Emperor, could achieve such a god-like undertaking alone. Hence you were created.'

'To conquer the galaxy for humanity,' said Horus.

'No, not for humanity, for the Emperor,' said Sejanus. 'You already know in your heart what awaits you when the Great Crusade is over. You will become a gaoler who polices the Emperor's regime while he ascends to godhood and abandons you all. What sort of reward is that for someone who conquered the galaxy?'

'It is no reward at all,' snarled Horus, hammering his hand into the side of the silver tank before him. The metal buckled and a hairline crack split the toughened glass under his assault. He could hear a desperate drumming from inside, and a hiss of escaping gas whined from the frosted panel of the tank.

'Look around you, Horus,' said Sejanus. 'Do you think that the science of man alone could have created a being such as a primarch? If such technology existed, why not create a hundred Horuses, a thousand? No, a bargain was made that saw you emerge from its forging. I know, for the masters of the warp are as much your father as the Emperor.'

'No!' shouted Horus. 'I won't believe you. The primarchs are my brothers, the Emperor's sons created from his own flesh and blood and each a part of him.'

'Each a part of him, yes, but where did such power come from? He bargained with the gods of the warp for a measure of their power. *That* is what he invested in you, not his paltry human power.'

'The gods of the warp? What are you talking about, Sejanus?'

'The entities whose realm is being destroyed by the Emperor,' said Sejanus. 'Intelligences, xenos creatures, gods? Does it matter what terminology we use for them? They have such incredible power that they might as well be gods by your reckoning. They command the secrets of life and death and all that lies between. Experience, change, war and decay, they are all are part of the endless cycle of existence, and the gods of the warp hold dominion over them all. Their power flows through your veins and bestows incredible abilities upon you. The Emperor has long known of them and he came to them many centuries ago, offering friendship and devotion.'

'He would never do such a thing!' denied Horus.

'You underestimate his lust for power, my friend,' said Sejanus as they made their way back towards the steps that led down to the laboratory floor. 'The gods of the warp are powerful, but they do not understand this material universe, and the Emperor was able to betray them, stealing away their power for himself. In creating you, he passed on but a tiny measure of that power.'

Horus felt his breath come in short, painful bursts. He wanted to deny Sejanus's words, but part of him knew that this was no lie. Like any man, his future was uncertain, but his past had always been his own. His glories and life had been forged with his own two hands, but even now, they were being stripped away from him by the Emperor's treachery.

'So we are tainted,' whispered Horus. 'All of us.'

'Tainted, no,' said Sejanus, shaking his head. 'The power of the warp simply *is*. Used wisely and by a man of power it can be a weapon like no other. It can be mastered and it can be a powerful tool for one with the will to use it.'

'Then why did the Emperor not use it well?'

'Because he was weak,' said Sejanus, leaning in close to Horus. 'Unlike you, he lacked the will to master it, and the gods of the warp do not take kindly to those who betray them. The Emperor had taken a measure of their power for himself, but they struck back at him.'

'How?'

'You will see. With the power he stole from them, he was too powerful for them to attack directly, but they had foreseen a measure of his plans and they struck at what he needed most to realise those plans.'

'The primarchs?'

'The primarchs,' agreed Sejanus, walking back down the length of walkway. Horus heard distant sirens blare and felt the air within the chamber become more agitated, as if a cold electric current whipped from molecule to molecule.

'What's going on?' he asked, as the sirens grew louder.

'Justice,' said Sejanus.

The reflective surfaces of the tanks lit up as an actinic blue light appeared above them, and Horus looked up to see a blob of dirty light swirling into existence just below the ceiling. Like a miniature galaxy, it hung suspended above the silver incubation tanks, growing larger with every passing second. A powerful wind tugged at Horus and he hung onto the railing as a shrieking howl issued from the spreading vortex above him.

'What is that?' he shouted, working his way along the railing towards the stairs.

'You know what it is, Horus,' said Sejanus.

'We have to get out of here.'

'It's too late for that,' said Sejanus, taking his arm in an iron grip.

'Take your hand off me, Sejanus,' warned Horus, 'or whatever your name is. I know you're not Sejanus, so you might as well stop pretending.'

Even as he spoke, he saw a group of armoured warriors rushing through the chamber's doorway towards them. There were six of them, each with the build of an Astartes, but without a suit of battle plate, they were less bulked out and gigantic. They wore fabulously ornate gold breastplates decorated with eagles and lightning bolts, and each wore a tall, peaked helm of bronze with a red, horsehair plume. Scarlet cloaks billowed behind them in the cyclone that swept through the chamber. Long spears with boltguns slung beneath long, crackling blades were aimed at him, and he instantly recognised the warriors for what they were – the Custodian Guard, the Praetorians of the Emperor himself.

'Halt, fiends and face thy judgement!' shouted the lead warrior, aiming his guardian spear at Horus's heart. Though the warrior wore an enclosing helm, Horus would have recognised his eyes and that voice anywhere.

'Valdor!' cried Horus. 'Constantin Valdor. It's me, it's Horus.'

'Be silent!' shouted Valdor. 'End this foul conjuration now!'

Horus looked up at the ceiling, feeling the power contained within that swirling maelstrom tugging at him like the call of a long lost friend. He forced its siren song from his mind, dropped to the floor of the chamber and took a step forward.

Ripping blasts of light erupted from the Custodians' spears, and Horus was forced to his knees by the hammering impacts of their shells. The howling gale swallowed the noise of the shots, and Horus cried out, not with pain, but with the knowledge that fellow warriors of the Imperium had fired upon him.

More blasts struck him, tearing great chunks from his armour, but none was able to defeat its protection. The Custodians advanced in disciplined ranks, pouring their fire into him and keeping him pinned beneath its weight. Sejanus ducked behind the stairs, sparks and smoking chunks ripping from the metal as the explosive bolts tore through it.

Horus roared in anger and surged to his feet, all thoughts of restraint forgotten as he found himself at the centre of the deafening storm. A bolt clipped his gorget and almost spun him around, but it was not enough to stop him. He ripped the guardian spear from the nearest Custodian and smashed his skull to splinters with a single blow from his fist.

He reversed his grip on the spear and slashed the next Custodian from collarbone to groin, the two shorn halves swept up by the howling winds and vanishing into the crackling vortex. Another Custodian died as Horus rammed the spear through his chest and split him in two.

A blade lanced for his head, but he shattered it with a swipe of his fist and ripped the arm from his attacker with casual ease. Another Custodian died as Horus tore his head off in his mighty fist, blood gushing from the neck, as if from a geyser, as he tossed the severed head aside.

Only Valdor remained, and Horus snarled as he rounded on the Chief Custodian. A blaze of light erupted from the barrel of Valdor's guardian spear. Horus grunted at the impacts and raised his fist to strike Valdor down, hearing metal squeal and tear as the force of the hurricane reaching from the vortex above finally achieved its goal.

Horus paused in his attack, suddenly terrified for the fate of those inside the tanks. He turned and saw one tank spewing gasses and screams as it was ripped from the ground, following others as they were torn from their moorings and swept upwards.

Then time stopped and a blinding light filled the chamber.

Horus felt warm honey flow through him, and he turned towards the source of the light: a shimmering golden giant of unimaginable majesty and beauty.

Horus dropped to his knees in rapture at the sight. Who would not strive to worship so perfect a being? Power and certainty flowed from the figure, the secret mystery of creation at his fingertips, the answers to any question that could be asked there for the knowing, and the wisdom to know how to use them.

He wore armour that gleamed a perfect gold, his features impossible to know, and his glory and power unmatched by any being in creation.

The golden warrior moved as though in slow motion, raising his hand to halt the madness of the vortex with a gesture. The maelstrom was silenced, the tumbling incubation tanks suspended in mid air.

The golden figure turned a puzzled gaze upon Horus.

'I know you?' he said, and Horus wept to hear such a perfect symphony of sound.

'Yes,' said Horus, unable to raise his voice above a whisper.

The giant cocked his head to one side and said, 'You would destroy my great works, but you will not succeed. I beg you, turn from this path or all will be lost.'

Horus reached out towards the golden warrior as he turned his sad gaze to the incubation tanks held motionless above him, weighing the consequences of future events in the blink of an eye.

Horus could see the decision in the figure's wondrous eyes and shouted, 'No!'

The figure turned from him and time snapped back into its prescribed stream.

The deafening howl of the warp-spawned wind returned with the force of a hurricane and Horus heard the screams of his brothers amid the metallic clanging of their incubation tanks.

'Father, no!' he yelled. 'You can't let this happen!'

The golden giant was walking away, leaving the carnage in his wake, uncaring of the lives he had wrought. Horus felt his hate swell bright and strong within his breast.

The power of the wind seized him in its grip and he let it take him, spinning him up into the air and Horus opened his arms as he was reunited once again with his brothers.

The abyss of the warp vortex yawned above him like a great eye of terror and madness.

He surrendered to its power and let it take him into its embrace.

SIXTEEN

The truth is all we have/Arch prophet/Home

For once Loken was inclined to agree with Iacton Qruze when he said, 'Not like it used to be, boy. Not like it used to be.'

They stood on the strategium deck, looking out over the ghostly glow of Davin as it hung in space like a faded jewel. 'I remember the first time we came here, seems like yesterday.'

'More like a lifetime,' said Loken.

'Nonsense, young man,' said Qruze. 'When you've been around as long as I have you learn a thing or two. Live to my age and we'll see how you perceive the passage of years.'

Loken sighed, not in the mood for another of Qruze's rambling, faintly patronising stories of 'the good old days'.

'Yes, Iacton, we'll see.'

'Don't dismiss me, boy,' said Qruze. 'I may be old, but I'm not stupid.'

'I never meant to say you were,' said Loken.

'Then take heed of me now, Garviel,' said Qruze, leaning in close. 'You think I don't know, but I do.'

'Don't know about what?'

'About the "half-heard" thing,' hissed Qruze, quietly so that none of the deck crew could hear. 'I know fine well why you call me that, and it's not because I speak softly, it's because no one pays a blind bit of notice to what I say.'

Loken looked into Qruze's long, tanned face, his skin deeply lined with creases and folds. His eyes, normally hooded and half-closed were now intense and penetrating.

'Iacton–' began Loken, but Qruze cut him off.

'Don't apologise, it doesn't become you.'

'I don't know what to say,' said Loken.

'Ach… don't say anything. What do I have to say that anyone would want to listen to anyway?' sighed Qruze. 'I know what I am, boy, a relic of a time long passed for our beloved Legion. You know that I remember when we fought without the Warmaster, can you imagine such a thing?'

'We may not have to soon, Iacton. It's nearly time for the Delphos to open and there's been no word. Apothecary Vaddon is no nearer to finding out what happened to the Warmaster, even with the anathame.'

'The what?'

'The weapon that wounded the Warmaster,' said Loken, wishing he hadn't mentioned the kinebrach weapon in front of Qruze.

'Oh, must be a powerful weapon that,' said Qruze sagely.

'I wanted to go back down to Davin with Torgaddon,' said Loken, changing the subject, 'but I was afraid of what I might do if I saw Little Horus or Ezekyle.'

'They are your brothers, boy,' said Qruze. 'Whatever happens, never forget that. We break such bonds at our peril. When we turn from one brother, we turn from them all.'

'Even when they have made a terrible mistake?'

'Even then,' agreed Qruze. 'We all make mistakes, lad. We need to appreciate them for what they are – lessons that can only be learned the hard way. Unless it's a fatal mistake, of course, but at least someone else can learn from *that*.'

'I don't know what to do,' said Loken, leaning on the strategium rail. 'I don't know what's happening with the Warmaster and there's nothing I can do about it.'

'Aye, it's a thorny one, my boy,' agreed Qruze. 'Still, as we used to say back in my day, "When there's nothing you can do about it, don't worry about it".'

'Things must have been simpler back in your day, Iacton,' said Loken.

'They were, boy, that's for sure,' replied Qruze, missing Loken's sarcasm. 'There was none of this quiet order nonsense, and do you think we'd have that upstart Varvarus baying for blood back in the day? Or that we'd have had remembrancers on our own bloody ship, writing treasonous poetry about us and claiming that it's the unvarnished truth? I ask you, where's the damn respect the Astartes used to be held in? Changed days, young man, changed days.'

Loken's eyes narrowed as Qruze spoke. 'What are you talking about?'

'I said it's changed days since–'

'No,' said Loken, 'about Varvarus and the remembrancers.'

'Haven't you heard? No, I suppose you haven't,' said Qruze. 'Well, it seems Varvarus wasn't too pleased about you and the Mournival's return to the *Vengeful Spirit* with the Warmaster. The fool thinks heads should roll for the deaths you caused. He's been on the vox daily to Maloghurst demanding we tell the fleet what happened, make reparations to the families of the dead, and then punish you all.'

'Punish us?'

'That's what he's saying,' nodded Qruze. 'Claims he's already had Ing Mae Sing despatch communiqués back to the Council of Terra about the mess you caused. Bloody nuisance if you ask me. We didn't have to put up with this when we first set out, you fought and bled, and if people got in the way then that was their tough luck.'

Loken was aghast at Qruze's words, once again feeling the shame of his actions on the embarkation deck. The innocent deaths he'd been part of would remain with him until his dying day, but what was done was done and he wouldn't waste time on regret. For mere mortals to decree the death of an Astartes was unthinkable, however unfortunate the events had been.

As troublesome a problem as Varvarus was, he was a problem for Maloghurst to deal with, but something in Qruze's words struck a familiar chord.

'You said something about remembrancers?'

'Yes, as if we didn't have enough to worry about.'

'Iacton, don't draw this out. Tell me what's going on.'

'Very well, though I don't know what your hurry is,' replied Qruze. 'It seems there's some anonymous remembrancer going about the ship, dishing out anti-Astartes propaganda, poetry or some such drivel. Crewmen have been finding pamphlets all over the ship. Called the "truth is all we have" or something pretentious like that.'

'The truth is all we have,' repeated Loken.

'Yes, I think so.'

Loken spun on his heel and made his way from the strategium without another word.

'Not like it was, back in my day,' sighed Qruze after Loken's departing back.

✠ ✠ ✠

IT WAS LATE and he was tired, but Ignace Karkasy was pleased with the last week's work. Each time he'd made a clandestine journey through the ship distributing his radical poetry, he'd returned hours later to find every copy gone. Though the ship's crew was no doubt confiscating some, he knew that others must have found their way into the hands of those who needed to hear what he had to say.

The companionway was quiet, but then it always was these days. Most of those who held vigils for the fallen Warmaster did so either on Davin or in the larger spaces of the ship. An air of neglect hung over the *Vengeful Spirit*, as though even the servitors who cleaned and maintained it had paused in their duties to await the outcome of events on the planet below.

As he walked back to his billet, Karkasy saw the symbol of the *Lectitio Divinitatus* scratched into bulkheads and passageways time and time again, and he had the distinct impression that if he were to follow them, they would lead him to a group of the faithful.

The faithful: it still sounded strange to think of such a term in these enlightened times. He remembered standing in the fane on Sixty-Three Nineteen and wondering if belief in the divine was some immutable flaw in the character of mankind. Did man need to believe in something to fill some terrible emptiness within him?

A wise man of Old Earth had once claimed that science would destroy mankind, not through its weapons of mass destruction, but through finally proving that there was no god. Such knowledge, he claimed, would sear the mind of man and leave him gibbering and insane with the realisation that he was utterly alone in an uncaring universe.

Karkasy smiled and wondered what that old man would have said if he could see the truth of the

Imperium taking its secular light to the far corners of the galaxy. On the other hand, perhaps this *Lectitio Divinitatus* cult was vindication of his words: proof that, in the face of that emptiness, man had chosen to invent new gods to replace the ones that had passed out of memory.

Karkasy wasn't aware of the Emperor having transubstantiated from man to god, but the cult's literature, which was appearing with the same regularity as his own publications, claimed that he had already risen beyond mortal concerns.

He shook his head at such foolishness, already working out how to incorporate this weighty pontificating into his new poems. His billet was just ahead, and as he reached towards the recessed handle, he immediately knew that something was wrong.

The door was slightly ajar and the reek of ammonia filled the corridor, but even over that powerful smell, Karkasy detected a familiar, pervasive aroma that could mean only one thing. The impertinent ditty he had composed for Euphrati Keeler concerning the stink of the Astartes leapt to mind, and he knew who would be behind the door, even before he opened it.

He briefly considered simply walking away, but realised that there would be no point.

He took a deep breath and pushed open the door.

Inside, his cabin was a mess, though it was a mess of his own making rather than that of any intruder. Standing with his back to him and seeming to fill the small space with his bulk was, as he'd expected, Captain Loken.

'Hello, Ignace,' said Loken, putting down one of the Bondsman number 7's. Karkasy had filled two of them with random jottings and thoughts, and he knew that Loken wouldn't be best pleased with what he must have read. You didn't need to be a student of literature to understand the vitriol written there.

'Captain Loken,' replied Karkasy. 'I'd ask to what do I owe the pleasure of this visit, but we both know why you're here, don't we?'

Loken nodded, and Karkasy, feeling his heart pounding in his chest, saw that the Astartes was holding his anger in check by the finest of threads. This was not the raging fury of Abaddon, but a cold steel rage that could destroy him without a moment's pause or regret. Suddenly Karkasy realised how dangerous his newly rediscovered muse was and how foolish he'd been in thinking he would remain undiscovered for long. Strangely, now that he was unmasked, he felt his defiance smother the fire of his fear, and knew that he had done the right thing.

'Why?' hissed Loken. 'I vouched for you, remembrancer. I put my good name on the line for you and this is how I am repaid?'

'Yes, captain,' said Karkasy. 'You did vouch for me. You made me swear to tell the truth and that is what I have been doing.'

'The truth?' roared Loken, and Karkasy quailed before his anger, remembering how easily the captain's fists had bludgeoned people to death. 'This is not the truth, this is libellous trash! Your lies are already spreading to the rest of the fleet. I should kill you for this, Ignace.'

'Kill me? Just like you killed all those innocent people on the embarkation deck?' shouted Karkasy. 'Is that what Astartes justice means now? Someone gets in your way or says something you don't agree with and you kill them? If that's what our glorious Imperium has come to then I want nothing to do with it.'

He saw the anger drain from Loken and felt a momentary pang of sorrow for him, but quashed it as he remembered the blood and screams of the dying. He lifted a collection of poems and held them out to Loken. 'Anyway, this is want you wanted.'

'You think I wanted this?' said Loken, hurling the pamphlets across the billet and looming over him. 'Are you insane?'

'Not at all, my dear captain,' said Karkasy, affecting a calm he didn't feel. 'I have you to thank for this.'

'Me? What are you talking about?' asked Loken, obviously confused. Karkasy could see the chink of doubt in Loken's bluster. He offered the bottle of wine to Loken, but the giant warrior shook his head.

'You told me to keep telling the truth, ugly and unpalatable as it might be,' said Karkasy, pouring some wine into a cracked and dirty tin mug. 'The truth is all we have, remember?'

'I remember,' sighed Loken, sitting down on Karkasy's creaking cot bed.

Karkasy let out a breath as he realised the immediate danger had passed, and took a long, gulping drink of the wine. It was poor a vintage and had been open for too long, but it helped to calm his jangling nerves. He pulled a high backed chair from his writing desk and sat before Loken, who held his hand out for the bottle.

'You're right, Ignace, I did tell you to do this, but I never imagined it would lead us to this place,' said Loken, taking a swig from the bottle.

'Nor I, but it has,' replied Karkasy. 'The question now becomes what are you going to do about it?'

'I don't really know, Ignace,' admitted Loken. 'I think you are being unfair to the Mournival, given the circumstances we found ourselves in. All we–'

'No,' interrupted Karkasy, 'I'm not. You Astartes stand above us mortals in all regards and you demand our respect, but that respect has to be earned. It requires your ethics to be without question. You not only have to stay above the line between right and wrong, you also have to stay well clear of the grey areas in-between.'

Loken laughed humourlessly. 'I thought it was Sindermann's job to be a teacher of ethics.'

'Well, our dear Kyril has not been around much lately, has he?' said Karkasy. 'I admit I'm somewhat of a late-comer to the ranks of the righteous, but I know that what I am doing is right. More than that, I know it's *necessary*.'

'You feel that strongly about this?'

'I do, captain. More strongly than I have felt about anything in my life.'

'And you'll keep publishing this?' asked Loken, lifting a pile of scribbled notes.

'Is there a right answer to that question, captain?' asked Karkasy.

'Yes, so answer honestly.'

'If I can,' said Karkasy, 'then I will.'

'You will bring trouble down on us both, Ignace Karkasy,' said Loken, 'but if we have no truth, then we are nothing, and if I stop you speaking out then I am no better than a tyrant.'

'So you're not going to stop me writing, or send me back to Terra?'

'I should, but I won't. You should be aware that your poems have made you powerful enemies, Ignace, enemies who will demand your dismissal, or worse. As of this moment however, you are under my protection,' said Loken.

'You think I'll need protection?' asked Karkasy.

'Definitely,' said Loken.

'I'M TOLD YOU wanted to see me,' said Euphrati Keeler. 'Care to tell me why?'

'Ah, my dear, Euphrati,' said Kyril Sindermann, looking up from his food. 'Do come in.'

She'd found him in the sub-deck dining area after scouring the dusty passages of Archive Chamber Three for him for over an hour. According to the iterators left on the ship, the old man had been spending almost all of his time there, missing his lectures – not that there were any students to lecture just now – and ignoring the requests of his peers to join them for meals or drinks.

Torgaddon had left her to find Sindermann on her own, his duty discharged simply by bringing her back to the *Vengeful Spirit*. Then he had gone in search of Captain Loken, to travel back down to Davin with him. Keeler didn't doubt that he'd pass on what he'd seen on the planet to Loken, but she no longer cared who knew of her beliefs.

Sindermann looked terrible, his eyes haggard and grey, his features sallow and gaunt.

'You don't look good, Sindermann,' she said.

'I could say the same for you, Euphrati,' said Sindermann. 'You've lost weight. It doesn't suit you.'

'Most women would be grateful for that, but you didn't have one of the Astartes fetch me back here to comment on my eating habits, did you?'

Sindermann laughed, pushing aside the book, he'd been poring over, and said, 'No, you're right, I didn't.'

'Then why did you?' she asked, sitting opposite him. 'If it's because of something Ignace has told you, then save your breath.'

'Ignace? No, I haven't spoken to him for some time,' replied Sindermann. 'It was Mersadie Oliton who came to see me. She tells me that you've become quite the agitator for this *Lectitio Divinitatus* cult.'

'It's not a cult.'

'No? Then what would you call it?'

She thought about it for a moment and then answered, 'A new faith.'

'A shrewd answer,' said Sindermann. 'If you'll indulge me, I'd like to know more about it.'

'You would? I thought you'd brought me back to try and teach me the error of my ways, to use your iterator's wiles to try and talk me out of my beliefs.'

'Not at all, my dear,' said Sindermann. 'You may think your tribute is paid in secret in the recesses of your heart, but it will out. We are a curious species when it comes to worship. The things that dominate our imagination determine our lives and our character. Therefore it behoves us to be careful what we worship, for what we are worshipping we are becoming.'

'And what do you think we worship?'

Sindermann looked furtively around the sub-deck and produced a sheet of paper that she recognised immediately as one of the *Lectitio Divinitatus* pamphlets. 'That's what I want you to help me with. I have read this several times and I must admit that I am intrigued by the things it posits. You see, ever since the… events beneath the Whisperheads, I… I haven't been sleeping too well and I thought to bury myself in my books. I thought that if I could understand what happened to us, then I could rationalise it.'

'And did you?'

He smiled, but she could see the weariness and despair behind the gesture. 'Honestly? No, not really, the more I read, the more I saw how far we'd come since the days of religious hectoring from an autocratic priesthood. By the same token, the more I read the more I realised there was a pattern emerging.'

'A pattern? What kind of pattern?'

'Look,' said Sindermann, coming round the table to sit next to her, and flattening out the pamphlet before her. 'Your *Lectitio Divinitatus* talks about how the Emperor has moved amongst us for thousands of year, yes?'

'Yes.'

'Well in the old texts, rubbish mostly – ancient histories and lurid tales of barbarism and bloodshed – I found some recurring themes. A being of golden light appears in several of the texts and, much as I hate to admit it, it sounds a lot like what this paper describes. I don't know what truth may lie in this avenue of investigation, but I would know more of it, Euphrati.'

She didn't know what to say.

'Look,' he said, pulling the book around and turning it towards her. 'This book is written in a derivation of an ancient human language, but one I haven't seen before. I can make out certain passages, I think, but it's a very complex structure and without some of the root words to make the right grammatical connections, it's proving very difficult to translate.'

'What book is it?'

'I believe it to be the *Book of Lorgar*, although I haven't been able to speak with First Chaplain Erebus to verify that fact. If it is, it may be a copy given to the Warmaster by Lorgar himself.'

'So why does that make it so important?'

'Don't you remember the rumours about Lorgar?' asked Sindermann urgently. 'That he too worshipped the Emperor as a god? It's said that his Legion devastated world after world for not showing the proper devotion to the Emperor, and then raised up great monuments to him.'

'I remember the tales, yes, but that's all they are, surely?'

'Probably, but what if they aren't?' said Sindermann, his eyes alight with the possibility of uncovering such knowledge. 'What if a primarch, one of the Emperor's sons no less, was privy to something we as mere mortals are not yet ready for? If my work so far is correct, then this book talks about bringing forth the essence of god. I must know what that means!'

Despite herself, Euphrati felt her pulse race with this potential knowledge. Undeniable proof of the Emperor's divinity coming from Kyril Sindermann would raise the *Lectitio Divinitatus* far above its humble status and into the realm of a phenomenon that could spread from one side of the galaxy to the other.

Sindermann saw that realisation in her face and said, 'Miss Keeler, I have spent my entire adult life promulgating the truth of the Imperium and I am proud of the work I have done, but what if we are teaching the wrong message? If you are right and the Emperor is a god, then what we saw beneath the mountains of Sixty-Three Nineteen represents a danger more horrifying than we can possibly imagine. If it truly was a spirit of evil then we need a divine being such as the Emperor, more than ever. I know that words cannot move mountains, but they can move the multitude – we've proven that time and time again. People are more ready to fight and die for a word than for anything else. Words shape thought, stir feeling, and force action. They kill and revive, corrupt and cure. If being an iterator has taught me anything, it's that men of words – priests, prophets and intellectuals – have played a more decisive role in history than any military leaders or statesmen. If we can prove the existence of god, then I promise you the iterators will shout that truth from the highest towers of the land.'

Euphrati stared, open mouthed, as Kyril Sindermann turned her world upside down: this arch prophet of secular truth speaking of gods and faith? Looking into his eyes, she saw the wracking self-doubt and crisis of identity that he had undergone since she had last seen him, understanding how much of him had been lost these last few days, and how much had been gained.

'Let me see,' she said, and Sindermann pushed the book in front of her.

The writing was an angular cuneiform, running up and down the page rather than along it, and right away she could see that she would be no help in its translation, although elements of the script looked somehow familiar.

'I can't read it,' she said. 'What does it say?'

'Well, that's the problem, I can't tell exactly,' said Sindermann. 'I can make out the odd word, but it's difficult without the grammatical key.'

'I've seen this before,' she said, suddenly remembering why the writing looked familiar.

'I hardly think so, Euphrati,' said Sindermann. 'This book has been in the archive chamber for decades. I don't think anyone's read it since it was put there.'

'Don't patronise me, Sindermann, I've definitely seen this before,' she insisted.

'Where?'

Keeler reached into her pocket and gripped the memory coil of her smashed picter. She rose from her seat and said, 'Gather your notes and I'll meet you in the archive chamber in thirty minutes.'

'Where are you going?' asked Sindermann, gathering up the book.

'To get something you're going to want to see.'

HORUS OPENED HIS eyes to see a sky thick with polluted clouds, the taste in the air chemical and stagnant.

It smelled familiar. It smelled of home.

He lay on an uneven plateau of dusty black powder in front of a long-exhausted mining tunnel, and felt the hollow ache of homesickness as he realised this was Cthonia.

The smog of the distant foundries and the relentless hammering of deep core mining filled the sky with particulate matter, and he felt an ache of loneliness for the simpler times he had spent here.

Horus looked around for Sejanus, but whatever the swirling vortex beneath Terra had been, it had evidently not swept up his old comrade in its fury.

His journey here had not been as silent and instant as his previous journeys through this strange and unknown realm. The powers that dwelled in the warp had shown him a glimpse of the future, and it was a desolate place indeed. Foul xeno breeds held sway over huge swathes of the galaxy and a pall of hopelessness gripped the sons of man.

The power of humanity's glorious armies was broken, the Legions shattered and reduced to fragments of what they had once been: bureaucrats, scriveners and official-dom ruling in a hellish regime where men lived inglorious lives of no consequence or ambition.

In this dark future, mankind had not the strength to challenge the overlords, to fight against the terrors the Emperor had left them to. His father had become a carrion god who neither felt his subjects' pain nor cared for their fate.

In truth, the solitude of Cthonia was welcome, his thoughts tumbling through his head in a mad whirl of anger and resentment. The Emperor tinkered with powers far beyond his means to master – and had already failed to control once before. He had bargained away his sons for the promise of power, and now returned to Terra to try once again.

'I will not let this happen,' Horus said quietly.

As he spoke, he heard the plaintive howl of a wolf and pushed himself to his feet. Nothing like a wolf lived on Cthonia, and Horus was sick of this constant pursuit through the warp.

'Show yourselves!' he shouted, punching the air and bellowing an ululating war cry.

His cry was answered as the howling came again, drawing nearer, and Horus felt his battle lust swim to the surface. He had the taste of blood after the slaughter of the Custodian Guards and welcomed the chance to spill yet more.

Shadows moved around him and he shouted, 'Lupercal! Lupercal!'

Shapes resolved from the shadows and he saw a red-furred wolf pack detach from the darkness. They surrounded him, and Horus recognised the pack leader as the beast that had spoken to him when he had first awoken in the warp.

'What are you?' asked Horus, 'and no lies.'

'A friend,' said the wolf, its form blurring and running with rippling lines of golden light. The wolf reared up on its hind legs, its form elongating and widening as it became more humanoid, its proportions swelling and changing until it stood as tall as Horus himself.

Copper skin replaced fur and its eyes ran like liquid as they formed one, golden orb. Thick red hair sprouted from the figure's head and bronze coloured armour shimmered into existence upon his breast and arms. He wore a billowing cloak of feathers and Horus knew him as well he knew his own reflection.

'Magnus,' said Horus. 'Is it really you?'

'Yes, my brother, it is,' said Magnus, and the two warriors embraced in a clatter of plate.

'How?' asked Horus. 'Are you dying too?'

'No,' said Magnus. 'I am not. You must listen to me, my brother. It has taken me too long to reach you, and I do not have much time here. The spells and wards placed around you are powerful and every second I am here a dozen of my thralls die to keep them open.'

'Don't listen to him, Warmaster,' said another voice, and Horus turned to see Hastur Sejanus emerge from the darkness of the mining tunnel. 'This is who we have been trying to avoid. It is a shape-changing creature of the warp that feasts on human souls. It seeks to devour yours so that you cannot return to your body. All that was Horus would be no more.'

'He lies,' spat Magnus. 'You know me, Horus. I am your brother, but who is he? Hastur? Hastur is dead.'

'I know, but here, in this place, death is not the end.'

'There is truth in that,' agreed Magnus, 'but you would place your trust in the dead over your own brother? We mourn Hastur, but he is gone from us. This impostor does not even wear his own true face!'

Magnus thrust his fist forward and closed his fingers on the air, as though gripping something invisible. Then he wrenched his hand back. Hastur screamed and a silver light blazed like a magnesium flare from his eyes.

Horus squinted through the blinding light, still seeing an Astartes warrior, but one now armoured in the livery of the Word Bearers.

'Erebus?' asked Horus.

'Yes, Warmaster,' agreed First Chaplain Erebus; the long red scar across his throat had already begun to heal. 'I came to you in the guise of Sejanus to ease your understanding of what must be done, but I have spoken nothing but the truth since we travelled this realm.'

'Do not listen to him, Horus,' warned Magnus. 'The future of the galaxy is in your hands.'

'Indeed it is,' said Erebus, 'for the Emperor will abandon the galaxy in his quest for apotheosis. Horus must save the Imperium, for it is evident that the Emperor will not.'

SEVENTEEN

Horror/Angels and daemons/Blood pact

WITH THE COMPACT edit engine tucked under one arm and a sense of limitless possibilities filling her heart, Euphrati Keeler made her way through the stacks of Archive Chamber Three towards Sindermann's table. The white haired iterator sat hunched over the book he had shown her earlier, his breath misting in the chill air. She sat down beside him and placed the edit engine on the desk, slotting a memory coil into the imager slot.

'It's cold in here, Sindermann,' she said. 'How you haven't caught a fever I'll never know.'

He nodded. 'Yes, it is rather cold, isn't it. It's been like this for days now, ever since the Warmaster was taken to Davin in fact.'

The screen of the edit engine flickered to life, its white screen bathing them both in its washed-out light as Keeler flicked through the images she had captured. She zipped through those she had taken while on Davin's surface and those of Captain Loken and the Mournival prior to their departure for the Whisperheads.

'What are you looking for exactly?' asked Sindermann.

'This,' she said triumphantly, angling the screen so he could see the image it displayed.

The file contained eight pictures, all taken at the war council held on Davin where Eugan Temba's treachery had been revealed. Each shot included First Chaplain Erebus, and she used the engine's trackball to zoom in on his tattooed skull. Sindermann gasped as he recognised the symbols on Erebus's head. They were identical to the ones in the book that he had shown Keeler on the sub-deck.

'That's it then,' he breathed. 'It must be the *Book of Lorgar*. Can you get any closer to get the symbols from all sides of Erebus's head? Is that possible?'

'*Please*, it's me,' she replied, her hands dancing across the keys of the edit engine.

Using all the various images, and shots of the Word Bearer from different angles, Euphrati was able to create a composite image of the symbols tattooed onto his skull and project it onto a flat pane. Sindermann watched her skill with admiration, and it took her less than ten minutes to resolve a high-gain image of the symbols on Erebus's head.

With a grunt of satisfaction, she made a final keystroke, and a glossy hard copy of the screen's image slid from the side of the machine with a whirring sigh. Keeler lifted it by the corners and waved it for a second or two to dry it, before handing it to Sindermann.

'There,' she said. 'Does that help you translate what this book says?'

Sindermann slid the image across the table and held it close to the book, his head bobbing back and forth between the book and his notes as his finger traced down the trails of cuneiforms.

'Yes, yes...' he said excitedly. 'Here, you see, this word is laden with vowel transliterations and this one is clearly a personal argot, though of a much denser poly-syllabic construction.'

Keeler tuned out of what Sindermann was saying after a while, unable to make sense of the jargon he was using. Karkasy or Oliton might be able to understand the iterator, but images were her thing, not words.

'How long will it take you to get any sense out of it?' she asked.

'What? Oh, not long I shouldn't wonder,' he said. 'Once you know the grammatical logic of a language, it is a relatively simple matter to unlock the rest of its meaning.'

'So how long?'

'Give me an hour and we'll read this together, yes?'

She nodded and pushed her chair back, saying, 'Fine, I'll take a look around if that's alright.'

'Yes, feel free to have a look at whatever catches your eye, my dear, though I fear much of this collection is more suited to dusty academics like myself.'

Keeler smiled as she got up from the table. 'I may not be a documentarist, but I know which end of a book to read, Kyril.'

'Of course you do, I didn't mean to suggest–'

'Too easy,' she said and wandered off into the stacks to browse while Sindermann returned to his books.

Despite her quip, she soon realised that Sindermann was exactly right. She spent the next hour wandering up and down shelves packed with scrolls, books and musty, loose-leaf manuscripts. Most of the books had unfath-omable titles like *Reading Astrologies and Astrotelepathic Auguries, Malefic Abjurations and the Multifarious Horrores Associated wyth Such Workes* or *The Book of Atum*.

As she passed this last book, she felt a shiver travel the length her spine and reached up to slide the book from the shelf. The smell of its worn leather binding was strong, and though she had no real wish to read the book, she couldn't deny the strange attraction it held for her.

The book creaked open in her grip, and the dust of centuries wafted from its pages as she opened them. She coughed, hearing Sindermann reading aloud from the *Book of Lorgar* as he translated more of the text.

Surprisingly, the words before her were written in a language she could understand, and her eyes quickly scanned the page. Sindermann's words came again, and it took Euphrati a moment to register that the words she was hearing echoed the words she was seeing on the page, the letters blurring and rearranging themselves before her very eyes. The faded script seemed to illuminate from within, and as she read what they said, the book's pages burst into flames. She dropped the book with a cry of alarm.

She turned and ran back towards where she had left Sindermann, turning the corner to see him reading aloud from the book with a terrified expression on his face. He gripped the edges of the book as though unable to let go, the words pouring from him in a flood of voices.

A crackling, electric sensation set Euphrati's teeth on edge and she cried out in terror as she saw a swirling cloud of bluish light hovering above the desk. The image twisted and jerked in the air, moving as though out of sync with the world around it.

'Kyril! What's happening?' she screamed as the terror of the Whisperheads returned to her with paralysing force and she dropped to her knees. Sindermann didn't answer, the words streaming from his unwilling mouth and his eyes fixed in terror on the unnatural sight above him. She could tell the same fear that she felt was also running hot in his veins.

The light bulged and stretched as though something was pushing through from beyond, and an iridescent, questing limb oozed from its depths. Keeler felt the anger that had consumed her in the months following her attack break through the fear and she surged to her feet.

Keeler ran towards Sindermann and gripped his skinny wrists, as the suggestion of a rippling body of undulating, glowing flesh began tearing through the light.

His hands were locked on the book, the knuckles white, and she couldn't prise them loose as he continued to give voice to the terrible words within its pages.

'Kyril! Let go of the damn book!' she cried as an awful ripping sound came from above. She risked a look upwards, and saw yet more tentacled limbs pushing through the light in an obscene parody of birth.

'I'm sorry, Kyril!' she shouted and punched the iterator across the jaw. He pitched backwards out of his chair, and the torrent of words was cut off as the book fell from his hands. She quickly circled the table and lifted Sindermann to his feet. As she did so, she heard a grotesque sucking sound and a hard, wet thud of something heavy landing on the table.

Euphrati didn't waste time looking back, but took off as fast as she could towards the stacks, supporting the lurching Sindermann as she went. The pair of them staggered away from the table as a glittering light behind them threw their shadows out before them, and a cackling shriek like laughter washed over them.

Keeler heard a whoosh of air and something bright and hot flashed past her, exploding against the shelves with a hot bang like a firework. The wood hissed and spat where it had been struck, and she looked over her shoulder to see a horror of flailing limbs and glowing, twisting flesh leap after them. It moved with a rippling motion, lunatic faces, eyes and cackling mouths forming and reforming from the liquid matter of its body. Blue and red light flared from within it, strobing in dazzling beams through the archive.

Another bolt of phosphorescent brightness streaked towards them, and Keeler threw herself and Sindermann flat as it blasted the shelf beside them, sending flaming books and splintered chunks of wood flying. The horrifying monster loped through the stacks on long, elastic limbs, its speed and agility incredible, and Keeler could see that it was circling around to get behind them.

She dragged Sindermann to his feet as she heard the monster's maddening laughter cackling behind her. The iterator seemed to have regained some measure of his senses after her punch, and once again, they ran between the twisting, narrow rows of shelves towards the chamber's exit. Behind her, she could hear the whoosh of flames as the horror squeezed its body into the row and books erupted into geysers of pink fire.

The end of the row was just ahead of her and she almost laughed as she heard the claxons that warned of a fire screech in alarm. Surely, someone would come to help them now?

They burst from the end of the row and Sindermann stumbled, again carrying her to the floor with him. They fell in a tangle of limbs, scrambling desperately to put some distance between them and the loathsome monster.

Keeler rolled onto her back as it pushed itself from the row of shelves, its rippling bulk undulating with roiling internal motion. Leering eyes and wide, fang-filled mouths erupted across its amorphous body, and she screamed as it vomited a breath of searing blue fire towards her.

Though she knew it would do no good, she closed her eyes and threw her arms up to ward off the flames, but a sudden silence enveloped her and the expected burning agony never hit.

'Hurry!' said a trembling voice. 'I cannot hold it much longer.'

Keeler turned and saw the white robed form of the *Vengeful Spirit's* Mistress of Astropaths, Ing Mae Sing, standing in the archive chamber's doorway with her hands outstretched before her.

'HORUS, MY BROTHER,' said Magnus. 'You must not believe whatever he has told you. It is lies, all of it. Lies that disguise his sinister purpose.'

'Those with courage and character to speak the truth always seem sinister to the ignorant,' snarled Erebus. 'You dare speak of lies while you stand before us in the warp? How can this be without the use of sorcery? Sorcery you were expressly forbidden to practise by the Emperor himself.'

'Do not presume to judge me, whelp!' shouted Magnus, hurling a glittering ball of fire towards the first chaplain. Horus watched as the flame streaked towards Erebus and enveloped him, but as the fire died, he saw that Erebus was unharmed, his armour not so much as scratched, and his skin unblemished.

Erebus laughed. 'You are too far away, Magnus. Your powers cannot reach me here.'

Horus watched as Magnus hurled bolt after bolt of lightning from his fingertips, amazed and horrified to see his brother employing such powers. Though all the Legions had once had Librarius divisions that trained warriors to tap into the power of the warp, they had been disbanded after the Emperor's decree at the Council of Nikaea.

Clearly, Magnus had paid that order no mind, and such conceit staggered Horus.

Eventually his cyclopean brother recognised that his powers were having no effect on Erebus and he dropped his hands to his side.

'You see,' said Erebus, turning to Horus, 'he cannot be trusted.'

'Nor can you, Erebus,' said Horus. 'You come to me cloaked in the identity of another, you claim my brother Magnus is naught but some warp beast set upon devouring me, and then you speak to him as though he is exactly as he seems. If he is here by sorcery, then how else can you be here?'

Erebus paused, caught in his lie and said, 'You are right, my lord. The sorcery of the Serpent Lodge has sent me to you to help you, and to offer you this chance of life. The serpent priestess had to cut my throat to do it and once I return to the world of flesh I will kill the bitch for that, but know that everything I have shown you is real. You saw it yourself and you know the truth.'

Magnus towered over the figure of Erebus. His crimson mane shook with fury, but Horus saw that he kept tight rein on his anger as he spoke.

'The future is not set, Horus. Erebus may have shown you *a* future, but that is only one possible future. It is not absolute. Have faith in that.'

'Pah!' sneered Erebus. 'Faith is just another way of not wanting to know what is true.'

'You think I don't know that, Magnus?' snapped Horus. 'I know of the warp and the tricks it can play with the mind. I am not stupid. I knew that this was not Sejanus just as I know that without a context, everything I have seen here is meaningless.'

Horus saw the crestfallen look on Erebus's face and laughed. 'You must take me for a fool, Erebus, if you thought that such simple parlour tricks would bewitch me to your cause.'

'My brother,' smiled Magnus. 'You are a wonder to me.'

'Be quiet,' snarled Horus. 'You are no better than Erebus. You will not manipulate me like this, for I am Horus. I am the Warmaster!'

Horus relished their confusion.

One was his brother, the other a warrior he had counted as a valued counsellor and devoted follower. He had sorely misjudged them both.

'I can trust neither of you,' he said. 'I am Horus and I make my own fate.'

Erebus stepped towards him with his hands outstretched in supplication. 'You should know that I came to you at the behest of my lord and master, Lorgar. He already has knowledge of the Emperor's quest to ascend to godhood, and has sworn himself to the powers of the warp. When the Emperor rejected Lorgar's worship, he found other gods all too willing to accept his devotion. My primarch's power has grown tenfold and it is but a fraction of the power that could be yours were you to pledge yourself to their cause.'

'He lies!' cried Magnus. 'Lorgar is loyal. He would never turn against the Emperor.'

Horus listened to Erebus's words and knew with utter certainty that he spoke the truth.

Lorgar, his most beloved brother had already embraced the power of the warp? Warring emotions vied for supremacy within him, disappointment, anger and, if he was honest, a spark of jealousy that Lorgar should have been chosen first.

If wise Lorgar would choose such powers as patrons, was there not some merit in that?

'Horus,' said Magnus, 'I am running out of time. Please be strong, my brother. Think of what this mongrel dog is asking you to do. He would have you spit on your oaths of loyalty. He is forcing you to betray the Emperor and turn on your brother Astartes! You must trust the Emperor to do what is right.'

'The Emperor plays dice with the fate of the galaxy,' countered Erebus, 'and he throws them where they cannot be seen.'

'Horus, please!' cried Magnus, his voice taking on a ghostly quality as his image began to fade. 'You must not do this or all we have fought for will be cast to ruin forever! You cannot do this terrible thing!'

'Is it so terrible?' asked Erebus. 'It is but a small thing really. Deliver the Emperor to the gods of the warp, and unlimited power can be yours. I told you before that they have no interest in the realms of men, and that promise still holds true. The galaxy will be yours to rule over as the new Master of Mankind.'

'Enough!' roared Horus and the world was silence. 'I have made my choice.'

KEELER HELPED KYRIL Sindermann to his feet, and together they fled through the archive chamber's door. Ing Mae Sing's trembling arms were still outstretched, and Keeler could feel waves of psychic cold radiating from her with the effort of holding the horror within the chamber at bay.

'Close... the... door,' said Ing Mae Sing through gritted teeth. Veins stood out on her neck and forehead, and her porcelain features were lined with pain. Keeler didn't need to be told twice, and she dropped Sindermann to get the door, as Ing Mae Sing backed away with slow, shuffling steps.

'Now!' shouted the astropath, dropping her arms. Keeler hauled on the door as the roaring, seething laughter of the beast swelled once again. Alarm claxons and its shrieks of insanity filled her ears as the door swung shut.

Something heavy impacted on the other side, and she could feel its raw heat through the metal. Ing Mae Sing helped her, but the astropath was too frail to be of much use and Keeler knew they couldn't hold the door for long.

'What did you do?' demanded Ing Mae Sing.

'I don't know,' gasped Keeler. 'The iterator was reading from a book and that... thing just appeared from nowhere. What in the name of the Emperor is it?'

'A beast from beyond the gates of the Empyrean,' said Ing Mae Sing as the door shook with another burning impact. 'I felt the build-up of warp energy and got here as quickly as I could.'

'Shame you weren't quicker, eh?' said Keeler. 'Can you send it back?'

Ing Mae Sing shook her head as a thrashing pseudo-pod of pinkish light flicked through the door and grazed Keeler's arm. Its touch seared through her robes and burned her skin. She screamed, flinching from the door, and gripped her arm in agony. The horror slammed into the door once more, and the impact sent her and the astropath flying.

Blinding light filled the passageway and Keeler shielded her eyes as she felt hands upon her shoulders, seeing that Kyril Sindermann was on his feet once more. He dragged her to her feet and said, 'I think I may have mistranslated part of the book...'

'You *think*?' snapped Keeler as they backed away from the abomination.

'Or maybe you translated it just perfectly,' said Ing Mae Sing, desperately scrambling away from the archive chamber's door. The beast of light oozed outwards in a slithering loop of limbs, each one thrashing in blind hunger. Multitudinous eyes rippled and popped like swollen boils across its rubbery skin as it came towards them once more.

'Oh Emperor protect us,' whispered Keeler as she turned to run.

The beast shuddered at her words, and Ing Mae Sing tugged on her sleeve, crying, 'Come on. We can't fight it.'

Euphrati Keeler suddenly realised that wasn't true and shrugged off the astropath's grip, reaching beneath her

robes to pull out the Imperial eagle she kept on the end
of her necklace. Its silver surfaces shone in the creature's
dazzling light, brighter than it had any reason to be, and
feeling hot in her palm. She smiled beatifically as she
understood with complete clarity that everything since
the Whisperheads had been preparing her for this
moment.

'Euphrati! Come on!' shouted Sindermann in terror.

A whipping limb formed from the horror's body and
another gout of blue fire roared towards her. Keeler
stood firm before it and held the symbol of her faith out
in front of her.

'The Emperor protects!' she screamed as the flames
washed over her.

RAIN FELL IN heavy sheets, and Loken could feel a tangi-
ble charge to the night air as dark thunderheads pressed
down on the tens of thousands of people gathered
around the Delphos. Lightning bolts fenced above him,
and the sense of anticipation was almost unbearable.

Nine days had passed since the Warmaster had been
interred within the Temple of the Serpent Lodge and
with each passing day the weather had worsened. Rain
fell in an unending downpour that threatened to wash
away the makeshift camps of the pilgrims, and booming
peals of thunder shook the sky like ringing hammer
blows.

The Warmaster had once told Loken that the cosmos
was too large and sterile for melodrama, but the skies
above Davin seemed determined to prove him wrong.

Torgaddon and Vipus stood with him at the top of the
steps and hundreds of the Sons of Horus followed
behind the three of them. Company captains, squad
leaders, file officers and warriors had come to Davin to
witness what would be either their salvation or their
undoing. They had marched through the singing

crowds, the dirty beige robes of remembrancers mixed in with army uniforms and civilian dress.

'Looks like the entire bloody Expedition's here,' Torgaddon had said as they marched up the steps, trampling trinkets and baubles left as offerings to the Warmaster beneath their armoured boots.

From the top of the processional steps, Loken could see the same group he had faced nine days previously, with the exception of Maloghurst who had returned to the ship some days before. Rain ran down Loken's face as a flash of lightning lit up the surface of the great bronze gateway, making it shine like a great wall of fire. The gathered Astartes warriors stood sentinel before it in the rain: Abaddon, Aximand, Targost, Sedirae, Ekaddon and Kibre.

None of them had abandoned their vigil before the gates of the Delphos, and Loken wondered if they had bothered to eat, drink or sleep since he had last laid eyes upon them.

'What do we do now, Garvi?' asked Vipus.

'We join our brothers and wait.'

'Wait for what?'

'We'll know that when it happens,' said Torgaddon. 'Won't we, Garvi?'

'I certainly hope so, Tarik,' replied Loken. 'Come on.'

The three of them set off towards the gateway, the thunder echoing from the massive structure's sides and the snakes atop each pillar slithering with each flashing bolt of lightning.

Loken watched as his brothers in front of the gate came to stand in line at the edge of the rippling pool of water, the full moon reflected in its black surface. Horus Aximand had once called it an omen. Was it again? Loken didn't know whether to hope that it was or not.

The Sons of Horus followed their captains down the wide processional in their hundreds, and Loken kept a grip on his temper, knowing that if things went ill here, there would almost certainly be bloodshed.

The thought horrified him and he hoped with all his heart that such a tragedy could be averted, but he would be ready if it came to war...

'Are you battle-ready?' hissed Loken to Torgaddon and Vipus on a discrete vox channel.

'Always,' nodded Torgaddon. 'Full load on every man.'

'Yes,' said Vipus. 'You really think...'

'No,' said Loken, 'but be ready in case we need to fight. Keep your humours balanced and it will not come to that.'

'You too, Garvi,' warned Torgaddon.

The long column of Astartes warriors reached the pool, the Warmaster's bearers standing on its opposite side, stoic and unrepentant.

'Loken,' said Serghar Targost. 'Are you here to fight us?'

'No,' said Loken, seeing that, like them, the others were locked and loaded. 'We've come to see what happens. It's been nine days, Serghar.'

'It has indeed,' nodded Targost.

'Where is Erebus? Have you seen him since you put the Warmaster in this place?'

'No,' growled Abaddon, his long hair unbound and his eyes hostile. 'We have not. What does that have to do with anything?'

'Calm yourself, Ezekyle,' said Torgaddon. 'We're all here for the same thing.'

'Loken,' said Aximand, 'there has been bad blood between us all, but that must end now. For us to turn on one another would dishonour the Warmaster's memory.'

'You speak as though he's already dead, Horus.'

'We will see,' said Aximand. 'This was always a forlorn hope, but it was all we had.'

Loken looked into the haunted eyes of Horus Aximand, seeing the despair and doubt that plagued him, and felt his anger towards his brother diminish.

Would he have acted any differently had he been present when the decision to inter the Warmaster had been taken? Could he in all honesty say that he would not have accepted the decision of his friends and peers if the situation had been reversed? He and Horus Aximand might even now be standing on different sides of the moon shimmered pool.

'Then let us wait as brothers united in hope,' said Loken, and Aximand smiled gratefully.

The palpable tension lifted from the confrontation and Loken, Torgaddon and Vipus marched around the pool to stand with their brothers before the vast gate.

A dazzling bolt of lightning reflected from the gate as the Mournival stood shoulder to shoulder with one another, and a thunderous boom, that had nothing to do with the storm, split the night.

Loken saw a dark line appear in the centre of the gate as the thunder was suddenly silenced and the lightning stilled in the space of a heartbeat. The sky was mystifyingly calm, as though the storm had blown out and the heavens had paused in their revelries better to witness the unfolding drama on the planet below.

Slowly, the gate began to open.

THE FLAMES BATHED Euphrati Keeler, but they were cold and she felt no pain from them. The silver eagle blazed in her hand, thrust before her like a talisman, and she felt a wondrous energy fill her, rushing through her from the tips of her toes to the shorn ends of her hair.

'The power of the Emperor commands you, abomination!' she yelled, the words unfamiliar, but feeling right.

Ing Mae Sing and Kyril Sindermann watched her in amazement as she took one step, and then another, towards the horror. The monster was transfixed; whether by her courage or her faith, she didn't know, but whatever the reason, she was thankful for it.

Its limbs flailed as though some invisible force attacked it, its screeching laughter turning into the pitiful wails of a child.

'In the name of the Emperor, go back to the warp, you bastard!' said Keeler, her confidence growing as the substance of the monster diminished, skins of light shearing away from its body. The silver eagle grew hotter in her hand and she could feel the skin of her palms blistering under its heat.

Ing Mae Sing joined her, adding her own powers to Keeler's assault on the monster. The air around the astropath grew colder and Keeler moved her hand close to the psyker in the hopes of cooling the blazing eagle.

The monster's internal light was fading and flickering, its nebulous outline spitting embers of light as though it fought to hold onto existence. The light from Keeler's eagle outshone its hellish illumination tenfold and the entire corridor was bleached shadowless with its brilliance.

'Whatever you're doing, keep doing it!' cried Ing Mae Sing. 'It's weakening.'

Keeler tried to answer, but found that she had no voice left. The wondrous energy that had filled her was now streaming from her through the eagle, taking her own strength with it.

She tried to drop the eagle, but it was stuck fast to her hand, the red hot metal fusing itself to her skin.

From behind her, Keeler heard the clatter of armoured ship's crew and their cries of astonishment at the scene before them.

'Please…' she whispered as her legs gave out and she collapsed to the floor.

The blazing light faded from her hand and the last things she saw were the disintegrating mass of the horror and Sindermann's rapturous face staring down at her in wonder.

✠ ✠ ✠

THE ONLY SOUND was that of the gate. Loken's entire existence shrank to the growing darkness between its two halves, as he held his breath and waited to see what might lie beyond. The gates swung fully open and he risked a glance at his fellow Sons of Horus, seeing the same desperate hope in every face.

Not a single sound disturbed the night, and Loken felt melancholy rise in him as he realised that this must simply be the automated opening of the temple doors.

The Warmaster was dead.

A sick dread settled on Loken and his head sank to his chest.

Then he heard the sound of footsteps, and looked up to see the gleam of white and gold plate emerge from the darkness.

Horus strode from the Delphos with his cloak of royal purple billowing behind him and his golden sword held high above him.

The eye in the centre of his breastplate blazed a fiery red and the laurels at his forehead framed features that were beautiful and terrible in their magnificence.

The Warmaster stood before them, unbowed and more vital than ever, the sheer physicality of his presence robbing every one of them of speech.

Horus smiled and said, 'You are a sight for sore eyes, my sons.'

Torgaddon punched the air in elation and shouted, 'Lupercal!'

He laughed and ran towards the Warmaster, breaking the spell that had fallen on the rest of them.

The Mournival rushed to this reunion with their lord and master, joyous cries of 'Lupercal!' erupting from the throat of every Astartes warrior as word spread back through the files and into the crowd surrounding the temple.

The pilgrims around the Delphos took up the chant and ten thousand throats were soon crying the Warmaster's name.

'Lupercal! Lupercal! Lupercal!'

The walls of the crater shook to deafening cheers that went on long into the night.

PART FOUR
CRUSADE'S END

EIGHTEEN

Brothers/Assassination/This turbulent poet

SILVER TRAILS OF molten metal had solidified on the breastplate and Mersadie Oliton had learned enough in her time with the Expedition fleet to know that it would require the aid of Legion artificers to repair it properly. Loken sat before her in the training halls, while other officers of the Sons of Horus were scattered throughout it, repairing armour and cleaning bolters or chainswords. Loken was melancholic, and she was quick to notice his sombre mood.

'Is the war not going well?' she asked as he removed the firing chamber from his bolter and pulled a cleaning rag through it. He looked up and she was struck by how much he had aged in the last ten months, thinking that she would need to revise her chapter on the immortality of the Astartes.

Since opening hostilities against the Auretian Technocracy, the Astartes had seen some of the hardest fighting since the Great Crusade had begun, and it was beginning to tell on many of them. There had been few opportunities to spend time with Loken during the war, and it was only now that she truly appreciated how much he had changed.

'It's not that,' said Loken. 'The Brotherhood is virtually destroyed and the warriors of Angron will soon storm the Iron Citadel. The war will be over within the week.'

'Then why so gloomy?'

Loken glanced around to see who else was in the training halls and leaned in close to her.

'Because this is a war we should not be fighting.'

Upon Horus's recovery on Davin, the fleet of the 63rd Expedition had paused just long enough to recover its personnel from the planet's surface and install a new Imperial commander from the ranks of the Army. Like Rakris before him, the new Lord Governor Elect, Tomaz Vesalias, had begged not to be left behind, but with Davin once again compliant, Imperial rule had to be maintained.

Before the fighting on Davin, the Warmaster's fleet had been en route to Sardis and a rendezvous with the 203rd Fleet. The plan was to undertake a campaign of compliance in the Caiades Cluster, but instead of keeping that rendezvous, the Warmaster had sent his compliments and ordered the 203rd's Master of Ships to muster with the 63rd Expedition in a binary cluster designated Drakonis Three Eleven.

The Warmaster told no one why he chose this locale, and none of the stellar cartographers could find reports from any previous expedition as to why the place might be of interest.

Sixteen weeks of warp travel had seen them translate into a system alive with electronic chatter. Two planets and their shared moon in the second system were discovered to be inhabited, glinting communications satellites ringing each one, and interplanetary craft flitting between them.

More thrilling still, communications with orbital monitors revealed this civilisation to be human, another lost branch of the old race – isolated these past centuries. The arrival of the Crusade fleet had been greeted with understandable surprise, and then joy as the planet's inhabitants realised that their lonely existence was finally at an end.

Formal, face-to-face contact was not established for three days, in which time the 203rd Expedition under the command of Angron of the XII Legion, the World Eaters, translated in-system.

The first shots were fired six hours later.

THE NINTH MONTH of the war.

Bolter shells stitched a path towards Loken from the blazing muzzle of the bunker's gun. He ducked behind a shell-pocked cement column, feeling the impacts hammering through it and knowing that he didn't have much time until the gunfire chewed its way through.

'Garvi!' shouted Torgaddon, rolling from behind cover and shouldering his bolter. 'Go left, I've got you!'

Loken nodded and dived from behind the cover as Torgaddon opened up, his Astartes strength keeping the barrel level despite the bolter's fearsome recoil. Shells exploded in grey puffs of rockcrete at the bunker's firing slit and Loken heard screams of pain from within. Locasta moved up behind him and he heard the whoosh of flame units as warriors poured fire into the bunker.

More screams and the stink of flesh burned by chemical flame filled the air.

'Everyone back!' shouted Loken, getting to his feet and knowing what would come next.

Sure enough, the bunker mushroomed upwards with a thudding boom, its internal magazine cooking off as its internal sensors registered that its occupants were dead.

Heavy gunfire ripped through their position, a collapsed structure at the edge of the central precinct of the planet's towering city of steel and glass. Loken had marvelled at the city's elegance, and Peeter Egon Momus had declared it perfect when he had first seen the aerial scans. It didn't look perfect now.

Puffs of flickering detonations tore a line through the Astartes, and Loken dropped as the warrior with the flame unit disappeared in a column of fire. His armour kept him alive for a few seconds, but soon he was a burning statue, the armour joints fused, and Loken rolled onto his back to see a pair of speeding aircraft rolling around for another strafing run.

'Take those ships out!' yelled Loken as the craft, sleeker, more elegant Thunderhawk variants, turned their guns towards them once again.

The Astartes spread out as the under-slung gun pods erupted in fire, and a torrent shells tore through their position, ripping thick columns in two and sending up blinding clouds of grey dust. Two warriors ducked out from behind a fallen wall, one aiming a long missile tube in the rough direction of the flier while the other sighted on it with a designator.

The missile launched in a streaming cloud of bright propellant, leaping into the sky and speeding after the closest flier. The pilot saw it and tried to evade, but he was too close to the ground and the missile flew straight into his intake, blowing the craft apart from the inside.

Its blazing remains plummeted towards the ground as Vipus shouted, 'Incoming!'

Loken turned to rebuke him for stating the obvious when he saw that his friend wasn't talking about the remaining flier. Three tracked vehicles smashed over a low ceramic brick wall behind them, their thick armoured forward sections emblazoned with a pair of crossed lightning bolts.

Too late, Loken realised the fliers had been keeping them pinned in place while the armoured transports circled around to flank them. Through the smoking wreckage of the burning bunker, he could see blurred forms moving towards them, darting from cover to cover as they advanced. Locasta was caught between two enemy forces and the noose was closing in.

Loken chopped his hand at the approaching vehicles and the missile team turned to engage their new targets. Within seconds, one was a smoking wreck as a missile punched through its armour and its plasma core exploded inside.

'Tarik!' he shouted over the din of gunfire from nearby. 'Keep our front secure.'

Torgaddon nodded, moving forwards with five warriors. Leaving him to it, Loken turned back towards the armoured vehicles as they crunched to a halt, pintle-mounted bolters hammering them with shots. Two men fell, their armour cracked open by the heavy shells.

'Close on them!' ordered Loken as the frontal assault ramps lowered and the Brotherhood warriors within charged out. The first few times Loken had fought the Brotherhood, he'd felt a treacherous hesitation seize his limbs, but nine months of gruelling campaigning had pretty much cured him of that.

Each warrior was armoured in fully enclosed plate, silver like the knights of old, with red and black heraldry upon their shoulder guards. Their form and function was horribly similar to that of the Sons of Horus, and though the enemy warriors were smaller than the Astartes, they were nevertheless a distorted mirror of them.

Loken and the warriors of Locasta were upon them, the lead Brotherhood warriors raising their weapons in response to the wild charge. The blade of Loken's chainsword hacked through the nearest warrior's gun and cleaved into his breastplate. The Brotherhood scattered, but Loken didn't give them a chance to recover from their surprise, cutting them down in quick, brutal strokes.

These warriors might look like Astartes, but, up close, they were no match for even one of them.

He heard gunfire from behind, and heard Torgaddon issuing orders to the men under his command. Stuttering impacts on Loken's leg armour drove him to his knees and he swept his sword low, hacking the legs from the enemy warrior behind him. Blood jetted from the stumps of his legs as he fell, spraying Loken's armour red.

The vehicle began reversing, but Loken threw a pair of grenades inside, moving on as the dull crump of the detonations halted it in its tracks. Shadows loomed over them and he felt the booming footfalls of the Titans of the Legio Mortis as they marched past, crushing whole swathes of the city as they went. Buildings were smashed from their path, and though missiles and lasers reached up to them, the flare of their powerful void shields were proof against such attacks.

More gunfire and screams filled the battlefield, the enemy falling back from the fury of the Astartes counterattack. They were courageous, these warriors of the Brotherhood, but they were hopelessly optimistic if they thought that simply wearing a suit of power armour made a man the equal of an Astartes.

'Area secure,' came Torgaddon's voice over the suit vox. 'Where to now?'

'Nowhere,' replied Loken as the last enemy warrior was slain. 'This is our object point. We wait until the World Eaters get here. Once we hand off to them, we can move on. Pass the word.'

'Understood,' said Torgaddon.

Loken savoured the sudden quiet of the battlefield, the sounds of battle muted and distant as other companies fought their way through the city. He assigned Vipus to secure their perimeter and crouched beside the warrior whose legs he had cut off.

The man still lived, and Loken reached down to remove his helmet, a helmet so very similar to his own. He knew where the release catches were and slid the helm clear.

His enemy's face was pale from shock and blood loss, his eyes full of pain and hate, but there were no monstrously alien features beneath the helmet, simply ones as human as any member of the 63rd Expedition.

Loken could think of nothing to say to the man, and simply took off his own helmet and pulled the water-dispensing pipe from his gorget. He poured some clear, cold water over the man's face.

'I want nothing from you,' hissed the dying man.

'Don't speak,' said Loken. 'It will be over quickly.'

But the man was already dead.

'WHY SHOULDN'T WE be fighting this war?' asked Mersadie Oliton. 'You were there when they tried to assassinate the Warmaster.'

'I was there,' said Loken, putting down the cleaned firing chamber. 'I don't think I'll ever forget that moment.'

'Tell me about it.'

'It's not pretty,' warned Loken. 'You will think less of us when I tell you the truth of it.'

'You think so? A good documentarist remains objective at all times.'

'We'll see.'

THE AMBASSADORS OF the planet, which Loken had learned was named Aureus, had been greeted with all the usual pomp and ceremony accorded to a potentially friendly culture. Their vessels had glided onto the embarkation deck to surprised gasps as every warrior present recognised their uncanny similarity to Stormbirds.

The Warmaster was clad in his most regal armour, gold fluted and decorated with the Emperor's devices of lightning bolts and eagles. Unusually for an occasion such as this, he was armed with a sword and pistol, and Loken could feel the force of authority the Warmaster projected.

Alongside the Warmaster stood Maloghurst, robed in white, Regulus – his gold and steel augmetic body polished to a brilliant sheen – and First Captain Abbadon, who stood proudly with a detachment of hulking Justaerin Terminators.

It was a gesture to show strength and backing it up, three hundred Sons of Hours stood at parade rest behind the group, noble and regal in their bearing – the very image of the Great Crusade – and Loken had never been prouder of his illustrious heritage.

The doors of the craft opened with the hiss of decompression and Loken had his first glimpse of the Brotherhood.

A ripple of astonishment passed through the embarkation deck as twenty warriors in gleaming silver plate armour, the very image of the assembled Astartes, marched from the landing craft's interior in perfect formation, though Loken detected a stammer of surprise in them too. They carried weapons that looked very much like a standardissue boltgun, though in deference to their hosts, none had magazines fitted.

'Do you see that?' whispered Loken.

'No, Garvi, I've suddenly been struck blind,' replied Torgaddon. 'Of course I see them.'

'They look like Astartes!'

'There's a resemblance, I'll give you that, but they're far too short.'

'They're wearing power armour... How is that possible?'

'If you keep quiet we might find out,' said Torgaddon.

The warriors wheeled and formed up around a tall man wearing long red robes, whose features were half-flesh, half machine and whose eye was a blinking emerald gem. Walking with the aid of a golden cog-topped staff, he stepped onto the deck with the pleased expression of one who finds his expectations more than met.

The Auretian delegation made its way towards Horus, and Loken could sense the weight of history pressing in on this moment. This meeting was the very embodiment of what the Great Crusade represented: lost brothers from across the galaxy once again meeting in the spirit of companionship.

The red robed man bowed before the Warmaster and said, 'Do I have the honour of addressing the Warmaster Horus?'

'You do, sir, but please do not bow,' replied Horus. 'The honour is mine.'

The man smiled, pleased at the courtesy. 'Then if you will permit me, I will introduce myself. I am Emory Salignac, Fabricator Consul to the Auretian Technocracy. On behalf of my people, may I be the first to welcome you to our worlds.'

Loken had seen Regulus's excitement at the sight of Salignac's augmetics, but upon hearing the full title of this new empire, his enthusiasm overcame the protocol of the moment.

'Consul,' said Regulus, his voice blaring and unnatural. 'Do I understand that your society is founded on the knowledge of technical data?'

Horus turned to the adept of the Mechanicum and whispered something that Loken didn't hear, but Regulus nodded and took a step back.

'I apologise for the adept's forthright questions, but I hope you might forgive his outburst, given that our warriors appear to share certain... similarities in their wargear.'

'These are the warriors of the Brotherhood,' explained Salignac. 'They are our protectors and our most elite soldiers. It honours me to have them as my guardians here.'

'How is it they are armoured so similarly to my own warriors?'

Salignac appeared to be confused by the question and said, 'You expected something different, my lord Warmaster? The construct machines our ancestors brought with them from Terra are at the heart of our society and provide us with the boon of technology. Though advanced, they do tend towards a certain uniformity of creation.'

The silence that greeted the consul's words was brittle and fragile, and Horus held up his hand to still the inevitable outburst from Regulus.

'Construct machines?' asked Horus, a cold edge of steel in his voice. 'STC machines?'

'I believe that was their original designation, yes,' agreed Salignac, lowering his staff and holding it towards the Warmaster. 'You have–'

Emory Salignac never got to finish his sentence as Horus took a step backward and drew his pistol. Loken saw the muzzle flash and watched Emory Salignac's head explode as the bolt blew out the back of his skull.

'Yes,' said Mersadie Oliton. 'The staff was some kind of energy weapon that could have penetrated the Warmaster's armour. We've been told this.'

Loken shook his head. 'No, there was no weapon.'

'Of course there was,' insisted Oliton, 'and when the consul's assassination attempt failed, his Brotherhood warriors attacked the Warmaster.'

Loken put down his bolter and said, 'Mersadie, forget what you have been told. There was no weapon, and after the Warmaster killed the consul, the Brotherhood only tried to escape. Their weapons were not loaded and they could not have fought us with any hope of success.'

'They were unarmed?'

'Yes.'

'So what did you do?'

'We killed them,' said Loken. 'They were unarmed, but we were not. Abaddon's Justaerin cut half a dozen of them down before they even knew what had happened. I led Locasta forward and we gunned them down as they tried to board their ship.'

'But why?' asked Oliton, horrified at his casual description of such slaughter.

'Because the Warmaster ordered it.'

'No, I mean why would the Warmaster shoot the consul if he wasn't armed? It doesn't make any sense.'

'No, it doesn't,' agreed Loken. 'I watched him kill the consul and I saw his face after we had killed the Brotherhood warriors.'

'What did you see?'

Loken hesitated, as though not sure he should answer. At last he said, 'I saw him smile.'

'Smile?'

'Yes,' said Loken, 'as if the killings had been part of his plan all along. I don't know why, but Horus *wants* this war.'

TORGADDON FOLLOWED THE hooded warrior down the darkened companionway towards the empty reserve armoury chamber. Serghar Targost had called a lodge meeting and Torgaddon was apprehensive, not liking the sensation one bit. He had attended only a single meeting since Davin, the quiet order no longer a place of relaxation for him. Though the Warmaster had been returned to them, the lodge's actions had smacked of subterfuge and such behaviour sat ill with Tarik Torgaddon.

The robed figure he followed was unknown to him, young and clearly in awe of the legendary Mournival officer, which suited Torgaddon fine. The warrior had clearly only achieved full Astartes status recently, but Torgaddon knew that he would already be an experienced fighter. There was no room for inexperience among the Sons of Horus, the months of war on Aureus making veterans or corpses of those raised from the novitiate and scout auxiliaries. The Brotherhood might not have the abilities of the Astartes, but the Technocracy could call on millions of them, and they fought with courage and honour.

It only made killing them all the harder. Fighting the megarachnids of Murder had been easy, their alien physiognomy repulsive to look upon and therefore easy to destroy.

The Brotherhood, though... they were so like the Sons of Horus that it was as though two Legions fought each other in some brutal civil war. Not one amongst the Legion had failed to experience a moment of pause at such a terrible image.

Torgaddon was saddened as he knew that, like the interex before them, the Brotherhood and the Auretian Technocracy would be destroyed.

A voice from the darkness ahead shook him from his sombre thoughts.

'Who approaches?'

'Two souls,' replied the young warrior.

'What are your names?' the figure asked, but Torgaddon did not recognise the voice.

'I can't say,' said Torgaddon.

'Pass, friends.'

Torgaddon and the warrior passed the guardian of the portal and entered the reserve armoury. The vaulted chamber was much larger than the aft hold where meetings had commonly been held, and when he stepped into the flickering candlelit space, he could see why Targost had chosen it.

Hundreds of warriors filled the armoury, each one hooded and holding a flickering candle. Serghar Targost, Ezekyle Abaddon, Horus Aximand and Maloghurst stood at the centre of the gathering; to one side of them stood First Chaplain Erebus.

Torgaddon looked around at the assembled Astartes and couldn't escape the feeling that this meeting had been called for his benefit.

'You've been busy, Serghar,' he said. 'Been on a recruiting drive?'

'Since the Warmaster's recovery on Davin our stock has risen somewhat,' agreed Targost.

'So I see. Must be tricky keeping it secret now.'

'Amongst the Legion we no longer operate under a veil of secrecy.'

'Then why the same pantomime to enter?'

Targost smiled apologetically. 'Tradition, you understand?'

Torgaddon shrugged and crossed the chamber to stand before Erebus. He stared with undisguised hostility towards the first chaplain and said, 'You have been keeping a low profile since Davin. Captain Loken wants to speak with you.'

'I'm sure he does,' replied Erebus, 'but I am not under his command. I do not answer to him.'

'Then you'll answer to me, you bastard!' snapped Torgaddon, drawing his combat knife from beneath his robes and holding it to Erebus's neck. Cries of alarm sounded at the sight of the knife, and Torgaddon saw the line of an old scar running across Erebus's neck.

'Looks like someone's already tried to cut your throat,' hissed Torgaddon. 'They didn't do a very good job of it, but don't worry, I won't make the same mistake.'

'Tarik!' cried Serghar Targost. 'You brought a weapon? You know they are forbidden.'

'Erebus owes us all an explanation,' said Torgaddon, pressing the knife against Erebus's jaw. 'This snake stole a kinebrach weapon from the Hall of Devices on Xenobia. He's the reason the negotiations with the interex failed. He's the reason the Warmaster was injured.'

'No, Tarik,' said Abaddon, moving to stand next to him and placing a hand on his wrist. 'The negotiations with the interex failed because they were meant to. The interex consorted with xenos breeds. They integrated with them. We could never have made peace with such people.'

'Ezekyle speaks the truth,' said Erebus.

'Shut your mouth,' snapped Torgaddon.

'Torgaddon, put the knife down,' said Horus Aximand. 'Please.'

Reluctantly, Torgaddon lowered his arm, the pleading tone of his Mournival brother making him realise the enormity of what he was doing in holding a knife to the throat of another Astartes, even one as untrustworthy as Erebus.

'We are not finished,' warned Torgaddon, pointing the blade at Erebus.

'I will be ready,' promised the Word Bearer.

'Both of you be silent,' said Targost. 'We have urgent matters to discuss that require you to listen. These last few months of war have been hard on everyone and no one fails to see the great tragedy inherent in fighting brother humans who look so very like us. Tensions are high, but we must remember that our purpose among the stars is to kill those who will not join with us.'

Torgaddon frowned at such a blunt mission statement, but said nothing as Targost continued his speech. 'We are Astartes and we were created to kill and conquer the galaxy. We have done all that has been asked of us and more, fighting for over two centuries to forge the new Imperium from the ashes of Old Night. We have destroyed planets, torn down cultures and wiped out entire species all because we were so ordered. We are killers, pure and simple, and we take pride in being the best at what we do!'

Cheering broke out at Targost's pronouncements, fists punching the air and hammering bulkheads, but Torgaddon had seen the iterators in action enough times to recognise cued applause. This speech was for his benefit and his alone, of that he was now certain.

'Now, as the Great Crusade draws to a close, we are lambasted for our ability to kill. Malcontents and agitators stir up trouble in our wake with bleating cries that we are too brutal, too savage and too violent. Our very own Lord Commander of the Army, Hektor Varvarus, demands blood for the actions of our grief-stricken brothers who returned the Warmaster to us while he lay dying. The traitor Varvarus demands that we be called to account for these regrettable deaths, and that we be punished for trying to save the Warmaster.'

Torgaddon flinched at the word 'traitor', shocked that Targost would openly use such an incendiary word to describe an officer as respected as Varvarus. But, as Torgaddon looked at the faces of the warriors around him, he saw only agreement with Targost's sentiment.

'Even civilians now feel they have the right to call us to account,' said Horus Aximand, taking up where Targost had left off and holding up a handful of parchments. 'Dissenters and conspirators amongst the remembrancers spread lies and propaganda that paint us as little better than barbarians.'

Aximand circled amongst the gathering, passing out the pamphlets as he spoke, 'This one is called *The Truth is all We Have* and it calls us murderers and savages. This turbulent poet mocks us in verse, brothers! These lies circulate amongst the fleet every day.'

Torgaddon took a pamphlet from Aximand and quickly scanned the paper, already knowing who had written it. Its contents were scathing, but hardly amounted to sedition.

'And this one!' cried Aximand. 'The *Lectitio Divinitatus* speaks of the Emperor as a god. A god! Can you imagine anything so ridiculous? These lies fill the heads of those we are fighting for. We fight and die for them and this is our reward: vilification and hate. I tell you this, my brothers, if we do not act now, the ship of the Imperium, which has weathered all storms, will sink through the mutiny of those onboard.'

Shouts of anger and calls for action echoed from the armoury walls, and Torgaddon did not like the ugly desire for reciprocity that he saw on the faces of his fellow warriors.

'Nice speech,' said Torgaddon when the roars of anger had diminished, 'but why don't you get to the point? I have a company to make ready for a combat drop.'

'Always the straight talker, eh, Tarik?' said Aximand. 'That is why you are respected and valued. That is why we need you with us, brother.'

'With you? What are you talking about?'

'Have you not heard a word that was said?' asked Maloghurst, limping over to where Torgaddon stood. 'We are under threat from within our own ranks. The enemy within, Tarik, it is the most insidious foe we have yet faced.'

'You'll need to speak plainly, Mal,' said Abaddon. 'Tarik needs it spelled out for him.'

'Up yours, Ezekyle,' said Torgaddon.

'I have learned that the remembrancer who writes these treasonous missives is called Ignace Karkasy,' said Maloghurst. 'He must be silenced.'

'Silenced? What do you mean by that?' asked Torgaddon. 'Given a slap on the wrist? Told not to be such a naughty boy? Something like that?'

'You know what I mean, Tarik,' stated Maloghurst.

'I do, but I want to hear you say it.'

'Very well, if you wish me to be direct, then I will be. Karkasy must die.'

'You're crazy, Mal, do you know that? You're talking about murder,' said Torgaddon.

'It's not murder when you kill your enemy, Tarik,' said Abaddon. 'It's war.'

'You want to make war on a poet?' laughed Torgaddon. 'Oh, they'll tell tales of that for centuries, Ezekyle. Can't you hear what you're saying? Anyway, the remembrancer is under Garviel's protection. You touch Karkasy and he'll hand your head to the Warmaster himself.'

A guilty silence enveloped the group at the mention of Loken's name, and the lodge members in front of Torgaddon shared an uneasy look.

Finally, Maloghurst said, 'I had hoped it would not come to this, but you leave us no choice, Tarik.'

Torgaddon gripped the hilt of his combat knife tightly, wondering if he would need to fight his way clear of his brothers.

'Put up your knife, we're not about to attack you,' snapped Maloghurst, seeing the tension in his eyes.

'Go on,' said Torgaddon, keeping a grip on the knife anyway. 'What did you hope it would not come to?'

'Hektor Varvarus claims to have spoken with the Council of Terra about events surrounding the Warmaster's injury, and it is certain that if he has not yet informed Malcador the Sigillite of the deaths on the embarkation deck, he soon will. He petitions the War-master daily with demands that there be justice.'

'And what has the Warmaster told him? I was there too. So was Ezekyle. You too Little Horus.'

'And so was Loken,' finished Erebus, joining the oth-ers. 'He led you onto the embarkation deck and he led the way through the crowd.'

Torgaddon took a step towards Erebus. 'I told you to be quiet!'

He turned from Erebus, and despair filled him as he saw acquiescent looks on his brothers' faces. They had already accepted the idea of throwing Garviel Loken to the wolves.

'You can't seriously be considering this, Mal,' protested Torgaddon. 'Ezekyle? Horus? You would betray your sworn Mournival brother?'

'He already betrays us by allowing this remembrancer to spread lies,' said Aximand.

'No, I won't do it,' swore Torgaddon.

'You must,' said Aximand. 'Only if you, Ezekyle and I swear oaths that it was Loken who orchestrated the mas-sacre will Varvarus accept him as guilty.'

'So, that's what this is all about, is it?' asked Torgad-don. 'Two birds with one stone? Make Garviel your scapegoat, and you're free to murder Karkasy. How can you even consider this? The Warmaster will never agree to it.'

'Bluntly put, but you are mistaken if you think the Warmaster will not agree,' said Targost. 'This was his sug-gestion.'

'No!' cried Torgaddon. 'He wouldn't…'

'It can be no other way, Tarik,' said Maloghurst. 'The survival of the Legion is at stake.'

Torgaddon felt something inside him die at the thought of betraying his friend. His heart broke at mak-ing a choice between Loken and the Sons of Horus, but no sooner had the thought surfaced than he knew what he had to do.

He sheathed his combat knife and said, 'If betrayal and murder is needed to save the Legion then perhaps it does not deserve to survive! Garviel Loken is our brother and you would betray his honour like this? I spit on you for even thinking it.'

A horrified gasp spread through the chamber and angry mutterings closed in on Torgaddon.

'Think carefully, Tarik,' warned Maloghurst. 'You are either with us or against us.'

Torgaddon reached into his robes and tossed something silver and gleaning at Maloghurst's feet. The lodge medal glinted in the candlelight.

'Then I am against you,' said Torgaddon.

NINETEEN

Isolated/Allies/Eagle's wing

PETRONELLA SAT AT her escritoire, filling page after page with her cramped handwriting, the spidery script tight and intense. Her dark hair was unbound and fell around her shoulders in untidy ringlets. Her complexion had the sallow appearance of one who has not stepped outside her room for many months, let alone seen daylight.

A pile of papers beside her was testament to the months she had spent in her luxurious cabin, though its luxury was a far cry from what it had been when she had first arrived on the *Vengeful Spirit*. The bed was unmade and her clothes lay strewn where she had discarded them before bed.

Her maidservant, Babeth, had done what she could to encourage her mistress to pause in her labours, but Petronella would have none of it. The words of the Warmaster's valediction had to be transcribed and interpreted in the most minute detail if she was to do his confession any justice. Even though his words had turned out not to be his last, she knew they deserved to be recorded, for she had tapped into the Warmaster's innermost thoughts. She had teased out information no one had contemplated before, secrets of the primarchs that had not seen the light of day since the Great Crusade had begun and truths that would rock the Imperium to its very core.

That such things should perhaps remain buried had occurred to her only once in her lonely sojourn, but she was the Palatina Majoria of House Carpinus and such questions had no meaning. Knowledge and truth were all that mattered and it would be for future generations to judge whether she had acted correctly.

She had a dim memory of speaking of these incredible truths to some poet or other in a dingy bar many months ago while very drunk, but she had no idea what had passed between them. He had not tried to contact her afterwards, so she could only assume that he hadn't tried to seduce her, or that she hadn't in fact been seduced. It was immaterial; she had locked herself away since the beginning of the war with the Technocracy, trawling every fragment of her mnemonic implants for the words and turns of phrase that the Warmaster had used.

She was writing too much, she knew, but damn the word count, her tale was too important to be constrained by the bindings of a mere book. She would tell the tale for as long as it took in the telling… but there was something missing.

As the weeks and months had passed, the gnawing sensation that something wasn't gelling grew from a suspicion to a certainty, and it had taken her until recently to realise what that was: context.

All she had were the Warmaster's words, there was no framework to hang them upon and without that, everything was meaningless. Finally realising what was amiss, she sought out Astartes warriors at every opportunity, but hit her first real obstacle in this regard.

No one was speaking to her.

As soon as any of her subjects knew what Petronella wanted, or who she was, they would clam up and refuse to speak another word, excusing themselves from her presence with polite abruptness.

Everywhere she had turned, she ran into walls of silence, and despite repeated entreaties to the office of the Warmaster to intervene, she was getting nowhere. Every one of her requests for an audience with the Warmaster was declined, and she soon began to despair of ever finding a means of telling her tale.

Inspiration as to how to break this deadlock had come yesterday after yet another afternoon of abject failure. As always, Maggard escorted her, clad in his golden battle armour and armed with his Kirlian rapier and pistol. After the fighting on Davin, Maggard had made a speedy recovery, and Petronella had noticed a more cocksure swagger to his step. She also noticed that he was treated with more respect around the ship than she was. Of course, such a state of affairs was intolerable, despite the fact that it made his vigour as her concubine that much more forceful and pleasurable.

An Astartes warrior had nodded in respect as Petronella despondently travelled along the upper decks of the ship towards her stateroom. She had made to nod back, before realising that the Astartes had been paying his respects to Maggard, not her.

A scroll upon the Astartes's shoulder guard bore a green crescent moon, marking him out as a veteran of the Davin campaign and thus no doubt aware of Maggard's fighting prowess.

Indignation surged to the surface, but before Petronella said anything, an idea began to form and she hurried back to the stateroom.

Petronella had stood Maggard in the centre of the room and said, 'It's so obvious to me now, shame on me for not thinking of this sooner.'

Maggard looked puzzled, and she moved closer to him, stroking her hand down his moulded breastplate. He seemed uncomfortable with this, but she pressed on, knowing that he would do anything for her in fear of reprisal should he refuse.

'It's because I am a woman,' she said. 'I'm not part of their little club.'

She moved behind him and stood on her tiptoes, placing her hands on his shoulders. 'I'm not a warrior. I've never killed anyone, well, not myself, and that's what they respect: killing. You've killed men, haven't you Maggard?'

He nodded curtly.

'Lots?'

Maggard nodded again and she laughed. 'I'm sure they know that too. You can't speak to boast of your prowess, but I'm sure the Astartes know it. Even the ones that weren't on Davin will be able to see that you're a killer.'

Maggard licked his lips, keeping his golden eyes averted from her.

'I want you to go amongst them,' she ordered. 'Let them see you. Inveigle yourself into their daily rituals. Find out all you can about them and each day we will use the mnemo-quill to transcribe what you've discovered. You're mute, so they'll think you simple. Let them. They will be less guarded if they think they humour a dolt.'

She could see that Maggard was unhappy with this task, but his happiness was of no consequence to her and she had sent him out the very next morning.

She had spent the rest of the day writing, sending Babeth out for food and water when she realised she was hungry, and trying different stylistic approaches to the introduction of her manuscript.

The door to her stateroom opened and Petronella looked up from her work. The chronometer set into the escritoire told her that it was late afternoon, ship time.

She swivelled in her chair to see Maggard enter her room and smiled, reaching over to pull her data-slate close and then lifting the mnemo-quill from the Lethe-well.

'You spent time with the Astartes?' she asked.

Maggard nodded.

'Good,' said Petronella, sitting the reactive nib on the slate and clearing her mind of her own thoughts.

'Tell me everything,' she commanded, as the quill began to scratch out his thoughts.

THE WARMASTER'S SANCTUM was silent save for the occasional hissing, mechanical hum from the exo-armature of Regulus's body, and the rustle of fabric as Maloghurst shifted position. Both stood behind the Warmaster, who sat in his chair at the end of the long table, his hands steepled before him and his expression thunderous.

'The Brotherhood should be carrion food by now,' he said. 'Why have the World Eaters not yet stormed the walls of the Iron Citadel?'

Captain Khârn, equerry to Angron himself, stood firm before the Warmaster's hostile stare, the dim light of the sanctum reflecting from the blue and white of his plate armour.

'My lord, its walls are designed to resist almost every weapon we have available, but I assure you the fortress will be ours within days,' said Khârn.

'You mean mine,' growled the Warmaster.

'Of course, Lord Warmaster,' replied Khârn.

'And tell my brother Angron to get up here. I haven't seen hide nor hair of him in months. I'll not have him sulking in some muddy trench avoiding me just because he can't deliver on his promises.'

'If I may be so bold, my primarch told you that this battle would take time,' explained Khârn. 'The citadel was built with the old technology and needs siege experts like the Iron Warriors to break it open.'

'And if I could contact Perturabo, I would have him here,' said the Warmaster.

Regulus spoke from behind the Warmaster. 'The STC machines will be able to counter much of the Mechanicum's arsenal. If the Dark Age texts are correct, they will adapt and react to changing circumstances, creating ever more cunning means of defence.'

'The citadel may be able to adapt,' said Captain Khârn, angrily gripping the haft of his axe, 'but it will not be able to stand before the fury of the XII Legion. The sons of Angron will tear the beating heart from that fortress for you, Warmaster. Have no doubt of that.'

'Fine words, Captain Khârn,' said Horus. 'Now storm that citadel for me. Kill everyone you find within.'

The World Eater bowed and turned on his heel, marching from the sanctum.

Once the doors slid shut behind Khârn, Horus said, 'That ought to light a fire under Angron's backside. This war is taking too damn long. There is other business to be upon.'

Regulus and Maloghurst came around from behind the Warmaster, the equerry taking a seat to ease his aching body.

'We must have those STC machines,' said Regulus.

'Yes, thank you, adept, I had quite forgotten that,' said Horus. 'I know very well what those machines represent, even if the fools who control them do not.'

'My order will compensate you handsomely for them, my lord,' said Regulus.

Horus smiled and said, 'At last we come to it, adept.'

'Come to what, my lord?'

'Do not think me a simpleton, Regulus,' cautioned Horus. 'I know of the Mechanicum's quest for the ancient knowledge. Fully functional construct machines would be quite a prize, would they not?'

'Beyond imagining,' admitted Regulus. 'To rediscover the thinking engines that drove humanity into the stars and allowed the colonisation of the galaxy is a prize worth any price.'

'Any price?' asked Horus.

'These machines will allow us to achieve the unimaginable, to reach into the halo stars and perhaps even other galaxies,' said Regulus. 'So yes, any price is worth paying.'

'Then you shall have them,' said Horus.

Regulus seemed taken aback by such a monumentally grand offer and said, 'I thank you, Warmaster. You cannot imagine the boon you grant the Mechanicum.'

Horus stood and circled behind Regulus, staring unabashedly at the remnants of flesh that clung to his metallic components. Shimmering fields contained the adept's organs, and a brass musculature gave him a measure of mobility.

'There is little of you that can still be called human, isn't there?' asked Horus. 'In that regard you are not so different from myself or Maloghurst.'

'My lord?' replied Regulus. 'I aspire to the perfection of the machine state, but would not presume to compare myself with the Astartes.'

'As well you should not,' said Horus, continuing to pace around the sanctum. 'I will give you these construct machines, but as we have established, there will be a price.'

'Name it, my lord. The Mechanicum will pay it.'

'The Great Crusade is almost at an end, Regulus, but our efforts to secure the galaxy are only just beginning,' said Horus, leaning over the table and planting his hands on its black surface. 'I am poised to embark on the greatest endeavour imaginable, but I need allies, or all will come to naught. Can I count on you and the Mechanicum?'

'What is this great endeavour?' asked Regulus.

Horus waved his hand and came around the table to stand next to the adept of the Mechanicum once more, placing a reassuring hand on his brass armature.

'No need to go into the details just now,' he said. 'Just tell me that you and your brethren will support me when the time comes and the construct machines are yours.'

A whirring mechanical arm wrapped in gold mesh swung over the table and placed a polished machine-cog gently on its surface.

'As much of the Mechanicum as I command is yours Warmaster,' promised Regulus, 'and as much strength as I can muster from those I do not.'

Horus smiled and said, 'Thank you, adept. That's all I wanted to hear.'

ON THE SIXTH day of the tenth month of the war against the Auretian Technocracy, the 63rd Expedition was thrown into panic when a group of vessels translated in-system behind it, in perfect attack formation.

Boas Comnenus attempted to turn his ships to face the new arrivals, but even as the manoeuvres began, he knew it would be too late. Only when the mysterious ships reached, and then passed, optimal firing range, did those aboard the *Vengeful Spirit* understand that the vessels had no hostile intent.

Relieved hails were sent from the Warmaster's flagship to be met with an amused voice that spoke with the cultured accent of Old Terra.

'Horus, my brother,' said the voice. 'It seems I still have a thing or two to teach you.'

On the bridge of the *Vengeful Spirit*, Horus said, 'Fulgrim.'

DESPITE THE HARDSHIPS of the war, Loken was excited at the prospect of meeting the warriors of the Emperor's

Children once again. He had spent as much time as his duties allowed in repairing his armour, though he knew it was still in a sorry state. He and the Mournival stood behind the Warmaster as he waited proudly on the upper transit dock of the *Vengeful Spirit*, ready to receive the primarch of the III Legion.

Fulgrim had been one of the Warmaster's staunchest supporters since his elevation to Warmaster, easing the concerns of Angron, Perturabo and Curze when they raged against the honour done to Horus and not them. Fulgrim's voice had been the breath of calm that had stilled bellicose hearts and soothed ruffled pride.

Without Fulgrim's wisdom, Loken knew that it was unlikely that the Warmaster would ever have been able to command the loyalty of the Legions so completely.

He heard metallic scrapes from beyond the pressure door.

Loken had seen Fulgrim once before at the Great Triumph on Ullanor, and even though it had been from a distance as he had marched past with tens of thousands of other Astartes warriors, Loken's impression of the primarch had never faded from his mind.

It was a palpable honour to stand once again in the presence of two such godlike beings as the primarchs.

The eagle-stamped pressure door slid open and the Primarch of the Emperor's Children stepped onto the *Vengeful Spirit*.

Loken's first impression was of the great golden eagle's wing that swept up over Fulgrim's left shoulder. The primarch's armour was brilliant purple, edged in bright gold and inlaid with the most exquisite carvings. Hooded bearers carried his long, scaled cloak, and trailing parchments hung from his shoulder guards.

A high collar of deepest purple framed a face that was pale to the point of albinism, the eyes so dark as to be

almost entirely pupil. The hint of a smile played around
his lips and his hair was a shimmering white.

Loken had once called Hastur Sejanus a beautiful
man, adored by all, but seeing the Primarch of the
Emperor's Children up close for the first time, he knew
that his paltry vocabulary was insufficient for the perfection he saw in Fulgrim.

Fulgrim opened his arms and the two primarchs
embraced like long-lost brothers.

'It has been too long, Horus,' said Fulgrim.

'It has, my brother, it has,' agreed Horus. 'My heart
sings to see you, but why are you here? You were prose-
cuting a campaign throughout the Perdus Anomaly. Is
the region compliant already?'

'What worlds we found there are now compliant, yes,'
nodded Fulgrim as four warriors stepped through the
pressure door behind him. Loken smiled to see Saul
Tarvitz, his patrician features unable to contain his relish
at being reunited with his brothers of the Sons of Horus.

Lord Commander Eidolon came next, looking as
unrepentantly viperous as Torgaddon had described
him. Lucius the swordsman came next, still with the
same sardonic expression of superiority that he remembered, though his face was now heavily scarred. Behind
him came a warrior Loken did not recognise, a sallow
skinned Astartes in the armour of an apothecary, with
gaunt cheeks and a long mane of hair as white as that of
his primarch.

Fulgrim turned from Horus and said, 'I believe you are
already familiar with some of my brothers, Tarvitz,
Lucius and Lord Commander Eidolon, but I do not
believe you have met my Chief Apothecary Fabius.'

'It is an honour to meet you, Lord Horus,' said Fabius,
bowing low.

Horus acknowledged the gesture of respect and said,
'Come now, Fulgrim, you know better than to try to stall

me. What's so important that you turn up here unannounced and give half of my crew heart attacks?'

The smile fell from Fulgrim's pale lips and he said, 'There have been reports, Horus.'

'Reports? What does that mean?'

'Reports that things are not as they should be,' replied Fulgrim, 'that you and your warriors should be called to account for the brutality of this campaign. Is Angron up to his usual tricks?'

'Angron is as he has always been.'

'That bad?'

'No, I keep him on a short leash, and his equerry, Khârn, seems to curb the worst of our brother's excesses.'

'Then I have arrived just in time.'

'I see,' said Horus. 'Are you here to relieve me then?'

Fulgrim could keep a straight face no longer and laughed, his dark eyes sparkling with mirth. 'Relieve you? No, my brother, I am here so that I can return and tell those fops and scribes on Terra that Horus fights war the way it is meant to be fought: hard, fast and cruel.'

'War *is* cruelty. There is no use trying to reform it. The crueller it is, the sooner it is over.'

Fulgrim said, 'Indeed, my brother. Come, there is much for us to talk about, for these are strange times we live in. It seems our brother Magnus has once again done something to upset the Emperor, and the Wolf of Fenris has been unleashed to escort him back to Terra.'

'Magnus?' asked Horus, suddenly serious. 'What has he done?'

'Let us talk of it in private,' said Fulgrim. 'Anyway, I have a feeling my subordinates would welcome the chance to reacquaint themselves with your... what do you call it? Mournival?'

'Yes,' smiled Horus, 'memories of Murder no doubt.'

Loken felt a chill travel down his spine as he recognised the smile on Horus's face, the same one he had worn right after he had blown out the Auretian consul's brains on the embarkation deck.

WITH HORUS AND Fulgrim gone, Abaddon and Aximand, together with Eidolon, followed the two primarchs, while Loken and Torgaddon exchanged greetings with the Emperor's Children. The Sons of Horus welcomed their brothers with laughter and crushing bear hugs, the Emperor's Children with decorum and reserve.

For Torgaddon and Tarvitz it was a reunion of comrades, with a mutual respect forged in the heat of battle, their easy friendship clear for all to see.

The apothecary, Fabius, requested directions to the medicae deck and excused himself with a bow upon receiving them.

Lucius remained with the two members of the Mournival, and Torgaddon couldn't resist baiting him just a little. 'So, Lucius, you fancy another round in the training cages with Garviel? From the look of your face you could do with the practice.'

The swordsman had the good grace to smile, the many scars twisting on his flesh, and said, 'No thank you. I fear I may have grown beyond Captain Loken's last lesson. I would not want to humble him this time.'

'Come on, just one bout?' asked Loken. 'I promise I'll be gentle.'

'Yes, come on, Lucius,' said Tarvitz. 'The honour of the Emperor's Children is at stake.'

Lucius smiled. 'Very well, then.'

LOKEN COULD NOT remember much of the bout; it had been over so quickly. Evidently, Lucius had indeed learned his lesson well. No sooner had the practice cage shut than the swordsman attacked. Loken had been ready for such a move, but even so, was almost overwhelmed in the first seconds of the fight.

The two warriors fought back and forth, Torgaddon and Saul Tarvitz cheering from outside the practice cages.

The bout had attracted quite a crowd, and Loken wished Torgaddon had kept word of it to himself.

Loken fought with all the skill he could muster, while Lucius sparred with a casual playfulness. Within moments, Loken's sword was stuck in the ceiling of the practice cage, and Lucius had a blade at his throat.

The swordsman had barely broken sweat, and Loken knew that he was hopelessly outclassed by Lucius. To fight Lucius with life and death resting on the blades would be to die, and he suspected that there was no one in the Sons of Horus who could best him.

Loken bowed before the swordsman and said, 'That's one each, Lucius.'

'Care for a decider?' smirked Lucius, dancing back and forth on the balls of his feet and slicing his swords through the air.

'Not this time,' said Loken. 'Next time we meet, we'll put something serious on the outcome, eh?'

'Any time, Loken,' said Lucius, 'but I'll win. You know that, don't you?'

'Your skill is great, Lucius, but just remember that there's someone out there who can beat you.'

'Not this lifetime,' said Lucius.

THE QUIET ORDER met once again in the armoury, though this was a more select group than normally gathered with Lodge Master Serghar Targost presiding over an assemblage of the Legion's senior officers.

Aximand felt a pang of regret and loss as he saw that, of the Legion's captains, only Loken, Torgaddon, Iacton Qruze and Tybalt Marr were absent.

Candles lit the armoury and each captain had dispensed with his hooded robes. This was a gathering for debate, not theatrics.

'Brothers,' said Targost, 'this is a time for decisions: hard decisions. We face dissent from within, and now Fulgrim arrives out of the blue to spy on us.'

'Spy?' said Aximand. 'Surely you don't think that Fulgrim would betray his brother? The Warmaster is closer to Fulgrim than he is to Sanguinius.'

'What else would you call him?' asked Abaddon. 'Fulgrim said as much when he arrived.'

'Fulgrim is as frustrated by the situation back on Terra as we are,' said Maloghurst. 'He knows that those who desire the outcome of war do not desire to see the blood of its waging. His Legion seeks perfection in all things, especially war, and we have all seen how the Emperor's Children fight: with unremitting ruthlessness and efficiency. They may fight differently from us, but they achieve the same result.'

'When Fulgrim's warriors see how the war is fought on Aureus they will know that there is no honour in it,' added Luc Sedirae. 'The World Eaters shock even me. I make no secret of the fact that I live for battle and revel in my ability to kill, but the Sons of Angron are… uncivilised. They do not fight, they butcher.'

'They get the job done, Luc,' said Abaddon. 'That's all that matters. Once the Titans of the Mechanicum break open the walls of the Iron Citadel, you'll be glad to have them by your side when it comes time to storm the breaches.'

Sedirae nodded and said, 'There is truth in that. The Warmaster wields them like a weapon, but will Fulgrim see that?'

'Leave Fulgrim to me, Luc,' said a powerful voice from the shadows, and the warriors of the quiet order turned in surprise as a trio of figures emerged from the darkness.

The lead figure was armoured in ceremonially adorned armour, the white plate shimmering in the candlelight, and the red eye on his chest plate glowing with reflected fire.

Aximand and his fellow captains dropped to their knees as Horus entered their circle, his gaze sweeping around his assembled captains.

'So this is where you've been gathering in secret?'

'My lord–' began Targost, but Horus held up his hand to silence him.

'Hush, Serghar,' said Horus. 'There's no need for explanations. I have heard your deliberations and come to shed some light upon them, and to bring some new blood to your quiet order.'

As he spoke, Horus gestured the two figures that had accompanied him to come forward. Aximand saw that one was an Astartes, Tybalt Marr, while the other was a mortal clad in gold armour, the warrior who had fought to protect the Warmaster's documentarist on Davin.

'Tybalt you already know,' continued the Warmaster. 'Since the terrible death of Verulam, he has struggled to come to terms with the loss. I believe he will find the support he needs within our order. The other is a mortal, and though not Astartes, he is a warrior of courage and strength.'

Serghar Targost raised his head and said, 'A mortal within the order? The order is for Astartes only.'

'Is it, Serghar? I was led to believe that this was a place where men were free to meet and converse, and confide outside the strictures of rank and martial order.'

'The Warmaster is right,' said Aximand, rising to his feet. 'There is only one qualification a man needs to be a part of our quiet order. He must be a warrior.'

Targost nodded, though he was clearly unhappy with the decision.

'Very well, let them come forward and show the sign,' he said.

Both Marr and the gold-armoured warrior stepped forward and held out their hands. In each palm, a silver lodge medal glinted.

'Let them speak their names,' said Targost.

'Tybalt Marr,' said the Captain of the 18th Company.

The mortal said nothing, looking helplessly at Horus. The lodge members waited for him to announce himself, but no name was forthcoming.

'Why does he not identify himself?' asked Aximand.

'He can't say,' replied Horus with a smile. 'Sorry, I couldn't resist, Serghar. This is Maggard, and he is mute. It has come to my attention that he wishes to learn more of our Legion, and I thought this might be a way of showing him our true faces.'

'He will be made welcome,' assured Aximand, 'but you didn't come here just to bring us two new members, did you?'

'Always thinking, Little Horus,' laughed Horus. 'I've always said you were the wise one.'

'Then why are you here?' asked Aximand.

'Aximand!' hissed Targost. 'This is the Warmaster, he goes where he wills.'

Horus held up his hand and said, 'It's alright, Serghar, Little Horus has a right to ask. I've kept out of your affairs for long enough, so it's only fair I explain this sudden visit.'

Horus walked between them, smiling and bathing them in the force of his personality. He stood before Aximand and the effect was intoxicating. Horus had always been a being of supreme majesty, whose beauty and charisma could bewitch even the most stoic hearts.

As he met the Warmaster's gaze, Aximand saw that his power to seduce was beyond anything he had experienced before, and he felt shamed that he had questioned this luminous being. What right did he have to ask anything of the Warmaster?

Horus winked, and the spell was broken.

The Warmaster moved into the centre of the group and said. 'You are right to gather and debate the coming days, my sons, for they will be hard indeed. Times are upon us when we must make difficult decisions, and there will be those who will not understand why we do what we do, because they were not here beside us.'

Horus stopped before each of the captains in turn, and Aximand could see the effect his words were having on them. Each warrior's face lit up as though the sun shone upon it.

'I am set upon a course that will affect every man under my command, and the burden of my decision is a heavy weight upon my shoulders, my sons.'

'Share it with us!' cried Abaddon. 'We are ready to serve.'

Horus smiled and said, 'I know you are, Ezekyle, and it gives me strength to know that I have warriors with me who are as steadfast and true as you.'

'We are yours to command,' promised Serghar Targost. 'Our first loyalty is to you.'

'I am proud of you all,' said Horus, his voice emotional, 'but I have one last thing to ask of you.'

'Ask us,' said Abaddon.

Horus placed his hand gratefully on Abaddon's shoulder guard and said, 'Before you answer, consider what I am about to say carefully. If you choose to follow me on this grand adventure, there will be no turning back once we have embarked upon it. For good or ill, we go forward, never back.'

'You always were one for theatrics,' noted Aximand. 'Are you going to get to the point?'

Horus nodded and said, 'Yes, of course, Little Horus, but you'll indulge my sense for the dramatic I hope?'

'It wouldn't be you otherwise.'

'Agreed,' said Horus, 'but yes, to get to the point. I am about to take us down the most dangerous path, and not all of us will survive. There will be those of the Imperium who will call us traitors and rebels for our actions, but you must ignore their bleatings and trust that I am certain of our course. The days ahead will be hard and painful, but we must see them through to the end.'

'What would you have us do?' asked Abaddon.

'In good time, Ezekyle, in good time,' said Horus. 'I just need to know that you are with me, my sons. Are you with me?'

'We are with you!' shouted the warriors as one.

'Thank you,' said Horus, gratefully, 'but before we act, we must set our own house in order. Hektor Varvarus and this remembrancer, Karkasy: they must be silenced while we gather our strength. They draw unwelcome attention to us and that is unacceptable.'

'Varvarus is not a man to change his mind, my lord,' warned Aximand, 'and the remembrancer is under Garviel's protection.'

'I will take care of Varvarus,' said the Warmaster, 'and the remembrancer... Well, I'm sure that with the correct persuasion he will do the right thing.'

'What do you intend, my lord?' asked Aximand.

'That they be illuminated as to the error of their ways,' said Horus.

TWENTY

The breach/A midday clear/Plans

THE VISIT OF the Emperor's Children was painfully brief, the two primarchs sequestering themselves behind closed doors for its entirety, while their warriors sparred, drank and talked of war. Whatever passed between the Warmaster and Fulgrim appeared to satisfy the Primarch of the Emperor's Children that all was well, and three days later, an honour guard formed up at the upper transit dock as the Emperor's Children bade their farewells to the Sons of Horus.

Saul Tarvitz and Torgaddon said heartfelt goodbyes, while Lucius and Loken exchanged wry handshakes, each anticipating the next time they would cross blades. Eidolon nodded curtly to Torgaddon and Loken, as Apothecary Fabius made his exit without a word.

Fulgrim and Horus shared a brotherly embrace, whispering words only they could hear to one another. The wondrously perfect Primarch of the Emperor's Children turned with a flourish towards the pressure door and stepped from the *Vengeful Spirit*, his long, scale cloak billowing behind him.

Something glinted beneath the cloak, and Loken did a double take as he caught a fleeting glimpse of a horribly familiar golden sword belted at Fulgrim's waist.

LOKEN SAW THAT the Iron Citadel was aptly named, its gleaming walls rearing from the rock like jagged metal teeth. The mid-morning light reflected from its shimmering walls, the air rippling in the haze of energy fields, and clouds of metal shavings raining down from self-repairing ramparts. The outer precincts of the fortress were in ruins, the result of a four-month siege waged by the warriors of Angron and the war machines of the Mechanicum.

The *Dies Irae* and her sister Titans bombarded the walls daily, hurling high explosive shells and crackling energy beams at the citadel, slowly but surely pushing the Brotherhood back to this, their last bastion.

The citadel itself was a colossal half moon in plan, set against the rock of a range of white mountains, its approach guarded by scores of horn-works and redoubts. Most of these fortifications were little more than smouldering rubble, the Mechanicum's Legio Reductor corps having expended a fearsome amount of ordnance to flatten them in preparation for the storm of the Iron Citadel.

After months of constant shelling, the walls of the citadel had finally been broken open and a half-kilometre wide breach had been torn in its shining walls. The citadel was ready to fall, but the Brotherhood would fight for it to the bitter end, and Loken knew that most of the warriors who were to climb that breach would die.

He waited for the order of battle with trepidation, knowing that an escalade was the surest way for a warrior to meet his end. Statistically, a man was almost certain to die when assaulting the walls of a well-defended fortress, and it was therefore beholden to him to make that death worthwhile.

'Will it be soon, do you think, Garvi?' asked Vipus, checking the action of his chainsword for the umpteenth time.

'I think so,' said Loken, 'but I imagine that the World Eaters will be first into the breach.'

'They're welcome to the honour,' grunted Torgaddon, and Loken was surprised at his comrade's sentiment. Torgaddon was normally the first to request a place in the speartip of any battle, though he had been withdrawn and sullen for some time now. He would not be drawn on the reasons why, but Loken knew it had to do with Aximand and Abaddon.

Their fellow Mournival members had barely spoken to them over the course of this war, except where operational necessity had demanded it. Neither had the four of them met with the Warmaster since Davin. For all intents and purposes, the Mournival was no more.

The Warmaster kept his own council, and Loken found himself in agreement with Iacton Qruze's sentiments that the Legion had lost its way. The words of the 'half-heard' carried no real weight in the Sons of Horus, and the aged veteran's complaints were largely ignored.

Loken's growing suspicions had been fed by what Apothecary Vaddon had told him when he had rushed to the medicae deck after the departure of the Emperor's Children.

He had found the apothecary in the midst of surgery, ministering to the Legion's wounded, the tiled floor slick with congealed blood.

Loken had known better than to disturb Vaddon's labours and only when the apothecary had finished did Loken speak to him.

'The anathame?' demanded Loken. 'Where is it?'

Vaddon looked up from washing his hands of blood. 'Captain Loken. The anathame? I don't have it any more. I thought you knew.'

'No,' said Loken. 'I didn't. What happened to it? I told you to tell no one that it was in your possession.'

'And nor did I,' said Vaddon angrily. 'He already knew I had it.'

'He?' asked Loken. 'Who are you talking about?'

'The apothecary of the Emperor's Children, Fabius,' said Vaddon. 'He came to the medicae deck a few hours ago and told me he had been authorised to remove it.'

A cold chill seized Loken as he asked, 'Authorised by whom?'

'By the Warmaster,' said Vaddon.

'And you just gave him it?' asked Loken. 'Just like that?'

'What was I supposed to do?' snarled Vaddon. 'This Fabius had the Warmaster's seal. I had to give it to him.'

Loken took a deep calming breath, knowing that the apothecary would have had no choice when presented with the seal of Horus. The months of research Vaddon had performed on the weapon had, thus far, yielded no results, and with its removal from the *Vengeful Spirit*, any chance of uncovering its secrets was lost forever.

A crackling voice in Loken's helmet shook him from his sour memory of the second theft of the anathame, and he focused on the order of battle streaming through his headset. Sure enough, the World Eaters were going in first, a full assault company led by Angron himself and supported by two companies of the Sons of Horus, the Tenth and the Second: Loken and Torgaddon's companies.

Torgaddon and Loken shared an uneasy glance. To be given the honour of going into the breach seemed at odds with their current status within the Legion, but the order was given and there was no changing it now. Army regiments would follow to secure the ground the Astartes won, and Hektor Varvarus himself would lead these detachments.

Loken shook hands with Torgaddon and said, 'See you on the inside, Tarik.'

'Try not to get yourself killed, Garvi,' said Torgaddon.

'Thanks for the reminder,' said Loken, 'and here was me thinking that was the point.'

'Don't joke, Garvi,' said Torgaddon. 'I'm serious. I think we're going to need each other's support before this campaign is over.'

'What do you mean?'

'Never mind,' said Torgaddon. 'We'll talk more once this citadel is ours, eh?'

'Yes, we'll share a bottle of victory wine in the ruins of the Brotherhood's citadel.'

Torgaddon nodded and said, 'You're buying though.'

They shook hands once more and Torgaddon jogged away to rejoin his warriors and ready them for the bloody assault. Loken watched him go, wondering if he would see his friend alive again to share that drink. He pushed such defeatism aside as he made his way through his own company to pass out orders and offer words of encouragement.

He turned as a huge cheer erupted from further down the mountains, seeing a column of warriors clad in the blue and white armour of the World Eaters, marching towards the approaches to the breach. The assaulters of the World Eaters were hulking warriors equipped with mighty chain axes and heavy jump packs. They were brutality distilled and concentrated violence moulded them into the most fearsome close combat fighters Loken had ever seen.

Leading them was the Primarch Angron.

ANGRON, THE BLOODY One: the Red Angel.

Loken had heard all these names and more for Angron, but none of them did justice to the sheer brutal physicality of the Primarch of the World Eaters. Clad in an ancient suit of gladiatorial armour, Angron was like a warrior from some lost heroic age. A glinting mesh cape of chain mail hung from his high gorget and pauldrons, with skulls worked into its weave like barbaric trophies.

He was armed to the teeth with short, stabbing swords, and daggers the length of an Astartes chain-blade. An ornate pistol of antique design was holstered on each thigh, and he carried a monstrous chain-glaive, its terrifying size beyond anything Loken could believe.

'Throne alive…' breathed Nero Vipus as Angron approached. 'I wouldn't have believed it had I not seen it with my own eyes.'

'I know what you mean,' answered Loken, the mighty primarch's savage and tribal appearance putting him in mind of the bloody tales he had read in the *Chronicles of Ursh*.

Angron's face was murder itself, his thick features scarred and bloody. Dark iron glinted on his scalp where cerebral cortex implants punctured his skull to amplify his already fearsome aggression. The implants had been grafted to Angron's brain when he had been a slave, centuries before, and though the technology to remove them was available, he had never wanted them removed.

The bloody primarch marched past, glancing over at the men of 10th Company as he led his warriors towards the bloodletting. Loken shivered at the sight of him, seeing only death in his heavy-lidded eyes, and he wondered what terrible thoughts must fill Angron's violated skull.

No sooner had the Primarch of the World Eaters passed than the bombardment began, the guns of the Legio Mortis launching rippling salvoes of rockets and shells into the breach.

Loken watched as Angron delivered his assault orders with curt chops of his glaive, and felt a momentary pity for the Brotherhood warriors within the citadel. Though they were his sworn enemies, he did not envy them the prospect of fighting such a living avatar of blood and death.

A terrifying war cry sounded from the World Eaters, and Loken watched as Angron led his company in a crude ritual of scarification. The warriors removed their left gauntlets and slashed their axes across their palms, smearing the blood across the faceplates of their helmets as they chanted canticles of death and bloodshed.

'I almost feel sorry for the poor bastards in the citadel,' said Vipus, echoing Loken's earlier thoughts.

'Pass the word to stand ready,' he ordered. 'We move out when the World Eaters reach the crest of the breach.'

He held out his hand to Nero Vipus and said, 'Kill for the living, Nero.'

'Kill for the dead,' answered Vipus.

THE ASSAULT BEGAN in a flurry of smoke as the World Eaters surged up the lower slopes of the breach with roaring blasts of their jump packs. The wall head and the breach itself were wreathed in explosions from the Titans' bombardment, and the idea that something could live through such a storm of shot and shell seemed impossible to Loken.

As the World Eaters powered up the slopes of rubble, Loken and his warriors clambered over the twisted, blackened spars of iron that had been blasted from the walls above. They moved and fired, adding their own volleys of gunfire into the breach before the assaulters reached their targets.

The slope was steep, but eminently climbable, and they were making steady progress. Occasional shots and las blasts ricocheted from the rocks or their armour, but at this range, nothing could wound them.

Five hundred metres to his left, Loken saw Torgaddon leading Second Company up the slopes in the wake of the World Eaters, both forces of the Sons of Horus protecting the vulnerable flanks of the assaulters and ready with heavier weapons to secure the breach.

Behind the Astartes, the soldiers of Hektor Varvarus's Byzant Janizars – wearing long cream greatcoats with gold frogging – followed in disciplined ranks. To march into battle in ceremonial dress uniforms seemed ridiculous to Loken, but Varvarus had declared that he and his men were not going to enter the citadel looking less than their best.

Loken turned from the splendid sight of the marching soldiers as he heard a deep, bass rumbling that seemed to come from the ground itself. Powdered rubble and rocks danced as the vibrations grew stronger still and Loken knew that something was terribly wrong. Ahead, he could see Angron and the World Eaters reaching the crest of the breach. Blazing columns of smoke surrounded Angron, and Loken heard the mighty primarch's bellowing cry of triumph even over the thunderous explosions of battle.

The rumbling grew louder and more violent, and Loken had to grip onto a rusted spar of rebar to hold himself in place as the ground continued to shake as though in the grip of a mighty earthquake. Great cracks split the ground and plumes of fire shot from them.

'What's happening?' he shouted over the noise.

No one answered and Loken fell as the top of the breach suddenly exploded in a sheet of flame that reached hundreds of metres into the air. Rocks and metal were hurled skywards as the top of the wall vanished in a massive seismic detonation.

Like the bunkers in the cities, the Brotherhood destroyed what they could not hold, and Loken's reactive senses shut down briefly with the overload of light and noise. Twisted rubble and wreckage slammed down around them, and Loken heard screams of pain and the crack of splintering armour as scores of his men were pulverised by the storm of boulders.

Dust and matter filled the air, and when Loken felt safe enough to move, he saw in horror that the entire crest of the breach had been destroyed.

Angron and the World Eaters were gone, buried beneath the wreckage of a mountain.

TORGADDON SAW THE same thing, and picked himself up from the ground. He shouted at his warriors to get to their feet and charged towards the ruin of the breach. Filthy, dust-covered warriors clambered from the wreckage and followed their captain as he led them onwards and upwards to what might be their deaths. Torgaddon knew that such a course of action was probably suicidal, but he had seen Angron buried beneath the mountain, and retreating was not an option.

He activated the blade of his chainsword and scrambled up the slopes with the feral cry of the Sons of Horus bursting from his lips.

'Lupercal! Lupercal!' he screamed as he charged.

LOKEN WATCHED HIS brother rise from the aftermath of the explosion like a true hero, and began his own charge towards the breach. He knew that there was every chance a second seismic mine was buried in the breach, but the sight of a primarch brought low by the Brotherhood obliterated all thoughts of any tactical response, except charging.

'Warriors of the Tenth!' he roared. 'With me! Lupercal!'

Loken's surviving warriors pulled themselves from the rubble and followed Loken with the Warmaster's name echoing from the mountains. Loken sprang from rock to rock, clambering uphill faster than he would have believed possible, his anger hot and bright. He was ready to wreak vengeance upon the Brotherhood for what they had done in the name of spite, and nothing was going to stop him.

Loken knew that he had to reach the breach before the Brotherhood realised that its strategy had not killed all the attackers, and he kept moving upwards at a fast pace, using all the increased muscle power his armour afforded him. A storm of gunfire flashed from above: las shots and solid rounds spanging from the rocks and metal rubble. A heavy shell clipped his shoulder guard, spinning him around, but Loken shrugged off the impact and charged on.

The roaring tide of Astartes warriors climbed the breach, the last rays of the morning's sun glinting from the brilliant green of their armour. To see so many warriors in battle was magnificent, an unstoppable wave of death that would sweep away all resistance in a storm of gunfire and blades.

All tactics were moot now, the sight of Angron's fall robbing each and every warrior of any sense of restraint. Loken could see the gleaming silver armour of Brotherhood warriors as they climbed to what was left of the breach, dragging bipod-mounted heavy weapons with them.

'Bolters!' he shouted. 'Open fire!'

The crest of the breach vanished as a spray of bolter rounds impacted. Sparks and chunks of flesh flew as Astartes rounds found homes in flesh, and though many were firing from the hip, most were deadly accurate.

The noise was incredible, hundreds of bolter rounds ripping enemy warriors to shreds and skirling wolf howls ringing in his ears as the Astartes swept over the breach and reverted once again to the persona of the Luna Wolves. Loken threw aside his bolter, the magazine empty, and drew his chainsword, thumbing the activation stud as he vaulted the smoking rocks that had crushed Angron and the World Eaters.

Beyond the walls of the Iron Citadel was a wide esplanade, its surface strewn with gun positions and coils of razor wire. A shell-battered keep was built into the mountainside, but its gates were in pieces and black smoke poured from its gun ports. Brotherhood warriors were streaming back from the ruin of the walls towards these prepared positions, but they had horribly misjudged the timing of their fallback.

The Sons of Horus were already amongst them, hacking them down with brutal arcs of chainblades or gunning them down as they fled. Loken tore his way through a knot of Brotherhood warriors who turned to fight, killing three of them in as many strokes of his sword, and backhanding his elbow into the last opponent's head, smashing his skull to splinters.

All was pandemonium as the Sons of Horus ran amok within the precincts of the Iron Citadel, its defenders slaughtered in frantic moments of unimaginable violence. Loken killed and killed, revelling in the shedding of enemy blood and realising that, with this victory, the war would be over.

With that thought, the cold reality of what was happening penetrated the red fog of his rage. They had won, and already he could see the victory turning into a massacre.

'Garviel!' a desperate voice called over the suit-vox. 'Garviel, can you hear me?'

'Loud and clear, Tarik!' answered Loken.

'We have to stop this!' cried Torgaddon. 'We've won, it's over. Get a hold of your company.'

'Understood,' said Loken, pleased that Torgaddon had realised the same thing as he had.

Soon the inter-suit vox network was alive with barked orders to halt the attack that quickly passed down the chain of command.

By the time the echoes of battle were finally stilled, Loken could see that the Astartes had just barely managed to hold themselves from plunging into an abyss of barbarity, out of which they might never have climbed. Blood, bodies and the stink of battle filled the day, and as Loken looked up into the beautifully clear sky, he could see that the sun was almost at its zenith.

The final storm of the Iron Citadel had taken less than an hour, yet had cost the lives of a primarch, hundreds of the World Eaters, thousands of the Brotherhood, and the Emperor alone knew how many Sons of Horus.

The mass slaughter seemed such a terrible waste of life for what was a paltry prize: ruined cities, a battered and hostile populace, and a world that was sure to rebel as soon as it had the chance.

Was this world's compliance worth such bloodshed?

The majority of the Brotherhood warriors had died in those last enraged minutes, but many more were prisoners of the Sons of Horus, rather than their victims.

Loken removed his helmet and gulped in a lungful of the clear air, its crispness tasting like the sweetest wine after the recycled air of his armour. He made his way through the wreckage of battle, the torn remnants of enemy warriors strewn like offal throughout the esplanade.

He found Torgaddon on his knees, also with his helmet off and breathing deeply. His friend looked up as Loken approached and smiled weakly. 'Well... we did it.'

'Yes,' agreed Loken sadly, looking around at the crimson spoils of victory. 'We did, didn't we?'

Loken had killed thousands of enemies before, and he would kill thousands more in wars yet to be fought, but something in the savagery of this battle had soured his notion of triumph.

The two captains turned as they heard the tramp of booted feet behind them, seeing the lead battalions of the Byzant Janizars finally climbing into the citadel. Loken could see the horror on the soldiers' faces and knew that the glory of the Astartes would be tarnished for every man who set foot inside.

'Varvarus is here,' said Loken.

'Just in time, eh?' said Torgaddon. 'This'll sweeten his mood towards us.'

Loken nodded and simply watched as the richly appointed command units of the Byzant Janizars entered the citadel, their tall blue banners snapping in the wind, and brilliantly decorated officers scanning the battlefield.

Hektor Varvarus stood at the crest of the breach and surveyed the scene of carnage, his horrified expression easy to read even from a distance. Loken felt his resentment towards Varvarus swell as he thought, *this is what we were created for, what else did you expect?*

'Looks like their leaders are here to surrender to Varvarus,' said Torgaddon, pointing to a long column of beaten men and women marching from the smoking ruins of the inner keep, red and silver banners carried before them. A hundred warriors in battered plate armour marched with them, their long barrelled weapons shouldered and pointed at the ground.

Robed magos and helmeted officers led the column, their faces downcast and resigned to their capitulation. With the storm of the esplanade, the citadel was lost and the leaders of the Brotherhood knew it.

'Come on,' said Loken. 'This is history. Since there are no remembrancers here, we might as well be part of this.'

'Yes,' agreed Torgaddon, pushing himself to his feet. The two captains drew parallel with the column of beaten Brotherhood warriors, and soon every one of the Sons of Horus who had survived the escalade surrounded them.

Loken watched Varvarus climb down the rearward slope of the breach and make his way towards the leaders of the Auretian Technocracy. He bowed formally and said, 'My name is Lord Commander Hektor Varvarus, commander of the Emperor's armies in the 63rd Expedition. To whom do I have the honour of addressing?'

An elderly warrior in gold plate armour stepped from the ranks of men, his black and silver heraldry carried on a personal banner pole by a young lad of no more than sixteen years.

'I am Ephraim Guardia,' he said, 'Senior Preceptor of the Brotherhood Chapter Command and Castellan of the Iron Citadel.'

Loken could see the tension on Guardia's face, and knew that it was taking the commander all his self-control to remain calm in the face of the massacre he had just witnessed.

'Tell me,' said Guardia. 'Is this how all wars are waged in your Imperium?'

'War is a harsh master, senior preceptor,' answered Varvarus. 'Blood is spilled and lives are lost. I feel the sorrow of your losses, but excess of grief for the dead is madness. It is an injury to the living, and the dead know it not.'

'Spoken like a tyrant and a killer,' snarled Guardia, and Varvarus bristled with anger at his defeated foe's lack of etiquette.

'Given time, you will see that war is not what the Imperium stands for,' promised Varvarus. 'The Emperor's Great Crusade is designed to bring reason and illumination to the lost strands of mankind. I promise you that this… unpleasantness will soon be forgotten as we go forward into a new age of peace.'

Guardia shook his head and reached into a pouch at his side. 'I think you are wrong, but you have beaten us and my opinion means nothing any more.'

He unrolled a sheet of parchment and said, 'I shall read our declaration to you, Varvarus. All my officers have signed it and it will stand as a testament to our attempts to defy you.'

Clearing his throat, Guardia began to read.

'We fought your treacherous Warmaster to preserve our way of life and to resist the yoke of Imperial rule. It was, in truth, not for glory, nor riches, nor for honour that we fought, but for freedom, which no honest man could ever wish to give up. However, the greatest of our warriors cannot stand before the savagery of your war, and rather than see our culture exterminated, we surrender this citadel and our worlds to you. May you rule in peace more kindly than you make war.'

Before Varvarus could react to the senior preceptor's declaration, the rubble behind him shifted and groaned, cracks splitting the rock and metal as something vast and terrible heaved upwards from beneath the ground.

At first Loken thought that it was the second seismic charge he had feared, but then he saw that these tremors were far more localised. Janizars scattered, and men shouted in alarm as more debris clattered from the breach. Loken gripped the hilt of his sword as he saw many of the Brotherhood warriors reach for their weapons.

Then the breach exploded with a grinding crack of ruptured stone, and something immense and red erupted from the ground with a bestial roar of hate and bloodlust. Soldiers fell away from the red giant, hurled aside by the violence of his sudden appearance.

Angron towered over them, bloody and enraged, and Loken marvelled that he could still be alive after thousands of tonnes of rock had engulfed him. But Angron was a primarch and what – save for an anathame – could lay one such as him low?

'Blood for Horus!' shouted Angron and leapt from the breach.

The primarch landed with a thunderous impact that split the stone beneath him, his chain-glaive sweeping out and cleaving the entire front rank of Brotherhood warriors to bloody ruin. Ephraim Guardia died in the first seconds of Angron's attack, his body cloven through the chest with a single blow.

Angron howled in battle lust as he hacked his way through the Brotherhood with great, disembowelling sweeps of his monstrous, roaring weapon. The madness of his slaughter was terrifying, but the warriors of the Brotherhood were not about to die without a fight.

Loken shouted, 'No! Stop!' but it was already too late. The remainder of the Brotherhood shouldered their weapons and began firing on the Sons of Horus and the rampaging primarch.

'Open fire!' shouted Loken, knowing he had no choice.

Gunfire tore through the ranks of the Brotherhood, the point-blank firefight a lethal firestorm of explosive bolter rounds. The noise was deafening and horrifyingly brief as the Brotherhood were mercilessly gunned down by the Astartes or hacked apart by Angron.

Within seconds, it was over and the last remnants of the Brotherhood were no more.

Desperate cries for medics sounded from the command units of the Janizars, and Loken saw a group of bloody soldiers on their knees around a fallen officer, his cream greatcoat drenched in blood. The gold of his medals gleamed in the cold midday light and as one of the kneeling soldiers shifted position, Loken realised the identity of the fallen man.

Hektor Varvarus lay in a spreading pool of blood, and even from a distance, Loken could see that there would be no saving him. The man's body had been ripped open from the inside, the gleaming ends of splintered ribs jutting from his chest where it was clear a bolter round had detonated within him.

Loken wept to see this fragile peace broken, and dropped his sword in disgust at what had happened and at what he had been forced to do. With Angron's senseless attack, the lives of his warriors had been threatened, and he'd had no other choice but to order the attack.

Still, he regretted it.

The Brotherhood had been honourable foes and the Sons of Horus had butchered them like cattle. Angron stood in the midst of the carnage, his glaive spraying the warriors nearest him with spatters of blood from the roaring chainblade.

The Sons of Horus cheered in praise of the World Eaters' primarch, but Loken felt soul sick at such a barbaric sight.

'That was no way for warriors to die,' said Torgaddon. 'Their deaths shame us all.'

Loken didn't answer. He couldn't.

TWENTY-ONE

Illumination

WITH THE FALL of the Iron Citadel, the war on Aureus was over. The Brotherhood was destroyed as a fighting force and though there were still pockets of resistance to be mopped up, the fighting was as good as over. Casualties on both sides had been high, most especially in the Army units of the Expedition. Hektor Varvarus was brought back to the fleet with due reverence and his body returned to space in a ceremony attended by the highest-ranking officers of the Expeditions.

The Warmaster himself spoke the lord commander's eulogy, the passion and depths of his sorrow plain to see.

'Heroism is not only in the man, but in the occasion,' the Warmaster had said of Lord Commander Varvarus. 'It is only when we look now and see his success that men will say that it was good fortune. It was not. We lost thousands of our best warriors that day and I feel the loss of every one. Hektor Varvarus was a leader who knew that to march with the gods, one must wait until he hears their footsteps sounding through events, and then leap up and grasp the hem of their robes.

'Varvarus is gone from us, but he would not want us to pause in mourning, for history is a relentless master. It has no present, only the past rushing into the future. To try to hold fast to it is to be swept aside and that, my friends, will never happen. Not while I am Warmaster. Those men who fought and bled with Varvarus shall have this world to stand sentinel over, so that his sacrifice will never be forgotten.'

Other speakers had said their farewells to the lord commander, but none with the Warmaster's eloquence. True to his word, Horus ensured that Army units that had been loyal to Varvarus were appointed to minister the worlds he had died to make compliant.

A new Imperial commander was installed, and the martial power of the fleet began the time-consuming process of regrouping in preparation for the next stage of the Crusade.

KARKASY'S BILLET STANK of ink and printing fumes, the crude, mechanical bulk printer working overtime to print enough copies of the latest edition of *The Truth is All We Have*. Though his output had been less prolific of late, the Bondsman number 7 box was nearly empty. Ignace Karkasy remembered wondering, a lifetime ago it seemed, whether or not the lifespan of his creativity could be measured in the quantity of paper he had left to fill. Such thoughts seemed meaningless, given the powerful desire to write that was upon him these days.

He sat on the edge of his cot bed, the last remaining place for him to sit, penning the latest scurrilous piece of verse for his pamphlet and humming contentedly to himself. Papers filled the billet, strewn across the floor, tacked upon the walls or piled on any surface flat enough to hold them. Scribbled notes, abandoned odes and half-finished poems filled the space, but such was the fecundity of his muse that he didn't expect to exhaust it any time soon.

He'd heard that the war with the Auretians was over, the final citadel having fallen to the Sons of Horus a couple of days ago in what the ship scuttlebutt was already calling the White Mountains Massacre. He didn't yet know the full story, but several sources he'd cultivated over the ten months of the war would surely garner him some juicy titbits.

He heard a curt knock on his door-shutter and shouted, 'Come in!'

Karkasy kept on writing as the shutter opened, too focused on his words to waste a single second of his time.

'Yes?' he said, 'What can I do for you?'

No answer was forthcoming, so Karkasy looked up in irritation to see an armoured warrior standing mutely before him. At first, Karkasy felt a thrill of panic, seeing the man's longsword and the hard, metallic gleam of a holstered pistol, but he relaxed as he saw that the man was Petronella Vivar's bodyguard – Maggard, or something like that.

'Well?' he asked again. 'Was there something you wanted?'

Maggard said nothing and Karkasy remembered that the man was mute, thinking it foolish that anyone would send someone who couldn't speak as a messenger.

'I can't help you unless you can tell me why you're here,' said Karkasy, speaking slowly to ensure that the man understood.

In response, Maggard removed a folded piece of paper from his belt and held it out with his left hand. The warrior made no attempt to move closer to him, so with a resigned sigh, Karkasy put aside the Bondsman and pushed his bulky frame from the bed.

Karkasy picked his way through the piles of notebooks and took the proffered paper. It was a sepia coloured papyrus, as was produced in the Gyptian spires, with crosshatched patterning throughout. A little gaudy for his tastes, but obviously expensive.

'So who might this be from?' asked Karkasy, before again remembering that this messenger couldn't speak. He shook his head with an indulgent smile, unfolded the papyrus and cast his eyes over the note's contents.

He frowned as he recognised the words as lines from his own poetry, dark imagery and potent symbolism, but they were all out of sequence, plucked from a dozen different works.

Karkasy reached the end of the note and his bladder emptied in terror as he realised the import of the message, and its bearer's purpose.

PETRONELLA PACED THE confines of her stateroom, impatient to begin transcribing the latest thoughts of her bodyguard. The time Maggard had spent with the Astartes had been most fruitful, and she had already learned much that would otherwise have been hidden from her.

Now a structure suggested itself, a tragic tale told in reverse order that opened on the primarch's deathbed, with a triumphal coda that spoke of his survival and of the glories yet to come. After all, she didn't want to confine herself to only one book.

She even had a prospective title, one that she felt conveyed the correct gravitas of her subject matter, yet also included her in its meaning.

Petronella would call this masterpiece, *In The Footsteps of Gods*, and had already taken its first line – that most important part of the tale where her reader was either hooked or left cold – from her own terrified thoughts at the moment of the Warmaster's collapse.

I was there the day that Horus fell.

It had all the right tonal qualities, leaving the reader in no doubt that they were about to read something profound, yet keeping the end of the story a jealously guarded secret.

Everything was coming together, but Maggard was late in returning from his latest foray into the world of the Astartes and her patience was wearing thin. She had already reduced Babeth to tears in her impatient frustration, and had banished her maidservant to the tiny chamber that served as her sleeping quarters.

She heard the sound of the door to her stateroom opening in the receiving room, and marched straight through to reprimand Maggard for his tardiness.

'What time do you call...' she began, but the words trailed off as she saw that the figure standing before her wasn't Maggard.

It was the Warmaster.

He was dressed in simple robes and looked more magnificent than she could ever remember seeing him. A fierce anima surrounded him, and she found herself unable to speak as he looked up, the full force of his personality striking her.

Standing at the door behind him was the hulking form of First Captain Abaddon. Horus looked up as she entered and nodded to Abaddon, who closed the door at his back.

'Miss Vivar,' said the Warmaster. It took an effort of will on Petronella's part for her to find her voice.

'Yes... my lord,' she stammered, horrified at the mess of her stateroom and that the Warmaster should see it so untidy. She must remember to punish Babeth for neglecting her duties. 'I... that is, I wasn't expecting...'

Horus held up his hand to soothe her concerns and she fell silent.

'I know I have been neglectful of you,' said the Warmaster. 'You have been privy to my innermost thoughts and I allowed the concerns of the war against the Technocracy to command my attention.'

'My lord, I never dreamed you gave me such consideration,' said Petronella.

'You would be surprised,' smiled Horus. 'Your writing goes well?'

'Very well, my lord,' said Petronella. 'I have been prolific since last we met.'

'May I see?' asked Horus.

'Of course,' she said, thrilled that he should take an interest in her work. She had to force herself to walk, not run, into her writing room, indicating the papers stacked on her escritoire.

'It's all a bit of jumble, but everything I've written is here,' beamed Petronella. 'I would be honoured if you would critique my work. After all, who is more qualified?'

'Quite,' agreed Horus, following her to the escritoire and taking up her most recent output. His eyes scanned the pages, reading and digesting the contents quicker than any mortal man ever could.

She searched his face for any reaction to her words, but he was as unreadable as a statue, and she began to worry that he disapproved.

Eventually, he placed the papers back on the escritoire and said, 'It is very good. You are a talented documentarist.'

'Thank you, my lord,' she gushed, the power of his praise like a tonic in her veins.

'Yes,' said Horus, his voice cold. 'It's almost a shame that no one will ever read it.'

MAGGARD REACHED UP and grabbed the front of Karkasy's robe, spinning him around, and hooking his arm around the poet's neck. Karkasy struggled in the powerful grip, helpless against Maggard's superior strength.

'Please!' he gasped, his terror making his voice shrill. 'No, please don't!'

Maggard said nothing, and Karkasy heard the snap of leather as the warrior's free hand popped the stud on his holster. Karkasy fought, but he could do nothing, the crushing force of Maggard's arm around his neck robbing him of breath and blurring his vision.

Karkasy wept bitter tears as time slowed. He heard the slow rasp of the pistol sliding from its holster and the harsh click as the hammer was drawn back.

He bit his tongue. Bloody foam gathered in the corners of his mouth. Snot and tears mingled on his face. His legs scrabbled on the floor. Papers flew in all directions.

Cold steel pressed into his neck, the barrel of Maggard's pistol jammed tight under his jaw.

Karkasy smelled the gun oil.

He wished…

The hard bang of the pistol shot echoed deafeningly in the cramped billet.

AT FIRST, PETRONELLA wasn't sure she'd understood what the Warmaster meant. Why wouldn't people be able to read her work? Then she saw the cold, merciless light in Horus's eyes.

'My lord, I'm not sure I understand you,' she said, haltingly.

'Yes you do.'

'No…' she whispered, backing away from him.

The Warmaster followed her, his steps slow and measured. 'When we spoke in the apothecarion I let you look inside Pandora's Box, Miss Vivar, and for that I am truly sorry. Only one person has a need to know the things in my head, and that person is me. The things I have seen and done, the things I am going to do…'

'Please, my lord,' said Petronella, backing out of her writing room and into the receiving room. 'If you are unhappy with what I've written, it can be revised, edited. I would give you approval on everything, of course.'

Horus shook his head, drawing closer to her with every step.

Petronella felt her eyes fill with tears and she knew that this couldn't be happening. The Warmaster would not be trying to scare her. They must be playing some cruel joke on her. The idea of the Astartes making a fool of her stung Petronella's wounded pride and the part of her that had snapped angrily at the Warmaster upon their first meeting rose to the surface.

'I am the Palatina Majoria of House Carpinus and I demand that you respect that!' she cried, standing firm before the Warmaster. 'You can't scare me like this.'

'I'm not trying to scare you,' said Horus, reaching out to hold her by the shoulders.

'You're not?' asked Petronella, his words filling her with relief. She'd known that this couldn't be right, that there had to be some mistake.

'No,' said Horus, his hands sliding towards her neck. 'I am illuminating you.'

Her neck broke with one swift snap of his wrist.

THE MEDICAE CELL was cramped, but clean and well maintained. Mersadie Oliton sat by the bed and wept softly to herself, tears running freely down her coal dark skin. Kyril Sindermann sat with her and he too shed tears as he held the hand of the bed's occupant.

Euphrati Keeler lay, unmoving, her skin pale and smooth, with a sheen to it that made it look like polished ceramic. Since she had faced the horror in Archive Chamber Three, she had lain unmoving and unresponsive in this medicae bay.

Sindermann had told Mersadie what had happened and she found herself torn between wanting to believe him and calling him delusional. His talk of a daemon and of Euphrati standing before it with the power of the Emperor pouring through her was too fantastical to be true... wasn't it? She wondered if he'd told anyone else of it.

The apothecaries and medics could find nothing physically wrong with Euphrati Keeler, save for the eagle shaped burn on her hand that refused to fade. Her vital signs were stable and her brain wave activity registered normal: no one could explain it and no one had any idea how to wake her from this coma-like state.

Mersadie came to visit Euphrati as often as she could, but she knew that Sindermann came every day, spending several hours at a time with her. Sometimes they would sit together, talking to Euphrati, telling her of the events happening on the planets below, the battles that had been fought, or simply passing on ship gossip.

Nothing seemed to reach the imagist, and Mersadie sometimes wondered if it might not be a kindness to let her die. What could be worse for a person like Euphrati than being trapped by her own flesh, with no ability to reason, to communicate or express herself.

She and Sindermann had arrived together today and each instantly knew that the other had been crying. The news of Ignace Karkasy's suicide had hit them all hard and Mersadie still couldn't believe how he could have done such a thing.

A suicide note had been found in his billet, which was said to have been composed in verse. It spoke volumes of Ignace's enormous conceit that he made his last good-bye in his own poetry.

They had wept for another lost soul, and then they sat on either side of Euphrati's bed, holding each other's and Keeler's hands as they spoke of better times.

Both turned as they heard a soft knock behind them.

A thin faced man wearing the uniform of the Legio Mortis and an earnest face stood framed in the doorway.

Behind him, Mersadie could see that the corridor was filled with people.

'Is it alright if I come in?' he asked.

Mersadie Oliton said, 'Who are you?'

'My name's Titus Cassar, Moderati Primus of the *Dies Irae*. I've come to see the saint.'

THEY MET IN the observation deck, the lighting kept low and the darkness of space leavened only by the reflected glare of the planets they had just conquered. Loken stood with his palm against the armoured viewing bay, believing that something fundamental had happened to the Sons of Horus on Aureus, but not knowing what.

Torgaddon joined him moments later and Loken welcomed him with a brotherly embrace, grateful to have so loyal a comrade.

They stood in silence for some time, each lost in thought as they watched the defeated planets turn in space below them. The preparations for departure were virtually complete and the fleet was ready to move on, though neither warrior had any idea of where they were going.

Eventually Torgaddon broke the silence, 'So what do we do?'

'I don't know, Tarik,' replied Loken. 'I really don't.'

'I thought not,' said Torgaddon, holding up a glass test tube with something in it that reflected soft light with a golden gleam. 'This won't help then.'

'What is it?' asked Loken.

'These,' said Torgaddon, 'are the bolt round fragments removed from Hektor Varvarus.'

'Bolt round fragments? Why do you have them?'

'Because they're ours.'

'What do you mean?'

'I mean they're ours,' repeated Torgaddon. 'The bolt that killed the lord commander came from an Astartes bolter, not from one of the Brotherhood's guns.'

Loken shook his head. 'No, there must be some mistake.'

'There's no mistake. Apothecary Vaddon tested the fragments himself. They're ours, no question.'

'You think Varvarus caught a stray round?'

Torgaddon shook his head. 'The wound was dead centre, Garviel. It was an aimed shot.'

Loken and Torgaddon both understood the implications, and Loken felt his melancholy rise at the thought of Varvarus having been murdered by one of their own.

Neither spoke for a long moment. Then Loken said, 'In the wake of such deceit and destruction shall we despair, or is faith and honour the spur to action?'

'What's that?' asked Torgaddon.

'It's part of a speech I read in a book that Kyril Sindermann gave me,' said Loken. 'It seemed appropriate given where we find ourselves now.'

'That's true enough,' agreed Torgaddon.

'What are we becoming, Tarik?' asked Loken. 'I don't recognise our Legion any more. When did it change?'

'The moment we encountered the Technocracy.'

'No,' said Loken. 'I think it was on Davin. Nothing's been the same since then. Something happened to the Sons of Horus there, something vile and dark and evil.'

'Do you realise what you're saying?'

'I do,' replied Loken. 'I'm saying that we have to uphold the truth of the Imperium of Mankind, no matter what evil may assail it.'

Torgaddon nodded. 'The Mournival oath.'

'Evil has found its way into our Legion, Tarik, and it's up to us to cut it out. Are you with me?' asked Loken.

'Always,' said Torgaddon, and the two warriors shook hands in the old Terran way.

✠ ✠ ✠

THE WARMASTER'S SANCTUM was dimly lit, the cold glow of the bridge instruments the only source of illumination. The room was full, the core of the Warmaster's officers and commanders gathered around the table. The Warmaster sat at his customary place at the head of the table while Aximand and Abaddon stood behind him, their presence a potent reminder of his authority. Maloghurst, Regulus, Erebus, Princeps Turnet of the Legio Mortis, and various other, hand picked, Army commanders filled out the rest of the gathering.

Satisfied that everyone who needed to be there had arrived, Horus leaned forwards and began to speak.

'My friends, we begin the next phase of our campaign among the stars soon and I know that you're all curious as to where we travel next. I will tell you, but before I do, I need every one of you to be aware of the magnitude of the task before us.'

He could see he had everyone's attention, and continued. 'I am going to topple the Emperor from his Throne on Terra and take his place as the Master of Mankind.'

The enormity of his words was not lost on the assembled warriors and he gave them a few minutes to savour their weight, enjoying the look of alarm that crossed each man's face.

'Be not afraid, you are amongst friends,' chuckled Horus. 'I have spoken to you all individually over the course of the war with the Technocracy, but this is the first time you have been gathered and I have openly spoken of our destiny. You shall be my war council, those to whom I entrust the furthering of my plan.'

Horus rose from his seat, continuing to speak as he circled the table.

'Take a moment and look at the face of the man sitting next to you. In the coming fight, he will be your brother, for all others will turn from us when we make our intentions plain. Brother will fight brother and the fate of the galaxy will be the ultimate prize. We will face accusations of heresy and cries of treason, but they will fall from us because we are right. Make no mistake about that. We are right and the Emperor is wrong. He has sorely misjudged me if he thinks I will stand by while he abandons his realm in his quest for godhood, and leaves us amid the destruction of his rampant ambition.

'The Emperor commands the loyalty of millions of soldiers and hundreds of thousands of Astartes warriors. His battle fleets reach across the stars from one side of the galaxy to the other. The 63rd Expedition cannot hope to match such numbers or resources. You all know this to be the case, but even so, we have the advantage.'

'What advantage is that?' asked Maloghurst, exactly on cue.

'We have the advantage of surprise. No one yet suspects us of having learned the Emperor's true plan, and in that lies our greatest weapon.

'But what of Magnus?' asked Maloghurst urgently, 'What happens when Leman Russ returns him to Terra?'

Horus smiled. 'Calm yourself, Mal. I have already contacted my brother Russ and illuminated him with the full breadth of Magnus's treacherous use of daemonic spells and conjurations. He was… suitably angry, and I believe I have convinced him that to return Magnus to Terra would be a waste of time and effort.'

Maloghurst returned Horus's smile. 'Magnus will not leave Prospero alive.'

'No,' agreed Horus. 'He will not.'

'What of the other Legions?' asked Regulus. 'They will not sit idly by while we make war upon the Emperor. How do you propose to negate them?'

'A worthy question, adept,' said Horus, circling the table to stand at his shoulder. 'We are not without allies ourselves. Fulgrim is with us, and he now goes to win Ferrus Manus of the Iron Hands over to our cause.

Lorgar too understands the necessity of what must be done, and both bring the full might of their Legions to my banner.'

'That still leaves many others,' pointed out Erebus.

'Indeed it does, chaplain, but with your help, others may join us. Under the guise of the Chaplain Edict, we will send emissaries to each of the Legions to promulgate the formation of warrior lodges within them. From small beginnings we may win many to our cause.'

'That will take time,' said Erebus.

Horus nodded. 'It will, yes, but it will be worth it in the long term. In the meantime, I have despatched mobilisation orders to those Legions I do not believe we can sway. The Ultramarines will muster at Calth to be attacked by Kor Phaeron of the Word Bearers, and the Blood Angels have been sent to the Signus Cluster, where Sanguinius shall be mired in blood. Then we make a swift, decisive stroke on Terra.'

'That still leaves other Legions,' said Regulus.

'I know,' answered Horus, 'but I have a plan that will remove them as a threat to us once and for all. I will lure them into a trap from which none will escape. I will set the Emperor's Imperium ablaze and from the ashes will arise a new Master of Mankind!'

'And where will you set this trap?' asked Maloghurst.

'A place not far from here,' said Horus. 'The Istvaan system.'

ABOUT THE AUTHOR

Graham McNeill has written many titles for
The Horus Heresy, including the Siege of Terra
novellas *Sons of the Selenar* and *Fury of Magnus*,
the novels *The Crimson King* and *Vengeful
Spirit*, and the *New York Times* bestselling
A Thousand Sons and *The Reflection Crack'd*,
the latter of which featured in *The Primarchs*
anthology. Graham's Ultramarines series,
featuring Captain Uriel Ventris, is now seven
novels long, and has close links to his Iron
Warriors stories, the novel *Storm of Iron* being
a perennial favourite with Black Library fans.
He has also written the Forges of Mars trilogy,
featuring the Adeptus Mechanicus, and the
Warhammer Horror novella *The Colonel's
Monograph*. For Warhammer, he has written
the Warhammer Chronicles trilogy *The Legend
of Sigmar*, the second volume of which won
the 2010 David Gemmell Legend Award.

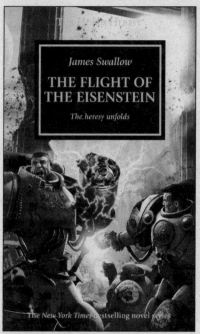

THE FLIGHT OF THE EISENSTEIN
by James Swallow

Having witnessed the terrible massacre on Isstvan III, Death Guard
Captain Garro seizes a ship and sets a course for Terra to warn the
Emperor of Horus's treachery.

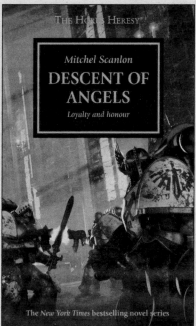

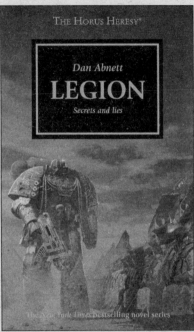

BATTLE FOR THE ABYSS
by Ben Counter

As Horus deploys his forces, a small band of loyal Space Marines from disparate Legions learn that a massive enemy armada is heading to Ultramar, home of the Ultramarines, headed by the most destructive starship ever constructed.